Deafened by Silence

A Dark Why Choose Academy Romance

DEDICATION

Whether we hear with our eyes, talk with our hands or read with our minds, we are all united by love.

Thank you to all of the ladies who gave up their time to be interviewed by the author as a part of her research, and for inspiring such a feisty female lead. You are all incredibly badass and I hope I have done you all proud.

Please check the Trigger Warnings below before diving in.
If you're a dark romance lover, you can skip through. You belong here.

- Orphaned FMC
- Stuck in the middle of a physical rivalry
- 1:1 Bullying
- Stalking
- Blackmail
- Gaslighting
- Invasion of Privacy
- Ableism / Discrimination
- Privilege Dynamics
- Eyes Open/Eyes on Me sex
- Open Door Sex
- Possessive behaviour
- Substance Use
- Party Culture
- Mentions of childhood trauma
- Battles with Depression
- Flashbacks/Nightmares from one of the MMC's

<u>Please Note:</u>

This novel is a piece of fiction, and the author's intention is to entertain you. Parts of this story have been exaggerated for the purposes of your enjoyment, such as the available technologies and studies around cochlear implants.

PROLOGUE

My phone won't stop vibrating against my thigh, no matter how long I pretend it doesn't exist. I don't even glance away from my book. I simply reach down, kill the power, and return to the world I'd much rather live in. I know today is my choice, but I need a little more time before I'm forced to play pretend again.

Through the attic window, once-luscious green has drowned in ice, the impending winter deemed to be the coldest in the last decade. Still beautiful, the frosted fields roll into the distance until they kiss the edge of the sea. The shimmer calms me, like a promise held just out of reach. A bookcase stands tall at the end of my padded bench, its faded turquoise cushion molded to the shape of my silence. Row after row of precious paperbacks, each one a passport to a world that doesn't require me to hear or speak to be understood. Places where I don't have to be *me*.

It's no surprise when Aunt Marg appears in the doorway, her eyes narrowing like she's trying not to sigh. She waves for my attention and points accusingly at the phone now clenched in her hand, doing her best to mime out her irritation. I don't fight the roll of my eyes.

It's been eight years since the car accident took my parents and my hearing, yet she's never once attempted to learn sign language with me.

My lip-reading skills have had plenty of practice, though, so every cloud and all that.

Marg crosses the wooden slats to the small table where my empty coffee cup awaits hopefully for a refill, but instead, she picks up the receivers for my cochlear implants. The same ones she forced me to get last year in preparation for today. It was give in to cochlears or remain here for the rest of my miserable existence.

Undeterred by my scowl, Marg brushes my hair aside, reaching to clamp them into place, but I slap her hand away and do it myself, jamming them in beneath my hairline with all the gentleness of a thunderclap. The weight is foreign and uncomfortable, but that's my own fault. I haven't worn them since the trial phase ended.

"Happy?" I ask, my voice weirdly clean for someone who hasn't even switched the damn things on yet. Marg's lips spread into that forced smile she always wears when she thinks she's fixed something. Label me fixed, I suppose. I scoop my book off the floor, slot it back into its place, and glance at my watch. Damn, I've lost half the morning already. As I start towards the stairs, Marg catches me by the arm.

"I really don't think this is a good idea, Harper," she mouths, panic flickering in her watery blue eyes. That look, the one she gave me after the accident, the one she's never quite stopped wearing, hits me like a blow to the sternum. Knowing this won't be a quick exchange, I relent and reach up, flicking my receivers on. The static of my hair brushing them sets me on edge.

"Really?" I say, letting sarcasm roll off my tongue like sugar-coated venom. "You've barely mentioned that every day for the past three months." Marg lets go of my arm, only to pull me into a bone-crushing hug that smells like lavender and guilt. At first I resist, stiff as a board, but eventually I let myself lean into the warmth of it.

Marg has done an excellent job of suffocating me with precautionary measures, hiding me away from the world, and, whether she means to or not, making me feel broken. But she's still my mom's sister. A kind-hearted, albeit batshit crazy, woman who's lost so much in her lifetime. For all her suffocating paranoia, my aunt *has* loved me. Fiercely, desperately, and maybe even too much. And now the day has come when she has to let me go, too.

"There are other schools, Harper," she whispers near my temple. "One's more appropriate for your condition."

This time, I don't bother hiding the scowl curling my lip. I shove out of her arms, standing straighter than I feel.

"And like I've told you a million times, there's *nothing* wrong with me. Waversea Academy has the best medical apprenticeship program in the country, and I've been busting my ass to get accepted there for *years*." Her lips part to protest, but I cut her off with a shake of my head. "I know you're worried, but you don't need to be. I've got everything under control."

She doesn't look convinced. But then again, neither am I. I sigh, knowing there's nothing left to say. I've already missed the first semester thanks to my aunt conveniently misplacing my application, and then another two weeks while the school board made *special arrangements* for me. The school year is in full swing, and no matter how much resource material I read, I'm already falling behind. Marg tries to argue that we can delay further but I've stopped listening. Sometimes it's better to simply rip off the band-aid.

"No more stalling. This is happening." I nod, striding for the stairs and descending them directly into the spare bedroom I was gifted. I'd like to say my aunt did her best, but a change in curtains and wallpaper can't compete with my childhood home, especially not when it's clear my mom got all the artistic flair in the family.

Marg's a mean cook, though. Even if her best meals are reserved for her dozens of feline companions, some of whom I'm sure are older than my nineteen years. Damn hissy bastards. She could've been a puppy breeder, or run a reptile sanctuary, but no. Freaking cats. I can't wait to wake up tomorrow without a hairball in my sheets or a dead bird on the doorstep.

Reaching for the sweatshirt draped over a wooden chair, I pull it on, careful not to knock my cochlears out of place. I straighten the hem to meet my ripped jeans. Aunt Marg follows me down, her eyes widening and a harsh gasp escaping her.

"Harper Addams! You can't wear that!" she shrieks in a pitch that causes me to wince. I frown, looking at the bare patches of creamy thigh sticking through the denim.

"Why not? I wear these all the time."

"Not your jeans," Marg flaps her hand toward my chest. "*That!*" My gaze drifts higher and I realize my aunt hasn't seen the new additions to my student wardrobe yet. I grin at the slogan on the grey sweater. '*I'm not ignoring you, I just don't want to listen to your bullshit*', is printed across the front, artfully bordered in a floral pattern that deceives the punch of the slogan. Well, if my aunt doesn't like this one, she definitely shouldn't look in my suitcase.

Quickly stopping in front of the full-length mirror, I check that my bouncy, brunette hair is concealing my hearing aids before painting on a more self-assured smile than I actually feel. I may only be five-four, but I have a killer imagination. If I believe myself to be the biggest personality in the room, I can damn-well fake it until I get home and cry myself to sleep. Yeah, like real women do.

Good pep talk Harp, I nod to myself, and then I heave my suitcase off the bed. It's natural to feel a little nervous after years of home-schooling and hiding away. My only sources of human contact have been Max, the engineer's son at the garage next door who routinely checked under my lady bumper, and Stewart, the sophomore who's been tutoring me in biology through many, many practical sessions. Both of my fuck buddies definitely went for extra credit, and I'd happily write each a reference for customer satisfaction if required.

I lift my chin with a confidence I'm still stitching together and move past Aunt Marg in the narrow hallway. She's clutching a fur-covered handkerchief, dabbing tears she tries to pretend aren't falling. My chest tightens as I head for the stairs, every step down feeling heavier than the last.

Honestly, I think this might be good for her. She's spent so long wrapped up in keeping me safe that I'm not sure she remembers how to just be *her*. Maybe now she'll breathe a little. Remember who she was before her world cracked open and she became the only guardian for her niece. She needs to find her own way again, maybe pick up a few hobbies that don't involve monitoring my every move or trying to force me into being someone I'm not. Maybe she'll pick up painting again. Or start Pilates. Or sleep in past six.

It'll be good for me too. It's time to step back into the real world. Not a world printed with magic and meaning like the ones I escape into between the pages. There's no carefully crafted backstory waiting for me, no thrilling plot twist to save the day. Maybe not even a happy ending. But it's mine, and I'm finally ready to start living it.

Her tattered slippers scuffle behind me all the way out the front door of our quaint little house to my beloved cherry-red Audi. I run my fingers along the smooth trunk in a soft caress before popping it open and loading my suitcase safely inside.

Marg *lost it* the day I booked my driving lessons, screeching so loud the cats started bolting around the house in a rush of limbs and panic. I was blissfully unaware until a furball cut in front of me on the stairs and I spent six hours in the emergency department. Luckily, my tumble only earned me a sprained wrist, but Marg wouldn't even look at me for weeks. Unfortunately for her, I had plans for my parents' life insurance hitting my bank account on my eighteenth birthday, and operation 'escape the crazy cat lady' meant I needed to drive.

Rounding the car, I pull my phone from my back pocket and type in the zip code from memory, connecting the GPS voice to my cochlear receiver. The advancements in technology are incredible. Bluetooth links to the inserted disc beneath my skin and feeds sound directly into my inner ear. Now I have a British woman in my head for the next five hours. Slipping into the driver's seat, I finally turn to face Marg, who is fully sobbing and leaning through my car window.

"I promise, if I didn't think I could do this, I wouldn't. I need to find my own way."

"I know, I know," she nods slowly, tears streaming freely down her cheeks. "I just...I hoped you would be able to find it here. You've done so well with the online learning, and these days, people work from home without needing to ever-"

I cut Marg a look and she catches herself, hastily looking down at the driveway. I get it. Me leaving is another adjustment for her, but I'll be coming back for the holidays. I just have this overriding fear that if I don't get out now, I never will.

Leaning in through the car window, Marg pulls me into one of her overly tight hugs, and I return it with everything I've got. She mumbles beside my ear to call every day, peppers my cheek with kisses, then hurries back inside with her face buried in her hands.

For a moment, I just sit there, staring at the closed door. I half expect it to fly back open and Marg to throw herself over my bonnet, but she doesn't. She's giving me the time to steel myself, until I'm finally ready to turn the key in the ignition. The Audi rumbles to life beneath me, humming with a barely contained excitement that trickles through my trepidation. I want this. My parents would want this. The vibrations thrumming through the steering wheel bolster me as a real, unstoppable smile spreads across my face.

This is the moment I've been dreaming about since a perfectly targeted online ad led me to the Waversea website. Since then, possibilities I'd long stopped considering have lit up my path like constellations. Opportunities of who I get to be have become limitless. That's what Aunt Marg couldn't seem to understand.

It isn't about leaving her. It's about finally choosing *me*.

CHAPTER ONE

It's official. I'm in love. Not with my overly peppy tour guide, an excitable blonde ballet major who vanished somewhere between nonfiction and fantasy, but with Waversea Academy.

The library breathes history, the kind that wraps around your ribs and holds you in its grip. I trail my fingers along the aged spines, following the shelves to a glass wall protecting a section of first editions. The paper inside appears brittle and worn, only to be handled with gloves and under supervision. Deeper inside, I happen upon a leisure area. Oversized armchairs nestled in a nook beneath a wooden sign that labels this as the *Silent Zone*. I smile to myself. Two hours on campus, and I've already found my sanctuary.

The bookcases part to reveal the heart of the library, a circle of tables and chairs beneath a domed glass skylight. Students fill every seat, hunched over their textbooks with headphones in. Across the open space, I spot my tour guide giving a hunk of tattooed muscle in a basketball jersey a tour of her mouth with his tongue. All of which provides me with the perfect cover to slip out unnoticed.

Outside, the courtyard thrums with life. Even just breathing it in fills me with a sense of wonder. Anything could happen here, and I can be whoever I want. Blend in or stand out, a decision I've yet to make.

I scan the people bustling in all directions. Despite the bite in the air, clusters of students lounge on the grass around a massive fountain, laughing and talking, while others rush by, checking their watches every five seconds. A flock of birds cuts across the cloud-covered sky, drawing several glances upward. I imagine there's high-pitched squawking, but I can't hear a thing. Just pure, sweet, blissful silence.

As soon as I parked behind the residence halls, I switched off my receivers, hoping to show myself around. Unfortunately, Miss High-on-Life intercepted me at the dorm entrance. One ID photograph and a whirlwind tour later, I'm counting down the seconds to be free again. However, time is creeping closer to my meeting with Dean O'Sullivan and the board of directors, putting yet another obstacle between me and my new dorm. A sigh expands my chest beneath the sweater. Might as well get this over with.

Descending the stone steps, I aim for the building that doesn't try to blend in. Unlike the sleek, recently-renovated halls, this one has gothic arches over the windows and entryway. A curved window sits dead center above it all, towering over the students below, definitely the kind of view a Dean's office would have.

An arm slips through the crook of mine, making me flinch until I notice the head of blonde hair I thought I'd left behind. My guide's eyes sparkle as she winks, a mischievous smile on her lips as I assess the sweatshirt she's now wearing. It reeks of male cologne, protectively wrapping her in the basketball colors of black and yellow. I suppose that's one way for her boyfriend to stake his claim.

With a small shake of my head, I let her veer me toward the fountain, past a statue of an aged, bearded man and into the looming structure. She leads me through rich mahogany corridors and up a curved staircase lined with Renaissance-worthy portraits, eventually depositing me in front of an open door.

"Best of luck," she smiles. My eyes remain on her mouth to read her lips, the door beside me opening before I can mutter more than a meager thanks. If she recognizes the trepidation in my expression, she doesn't show it. I turn to face my awaiting audience, scanning their faces in turn.

Five sharply dressed individuals seated behind an oval table turn in unison to scrutinize me. Staying impassive, I pull out my phone, unmute my receivers, and open the app to activate the microphone with a mental groan. The door closes behind me as I straighten my spine and walk across the sunlit room, placing my phone in the center of the table. Only then do I sink into the armchair that's clearly meant for me.

A dark-haired man seated at the head of the table clears his throat beneath a thick turtleneck sweater, his brown eyes pinning me with a forced smile. "Hello, Harper. I'm Dean O'Sullivan. Opposite you is Professor Lawrence, Head of Sciences, who will be overseeing most of your studies here with us."

He gestures toward a woman in a lovely blouse and a kind face, although the Dean's attention is on another. He jerks his head to an interpreter standing in the corner, who hastily begins to move her hands and sign back the sentence to me. I freeze for a moment, torn between correcting her or just rolling with it.

"Oh, um, that's really not necessary." I gesture vaguely in her direction. "My phone mic transmits directly to my receiver. I can hear you just fine." I pull my hair aside briefly to give the board a quick look, then let it fall back into place. After a few impressed and confused glances are exchanged, the Dean dismisses the interpreter and turns back to me with another tight smile.

"Very well. Let me start by saying it is a pleasure to finally meet you. I was intrigued by your entry video and even more impressed by your MCAT score. We're expecting great things from you during your time at Waversea. Now, as for the accommodations for your condition–"

For the next thirty-seven minutes, I watch the clock on the far wall and half-listen to the endless risk assessments and safety protocols being read aloud from a thick document laid across the table in front of me. My tapping toes are the only thing keeping me awake, though

I've let out a few yawns I didn't bother to stifle. Only Dean O'Sullivan speaks, although Professor Lawrence smiles at me warmly throughout. The other three directors present nod occasionally, like ornamental yes-men, but otherwise seem entirely pointless. Finally, the Dean shuts the booklet, and I stretch my arms out in front of me.

"Thank you all, but there's really no need for any extra hassle. I've already emailed all my individual professors with tips on how to accommodate me and asked them to pre-send class topics so I can prep ahead. As long as I've got my phone or one of the backup mic clips in my bag, I'll be just like any other student." I reach for my phone, yearning to get back in that library. "And to that end, all I want is to be treated like everyone else." I fix the Dean with a stern look that would have made Aunt Marge proud.

"It seems like you have everything under control. We'll leave you to it." Dean O'Sullivan watches me with a hawk-like gaze, his smile tight. Finally feeling dismissed, I'm on my feet, phone in hand, and halfway across the room when the Dean's booming voice speaks again. "Oh, there's just one more thing-"

I groan out loud, slowly turning to rest my back against the door. I was so close.

"The CEO, Mr. Waversea, is extremely invested in your success here and wants to ensure you feel supported. To that end, he's personally assigned his son to be your mentor. Rhys is already enrolled in several of your classes, so if you need anything, don't hesitate to reach out to him."

The Dean's lips twitch upward and for the first time, his expression doesn't seem so forced. There's genuine mirth in his features, and I have no idea what that means for me. I catch a few nervous glances ripple through the board members before they all scramble to their feet and rush past me, muttering low enough that I can't catch a single word. Both the Dean and Professor Lawrence stare at me, giving the impression I've overstayed my welcome so I too leave, closing the door behind me.

There's something to be said about heightened senses when one is lacking, and currently, my sixth sense is blaring like a foghorn in my skull. That lasting impression weighs on me, and instead of turning left toward the main entrance, I turn right, following the *fire exit* signs to the bottom floor.

The hallway floor feels slick, freshly polished maybe, causing my sneakers to tap softly as I walk. My phone's still in my hand, faintly filtering the ambient noise into my inner ear. Pushing heavily on the metal door handle, I step into the dusky chill of early evening to realize I've missed most of the day and I've yet to see my dorm. The street-lamps lining the rear car park flicker on, casting shadow over an approaching figure.

I don't fully register him until he's right in front of me. Tall, lean, tattooed. He's my every weakness wrapped into one delicious package. He towers over me, phone pressed to one ear, blue eyes seeming to look straight through me. His hair is longer on top, thrown back haphazardly from the sharp lines of his razor-edged jaw and ink that traces the sides of his neck, dipping down over a broad Adam's apple hidden underneath. Whether he notices my staring or not, he swallows slow and I swear my mouth waters.

"Yeah, yeah, Dad. I'm here, alright? Stop riding my balls," he huffs, looking directly over my head. His voice is low and rough, the kind that makes your stomach flip if it says your name the right way, but my common sense starts to trickle back in. He is completely ignoring my existence.

Ending the call, the guy looks up at the gothic building and eventually, he lowers his head to address me.

"You haven't seen a new girl walking around, have you?" he asks, causing his lip ring to glint. I blink, withdrawing from whatever daze I lost myself in. Oh damn, this is him. Rhys, the CEO's son. I lick my lips, trying to find the words to sound nonchalant when he steps even closer, his cologne wrapping around me like invisible shackles. "She's probably wandering around looking lost and shaking like a leaf. Maybe with a white stick or something. I don't know, I wasn't really listening."

A wash of ice-cold water douses my libido. A white stick? Is he for real? I'm deaf, not blind. Whatever hold he had on me instantly snaps, and I sidestep him with a casual shrug.

"Nope. No idea." I force my legs to move, despite the weight of his lingering gaze dragging down my spine. A shiver threatens to pass through me but I hold onto it until I've rounded a corner when I can slump against the building. I can still smell his cologne as if it's branded on me. Looking directly at my jeans crotch, I hold my hands out.

"*What the fuck is wrong with you?!*" I whisper to my vagina. I may be sheltered, but I hope, or more rather I hoped, I had more willpower than that. I can't lose my mind over the first tattooed, arrogantly hot guy who crosses my path. Especially one who would chew me up and spit me out before I've had the chance to prove I even existed.

CLAYTON

CHAPTER TWO

My fist connects with his smug face right before I tackle him onto the wood flooring. Every time my knuckles crash into his skin, a shiver of delight ripples through my arm and down my spine. Fuck, what I'd give to never stop. To keep pounding the smirk cemented on his face until his blood coats my hands and his last breath rings in my ears like the purest melody. I jab his ribs hard enough to bruise but hold onto the last sliver of restraint not to break a bone.

Even before my two-year stint in the Juvenile Detention Center, labeled the JDC, I was accustomed to violence. Born in the slums and raised on scraps and survival. Fighting is part in my DNA, so if I wanted this asshole dead, he'd already be a goner. And as much as I hate the entitled shithead he is, I'm not about to get myself expelled because he seems to be in an even more irritable mood today than usual.

He slips out from under me on the slick, polished court and lands his elbow square on my jaw. I use my forearm to pin the squirmy fucker back in place. He tries to jerk his knee up into my balls. The cheap-shotting, over-privileged, cop-out motherf–

"I said, that's *enough!*" Coach bellows. I'm yanked into the air by several sets of hands and thrown aside like the trash they think I am.

Coach's face is the color of a goddamn beetroot as he helps Smirky-McShit-Face to his feet, even brushing off his jersey as if my germs might still be clinging to it. Once he's satisfied I haven't caused any real damage, Coach turns to me and jabs a finger into my heaving chest.

"Clayton! On this court, we're a team. Leave your personal shit at the door or you won't make it to your first game!" My jaw clenches and I refuse to be pushed back into line. Standing firm at two inches taller than the coach, my chest pushes against his.

"He shot from outside the line and you won't call him out because his family signs your paycheck. He doesn't even have a shred of talent," I seethe, holding Coach's hard stare. In my peripheral, the rest of the team steps away from me like I've grown horns, a sharp inhale cutting through the silence. I don't give a shit how well-bred Rhys fucking Waversea is. If I had to earn my spot on this squad, then so should he.

Coach starts shaking with fury, bringing his whistle up to blare it in my face, and I can't stop the roll of my eyes. "That's it! Report back here after your classes today. You can run drills alone until you learn to be a valued team player!"

I shrug, making every effort to mask my annoyance. I guess I can kiss goodbye to my pre-booked slot in the boxing ring this afternoon. It's always fully booked out on weekends, so I'll have to wait an entire week, strung tighter than a lonely nymphomaniac who's run out of batteries.

Maybe I could coax Coach into a little one-on-one as punishment, though for me, it'd be the exact opposite. The throbbing of my flesh after a decent pounding is the only time I feel remotely alive anymore. Still, beating my coach within an inch of his life probably isn't the best long-term strategy. He may be bulky, but he's slow and clumsy, too easy a target to be any fun.

On his command, the rest of the team jogs back to the center of the court and fall into line like the obedient lapdogs they are. The ball moves back and forth between black and yellow jerseys, only the occasional bounce echoing through the empty gym like a thunderclap.

Over his shoulder, Rhys lifts his busted lip into another smirk, reminding me exactly why I smashed it in the first place. My fists clench on instinct.

I drop heavily onto the side bench, dragging my gym bag closer and tugging my sports jacket over my shoulders. I've only been on the basketball team officially for two weeks, and already I'm over these five a.m. drills. The fact that we have to wear the matching uniforms this early in the morning is a whole other level of stupid. Coach says they're supposed to 'unite' us. Well, I say screw that. I don't want to be united with any fucker who has as much privilege as *Wavershit*. Just being in the same room as him pisses me off.

He and I have clashed and fought ever since our first semester. The bastard seems to show up wherever I go, somehow always managing to scribble his name on every sign-up sheet right below mine. He's goading me. I'm sure of it. Our hatred sparked immediately. Well, *that*, and the fact that on day one, I caught him pinning another scholarship student to the ground while he rubbed dirt into her face. So yeah, I took it upon myself to knock him off his diamond-studded pedestal.

Rhys is my polar opposite in every way. Where my hair is shaggy and sun-bleached, his is dark brown and cropped short on the sides and back. Where I'm six-two, muscled and broad, he's an inch shorter and lean. From his knuckles to his jawline and every inch in between, his skin is inked in shitty black lines that hold no meaning. A silver ring clings to the side of his bottom lip, matching the one in his eyebrow. Rhys might have a high pain tolerance, but he still punches like a little bitch scared to chip one of his manicured nails.

The fourteen players left on the court run back and forth at Coach's whistle, dropping at the back line for sets of push-ups like clockwork. My eyes track them, not envious in the slightest to be watching from the sidelines. Wait a minute...why am I watching from the sidelines? Coach has his back to me and it seems the only reason I'm sitting here like a wounded puppy is because I'm an idiot. Sliding down the bench, I sling my bag over my shoulder and wait for the next whistle to mask the sound of my sneakers squeezing against the lino as I dart for the sport's hall exit.

In the far corner of the hall, a pair of sophomores lounge against the bleachers. It's a joke really, us down here busting our asses each morning whilst they stick to their private practices, only to be the star players on the court whenever we have a match. Rumor is they are scouting new talent, seeing who can take their place once they leave. Their gazes trail after me in silence, the one with hazel eyes and blond hair quirking a brow. I look straight ahead and keep walking.

I don't do friends, and I definitely don't have the patience to be part of the group he keeps trying to recruit me into. I have one goal here and one goal only, to make a better future for my mom. That's why I'm starting at the academy a year late, thanks to my cell-block vacation. That's why I have to bust my ass to maintain my scholarship. That's why I can't beat the life out of the guy whose family owns the same school that offered me a second chance.

All I can do is keep quiet and keep acing my classes. Otherwise, it's game over.

Stepping outside, the cold air slaps me across the face, goosebumps prickling my arms within the jacket. I stall long enough to pull a gray beanie over my head, and then head down the hill to cut across the deserted campus. I pass silent buildings and locked doors, their windows blank like watching eyes. The sky overhead is heavy and ominous, promising another unforgiving winter's day.

Crossing the central quad, flanked by towering stone buildings, my thoughts drift to those back home. The ones who won't be able to afford heating, who'll line up outside the soup kitchen hoping for a hot meal to carry them through another frozen night.

I stuff my hands deep into my pockets and force the guilt down. Guilt is a pointless emotion when I've worked this hard to claw my way out of a dead-end, but my loyalty to the streets still runs deep. Deep enough that catching the first bus home is always sitting at the back of my mind. Back where people actually look out for one another. Back to where gratitude exists. Not like at Waversea, where students only care about getting high, partying hard, and scraping by on the bare minimum. Not me. I need to focus.

As I enter the main courtyard, I glance toward the giant fountain that marks the center of campus. The lip around the base is wide enough to sit on, and I imagine in the summer, students flock here, cramming around the tiered sculpture praying for a little mist to cool off. Four neatly paved paths branch out from the fountain in all directions, cutting through perfectly maintained lawns.

Massive buildings stand on each side, a concrete ribcage protecting the pulsing heart of the campus. The cafeteria, the main hall, and the library are all buried within them, meaning every student will pass through this quadrant at some point today. To my left is the grand entrance to the Dean's and faculty offices, guarded by a proud, bronze statue of the academy's founder. Great grandaddy Waversea.

Instead of taking the usual path, I veer off across the grass beside it, leaving a trail of flattened blades behind me. Maybe it's the only trace I'll ever leave here, but it makes my chest feel a little lighter anyway.

Exiting through a gap in the upper corner, Bolton Halls comes into view. My dorm lies within the long rows of windows and aged brick. It's one of nine freshman dorm buildings on campus, but the only one reserved for scholarship students or those with grants covering their housing. In other words, if you live here, you're poor as shit, and everyone knows it.

Taking the nearest door, I slip inside as the motion-sensor lights flicker on to greet me. I'm on the fifth floor, same as back home, but here that's only halfway up instead of the top floor. My footsteps echo off the stairwell as I take the stairs two at a time, wanting just a sliver of time to myself before another long-ass day of lectures.

Most of the residents are already up, light seeps under doors, and the frantic tapping of keyboards filters into the hallway. Grabbing my key from my bag, I hear the telltale shuffling of my assigned roommate and let out a quiet sigh. I pause, key poised in the lock, and lean my forehead against the wood.

On second thought, maybe I'll just skip the nap I'd had in mind. Head straight to the cafeteria, stay in my sweat-soaked jersey all day instead. At least then people will steer even further away from me than usual.

The door swings open before I can decide, and I stumble forward, catching myself on a wide-eyed Kenneth Dockerson. His glasses sit crooked on his freckled nose, and his fiery red bedhead sticks out in every direction like he lost a fight with a hairdryer.

"Hey, Clayton! I saw a shadow under the door and I was like *mmm who's that?* Then I thought maybe you forgot your key again but then I was like no way, it's way too early for practice to be done, but I figured I'd check and–"

I cover his mouth with my hand, ignoring the way his lips feel too wet with spittle. Kenneth always talks a thousand miles a fucking hour and never leaves time to swallow or breathe. Lifting my free index finger to my own lips, I signal for him to *shh*, eyebrows drawn tight in warning. When he nods quickly, I slowly peel my hand away and shut the door, keeping my gaze locked on his until I've lowered myself onto my bed and closed my eyes.

A metallic crash sounds a second later, jolting me upright with clenched fists. Kenneth freezes, turning an impossible shade paler as he hovers over the pile of empty soda cans he just knocked off my desk. I'd been working on that can tower for weeks.

Pressing my fingers to my temple, I will myself to find some shred of inner strength. This kid is going to be the death of me. Back home, I would've been the first to protect people like him from the vicious world outside. But this isn't the cutthroat streets. He made the choice to come here, just as I did, so I'm not about to fall into the role of his bodyguard. Or his friend.

"Kenneth, either leave or shut. The. Fuck. Up."

He nods like a rabbit on crack, grabbing his backpack, shoes, and coat and bolting from the room, without putting any of them on first.

I stretch out, hands tucked behind my head, and let out a long breath. Finally, peace and quiet. Well, aside from the morning workout DVD blaring from upstairs and the vocal warmups from a music undergrad down the hall. But that's nothing compared to sirens or gang fights outside my bedroom window.

My mind conjures up my mother as I start to drift into a light doze, her beautiful smile that is always in place. I get my coloring from her. The blonde hair and eyes so dark they look black. I inherited her tenacity and unwavering inner strength too. I'm lucky in that aspect. We were happy once, the three of us. That was before Mom got sick. Before the weight of everyone else's burdens landed on my shoulders. But I can't think about any of that now.

This is my chance to fix everything. I just have to keep attending my classes. Keep my head down, get my degree, finally clean up the mess my worthless old man left behind, and make my mom proud.

That's all that matters, and I won't let anything, or anyone, distract me.

CHAPTER THREE

Shit on it.

So much for the epic new start I promised myself when curling up in bed last night. This morning, I was jolted from a fitful sleep by the sunlight glaring impatiently through the open curtains, my back aching from adjusting to a foreign mattress. The unmade bed and pile of brightly-colored abandoned outfits opposite were the only evidence my roommate had returned so late last night that I have yet to meet her. Hunting for my phone, my heart plummeted to find it had fallen through the gap between the mattress and headboard, vibrating soundlessly on the carpet beneath the bed.

Realizing I was running an hour late, I'd mentally slapped myself, skipped breakfast and it's all gone downhill from there. I bet my implant receivers are having a lovely day though, chilling on the dresser where I stupidly left them. But I did manage to dress appropriately, my #Antisocial t-shirt reflecting my current mood perfectly.

Despite sending several emails to the professors about not needing any special treatment, I knew starting in a new school wouldn't be a smooth process. For the most part, people generally go out of their way to make anyone remotely different feel included, which is great for others. Not for me. I've had to stay behind with two separate professors this morning for a discussion about unnecessary over-pronuncia-tions, and speaking in slow motion with a tone only whales could understand. My phone has been working hard duetting as a micro-phone and Aunt Marge gave me plenty of lip-reading practice over the years.

Currently, I'm sat in physiology, where the professor is dragging her feet back and forth behind her desk with the slowness of an elderly slug. Professor Vickers is a frail woman, with giant circular glasses and even bigger hair. Her greyed curls stick out in all directions and bounce as she steps, appearing as if she's been electrocuted. Physiology isn't the most appealing of subjects at the best of times, but with her brittle tone, I might just about die of boredom each and every day. I stopped listening to her voice filtering through my phone a little while back and started doodling an image of me being hung on an execution dock instead.

Bodies all around suddenly begin to pack up, signaling the end of this torture. Gathering my books into my backpack, I slump down the wooden steps of the curved lecture hall and grab my phone from the professor's desk. She catches my eye, seeming to want to speak to me but I avoid any further conversation with a solid thumbs up before ducking out of the room. There's a bustling line of students filing the hallway, all seeming to head in the same direction that I want to go – to the cafeteria.

The walls are thrumming with laughter, my vision filled with easy smiles and playfully bumping shoulders. I'm quick to shut off my phone, preferring to shuffle along in blissful silence. Maybe I've become prejudiced, or maybe I'll just never forget the overwhelming crush of metal on metal and the high-pitched screech from my mother before my hearing cut me off from the world around me. But I prefer my solitude. No matter where I am, I have my own cocoon of peace. No false words or bitchy comments or ill intentions. I'm oblivious to it all.

I follow a group through the double doors and across the courtyard. The sun has already begun to set, leaving heavy, grey clouds behind for another dismal evening. The four buildings surrounding us in a rectangle fall into shadow so they look more like haunted halls than the vibrant college from the online brochure. Fat raindrops land on my face and create a growing constellation across the path as the hurried footsteps ahead come to an abrupt stop by the central fountain.

I pull up short, straining to see what the holdup is. There's an awkward dance of bumping bodies and sidestepping, surely encased in confused chatter I can't hear. Ducking aside, I swing myself up onto the lip of the fountain. The vantage point provides a much clearer view of what's causing the chaos, and it doesn't surprise me in the slightest. I've only met him once, but I recognize him in an instant. Rhys Waversea is standing in front of the cafeteria entrance, his arms crossed as he shrewdly scans the masses of students before him. He has an entourage of bulky jocks, permitting entry to only a few a time.

Three guesses who he's looking for.

The cold bites through my jeans. Rain is falling harder now, fat drops smacking my hood and slickening the courtyard. The clouds are ready to split open. And I am so not ready to be caught in the middle of whatever the hell this is.

I turn to hop down from the fountain, every instinct screaming at me to slip away unnoticed before Rhys's calculating eyes sweep the crowd and land squarely on me, the new girl already drawing more attention than she ever wanted. But fate isn't on my side today. My foot slips on the slick edge of the stone twisting sharply beneath me. A jolt of pain rushes up my leg so sudden and sharp that I barely have time to gasp before I lose all sense of gravity.

My balance vanishes completely in a breathless moment, the world tipping sideways, the blur of students and grey sky rushing past me as I brace for the unforgiving impact of the cold, hard floor. Although, the impact never comes.

Instead, I crash against a solid weight which grabs onto me without falter. Strong arms wrap around my body like a shield, sheltering me from the rain and nearby stares. It might be that the air is already knocked from my lungs, but staring up into the face of my hero, I forget how to breathe.

He's tall and broad, sandy blonde hair poking out of a beanie hat. His jaw is sharp, his muscles evident by the way he's holding me without any sign of strain, but it's his eyes that captivate me. Endless, black eyes like that of a wild animal, dangerous yet oddly reassuring.

Rain soaks through both our clothes, the shift of movement closing in all around, but I let him hold me for longer than necessary. For the first time since I stepped foot on this campus, I feel completely still, cocooned and protected from the world I've learnt to fear.

"Are you okay?" his lips say. My gaze lingers on his mouth before flicking back up to his eyes. He's watching me with quiet focus and growing concern. I manage to nod, remembering myself and what I was originally running from. Shit, Rhys might have seen or heard the commotion building around us.

I pull away with a desperate sort of urgency, stumbling slightly as I untangle myself from the stranger's arms and murmur something I doubt he even hears before I turn and disappear into the crowd. My ankle aches with each step but I don't slow down, weaving between bodies and darting beneath the shelter of the courtyard's archway, my hood pulled low to hide the flush burning in my cheeks.

The rain has picked up now, falling in thick sheets that blur the lights above and soak the path ahead. I jog all the way to McAllister Halls with the growing wind knocking off my hood and raindrops striking my eyes like spears. Once inside, the lights flicker on as I use the banister to pull myself up to the first floor. I can't tell if I'm trembling from the cold or lack of food as I pull the key from my backpack with shaky fingers. Pushing inside the door, I stop short as a head of fuchsia pink hair twists to look at me.

Her warm, brown eyes soften as she smiles, silver dermal studs creating dimples on either cheek. Colorful tattoos are poking out from the neckline of her blue onesie, the face of Stitch hanging loosely on the hood. But none of that is what caught my attention. An open pizza box is laying upon her crossed legs, the smell drawing into the room.

"*Want some?*" She signs and it takes me a moment to realize she knows more about me than I do her. Pressing the door closed with my back, an awkward moment passes between us until she points to my receivers sitting on the desk. "*I took ASL in high school for extra credit,*" she shrugs and offers me the pizza box again. Too hungry to question the coincidence, I wriggle out of my hoodie and lift a slice to my mouth. Holy mother of grease, it's like a cheese topped medal after the marathon of a day I've had.

I know I'm moaning despite not being able to hear it. After demolishing the first and a second piece, I quickly shower and change into my softest pajamas before dropping down on my roommate's bed. Any hesitation about meeting my roommate fled when I let my blood sugars run too low, not that she seems to mind. Her smile is still in place as I continue to moan around mouthfuls of gooey goodness.

"*I'm A-D-D-Y,*" she finger spells, "but this is my sign name." Addy holds one hand palm up and cups the other into a C, rounding it above slowly whilst mouthing 'chalk'. "*Given to me by a six-year-old at deaf camp I volunteered in last summer. She thought I colored in my skin each morning with the sidewalk chalks.*" I grin along as Addy lifts her sleeves to reveal each arm covered in vibrant flowers and patterns.

When she looks back to me, I suddenly realize I have yet to respond. "I'm Harper, no sign name." I say out loud and look away to avoid her frown. Sign names are one of the highest forms of honor amongst the deaf community, and since I've been hidden away for most of the last decade, I haven't had the chance to meet others like me except for online courses and video calls.

Our phones vibrate at the same time beside the now empty pizza box, the college's app I was told to install flashing up on my screen. As well as delivering general news, the app allows all students to communicate anonymously on its own messaging platform.

Addy tosses her phone aside with a roll of her eyes. *"If Rhys were lucky enough for one, his sign name would be-"* she shakes her closed hand back and forth to mimic masturbating and then signs for a stain. I burst out laughing, my hair failing forward to tickle my ankles. I've never hung out with a girl like this, yet it feels so casual. Even before the accident, I would have sooner been tree climbing with the boys from the neighborhood than window shopping in the mall.

"He's looking for me," I sign back. *"He was assigned as my mentor but he thinks I'm blind."* Addy's eyebrows rise as she giggles, sitting forward as if I just became her new favorite sitcom. Unnerved by the idea, the smirk drops from my face. *"You won't.... tell anyone, right? I'm not ashamed, the opposite actually. I love myself the way I am. But I hate when people treat me differently for no reason."*

Addy is already nodding before I've finished signing, her eyes glistening with understanding. Taking my hands in hers, I read her lips as they move. *"Not my business to tell."* I sag forward in relief, which Addy takes as an opportunity to pull me into a hug. It's an odd sensation I lean into, using her comfort to chase away the heaviness of my shitty day.

I'd prepared myself as much as possible to enter the real world, to be shunned by most while powering through my degree. Many evenings of catch-up revision in my dorm and sitting alone at mealtimes, but I hadn't considered I might actually make a friend so easily. One who is my roommate no less. Maybe I don't have to remain so guarded all the time. Just maybe, I might not have to simply survive. I might actually be accepted.

RHYS

CHAPTER FOUR

Leaning back against the lockers, I take a long drag of my cigarette and blow out a perfect stream of O's to pass the time. The hallway is empty, sterile white walls glowing under the fluorescent lights. Every classroom door is shut tight, muffled lectures echoing faintly from behind them. Even though it's the middle of winter, the tall windows lining the opposite wall are cracked open just enough to let in the icy wind. It whistles through eerily, haunting the halls alongside me. I tug the fur collar of my parka tighter and wonder for the hundredth time this morning, why I even got out of bed.

Although, the answer to that is almost instantaneous. The buzzing in my pocket hasn't stopped since sunrise. I pull out my phone, only to cancel the call and put it away again. My father should get the memo soon enough. I'm not his little lap dog and I don't give a shit for his demands.

I've been the same since I was a kid. Well, more like I've been conditioned to be this way. Spoilt, entitled, refuse to do as I'm told. In fact, I make a point of doing the *exact* opposite.

So whatever reason I combed this campus twice last night and once again this morning looking for this charity case girl is beyond me. Maybe I wanted to check out the freak show before anyone else. Maybe

I'd scare her off with some hazing, but she's a ghost. I couldn't find her anywhere. It's not like I know every student by name, but surely she should've stood out. Aside from the scholarship scum, the students here come from prestigious families. I can sniff out a lost cause like a crack addict, usually.

I groan, dropping my head back against the lockers with a clang. I detest waiting around. Sure, I *could* go to one of my lectures, but what's the point? My last name is basically a golden ticket. I don't need to show up to pass, I just need to keep up with assignments in case my father ever decides to take a closer look at how I'm spending my days.

Speaking of which, a sharp squeak of rubber on tile snaps my attention to the end of the corridor. A barely five foot nerd is sprinting toward me like her life depends on it, frantic and clearly out of breath. Her ponytail swings wildly behind her as she faceplants the floor right by my feet. I sidestep with a sneer, not letting a single thread of her ragged secondhand hoodie touch me. She stammers out an apology and thrusts a plastic sleeve into my hand. I take a quick glance at my biology assignment.

"You were supposed to slide this under my door before sunrise," I say coolly, staring her down until she drops her gaze. "Next time you're late, I'll have you out on your ass faster than you can say, *'but Rhys, I'm your cousin'.*" Her cheeks flush crimson and her nostrils flare but she doesn't say a word.

Scrambling to her feet, she scurries past me, the flap of her sickly pink backpack hanging open. I follow behind, taking one last toke before flicking the last of my cigarette inside. A thin line of smoke has already begun trailing her as she veers around a corner and I pause outside the biochemistry lab.

Kicking my foot back on the wall, I scrub a hand down my face just as the door beside me opens and streams of students pile out into the corridor. I spot a beanie hat an inch above everyone else and stick out my leg to trip him up. An elbow is thrown into my gut before he darts off in the crowd and I chuckle to myself.

Toying with the trash almost gets me off more than the monthly three-way with the Brent twins, but there's something different about Clayton Michaels. He has a backbone and the fists of steel to match. Dare I say, I've finally found a worthy nemesis and I'm genuinely looking forward to spending the next few years fucking with him.

Swerving into the room as the last person leaves, my eyes fall on the pretty brunette from last night. Her waves tumble down her back, the strong lighting bouncing off her alabaster skin. Her pale green eyes flick to me instantly as if she can sense my presence, subconsciously biting down on her lower lip.

Snatching her phone from the professor's desk, she pulls a mask of indifference over her features and shoulders past me on her way out. I smirk as I watch her go, blue jeans hugging her rounded backside perfectly. Damn, maybe I should start going to my classes after all.

"Nice of you to show your face but you've missed class – again." A whiney voice snides. I turn back to the stick of a man behind a large desk with narrowed eyes. Hunched over to peer at a laptop screen through his thick-rimmed glasses, a white lab coat swamps his frame like the failed scientist he is. Stalking closer, I trail my finger across the wood and push his laptop closed.

"Remember who you are speaking to, Peterson." I slam my freshly printed assignment onto the table and lean forward, hardening my features enough to make him swallow hard. "I'm only here now as a courtesy. How are my grades looking?"

"Top marks, as usual," he grumbles with a clenched jaw. I drink in his hate, thriving on the high of control. I have the entire faculty firmly beneath my heel, forced to dance to whatever tune I feel like. I take a long inhale, the crisp air of being untouchable filling my lungs before striding out with a huge grin on my face.

A flash of blonde whips into view, slender arms snaring around my neck. Klara. Her full chest pushes against me as she bobs up and down excitedly, as if that might persuade me to hug her back. Settling on staring at a spot on the ceiling, I wait out the daily torture that comes with having a so-called girlfriend. Even the term is offensive, but this is one of two aspects of life my father thinks he controls.

Klara Kavanagh is the daughter of the college's most generous investor, so it's expected for her to be my date to all of the high society galas we attend together whilst her mom not-so-secretly screws my father in the cloakroom and her dad acts none the wiser. I can't stand upper-class politics, but I have a plan and a hefty allowance which funds my ink addition so for now, I'll play along.

Finally peeling Klara off me, my hands braced on her shoulders, I glance at the hourglass inked onto the back of my left hand. The sand's long gone, replaced by a mound of tiny skulls. In the upper half, only one remains, a golden crown balanced on its bony head like it's seconds from falling. That one's me, because time doesn't wait for anyone, king or otherwise.

Klara crosses her arms and stamps her foot, trying her hardest to look intimidating in heels that cost more than most people's rent. I drag my gaze back to her, the ring in my eyebrow tugging as I cock it and wait for her to drop the pout.

"I've got a free period," she purrs, unzipping her white fur coat to reveal she's wearing absolutely nothing underneath. "Want to head back to yours?"

Her body's objectively perfect. A huge, perky rack, toned stomach, and that cliché Barbie-blonde hair and ice-blue eyes combo that's supposed to short-circuit male brains. But it does nothing for me. There's no thrill in having my meal served on a silver platter. I want to chase it through the woods, corner it, sink my teeth in, and ruin it for anyone else.

"If you spent more of your free periods in the library instead of lying beneath me like a dead fish," I murmur, brushing past her, "maybe there wouldn't be so many rumors flying around about me dating a ditsy slut." Klara freezes, her jaw going slack and tears instantly welling, but they don't fall. Not real ones, anyway. I don't look back as I shove through the nearest door and straight into the bitter cold.

Preemptive trickles of snow drift through the courtyard, lazily speckling the ground between shoeprints. I yank the neck of my parka tighter as I push through a group of sophomores blocking the path. They don't register me until my shoulder clips a linebacker built with a brain to match. He takes a step toward me, but the look I shoot over my shoulder makes him think twice. Coward. I bite down on my lip ring and keep walking, the coppery taste of blood sinking into my mouth. It's not as thrilling as a fight, but it takes the edge off.

Cutting across the main quad and through alleyways, I don't stop until my place comes into view. My personal kingdom, and the best damn party pad in the state. Tucked away on the edge of campus, the two-story whitewash house is all mine, although it's never empty.

Even now, when most people are locked away in classrooms, there will be half-naked girls snoring on the sofas, some randoms tangled in upstairs beds, stoners hotboxing the porch, and more than likely a bunch of guys kicking a ball around the backyard. I don't know their names. Don't need to. They know *mine*, and that's what counts. I'm the fucking king, and they are my desperate, eager subjects. I come and go as I please, and they keep the house pristine, hoping I'll toss them a scrap of acknowledgment.

My boot hits the bottom step just as my phone starts vibrating again. I sigh, head drooping forward. If I don't answer, there's a real risk he'll show up in person, and after spending the holidays locked in the mausoleum we call home, I've earned at least three months of peace.

"What?" I answer without checking the caller ID, even though I already know.

"Have you found her yet?" my father's voice crackles down the line, cold and clipped as usual.

"I've been busy with my studies," I say, stretching lazily and yawning into the receiver. "I'll track down your precious little charity case when it suits me."

"Don't bullshit me. You haven't stepped foot in a classroom all semester." That gets my attention. I tune out the rest, mentally tallying which rat-faced professor is brave, or dumb, enough to tattle. Could be Vickers, that twitchy rodent of a woman who gossips like it's oxygen. Or Polesdon, who practically wets herself every time my dad darkens her doorway. "–your allowance," he finishes.

"Yeah, yeah, I heard the threats yesterday. Human experiment. Bigger research budget. Caribbean villa. Boo hoo." I lift my free hand to catch a flake of snow, then crush it in my palm.

"Just do it. Be the most *hospitable* version of yourself you can manage."

I actually laugh at that. Coming from a man who wouldn't let his own mother stay over Christmas because she'd 'clash with the decor.' Sensing the call's about to end, I speak quickly.

"You're wrong, by the way. I *do* attend one class, I haven't missed a single ass-crack-of-dawn basketball practice." A beat passes as my smug grin takes back position on my face. Screwing with my dad is a sure-fire way to brighten my day every damn time.

"Well, at least you'll have a backup when I disown you." I chuckle as the line clicks dead. That "when" is the only thing keeping me going. Once it happens, I'll finally be free to burn this entire world to the ground.

Pocketing my phone, I whistle at a group of jocks through the window. They leap to their feet like Pavlov's dogs and stand to attention on the porch. The kind of power that buzzes through me, lighting every nerve ending in my body, can only come from this level of control. "There's a new scholarship girl on campus. You find her and you bring her to me." I push my tongue against my lip ring, watching them nod and run down the road like a pack of wolves out on a hunt. I feel like an idiot now for trying to track her down myself, but at least this way, the job gets done.

My father's eyes actually lit up the day I handed him my Waversea application to sign his approval. Well, one eyebrow twitched and the corners of his mouth uncurled slightly, which is the proudest I've ever seen him. I'm sure he had long, sleepless nights picturing me derailing his legacy. He would've been right, if not for one inconvenient truth. I loathe him too much to simply sit home and be stubborn.

I loathe every word out of his smug mouth. Every ounce of deluded self-worth. Every disgusted glare he's ever flicked in my direction. And more than anything, I loathe this academy that he worships like a goddamn shrine. Waversea is a rotting temple of legacy and lies. It's filled with rejects and overachievers and charity cases who somehow, against all logic, have managed to win more of his attention than I ever have.

Fuck that.

Instead of following in my father's footsteps, as expected, I'm going to become a man of my own creation, as close to a God as any mortal has ever been. They will worship me, falling at my feet and begging for any scrap of attention I can be bothered to give. Then he will know not to underestimate me. His legacy will crumble into dust as I devote my life to destroying his.

Piece by piece, brick by brick, I'm going to tear this college apart from the inside out and set alight to any buildings that dare to remain standing. Only once the flames are reflected within my eyes and warming my cheeks will I be happy, and I don't give a fuck who's stuck inside when it goes down.

CLAYTON

CHAPTER FIVE

"Again!"

I scoop the ball from the floor, dribbling it across the empty court and shooting it into the basket for the hundredth time. Sweat pours down my forehead, my damp hair falling forward into my eyes as Coach shouts orders at me from the side bench. I'd be pissed about being stuck in here so late in the evening, if I wasn't fucking loving it. As long as I can tune out Coach's voice, I relish having the court to myself. The smooth wooden flooring, the fluorescent lightening and citrus scent of recently cleaned bleachers. Luxuries I could have only dreamed of whilst locked up.

I hadn't planned on having a criminal record before turning twenty, but life doesn't give a shit for the plans of the poor. We get tossed aside from society, our only two options being drugs or crime. Although it wasn't my fault I ended up in a youth detention center, at least I used that time to my advantage.

I took every crumpled worksheet on offer, read every faded textbook whilst working in the miniscule library, encouraged myself to be better when everyone else had given up on me. Using the hallway's dim light filtering through the tiny window, I filled out the scholarship application and used my commissary to buy the damn stamp.

The ball slips through the net with another clean whoosh, landing straight back in my hands. I dribble between my legs, weaving around invisible teammates as I race down the court and back. I fake a chest pass, laughing quietly to myself, before I spring up and sink another perfect shot. It's too easy. Who needs anyone else? The thought hits harder than expected, dragging a shadow from the past into the light, and my grin fades.

Coach's whistle snaps me out of it, a harsh sweep of his hand ordering me to join him on the bench. Passing him the ball and pulling the jersey over my head, I wipe my face and chest with the black material before taking a seat beside him. My last name is printed across the back in yellow, with a large number seven in the center. A sight which should fill me with pride, if it wasn't for the overriding guilt I can't shake.

"That was good. You're as ready as you can be for Friday's game. But eventually, good won't cut it. You could be a great addition to this team, if only-"

"I'm not the one who needs to hear this pep talk." I interject, feeling the instant clench of my shoulders. Just like that, all of the stress I've been trying to exude comes rushing back. "I can't be on a team with someone who doesn't know the meaning of the word."

"I know," Coach breathes, then instantly looks around wide-eyed as if he didn't mean to say that out loud. I shake my head knowing it's pointless. Rhys is untouchable and he knows it.

Joining the basketball team was supposed to help. Work off some frustration, maybe make a couple of friends. But then that entitled prick added his name just below mine on the sign-up form and all of my hopes went up in flames. I'm sure he did it just to mess with me, being the scholarship jock. Now I'm trapped in a vicious cycle. Unable to drop out and let him win, but also unable to stand being near him without raising my fists.

It took me a whole three seconds to figure out Wavershit when I first met him. The classic rich kid yes, but beneath the bullshit there's something darker lurking. He starts fights for sport, picking on the weak and vulnerable who don't stand a chance. He smiles in the face of pain, getting off on himself being hurt just as much as when he hurts other. No conscience or concept of remorse, no sense of authority. He is backed and fully supported by his father's title and wealth, which makes him far more dangerous than people realize.

Coach is just another pawn playing his game. I rise from the bench without waiting to be dismissed and stride towards the locker room door. My footsteps echo against the lino, bouncing with finality that my reprieve is about to end. I throw open the door, recognizing a moment too late that the hairs on the back of my neck have prickled. I pull up short, assessing the empty room in the same way I used to gauge the JDC rec rooms. There was always someone waiting to jump you from behind or hold a handcrafted weapon to your neck, and those instincts still ride me hard now.

The air is thick with disinfectant, a discarded mop bucket suggesting the cleaners were in recently. Fluorescent lights buzz against metal lockers lined in uniform rows, the room hollow in the center aside from a single, wooden bench. The showers are tucked out of sight around the corner.

Nothing jumps out immediately. No sound, no movement, yet the unease tightens in my gut like a fist, coiled and ready to strike. I visually sweep the room again, slower this time, allowing my eyes to catch on the one detail that doesn't belong. My grey locker, number seven the same as my jersey, is cracked half-open, the metal lock I'd secured hours earlier now hanging useless and open on the vinyl tile below.

I don't call out to ask who's there. Instead, I ease into the room with a measured, predatory pace, hugging the edge of the room. My shoulders are drawn tight with tension, my hands curled into fists at my sides, ready for whoever's dumb enough to hide in here and think I won't find them.

Keeping my breath measured and my steps silent, I ignore the desire to check my lockers contents, keeping my shoulders bunched and fists at the ready. At my back, Coach's office is empty and cloaked in darkness behind a metal grate. A perfect hiding place if it weren't for the chunky lock on the exterior. That only leaves the showers.

Crouching slightly by the last corner to investigate, a shaky exhale sounds from behind and I grin. Gotcha. In one swift pounce, I've pivoted around the corner and closed my fingers around a scrawny neck as an actual squeak leaves my stalker. I slam him into the tiled wall. A pair of glasses fly from a freckled face and shockingly red hair catches my attention.

"Kenneth?!" I bellow, tightening my grip on his throat for a millisecond before releasing him. He stumbles to the floor, coughing and scrambling after his glasses. I follow behind, retrieving the frames much easier than his blurred vision can manage, and press them firmly into his sweaty, trembling palm. Once my roommate has adjusted himself, I step back to fold my arms across my bare chest and stare him down like I'm deciding whether or not to snap his neck.

"What the fuck are you doing creeping around in here?"

"Um, well, see it's almost ten o'clock." Kenneth points to his Velcro strap watch on his equally freckled forearm as if that explains everything. His eyes flick to the clench in my jaw and widen, a jumble of word vomit falling from his lips.

"I didn't see you in your usual spot in the library and then you weren't in our room and it was getting late so I thought mmm, Where's Clayton? So I checked the calendar on your emails but they were blank and then I thought I know! I have the tracking app linked to your phone which said you were here, so I ran to the cafeteria and have put dinner in your locker-"

"Stop," I hold up a flat palm and then push my fingers against my temple. There is so much wrong with everything he just said. "You're giving me a headache. How did you get into my locker?" Pushing his glasses back up his nose, Kenneth's bulged eyes flick between me and the lock on the floor behind me.

"The code is your mom's birthday," his voice trails off as I stare at him dumbfounded. How in the hell...actually, I can't even deal with this tonight. At the mention of food, my stomach growls on cue and a low pounding starts to settle at the base of my skull. I need to eat, shower and sleep in that order.

Backtracking across the room, I remove the takeout box from my locker along with my clothes and slam it shut. Kenneth appears by my side, pulling one of my black beanies from his coat pocket as I quickly change.

"We are going to have a serious talk about boundaries later," I grumble, snatching the hat from him and stuffing it over my sweaty hair.

Pushing the takeout box, which smells heavenly by the way, into his hands, I shove my arms into my military style jacket and head for the exit. Kenneth shuffles along behind me, remaining unusually quiet for the entire walk. Even though I hate people tampering with my stuff, I find I'm not as pissed at him as I should be. Ignoring his creepy stalkerish ways, it's been far too long since someone has looked out for me. Everyone from my old neighborhood turned their back on me the day I was incarcerated, which is fine. But what I can't forgive is how they turned their back on my mom too.

My eyes prickle with sentiment ever so slightly at the thought, which has nothing to do with the sub-zero temperature of the night. Reaching the entrance of Bolton Halls several seconds before Kenneth manages to catch up, I tell him to go ahead with a scowl.

His scrawny legs have climbed the first staircase before I pull out my phone and hit the call button for mom's care facility. I'm sure the dial tone is about to cut to voicemail when the grouchy voice of the receptionist snarls the opening hours at me for the dozenth time but patches me through anyway. Despite most likely being tucked up in bed, my mom's sweet voice echoes through the speaker on the third ring.

"Is that you Jellybean?" I smile, ignoring the painful tug in my chest.

"Yeah mom, it's me. How are you keeping?"

"Oh you know me, soldiering on." There isn't a truer truth in the universe than that. My mom is a soldier. For as long as I can remember, my mom has carried herself as effortlessly as an angel, despite the hellish hands she's been dealt throughout her life. Through every winter without heating or every Christmas without presents, she filled our hearts with her warmth and gifted us with her laughter. "And how's my darling boy? Excited to start college?" I crouch down before my knees have the chance to give out, pulling my beanie lower over my forehead.

"I started already, remember mom? But everything's great. Classes are easy enough, everyone's really friendly and there's a basketball game at the end of the month." My mouth fills with acid, the lies pouring out with far too much ease at this point.

"Oh, lovely! And you know I'll be in the front row cheering you on. I've always been your number one fan." I can hear the smile spread across her face. I stuff my fist into my mouth, choking back the sob trapped in my throat.

"That'll be great, I'll save you a seat. I have to go, I have ball practice early," I mutter, unable to keep up this charade any longer.

"Of course Jellybean. But before you go, do me a favor and check in on Clayton. I don't like the crowd he's hanging out with. He needs his big brother to keep him on track." Tears spring from my eyes, wetting a trail to my chin.

"I'll talk to him, Mom. Love you."

"I love you Jellybean."

I end the call before she can hear the crack in my voice, a sharp hitch that slices through the back of my throat like broken glass. A following guttural sound wrenches free from my chest, somewhere between a gasp and a groan, and I press a fist to my sternum like I can hold myself together with sheer will. Cold air rushes from my lungs in short, panicked puffs, fogging up the night in front of me, blurring the world just enough to pretend I'm not coming undone.

But I am. The wall I've spent months building, brick by stubborn brick, silence mortared between the cracks, is crumbling under the weight of his name. Jeremy. My mom may not remember much, but she would never forget her son, my brother. Just hearing her say it is like stepping on a landmine I planted myself and forgot to mark.

I can't squeeze the sides of my head tight enough to erase the mental image of Jeremy from behind my eyelids. The broad frame and features we share, our pitch black eyes and full lips. His easy smile and the blonde locks he secretly dyed the same shade as mine. Mom struggled to tell us apart most the time, and that was before the dementia set in.

Her words play around my mind on an endless loop. *'He needs his big brother.'* Damn if that isn't the truth. I lost him and my future in the same night, unable to mourn him properly until I was alone in a darkened cell. The downward spiral only worsed from there. I was drowning in a void of failure. Refused to eat or sleep. I existed in a hidden hole in the ground, serving my time until I could return home.

But such a time would never come, and I had no home to go back to. Mom's illness took her frighteningly fast after Jeremy's death, her mind pulling her into a retreat where he not only still lived but is thriving. She's stuck in the summer before he was due to start at Waversea Academy, making us all proud as the basketball playing protégé he was.

It was due to her confusion that I ended up here. She thinks I'm him, and there's only so many times I can tell her he's gone. So the logical thing to do at the time was to take his place. Study hard, prove I'm not the fuck-up I've always been and live out Jeremy's future in his place, achieving the goals he didn't get a chance to see through.

For a while, I was able to trick myself into feeling closer to him. But now I feel like a fraud. I'll forever be stuck in my brother's shadow. No matter what I manage to accomplish, no matter how much I prove myself, in my mom's rare moments of clarity she will still see me for what I really am. The waste of space who is responsible for his brother's death.

CHAPTER SIX

A light tap touches my shoulder, Addy giving me another nudge to get up. I swat her away, putting my roommate back on snooze for another ten minutes. True, it's already past lunchtime but I'm still adjusting to a steady routine. Luckily, everyone was gifted free periods this morning for some ball game which has put education on hold for a day. Art students are decorating, the marching band is performing alongside the cheerleaders and other dance majors, and anyone who doesn't like sport can use the time to study in peace.

Remaining curled up in bed with my phone, I put an old-school playlist on, playing it directly into my implants whilst I scroll through Waversea's school app. The home page displays main news, which apparently consists of upcoming sports rallies and a huge party at the end of year that is already being planned. There's a section for each subject containing resources from lessons, a forum for general questions and the option for profiles to anonymously connect under screennames. I'd spent far too long on mine, but eventually settled on simply **Readmylips44**.

Another tap on my shoulder becomes a full shake and the covers are whipped off me. Uh oh, I've triggered Addy's domineering side.

Hiding my grin, I grab some clothes and head for the shared bathrooms down the hall, leaving her to fuss over my unmade bed.

Over the past few nights, I've spent more quality time with Addy than any other person in years, and it feels amazing. Addy has told me about her childhood, family, hobbies and her love for musical theatre while I soaked in her vibrant personality. She also warned me she won't be around much due to her busy timetable, but to message if I need anything. Technically she's only studying drama, but has taken on various extra classes in singing, dancing and set design to boost her resumé.

I shower and change, stretching my arms and back several ways for a ripple of satisfying cracks to pop along my spine. After throwing on a quick layer of make-up and mascara, I emerge in my '*I don't listen to assholes*' t-shirt and ripped black jeans, my stomach growling on cue. I take the time to push my aids over my ears, the receivers snapping onto my scalp softly before I cover them with my hair.

I've made the decision that I will experience campus life the way everyone else does. Even if only for today. Sharing pizza and laughing with Addy has given me a glimpse of the life I could have had if it wasn't for the accident. But more than that, it has made me wonder if instead of being strong like I thought, I may have been shutting the world out. In convincing myself I don't need emotional connections, I might have been holding myself back from being happy.

"Ready?" Addy asks, her body language much more impatient than her tone. I smile guiltily and nod, taking her arm after she's locked our dorm room door.

The sun is shining brightly outside, penetrating the clouds to brighten the pathway and mirror my mood. A glistening layer of frost coats the central fountain like thousands of tiny diamonds forming an outer shell on the sandstone. The courtyard is almost empty with the odd person milling in and out of the library. The books beyond the closing door beckon me as I pass, but I resist. Just. Today is for pushing the boundaries I've grown comfortable hiding behind.

Thankfully, the lack of other bodies continues into the cafeteria. I line up, rubbing my hands over my jeans to fight the chill from them. Selecting our options from the length of the back-cafeteria wall, I spare a glance around at the unusually empty hall. Trays sit stacked beside a silent buffet, the lingering scent of coffee and grease the only sign of this morning's early rush. Sunlight continues to spill through tall windows onto vacant benches and polished floors. The Waversea's spared no expense on their latest renovations, although I expect that's usual when converting a public school into a private one.

I stumbled across many articles about it when researching my college options. Apparently it was a huge scandal over a decade ago. Thousands of students were forced out if they couldn't afford to pay the new fees and their years of hard-earned grades suddenly meant nothing. Now, only four people a year are awarded a full scholarship. I hate to think of myself as lucky, but without the life insurance left to me by my parents, I would have been stuck at the state college down the road from our old house. But in turn, I wouldn't strive to be a clinical scientist in audiology if it weren't for the loss of my hearing so it's all swings and roundabouts.

Devouring a heavily iced bear claw and grabbing a coffee to go, Addy and I head directly towards the dome-topped building in the distance. Every streetlamp and fence beyond the courtyard is dripping with the college colors of yellow and black, banners hanging all-around of the elite Waversea Warriors. Many of their players go pro straight from graduation, the academy's reputation opening doors for them which others could only dream of.

Addy's arm is looped through mine again as we fall into step, her long legs pulling me faster than I'd normally go, but I let her lead. The closer we get to the stadium, the more students flood in from every direction, laughter and shouts ricocheting between the tall buildings like echoes trapped in a canyon. I can feel the thrum of the crowd under my Doc Martens before we even reach the main doors, a low, vibrating pulse that hums along my spine.

The second we step into the stadium, the atmosphere slams into me like a wave. A sharp whistle bounces off every surface and the speakers overhead rumble out the latest pop remix. The collision of sound that feels too wide and too fast, even with my implants turned low.

I flinch. Just once. Just enough that Addy squeezes my hand and checks on me with her eyes. I nod again, more firmly this time, and shake out my shoulders as if that can loosen the nerves curling around my ribs. I can do this. I need to do this. I need to be normal.

The whole stadium is bathed in gold light, banners draped from every beam, crowds already gathering in the stands even though tipoff isn't for another twenty minutes. We spot seats halfway up the bleachers, angled just enough for a clear view of the court. The floor is polished to a perfect gleam, reflecting the lines of the hoops and the oversized 'W' in the center like a mirror trying to convince me that this place is beautiful instead of brutal. It's not working.

I shrink into my seat, anxiety overriding my confidence. It's so much bigger and louder than I expected. Not the ideal place or time for me to embrace being a fully fledged student. I reach up to turn off my cochlears when Addy nudges me, gesturing toward a group of cheerleaders stretching on the sidelines.

"See that girl with the platinum braid?" she says close to my ear, pointing discreetly. "She hooked up with Coach's son last week. Cried about it in Art History, then did it again two nights later." I grin despite myself, lowering my arm. "And that ginger guy with the glasses down at the front, he's roommates with one of the players on the team. Weird kid, has a strange fascination for fire apparently. Someone in my dance class offered to go out with him once, but all he seemed to be interested in was how flammable her dress was. She had to have skin grafts on her thighs."

My eyes flash wide, a shudder rolling down my spine. I'm pretty sure that boy is in my biochem class. Addy is distracted from her stories by a tray of popcorn being marched up and down the stands. She calls out, grabbing us both a box and settles in just as the doors at the far end of the court open. I pop a piece into my mouth, watching two figures stride out ahead of the team. The marching band strikes up a loud rachet and the cheerleaders become hysterical. Whereas my heart nearly falls out of my ass.

I know them. Both of them. On the left is my hero, although I should really stop calling him that. I mean the man that stopped me from plummeting to the ground and breaking my neck. He is the taller of the pair, much broader. The kind of athlete who is sculpted by obsession, not just training. His eyes are narrowed, his posture tense as if he's walking into a boxing ring, not a basketball court.

The other is Rhys. A little leaner but by no means weaker, covered in ink from his knuckles to his jawline, disappearing behind his black and yellow jersey displaying the number one. Unsurprisingly, there's a confidence in the way he walks. A cockiness is his smirk. I'm not fooled by the volatile calm he exudes, like a lit match walking into a fireworks factory.

Everyone sits a little straighter when they appear, like the air itself has shifted. Like everyone is hoping to be noticed. I nudge Addy.

"Who is the blond?" I mutter quietly. Addy's eyes fly up to the court and raises a brow.

"Clayton Michaels? Do you know him?"

I quickly shake my head. A voice screams through the speakers, introducing the Waversea Warriors, and the crowd erupts on cue. This time, I do shoot my hands to my receivers and rip them off, but not before I catch a full-bodied roar echoing off every metal beam in the ceiling.

The rest of the team takes their places on the court, but I hardly notice because my heart is racing louder than any drumbeat. It hammers against my ribcage, the tremors of what could quite possibly be a panic attack starting. I will take full praise for my optimism, that I could walk into a ball game after years of silence and just get used to it, and I'll also take the constructive criticism that it was a really stupid fucking idea. The headache growing at the base of my skull will surely punish me for it later.

Addy says something beside me, maybe a joke, maybe a warning, I don't know, because the popcorn box is trembling in my lap and my spine has fused to the backrest as I watch them move onto the court. A pair of sophomores are in tow, a clear bromance happening between them. It makes the frostiness between the two front runners even more obvious.

Clayton is already in position, stretching his arms overhead in one long, fluid motion that makes the hem of his jersey ride up, revealing the carved ridges of a stomach that could shame a Grecian statue, and the girls in the rows below us lose their collective minds. I hate that I notice. I hate that it does something to me. I hate that I want to see if he looks this solid up close, if he smells like rain again, if his voice rumbles like thunder just before the storm hits. All things I blame my overactive brain for dreaming up last night.

Rhys is dominating his playground. Making the cheerleaders swoon and most of the guys insecure. A group over the far side, who are clearly his boys, are riled up, fists in the air and chanting what I believe to be his last name. *Waversea, Waversea, Waversea.* I hear the chant in my head as clearly as it's being shouted.

After receiving some roughhousing, Rhys circles back to talk trash, causing Clayton to bristle and seeming to want to swing at him before the ball's even been thrown. There is no friendliness between the two, that's obvious. I'd hazard a guess that they fully hate each other, but that doesn't stop my mind running away from me.

Seeing them side by side, shoulder to shoulder, swaggering across the court as if they own it, they look like sin dressed in school colors. I swallow, blinking away the vision of me squeezing in between the pair of them and seeing just how good their teamwork could be. Damn, I need to stop reading dark romance.

Instead, he grits his teeth and turns his back on Rhys, taking another gaze out into the crowd. I don't think I'll ever bore of looking at him. Blond, stoic, with a face so cold it's beautiful. Not the soft kind of beautiful. The kind you'd only ever describe once, because it would haunt you afterwards.

His eyes scan the bleachers, uninterested and unreadable, until he sees me. I would have been able to convince myself that I'd imagined the flash behind his eyes, if Addy didn't catch my eye and mouth, 'what the fuck was that?' I shrug, turning my focus to inspecting my popcorn individually while the blaze in my cheeks calms down.

Thankfully, he's soon distracted by the start of the game. The ten players on the court are split into two teams, pitting Clayton and Rhys against each other. No surprise to them, apparently. It's like watching two wolves in the same pack circle each other with barely hidden teeth, waiting for the excuse to bite. They don't speak, but remain constantly aware of where the other is. The whistle is blown, the ball launched into the air, and chaos ignites across the court.

Rhys' elbow snaps out, catching Clayton in the face before he steals the ball and ducks away. Clayton doesn't falter, remaining on Rhys' tail with confident strides. He yanks Rhys to the ground by the back of his jersey, to which the coach issues a warning.

I expect to see a round of boo's pass through the audience, but the opposite happens. The cheering is wild, and I don't understand it. Addy tosses popcorn into her mouth, not a trace of surprise passing through her features. I blink several times, watching the rest of the players shove and shoulder barge Clayton around the court. The only exaggerated jeers and taunts are being hurled his way, both on and off the court. That's when I realize the crowd hasn't come to watch a match. They've come to see a blood bath.

RHYS

I spotted her the moment I stepped onto the court. Or maybe I felt her presence. Like water amongst an oil spill, there's a purity surrounding her I'm unfamiliar with. She's the girl from the other night, a foreign, beautiful face that has lingered in my thoughts. Why don't I know her?

At least she's about to know me.

The game picks up speed like a car without brakes. I've played rough before, but this time feels different. There's something feral under my skin, like I'm trying to claw my way out of it, and every time I look across the court and see *him*, the need to swing instead of dribble takes over.

Clayton doesn't belong on this floor. Not because he isn't good, annoyingly he is, but because his self-righteous silence pisses me off. He's the one who's crawled out of the gutter, yet he acts as if he's better than me. Every time I drive the ball past him, I can feel his judgment. I get enough judgement at home, I refuse to accept it here. On my campus, in my kingdom.

The crowd doesn't hesitate to give me that validation, however. They roar for me, urging me to push it further. To prove my ruthlessness. I duck and spin, cutting through the court like a blade. Clayton blocks one of my shots. He doesn't gloat, which somehow makes it worse. His restraint is infuriating. It's all shoulders, silence and tightly wound discipline. Still, I don't hide the smirk as I stumble back, knowing how to get under his skin. It's my mission to find that breaking point.

I throw elbows without a care. I taunt with words only he can hear. I slam into him hard enough that the floor reverberates beneath our sneakers. The ref whistles, but we're past the point of rules now. This isn't basketball anymore. It's something else, something primal. The crowd feels it, too. Their cheers get louder, their gestures becoming messier. Most are already on their feet, shouting over each other, more excited for violence than victory.

The ball makes a clean bounce, landing directly in my hands and evidently, putting a target on my back. Clayton is done practising restraint, running full speed with his shoulder aimed at my stomach. I throw the ball just before he collides with me, taking us both to the ground hard. Laughter bursts from my lips, despite the air knocked from my lungs. His weight is crushing, pinning me down whilst slamming his fist into my ribs. It should be enough to keep me stuck in place, and although I'm lean, I'm agile.

Twisting, I force my shoulder between us, using my elbow to shift his weight aside. I can hear my boys chanting from the sidelines, voices raspy with excitement, hands pounding the edge of the stands. They want blood, or at least a good show. I aim to give them both.

Rolling rapidly, my back takes the brunt of multiple punches until I throw my head backwards. A delightful crack is followed by a bellow which echoes around the domed ceiling, enough weight lifting for me to army crawl free. An arm slips around my neck to hold me in place, tightening as I chuckle. Should it be embarrassing or impressive that I could easily get off on this? I'm getting hard either way.

Tucking my legs beneath me, I buck upwards and dislodge my attacker in one, swift move. In the next moment, I've bent forward to throw him over me, aiming a punch for Clayton's throat. The swoosh of a basket rings through the crowd's booming noise, but I don't bother looking up to see who scored. The game is mute at this point, my ego needing to be stroked by those cheering me on. Call it desperation, but the validation ripples over me like a caress.

My sneakers squeal against the court as I lunge to my feet. My jersey clings to my back, damp with sweat, every muscle in my torso aching from the impact, but I don't care. Clayton's already pushing himself up, wiping blood from his nose like it's nothing. I hate him for that. The cold stoicism that never cracks.

We're circling each other now, not even pretending to play. The ref is yelling something about technical fouls, about warnings and benches and ejections, but his voice is barely audible over the roar of the crowd. It pulses through the walls, through the floorboards, through my skull. My body vibrates with it. The band's stopped playing. The cheerleaders have stopped cheering. The game has stopped, except for us.

My gaze is drawn upwards, over Clayton's head to the brunette who has been staring intently this entire time. I felt her gaze, felt it warming my blood and urging me onwards. Except when I look now, the space where I expected her to be is empty.

Clayton feints left. I don't fall for it. I lunge forward instead, gripping his jersey in both fists and driving him back a step, just to feel the resistance. His hands grab for my arms, and we're locked, shoulder to shoulder, nose to nose, breathing each other's heat and hatred.

"You act like you're better than me," I mutter, low and guttural. "But I know what you are. Gutter scum."

Clayton's black eyes flicker, just barely. Just enough to prove I've struck a nerve. I shove him backward and he stumbles, but he doesn't go far before he's swinging again. His punch lands just below my jaw. It's not clean, more of a graze, but it splits the skin, the taste of copper flooding my mouth. My head jerks sideways, and then I see her.

She's halfway down the bleachers, hood drawn over her hair, chin tucked low, threading between bodies like she can disappear. But I know it's her. Even with her face hidden, the weight of her absence hits me in my chest the second she disappears through the arched exit. She didn't stay to watch me win, and for some reason that cuts deeper than Clayton's fists.

My feet are moving, no fucks given for the man staring me down and waiting for my next attack. Clayton doesn't deserve my explanation, or my time for that matter. Abandoning the court, I shove past those who reach out and try to urge me to stay. The stadium entrance is just as bright, flooded with fluorescent lighting that bounces off the black hoodie half-running out of the door. I catch up to her outside, the cool air slamming through my light jersey and freezing the sweat on my body.

"Where do you think you're going?" I ask far too harshly. She blinks up at me, shock passing through her delicate face. Her pale green eyes linger on my lips as I tongue my lip ring. "The show was just about to get started." Her cute button nose scrunches up.

"I'm not a fan of pointless violence," she replies flatly. I pause. Not because I don't have a dozen cocky responses lined up, I always do, but because I wasn't expecting that. Most girls would've swooned by now. Blushed. Giggled. Asked me to sign something, or better yet, asked to wear my jersey. But this girl just looks through me like I'm just another idiot bleeding on a sidewalk.

I drag the back of my hand across my lip, smearing the blood that's still leaking from where Clayton caught me.

"It's not pointless if he deserves it," I say, my voice low, matching the quiet crackle in the air between us. "And trust me, he does."

She doesn't look impressed. She crosses her arms instead, the movement sharp and fluid. The fabric of her hoodie stretches over her chest, and I'm doing my best not to stare.

"Well, then congratulations," she replies, arching a brow. "You beat a guy up in front of an entire school. Real impressive." My tongue rolls between my teeth. I don't bother pointing out that Clayton got just as many punches on me as I did him. It's obvious this girl doesn't care for me, and for some reason, that pisses me off and turns me on all at once.

There's a glint in her eye. Not fear. Not even judgment, really. Just boldness. The kind that comes from someone who knows their worth and doesn't need to flaunt it. I take a step closer, slow and deliberate, reaching out to grip her waist as she tries to sidestep me like I knew she would. Her eyes track mine, refusing to back down.

"We both know you couldn't take your eyes off me."

A small laugh huffs out through her nose. "Maybe you're not as hot as you think you are," she lies. Filthy dirty lies. Stepping closer, my chest brushes against the cotton of her hoodie as I trap her in place. She swallows thickly and her pupils dilate the tiniest amount in her pale eyes, but it's enough to prove my point. I can practically feel her arousal pulsing beneath my fingertips.

"I like your spirit, but I'd prefer to break it." Running my tongue across my bottom lip to draw her in, she watches my lips as I speak. "I'm throwing a party tomorrow night. You should come."

"And why would I want to do that?" her voice is barely a hoarse whisper.

"You might see a different side of me."

"I seriously doubt it," she half rolls her eyes. A bolt of electricity rushes through me, her insolence sending an arrow of desire straight to my dick. My smirk comes back around, the coppery taste lingering in my mouth starting to ebb.

"Let me guess, you're not a fan of parties either?" I cock a brow, intending for my question to be rhetorical. I should have known this girl has an answer for everything.

"I'm not a fan of assholes who are all big talk and tiny dick." I choke on my next breath. Most girls fall in line when I get close. They smile and preen and pretend not to notice how intense I get. They beg for scraps of my attention. This one? She just called me out and looked bored doing it. I glance up at the sky, biting back a laugh, and then refocus on her.

"You're different," I comment, cocking my head to the side. A flare of her nostrils and a clench of her jaw give her away. Ooh, I've just found a sore spot. A slow grin creeps across my face, the air around us stalling in a crossfire.

For the first time in a long time, I'm not sure how this ends. I don't know her name, don't know why she was at the game, don't know why I care that she walked out. She's fire, wrapped in a quiet challenge. Using my index finger, I tilt her chin upwards so she's staring directly at me.

"I'll see you at the party. Don't be late." Backing up a step, I hold her gaze, my smile growing in intensity. She gave no indication she'll turn up. No fluttering lashes or empty promises, but I know she'll come.

She shrugs, pushing her hands into her pockets. Calm as ever, I watch her step around me and walk away. Like a fool, I linger, standing in the cold, bloodied and breathless. She doesn't look back. An explosion of feelings detonates within me, the first demanding I march after her and drag her to me kicking and screaming. No one has turned me down before. But there's a quieter voice at the back of my mind slowly growing louder.

It looks like I have a new game to play.

Turning back toward the stadium, a smug little spring in my step, I barely make it ten paces before I'm intercepted, cut off by two sophomore boys and their girlfriend. Apparently she has five boyfriends in total, although these two are the only ones who still attend the academy. The others flunked out over some big scandal at the end of the previous semester.

The three of them stop in the entrance, barring my reentry. I nod to the guys, familiar with them from ball practices when they deem it worth their while to join in. They don't nod back. In front, their petite dancer girlfriend plants her hands on her slender waist, swishing her long blonde ponytail with the pop of her hip.

"You leave that girl alone," she snaps, jabbing a finger hard into my chest. I take a dramatic step back, hand flying to my heart like I've just been shot and blink in mock confusion.

"Girl? What girl?"

"Harper Addams," she spits. "I *saw* you talking to her just now." Ignoring the three looks of accusation, I file that name away for a little cyber stalk later. For now, I have a ballerina with the attitude of a feral feline who seems to have all the answers I need.

"And what do you know of her? Maybe she likes my attention." I raise a brow, letting the edge creep in. The two men behind stiffen, not taking nicely to my teasing tone. Blondie narrows her eyes, fury curling her glossy lips.

"I was her tour guide the other day. The last thing any new student needs is someone like you dragging her down to your level. Especially when she can't even hear a word you're saying." Crossing her arms dramatically with an angry flounce of her micro-skirt, Blondie remains oblivious to the trip my mind is taking.

Can't hear me? A weight in my gut shifts. Harper ignored me until I was right in front of her. She stared at my mouth, keeping close when I expected her to pull away. Holy shit, she's the charity case. I keep this revelation locked behind a mask of indifference. I take a slow breath, dialing down the flicker of something I don't recognize. Guilt? Definitely not. Curiosity.

"For your information," I say smoothly, "my father is the reason I've been searching for her. He's named me her personal mentor." Blondie gapes, wanting to say something, but her dark-haired boyfriend mutters in her ear and manages to shift her along. The three pin me with death stares as they pass, an attempt to intimidate me. As if that's what will keep me away from Harper now. She's been hiding in plain sight, flying under my radar whilst being at the forefront of it. Sneaky little minx.

I promised my father to look out for her, and promised myself to do whatever it took to sabotage my father's every whim. I'm not certain how those two things will play out, especially since I can't judge how Harper will act or what she'll say. But one thing is for sure. This academy just got a hell of a lot more entertaining.

CHAPTER EIGHT

A spoonful of granola is halfway to my mouth when I realize everyone is staring at me. As in, *everyone*. A whole cafeteria's worth of eyes focused on my face, some with open mouths, some with bitchy stares. My receivers are safely tucked away in my jacket pocket, but even without them I can tell the atmosphere in here is deafeningly quiet. What did I miss?

Placing the spoon down, I ignore the blush igniting on my cheeks and silence the podcast streaming into my implants. I spot a notification on the screen just before a flash of fuchsia catches my attention across the table. A panicked-looking Addy signing *'Cum Stain knows about you,'* a moment before Rhys shoves his way through the crowd. Oh shit.

He stops right in front of the table, his light blue eyes assessing me as if seeing me for the first time. For some inexplicable reason, his thick parka jacket is wide open, framing a bare chest inked in sprawling tattoos. The longer I'm unable to look away, the clearer his defined abs become visible like a hidden illusion. Remembering we are not alone, I force myself to refocus on his face.

His hair is ruffled as if he's either barely slept or rolled out of bed late. The blonde rushing up behind to cling onto his arm suggests that he didn't wake up alone. I'm not surprised by his actions, but I am surprised by the punch of jealousy I feel in my gut.

The moment stretches on under the weight of everyone watching, my fingers fidgeting beneath the table. Chewing on his lip ring, Rhys finally speaks, although the words that leave his mouth are ones I loathe more than anything in the world.

"You don't look disabled."

My teeth grit instantly, my appetite vanishing. This is it, the moment I knew would come. Everyone is watching, waiting for me to show the cards I've been holding close to my chest. As if the second I've been publicly called out, I'm going to become the incompetent deaf mess they expect. Slurring my words and fumbling with my fingers, no thank you. I've spent far too long working myself up to be here, and the last person who is going to make me doubt myself is Rhys.

I stand on a long exhale. Narrowing my eyes on his, I speak as clearly as I am able without hearing myself.

"And you don't look like a judgmental cock but here we are." There's a collective inhale around us. I don't have to hear it to feel it. In my mind, I can picture the sharp clatter of cutlery dropping. The wide-eyed, open-mouthed whispers.

The blonde clutching his arm shoots daggers at me but her companion doesn't seem to notice she's even there. Instead his smile is widening, until his whole face has lit up like a psychotic Christmas tree. I hold my nerve, no matter how long Rhys holds my stare, smiling like a damn clown.

Suddenly, he throws his head back and laughs. His entire chest rumbles, his shoulders shaking as he shrugs out of the blonde's grip. I glance back to Addy, who shrugs with the same confusion I'm feeling. That everyone in the room is feeling. My eyes fall back upon the man still laughing at his own joke, creating an atmosphere that starts and stops around himself, and that's when I realize what he's doing. What he always does. Rhys is putting on a show.

Ignoring the hundred or so gawking spectators and the girl with designer nails still trying to stake a claim, Rhys steps towards me. I brace myself, for what I'm not sure, but not for the heavy arm he drops around my shoulders. His rich scent wraps around me instantly. The fur of his jacket hood tickles my face, the warmth radiating from him lighting me on fire. Pushing through the gawking crowd, Rhys drags me along in his hold, strings of laughter still rumbling through his chest.

It doesn't occur to me to dig my heels in, wanting to be out of the public eye in any way possible. Thankfully, Addy has her brain switched on. She intercepts us near the open doorway, swiftly planting herself in the way. She jabs a finger into Rhys's chest, venting at him whilst I use the distraction to sneak my receivers beneath my hair and snap the magnets softly into place.

"-needs to be in Peterson's class in ten minutes so save your bullshit until later." Addy pops her hip and reaches out to grab my hand. I'm surprised Rhys allows her to pull me out of his hold so easily. Trying not to dwell on the sudden loss of his warmth beside me, I brave a glance up to his humored expression.

"Don't forget you're my date for tonight's party, Babygirl." He winks. A fresh wave of heat colors my cheeks as Addy pulls me away. We escape into the crisp morning and follow the building round to a hidden alcove at the back.

"Holy shit, that was incredible!" Addy bops up and down, shoving my forgotten backpack into my arms. "I don't think anyone has ever spoken to Rhys like that before! I didn't know if he was going to kiss or strangle you." I blink several times as those images get crossed in my mind and force out a shaky laugh.

"Yeah well, I'm not going to stroke his ego like everyone else around here. Although, I do actually have to get to class," I go to take a step but Addy yanks me back. The flicks of her pink waves brush my cheeks as she leans into me, her voice dropping.

"Before you go, just let me say this. Do be careful. Rhys may seem impressed this time, but I've heard stories. Apparently in fresher's week, he trapped a girl in a coffin and sat on top of it all night while she screamed to be let out. He can be a real nasty piece of shit when he wants to be." Her chocolate eyes level me with an even stare, no trace of humor in her tone. My stomach flips but I manage to nod easily.

"I plan on staying as far away from him as possible, but thanks for the heads up." Releasing my hand, Addy blows me a kiss and heads towards the drama block across campus while I slump back to the science building.

Students fill the corridors, bustling by to get to class but I don't miss the curious glances thrown my way. So much for staying under the radar. Heat begins to crawl up the back of my neck, the urge to run away from prying eyes growing. Slipping into the girl's bathroom, I duck into a cubicle and lean against the closed door.

Just breathe, Harper.

It's probably best this way. Once the fascination has passed, everyone can go back to ignoring me and I can have a half-decent college experience from the shadows. Wait, no. That's not why I came here. I won't hide. I will thrive on their misconceptions, prove to everyone I don't need my hearing to succeed.

Squaring my shoulders, I throw the door open and come nose to nose with a blue-eyed glare that could cut glass. I recognize her as the girl hanging from Rhys' arm. Her hair shines like liquid gold spilling onto her unnecessarily exposed cleavage. Her pink lipstick matches the barbie-style mini dress she must be freezing in beneath a white fur coat, but her hands-on-hips stance doesn't show it.

When she doesn't move or speak, I step around her until she snatches my arm tight enough for her talons to mark my leather jacket.

"What the hell is your problem?" I yell. She grabs a chunk of my hair to tug me back to face her sneer, her chest heaving.

"Keep your hands and eyes off my boyfriend," she barks. I'm momentarily struck speechless, unsure at what point of the exchange in the cafeteria she thought I was making a move on Rhys.

"Are you serious right now?!" Twisting my hair free, I shove her hard. She stumbles in her heeled boots, knocking against the basins. "Trust me, he's all yours. Every bitter word and pathetic payback. You suit each other."

Her screech hurts my head as she lunges for me again, but I manage to duck aside and witness her falling into the cubicle doors. Leaving her screaming behind the closed door, I jog through the now empty hallway to class.

I'm not used to so much, if any, drama before ten in the morning but at least it's done with now. No more lies or secrets. Everything is out in the open for the world to take or leave, I'm just going to keep being me. At least I have the distraction of Biochem and an afternoon of lectures to distract me.

Reaching the lab, I mutter an apology for being late, turning on my phone's mic and placing the device on the professor's desk. Rushing for my usual stool, I pull up short to find it occupied by the still-bare tattooed torso I was hoping to avoid. Thrumming his tattooed fingers on the desk, Rhys is smirking mischievously as Peterson walks over to greet me.

"Ahh, there you are." The professor shifts from foot to foot nervously, his hands wringing the edge of his white coat. "Master Waversea has decided to rejoin our classes, and has requested you to be his lab partner for the remainder of this semester."

Rhys's smile grows impossibly wider, his lip ring glinting in the light. I'm sure it's thrilling to have the power to control people like puppets, or to have the amount of money that makes others feel inferior. But if there's one lesson *Master Waversea* is going to learn today, it's that I won't be intimidated or bought by him.

"Is that so? Well, unfortunately, I would like a partner who will put in half the effort so I'll graciously decline."

Rhys's eyebrow raises but he only appears more interested as I curtsey in mockery. Peterson's voice fills my head and blocks out everyone else as I stride through the tables, heading for an empty stool at the back of the room.

Taking my notebook and highlighters from my bag, I sit to listen to the lecture, despite the prickling apprehension I'm being watched. A certain type of heat is beaming over the left side of my face, drawing my attention to my neighbor. My gut flips and the air locks in my lungs.

Orbs of onyx black trap me, holding me captive. Stubble trails his strong jawline, his full lips sit slightly parted. His blond hair is trapped beneath a beanie hat, like the first time I laid eyes on him.

"-did you catch that, Miss Addams?" Peterson's voice filling my head jars me from my exploration of Clayton's broad shoulders in an army jacket. Giving myself a little shake, I quickly relay the parts which filtered through my daze and he continues his lesson with a small nod. Daring another look sideways, Clayton has hunched over his workbook in a way that totally blocks me from his view.

That's for the best. My libido is telling me all sorts of conflicting stories right now.

I lose myself in the study of enzyme reaction rates, preferring what's written in black and white. What's clinical and factual. I underline keywords in violet, highlight transitions in gold, and circle concepts I don't quite grasp yet, etching asterisks in the margins to come back to later. Thankfully, time slips past unnoticed, my page now a battlefield of arrows and color-coded logic.

It's only when a wall of bodies blocks the whiteboard that I realize the lesson's over. Chairs scrape. Voices rise. The lecture hall begins to empty, everyone knowing they have other places to be. Except for Rhys.

Spinning around on his stool, he kicks his feet up on the desk and watches me, his usual smirk in place. I try to ignore him, but as the class files out, my attention is drawn back to the way he is dragging his thumb along his bottom lip. Peterson rushes passed in a flurry of white, dropping my phone before me and scurrying out of a fire door at the back of the room as if a bomb is about to detonate. Perhaps I should take the hint.

"It's about time you fucked off too," Rhys's deep voice makes me jump as it filters across the room. Opening my mouth in protest, movement shifts to my left and I realize Mr. Broad and Brooding is still sitting beside me.

"Nah, I'm good here," Clayton replies, nonchalantly. His voice sounds much louder as my phone is sitting directly between us, his rich baritone rolling through my skull. It's smooth, and considering it's the first time I've heard him speak, rather delicious. Enough of that.

Deactivating my phone's mic, I switch to my receivers. My hair rustles against them in a way that still makes me cringe. Rhys pushes himself upright and moves towards us in a slow prowl, knocking every book off each desk as he goes. Stopping at the edge of my table, Rhys cracks his inked fingers together in a clear threat, his eyes narrowing on the guy to my left.

"I said, fuck off."

"And I said no."

I barely manage to suppress the shudder that rolls down my spine. Attempting to rise from my stool, a hand from either side lashes out to clamp down on my shoulder or thigh to hold me in place. I gasp, both at the atmosphere and at their desires to keep me here, acting as the buffer between them. Heat oozes from each tensed palm, colliding with a mix of raw masculine power and a darker undertone. The air crackles with tension as the moment stretches out, the feeling that I'm a chunk of meat sitting in the middle of two lions seeping into my bones.

Eventually, Rhys releases my shoulder and slides himself forwards until he's resting on his forearms on the desk in front of me, his face inches from mine. With the slightest tilt of his head to look directly into my eyes, his lips are merely a breath away.

"Tell him to leave," he says in a little more than a whisper. The hand on my thigh retracts, Clayton's back straightening in determination as if he's decided to remain no matter what I say. Opening and closing my mouth, I give Rhys a barely visible shake of my head which causes him to sigh dramatically. Then the smile rolls back around, this one holding the threat of malice.

"Oh, Babygirl. I don't think you meant to, but you've just picked a side. And it's the wrong one."

CLAYTON

CHAPTER NINE

I clench my jaw, watching Wavershit take his sweet fucking time to saunter out of the lab. The door finally clicks shut, the atmosphere inside tripling as neither of us wants to move first. Eventually, my companion forces a shaky laugh.

"Well, that was awkward," she mumbles, pulling her hair over her shoulder to play with it.

I have managed to resist looking at her again for the entire lesson, which was a torture in itself, so I refuse to do so now. Her large green eyes are embedded in my memory anyway, the way she looked up at me, the way she felt in my arms. Unlike the other girls here who judge my non-designer clothes, those who sneer or ignore my existence completely, she gazed at me as if I were her savior. It was nice to be seen for once, to be needed.

I shake my head at the ridiculous thought and start to pack away my textbooks. Clearly it's been far too long since I've had the company of a female. Naturally, the first agenda on my mind when I left Juvie was to fuck my way through as many women as were willing, and thanks to my vigorous cell workouts, many were willing. But no matter how hard I tried, nothing could fill the empty void I've learnt to live with.

From then on, I decided I would only take a girl to bed if we had a meaningful connection, which conflicts with my urge to push everyone away so my right hand and I have had to become very well acquainted. Zipping up my backpack, I shove one strap over my shoulder and stand to leave.

"I'm Harper, by the way, if you remember me," her hand touches my arm. I still, and she quickly removes it. "I'm deaf by the way, if you didn't see the commotion in the cafeteria this morning. Just so you know. And I...um, I didn't say thank you, for the other day with the rain and the fountain," Harper rambles. Her long lashes flutter slightly as she looks up at me and I fall into her gaze again.

Her face is flawless, not a freckle or blemish in sight. Her nose turns up slightly at the end, a tiny smile sitting on her full lips. But her eyes, so wide and willing, so accepting and raw. I could stare into her eyes for hours, spilling every secret and thought I've ever had. I'd give her whatever she wanted while she's looking at me like that.

Fuck, nope, not going to happen. There's too much riding on my shoulders to step into a pissing contest against Wavershit. Moving into the central aisle, I notice Kenneth's notebook amongst the pile on the floor, his tell-tale animated doodles covering over half of the front cover. Picking it up, I rip a page out of the back and scrawl a message across it.

'Gone to the gym, don't stalk me.'

Tucking the note inside the pad, I leave it on his table for him to find when he realizes he's missing all of his notes from class. I make it two more steps towards the door when something strikes hard, hitting me square in the back. A book drops to the floor, its hard edge resting innocently as if it didn't just leave a mark between my shoulder blades.

"Didn't your mother teach you any manners?" Harper shouts from her seat at the back of the room. I freeze in place, half impressed at her throwing arm and half needing to take a deep inhale to remain calm. Spinning slowly, I keep my voice steady because I did in fact catch the drama from the cafeteria this morning.

"She did, before the dementia robbed her from me. What's your mom's excuse?"

"Dead," Harper deadpans and raises a brow. She hastily stuffs her belongings away. "So I win this pity party and you should still know better. I was being nice. The least you could do was acknowledge me." Pushing her phone into her back pocket, she grabs her bag and strolls past me. Pausing by the door, she turns back to face me. "I hope you manage to pull the stick from your ass and have a good day-"

"I'm Clayton, by the way," I interrupt, half mocking the way she introduced herself to me. She's right, my manners are lacking. I'll put it down to barely being spoken to for months aside from a threat or insult. Harper's resulting smile strikes me directly in the chest.

"I know," Harper breathes. With an approving nod, she's gone. I wait a few more moments to quiet the turbulent emotions battling within before leaving myself, pleased to find the hallway is empty. Walking along the rows of lockers, I stop at mine to retrieve the gym kit stashed inside for times like this. The class I'm supposed to have in ten minutes is a write-off, the emotions within needing to be expelled through grueling physical exercise.

Crossing the campus with long strides, I can already sense the undercurrent of excitement that comes to life every Friday . Wavershit's weekly parties. Or maybe, night of utter chaos and carnage would be more fitting. The blearing of music can be heard across the entire academy, mixed with sporadic explosions and high-pitched screams filling the night's sky. Anything could be happening but the staff turn a blind eye. Once again, money surpassing sense.

Down the central walkway, a large group of chittering cheerleaders spilt to let me pass, some scoffing with looks of disgust and hair flicks. Others sneak an appreciative eye when they think their friends aren't looking, a rogue hand reaching out of the crowd to squeeze my ass. I whip round on a snarl, forcing them all to jerk back and squeal in alarm.

Obviously there was always going to be a divide between me, living on hand outs, and the ones who can actually afford to attend Waversea. But that doesn't mean I will be equally scorned and groped on a daily basis by those who think their undeserved inheritances make them better than me. I don't have a cent to my name but hold onto the knowledge I have qualities they will never be able to possess.

"Don't think I'm beyond snapping a few of your precious fingers the next time one of you touches me without an invitation," I growl.

As if I would extend such an invitation to those shallow airheads. If I'm ever blessed with a woman tough enough to handle me, she'll know what it means to be worshipped. *If.* If I manage to surface from the debts my mom's care home is drowning me in. If I make something of myself worth loving.

Unable to stay in their presence a second longer without losing it, the narrowed eyes and curled upper lips adding to my inner-hatred, I force myself to turn away. My feet move quickly now, the release of exercise coming into view in the form of a heavily windowed white building. Shoving past a sophomore hovering in the doorway, I scan my college ID card and push against the metal barrier which doesn't budge. Groaning, I try again for the same red flashing light to appear on the touchpad.

"You've exceeded this month's sessions," an already-smirking redhead says from behind the counter, popping a bubble of gum. Not this bullshit again. I swear the gym staff have a bet going on how long before I utterly lose my shit and break the barrier. But they know as much as I do, I can't afford to fix it. "You can upgrade to a gold membership for-"

"I'm on a scholarship plan. I get as many visits as I want. *Look closer,*" I grit my teeth in an attempt to withhold the threat in my tone. Any other college treat their scholarship students like royalty, accepting the skill that it takes to receive such a chance. But not here. Here I'm filth. Undeserving. Unworthy. Red curtains my vision, a tremor raking through my arms.

Chewing her gym noisily, the redhead bends forward in her black uniform featuring the college crest on the bust and squints at the screen exaggeratingly. "Oh yes, so you are," she sniggers and pushes the button to let me enter. I withhold the names I'd like to call her, jogging up the first flight of stairs. I change in record time and burst into the gym with a tightness in my chest making it difficult to breathe.

Shining chrome and the tang of sweat greet me like old friends. Dropping into the seat of a recently vacated rowing machine, I instantly push myself into a vigorous workout without wasting time warming up. Every reel of the cord quells the rage that was close to taking over, the burn in my chest spreading into my biceps and thighs.

Images flash through my mind with each heave on the handle. Jeremy laughing easily, mom kissing our foreheads with a twinkle in her dark eyes. Fond memories which have become tainted. When it all becomes too much, the bitter grief I often succumb to, I switch my focus to another aspect of my life. The scoffs and jeers I get from everyone each and every day. I hate the world, and welcome it's hatred right back.

Suddenly a face appears in my mind's eye, sea foam green framed by thick eyelashes. A heart shaped face that doesn't twist up, lips that don't curl. Even better, she stood up to me. Called me out on my bullshit.

The last of my anger snaps like an elastic band, rushing from me on a ragged breath that has me stopping mid-thrust. Leaning forward with my elbows on my knees, I try to make sense of whatever just happened but come up blank. She managed to soothe me without even being here. Without doing anything.

Rain begins to pound against the glass-covered exterior, the sky a sea of charcoal grey clouds I hadn't noticed rolling in. Water thunders against the windows, filling the gym with a pounding similar to the hooves of a hundred horses trying to break in. Everyone present turns to look at the sudden downpour, more than a few groaning about tonight's party likely being cancelled.

On the other hand, I feel myself relax. I could sit and watch the rain all day, the cleansing of the earth resonating in ways I can't put into words. I wish I could cleanse myself just as easily, washing away all of the bad I've done and the pain I've caused. I grip the edges of the rowing machine, fingers flexing as though they need something more to hold onto.

Damn, I need to get my head straight. Pushing upright, I head towards the weight benches as a distant thud pulls me from the lull. At first, I believe it to be a noise lost to the rain. Then another comes, and another, pads and mats being thrown to the ground. A squeal of sneakers against slick rubber and an eruption of excited voices ricochets off the walls. I turn back, a frown pulling my brow tight.

Despite knowing I'm not in the JDC anymore, any sudden commotion has my fists clenching, setting my instincts on high alert. A pack of bodies explodes through the gym like they've been let loose from a cage. I'm assaulted by a swarm of Lycra. Dodging out the way, I reach out and catch the back of the first sweatshirt my hand comes in contact with.

"What the fuck's going on?" I growl, dragging him backwards with more force than necessary.

"Rhys cancelled his party. Apparently there's a new girl he's going to initiate, '*Hog Roast style*'." His curls bounce as he bobs excitedly, eager to join the rest of the crowd piling through the exit doors. Pulling my phone out of my sweatpants pocket, I see the alert which has sent everyone else crazy.

He's pinned it to the fucking main newsfeed.

"Dammit!" I shout to no one in particular. Falling in with the crowd, for once, I elbow my way into the locker room and retrieve my stuff. I've barely pulled my sweatshirt over my head by the time I step out into the rain, my heart in my throat as I rush to get to the front of those racing towards Rhys' frat house. The only pleasure I get is from shoving and elbowing the assholes hoping to get a front row seat to Harper's impending torture.

All I've desired since setting foot on this campus is to be alone.

When friends weren't an option, I chose solidarity. Keep my head down, do Jeremy's dreams justice and make my mom happy one last time. But I can't leave old habits behind. I can't leave a little mouse in the jaws of a snake. Call me her savior if that's what she needs me to be, but my intentions are also selfish.

I've never needed a better excuse to finally give Wavershit exactly what he's deserved for far too long.

CHAPTER TEN

I pull the textbook closer, doing everything in my power to focus on the words melting from the page. In the background, Addy is tugging on outfits, huffing in frustration and yanking them back off again. She clanks and clammers, not realizing how loud she's dropping the hairbrush or slamming her dresser drawers.

It's taking everything in me not to shut my cochlear implants off, but I made a promise to myself to adjust to living in a world dictated by sound. Since diving in at the deep end was an epic fail, building up slowly in the confines of my dorm room seemed like a better idea.

"What about this one?" Addy asks, a frown tugging at her mouth as she twirls for the seventh time in what must be her entire closet. I blink, startled back into the present by the rustle of skirts and the sound of fabric brushing against skin. The pile of discarded outfits behind her tells me I've missed most of the show, lost in the tangle of my psych textbook and the mental math of how many chapters I still have to get through before Monday.

She's wearing a steampunk dress now. Rich purple satin at the bust, black corset cinched tight around her waist, layers of lace and leather creating an otherworldly silhouette. She looks stunning. Her lean frame carries it like she just stepped out of some dystopian fairytale.

"Yes, that one's perfect," I say automatically, eyes darting back to the page, but I can hear the exaggerated sigh that follows. Addy flops down beside me with all the drama of someone who knows she looks amazing and still needs reassurance.

"You say that to every outfit." I glance at her from the corner of my eye, hiding a smile. "Are you sure you aren't going to come to the party?"

I twist my lips, pretending to read. Addy knows my answer already. I didn't come here to party, I came to make something of myself. Something that I would never have been able to achieve with online learning. And yes, maybe I should give myself some grace to be a normal nineteen year old, partying with my roommate. But the thought of walking into that house, of the eyes, the whispers, the snap judgements and Rhys' cocky smile that I bent to his will, nah I think I'm good.

Giving me a little twirl, her skirt and hair shift back and forth in time with each other before she dances her way down the hall towards the bathroom. Shaking my head, I lift my book and sigh as the words blur into each other from exhaustion. I would happily curl into bed and leave this for another day, if I didn't have an assignment due on Monday and a full weekend of revising to catch up on.

Before our door slams closed, scaring the shit out of me, noise filters in from the hallway and now that I've latched on, I can't seem to ignore it. Excited chatter and music from the surrounding dorms close in, causing my shoulders to shrink inwards as if I can escape. It's no use, and I quickly give up, jotting Addy a note.

I'll be at the library.

Stuffing my phone, stationery, and books into my backpack, I cram my feet into my biker boots and yank a thick hoodie over my head. The leather jacket goes on last, less for warmth and more for armor. Pausing to turn off my receivers, I leave them on the dresser. That's enough auditory practice for tonight.

Without a backward glance, in fear I'll change my mind and flop back into bed, I close the door and head out. The wind bites as I step outside, slicing through the fabric of my hoodie like tiny knives. A sliver of crescent moon hangs above, dimmed behind a veil of clouds. I tug the hood higher and add *'buy a decent coat'* to the ever-growing mental to-do list. Back when I was home-schooled, I didn't have to deal with freezing night air just to swap out a textbook.

I take the main path to the courtyard, keeping to public routes as much as possible. It should be safer that way, except there isn't another soul about. Anywhere. No bodies. No movement. No flickers of phone light bouncing between brick walls. The campus is... empty. The kind of empty that makes your skin crawl.

The hairs on the back of my neck stand on end as I walk faster, my boots thudding against the stone like warning drums. The courtyard opens up ahead, swallowed by shadow and dimmer than I was expecting. Lamp posts flicker behind me, my breath fogs in front of me. Shadows appear on the edge of my vision, only to vanish when I chase them with my eyes.

I climb the wide library steps two at a time, my safe haven within arm's reach. I'm being paranoid, I know that. My vivid imagination likes to play tricks on me. Grasping the door's thick handle, a shadow grows across the wood. Not mine, one much taller.

Before I can whip around, before I can so much as gasp, the straps of my backpack are tugged downwards, pinning my arms at an awkward angle. At the same time, my world goes completely dark. I twist, testing the strength pinning me in place. It doesn't budge. I'm shoved back down the stone steps, fumbling for my footing as the heat of my breath bounces back from the material covering my face.

Dread curdles in my stomach, a useless attempt of maintaining some type of dignity making me far too compliant. I'll blame it on the shock that's currently seizing my brain. Is this a prank, or should I be screaming my lungs out? A tiny voice in my head provides the answer, reminding me of who threatened me earlier today.

'You've just picked a side. And it's the wrong one.'

My jaw clenches. Being two senses down, I jerk and stumble, half through panic and half from being dragged along for what seems like hours but could be mere minutes. My fingers start to tingle from their strained position, my legs as heavy as lead as I try to keep up. I don't bother calling out, since I'm unable to hear any response I may be given. Instead I try to comply as much as possible, my mind and heart racing as fingernails bite into my upper arms.

I'm going to kill him for this. Murder him dead.

My boots graze on rockier terrain which makes finding my footing almost impossible. The hands on me are all that keep me upright, and I don't make their job easy. Dragging my weight down, they're forced to drag me the rest of the way. I may not be a good prisoner, but I sure am a passive-aggressive one.

Before long, I'm thrown forward and fall heavily to the ground, my left shoulder taking most of the impact. I groan at the pain, only sparing a moment before scrambling back and shoving the sack from my head. Frigid air slices through my throat as I gulp down ragged breaths, blinking hard to clear my vision.

Shapes moving around me blur into one. Patches of orange flicker in the wind, bouncing against a sea of hooded silhouettes holding the flame-lit torches in their hands. Barren trees stretch overhead in a network of branches trying to block out the hint of the moon and cage me inside. The ground is damp beneath my fingers, an underlying scent of disturbed soil speaking of a recent downpour I must have missed whilst studying.

At my feet, a figure looms over me. Beneath the hood, which is pitch black like its adjoining robes, sits the full-face mask of a mutilated pig. It's horrific, converted into a scowl with evil eyes and blood dripping from its silicone ears and nostrils. I'm disturbed by it, but I don't recoil in the way that I'm sure is intended.

Suddenly, a shape lunges from the corner of my vision. This time, at long last to those watching, I scream. There's nothing fake about the animal snarling and huffing inches from my face. Saliva coated teeth and a thick silver chain glint in the faint light, a hog as big as a wolf jolting with silent grunts. At the end of the chain, another masked man stands, not making much effort to control his beast.

Every instinct screams at me to move, to run, to *do something*, but I'm rooted to the soaked earth, limbs locked by a creeping dread I've only felt once before in my life. The figure before me, still as death in his dark robe, reaches inside the folds of fabric with deliberate slowness. My breath catches. His gloved fingers pull out a single sheet of paper and unfold it with care, like he has all the time in the world. One word is printed in bold, black ink across the center.

RUN.

Dropping the sheet, it flutters gently to the ground in an oddly graceful motion, despite the tension rippling beneath my skin. My tormentor watches it land at my feet before holding up ten fingers to start a countdown. By the time I realize I'm still cemented in place, paralyzed by shock, he's already on eight.

Panic spikes through me like electricity, and I shove myself upright, boots slipping slightly in the wet earth as I dart into the darkness of the woods. I didn't pause to think, otherwise I may have stood my ground and refused to participate in this idiocy. Instead, I'm stuck in the world of silence that I usually prefer, that often soothes me. But now, I'm disoriented by it. I don't know if the countdown has finished, if the hog has been released, if someone or *something* is right behind me. So I just keep running.

My boots land heavily with every pounding step, my heart ready to explode. Thick tree trunks jump out from nowhere, several taking the brunt of my weight as I rebound from one to the next. The mud tries to slow me down and branches claw at my hair, my only glimpse of light hanging uselessly overhead.

When my lungs are burning, fire licking up my sides, and a stitch clenches like a vice in my abdomen, I hurl myself over a fallen log and crouch behind it, panting. Hiding feels just as hopeless as running when I know my labored breaths and the sobs I can't hold back any longer will give me away.

Is this a game? Would they really let a crazed animal maul me just for a sick laugh?

Peering over the log, everything is as still as it is dark, but that doesn't mean they're not out there. Watching. Waiting. I tuck back into a tight ball out of sight, rubbing my side to work out the cramp. A shiver races down my spine from the plummeting temperature. If the frenzied hog doesn't get me, the luring caress of winter sure will. I need to find my way back to campus, find a professor or better yet, the Dean. How would the board feel if they knew their precious heir was delivering threats by day and hazing students by night?

Flexing my fingers, I hop up and start to run again. The short stop has cost me vital body warmth as I stumble onwards, using my hands to feel for wooden barricades blocking my way. I'm forced to slow, winding my way through the maze of the forest while pointlessly looking back. If I haven't been caught by now, surely no one is coming after all?

A body collides with mine in the next instant, all the air in my lungs forced out as my chest slams into a trunk. Colors burst behind my eyes, my temple slamming into the bark, heat flooding to a graze scraping across my cheek as I'm held in place. Pinned in place by a body at my back, I shout for someone to help me. Someone. *Anyone.* I scream until my voice feels raw, the silence in my head echoing.

An arm snakes around my upper arms and yanks backwards, arching my back. The pig's mask brushes my cheek, nudging my hair aside with their silicone nose. Heated breath huffs out of the nostril holes and fills my ear. My stomach flips. Not today, asshole. Bucking violently, I manage to jolt my captor off balance. It's easier than I expected, which somehow makes it worse. Like he *wants* me to fight. Then, *crack.*

A sharp sting explodes across my thigh. I scream from pain this time, the sting bursting like fireworks beneath my skin. My hand flies to the spot, blood instantly rushing to my throbbing thigh. In the slight shine from the moon, the object is brought up to my face, sturdy yet smooth leather being dragged across my cheek. A paddle.

Pushing me forward again, grinding his hips against my ass, I don't have to fake the retch from an uninvited erection pressing against me, which earns a second whack of the paddle on my still sore thigh. On what I'm sure sounds like a banshee's battle cry, I throw myself backwards and put all of my energy into elbowing my way free. Pure adrenaline fuels me to land blows wherever I can and bolt the second I have enough freedom to make my escape.

This time, I don't attempt to be cautious, blindly running into trees and falling over shrubs, but never stopping. My feet fall into several holes, raised roots trying to hold me back as I'm in full fight or flight mode. With every panted breath and panicked step further away from campus, the surer I become that I'll never find my way back.

I slam into another obstacle, becoming accustomed to the pain blossoming across my front, but this one isn't like the unforgiving trees. Warmth pushes back against me, hands grabbing my hips and throwing me upwards. I squeal, my flailing hands connecting with a branch, which I cling to with all my might. Pulling myself up, I attach myself to the thick branch in desperation to escape this horrendous night. The wood beneath me bows as whoever threw me up here also climbs up and nudges me over. Once we've shifted into a dip where the trunk meets the branch, I'm lifted into a lap in one easy move.

I struggle at first, shoving against him until the smooth material of his t-shirt gives me pause. A strong, musky smell fills my senses, a solid chest beneath my fingers rising and falling evenly. The darkness of the night is all-consuming, my eyesight failing me even this close.

Using my palms, I feel the outline of his shape, from broad shoulders to huge biceps. Trailing my fingers upwards, he allows me to explore the strength of his jawline and the stubble coating it. No robes, no mask. Not one of the assholes trying to scare the shit out of me and strike me with a paddle.

"Who are you?" I whisper shakily. With the gentlest touch, he pulls my hand from his face and holds it palm up with the utmost care. Using a finger from his other hand, he slowly writes letters upon my palm one by one. C-L-A-Y-T-O-N.

A rush of relief floods me, tears instantly prickling behind my eyes. Clayton is here. He came for me.

Closing my hand as if I can somehow capture the soft tingling he's left there, I press it to my chest and lean into his warmth without hesitation. My body begins to tremble, as much from the cold as from the creeping spill of fear that continues to seep into my bones. Clayton winds his arms around me, pulling me close, holding me steady as the first tear slips free.

Squeezing my eyes shut, the image of that pig-faced figure waits for me behind my lids, grotesque and grinning. A sob bursts from my throat as I fist Clayton's shirt in my grip, clinging to him as though the world might fall apart if I let go. The weight of what has just happened crashes over me with brutal clarity, the realization of how far it could have gone slamming into my chest. I can't breathe, I can't think. I can only hold on, shivering and aching in ways I don't yet have words for.

This was supposed to be my new beginning. The chance to make something of myself, to leave a mark on the world. Rhys Waversea has stolen that from me. He's playing a game in which no one knows the rules, making decisions based on a whim and a wounded ego.

I don't know how long we stay like that, but Clayton doesn't shift away. He doesn't try to communicate any further, just waits with a kindness I've come to realize is rare around here. I've soaked through his shirt, stolen every bit of warmth from his body, but he doesn't pull back.

In the thick blackness of tonight, I allow myself this one moment where I don't have to pretend I'm strong. I don't have to be composed. I don't have to carry it alone. I hate the way vulnerability feels like a bruise, but right now, I need it. I need him. I don't know where he came from or how he found me, but for once, I don't care.

Shifting slightly, my side still leaning against his front, my fingers brush against the firm plane of his abdomen. The contact is accidental, but I don't pull away. Instead, shielded by darkness and fueled by the flicker of recklessness rising in my chest, I trace the hard lines of his abs and the subtle divide between his chest muscles. He doesn't stop me. He lets me touch, lets me explore, my hand drifting upward with a boldness I shouldn't feel after everything I've experienced tonight. Or perhaps I feel this way in spite of it. A huge middle finger to Rhys that proves I can't be broken so easily.

Curling my fingers around the back of Clayton's neck, I lean forward just enough to offer the invitation of a kiss. He inclines his head and my blood remembers heat. A quiet ache stirs beneath my skin, a hunger not just for closeness but for comfort. I want to be wanted. I want to feel like more than something discarded and damaged.

His fingers skim the edge of my jacket, his palm inching upwards until he closes it around mine, making my breath catch in my throat. I close my eyes needlessly and tilt my head upward just as he gently peels my hand away from his neck.

Bracing his arms tighter around me, Clayton pushes us both from the branch, causing my hair to rise, my gut to plummet and a scream to become caught in my throat. Landing on his feet with bent knees, it takes me a second to release the way I've coiled myself around his shoulders. He places me down on shaky legs and steps away immediately, leaving me to steady myself.

Using the briefest of touch to turn me in the opposite direction, he places a hand on my shoulder to direct me forward and walk me through the wood like a dog on a leash. Embarrassment claws at my cheeks, a blush consuming my entire face. My nostrils flare in frustration at the complete fool I've just made of myself. The man came to save me and I threw myself at him. *Could I be any more desperate?*

Shrugging out of his grip, I pull the collar of my jacket higher around my neck and storm onwards. I don't need to see his body language or hear his false words to understand his kindness was purely for my benefit. And if there's one thing I hate above all else, it's other people's charity. Sure they mean well, using my needs to boost their own self-esteem or to validate all the shitty things they may have done, but this is my life. I'll fight my own battles, and I'll manage alone if that's what it takes.

The moon has decided to finally grace us with its presence, breaking clear of the clouds for long enough to illuminate the woodland around me. Even if I had a choice, we would be walking back in silence as there's nothing I have to say. Nothing I could hear to make me feel any less like an idiot.

Nevertheless, I sneak a glance back every so often to check Clayton is still following, just in case the crowd of pig-faced jocks return. I hate that I'm still hyper-aware, flinching at the shadows. I hate that I was coaxed into Rhys' weird hog fantasy. But that's fine. I can use my humiliation and channel my frustrations for a better cause, one that will see Rhys freezing his balls off and face-down in the mud.

Revenge is a mean bitch, and this one might just be his downfall.

RHYS

CHAPTER ELEVEN

Weaving a cigarette between my fingers, I tune out Professor Hargreaves' coma-inducing drone and start questioning my life choices. This is the third class I've sat through today, all with the same unspoken hope that Harper might show up for reasons I haven't quite admitted to myself. At first, I'd told myself it was just to see her expression when she realized her worst nightmare was planted in the front row, watching her every time she dared to walk through the door.

But as the day drags its sorry ass forward, I'm starting to wonder if she ever made it out of the woods. Maybe I should've sent a search party instead of spending the weekend stoned out of my skull, eating my way through the daily buffet my ever-loyal disciples laid at my feet.

I snort, remembering the way the other stoners had stared at my toffee cheesecake like starving orphans, praying I'd spare them a crumb. I didn't. I finished every cloying, sickly-sweet bite with the kind of spiteful determination reserved for kings and sociopaths. Even now, the sugar sludge coats the back of my throat like regret, but I devoured that whole damn thing out of principle. The only scraps I leave behind are the ones crying for just one more taste of my cock. Even that became boring rather quickly, but my reputation needed to be upheld.

Besides, I had cause to celebrate. From the haunted look in Harper's eyes on the forest floor, she's probably halfway back to whatever deadbeat town vomited her out, and her no-show today is the confirmation I needed. One small step closer to burning down everything my father built, one scorched soul at a time. Still a mountain to climb, but the smoke at the top is starting to smell a little sweeter.

Although, if I'm being brutally honest, and I always am, some small, pathetic part of me thought she'd put up more of a fight. I'd actually looked forward to dragging this little game out. I guess I overestimated her. Now I'm back to tormenting the scholarship scum, which doesn't quite thrill me the way it did last week. Back to tedious basketball practices, which did nothing to rid the tension corded tightly between my shoulders. There's something numb in the predictability of it all.

Even now, as Clayton stares daggers into my back, there's no sense of accomplishment to help drag me through this lecture. Dude is like a dog with a bone. Just by being in the same room, I can feel his anger rising, tiptoeing closer to breaking point. It's the only reason I'm still sitting here. Again, the things I do to uphold my hard earned reputation.

Smirk held firmly in place, I slot the cigarette between my lips and lean back, kicking my feet up onto the desk. Flicking open my lighter, a flame snaps to life, burning with that familiar hiss as I spark up and inhale. Professor Hargreaves clocks me immediately, her beady eyes narrowing before she rolls them with theatrical exhaustion and carries on rambling about the effects of embryonic development when exposed to smoke. The irony isn't lost on me. My smart watch buzzes with a message from Klara, no doubt dripping in desperation, asking to meet later. I delete it without opening.

The door creaks open to my left and my cigarette slips from between my lips before I even register what's happening. It hits my thigh, ember-side down, searing a hole into my jeans and scorching skin beneath. Fuck, *not the Armani*. I clamp a hand over the burn, cursing under my breath, but my eyes are already locked on the girl who just walked through the door.

Harper is standing there, pale eyes locked on mine, a scowl possessing her features that is fierce enough to turn a lesser man into dust. But not me, never me. She doesn't blink, just radiates unfiltered fury so sharp, it cracks through the mundane haze I'd become victim to.

Her legs are clad in high-waisted leggings, a glimpse of abdomen showing beneath a black crop top and leather jacket. Hmm, resilient I see. A purple bruise has bloomed on her forehead and there's a raw graze across her cheek. I can't hold back my grin, envisioning her hair matted with dead leaves, her skin coated in filth, tears cutting tracks down her face while she curses my existence in the dark.

"What the hell happened to you? Pick a fight with a tree?" I ask, just loud enough to carry. Harper doesn't react aside from flipping me off. My chest lightens with giddy excitement. She strides past, keeping her spine straight. And just like that, something shifts in my psyche. Something crazed and dangerous. *The game's back on.*

I tune out Hargreaves completely for the rest of class, my hand moving of its own accord as I doodle in the margins of my textbook. A few rough sketches of new tattoo designs. Then, without meaning to, a cartoon Harper strung up like a marionette starts taking shape, her limbs pulled by my inked fingers.

One minute before the end of class, I stand with a tall stretch and saunter to the back of the room just before everyone else begins to pack up and pile out. Perching on the edge of Harper's desk, I notice she's chosen a table in the opposite corner to Clayton. *Interesting.* They were best buddies the other day. Leaning over her scattered belongings, I spot a small black microphone tucked beside her notebook and lift it between my fingers. My thumb finds the 'on' switch.

"I hate to say I told you so," I say into the mic, amused by her sudden flinch, "but you really should've accepted my party invite."

Harper stands, snatching the mic from my grip and shoves it deep into her jacket pocket.

"I have my receivers on, you idiot. And what are you, twelve?" she snaps, pulling on the backpack I *generously* had delivered back to her dorm. She winces, clearly sore beneath her layers of stubborn pride, but it does nothing to quell her set jaw and smart mouth. "Clearly there's been some gaps in your social maturity, which is evident by your lack of friends."

I barely have time to frown. Before Harper can slip away, I grab a hold of her wrist and tug her back to face me with enough force to have her between my legs in an instant. Her breath catches somewhere in her throat. Her pulse thrums beneath my fingers, defiance crackling in her eyes like live wire.

Clayton is over her shoulder in the next second, his black eyes blazing with the promise of pain I would enjoy more than he can comprehend. Ignoring him, I center my attention on Harper. She lifts her chin defiantly, my dick jumping at the sight.

"I have friends," I scoff, sounding every bit like the petulant child she's painting me to be. "So many, I don't even know any of their names."

Harper just shrugs, twisting her wrist free from my grip. She steps back and collides with Clayton's chest. I watch amused, as her whole body tenses. She whips around with a snarl and shoves him as far as he's willing to move. A standoff takes place, the two of them locked in some silent tug-of-war I'm suddenly excluded from. Harper decides to ignore Clayton but finds herself still boxed in on both sides with no room to breathe. She releases a pitiful sigh.

"Whatever." Those green eyes roll. "All I know is, I'd rather have no friends than fake ones. If you went bankrupt overnight, I wonder how many of your *friends* would still be there in the morning."

Her words sink into me before I can swat them away. The thought of waking up broke and alone in an empty frat house with echoes for company doesn't sit well. I chew my lip ring like it'll anchor me back into the version of myself that doesn't care.

"Why does having friends matter anyway?" I frown. "I have everything I need. More money and women than I could ever possibly use. I love my life." I raise an eyebrow, challenging her to disagree. Harper shrugs again, but this time it's slower, more condescending. Her eyes shift, something distant moving across her face, and then she hits me with it. That look. Like I'm a wounded dog bleeding out on the sidewalk and she's debating whether to put me out of my misery.

"If that's really true," she says, her voice maddeningly gentle, "then I'm genuinely happy for you." She tilts her head slightly. "But something tells me it's not."

The moment Harper finishes speaking, I lash out. My fingers find a handful of her hair, yanking her forward and holding her exactly where I want her. Clayton grabs my throat from behind in some strange attempt at restraint, but I barely register it. All he's achieved is trapping Harper between us.

She's close. So goddamn close. Her breath brushes my face and her stubborn refusal to cower has a low, primal feeling stirring in my chest. She's still not afraid, and that won't do. Resolve so strong needs to be shattered, one crack at a time. If I'm going to maintain control at Waversea, she has to fall. She has to beg. She has to *break*.

"I'm going to be your worst nightmare," I breathe, the words laced with promise. Despite her injuries, Harper scoffs right in my face.

"Not likely." My smirk returns, creeping across my face. I release her and Clayton releases me. Shifting back on the table, I swing my legs like a bored kid in detention. Her useless shadow remains looming behind her.

"Is that so?" I hum. "Tell me, then, Harper Addams. What are you scared of?" She doesn't answer straight away. Instead, her eyes lift to the ceiling, thoughtful, almost amused.

"Oh, well, if you *really* want to know..." She drags it out, hanging on every syllable. I lean forward on my thighs, hanging on her next words. Needing this piece of key information to destroy her for good, but there's more to it than that. I want to feast on her fear and bathe in her pain.

"What truly terrifies me is knowing that insults to society like you don't get the karma they deserve," she finishes, eyes locked on mine. "Which is exactly why I'm going to give it to you." Before I can even process her threat, her fist connects with my jaw.

My head whips sideways and I topple off the edge of the table with a crash that echoes around the room. It wasn't the pain that knocked me sideways, but the shock of it. This girl, this new girl who was supposed to be meek and timid, just struck me. Despite the pleasure of a caress curving around my cheek, I jump up, shoulders bunched and fists clenched. I won't be disrespected so easily.

Hunting around the room, there's no sign of Harper. Clayton is still rooted in place like a useless lemon, arms folded, eyes on the swinging door she disappeared through. For someone who plays body-guard, he's spectacularly shit at actually guarding anything.

I shoulder past the scholarship scum clogging the aisle, refusing to remain standing there with a hard-on and a bruised ego next to my nemesis. Catching Hargreaves' narrowed gaze, she doesn't try to stop me, returning to her screen like nothing happened.

By the time I reach the courtyard, she's vanished. Lost to a sea of faces I've refused to learn. People are expendable, everyone's replace-able. After growing up with only my father present, I've seen first-hand how people can be used as pawns for personal gain. The rich and ruth-less are hardwired to reach for unimaginable wealth and nothing else, even if most don't know what to spend it on.

We are disciplined in the art of spotting and exploiting weaknesses in such a way, people don't even realize until it's too late. Once the viper's fangs are embedded, they are hooked on our poison, eager to please. No matter what is asked of them, they always come running back, their loyalty emanating from greed.

Rain needles down on me as I stalk the path between the fountain and main hall, glowering at anyone foolish enough to drift into my orbit. I don't know where the fuck to go, or what to do next, and I hate the unfamiliar itch of indecision crawling under my skin. One more minute in a lecture hall and I'll combust. My patience is shot, my mood's in the gutter, and if I keep playing the model student, someone's bound to notice I've gone soft.

"Hey Rhysie," a sickly-sweet voice sings from behind.

"Fuck off," I hiss without even looking. If my father didn't insist I accompany Klara to all of her family's high-class functions, and I wasn't appeasing my father so that he doesn't see the bigger picture, I would have scared her off a long time ago. Not that I'm particularly pleasant to her now, but she doesn't seem to take the hint. She's a means to an end, a necessity, but if she calls me *Rhysie* again I might just snap.

"Oh, come on baby, how about we—"

Whipping around, I lunge at her and knock us both to the ground. Closing my hand around her throat, her eyes dilate and a coy smile plays about her lips. She's more deluded than I thought, and if I hadn't already decided to never take her to bed again, this would have done it. There are only so many fake orgasms I can moan into a pillow before I start reconsidering celibacy. Her shrieking could raise the dead and kill them again in the same breath.

"Don't approach me unless I specifically ask you to. You play by my rules, or you can attend the Winterfest Ball alone. Got it?" Klara nods with a wink and giggle that has me rolling my eyes. Leaving her behind on the dampening grass, her friends dive in to help her up as I walk away. Her giggle chases me, engrained in my damn ears, and her words float on the wind.

"He just can't keep his hands off me."

I halt with clenched fists, having to force the next breath to pass my lips. Rage bubbles dangerously close to the surface, the image of Harper's sympathetic look filling my mind. Her condescending tone pointing out what no one else would dare voice. My power is a fragile illusion. There's an extremely thin line between who's the puppet and who's pulling the strings, and I haven't questioned where I fit on that line before today.

This is ridiculous. I can't let her crawl beneath my skin for a second longer. I need to recalibrate, refocus. Scare her off so thoroughly she begs to transfer before midterms. Then I can get back on track. Wipe out the charity cases, cripple the funding, tear down everything my father's built with the investors he's so smug about. One scholarship dropout at a time.

As if believing one into existence, I spot a grey beanie hat further down the pathway, heading directly towards the basketball court, most likely for his private afternoon session. Taking off in the same direction, I struggle to keep to a regular pace as my mouth stretches into its usual smirk. It feels familiar, safe. Like a mask I can conceal myself behind. Then it doesn't matter what is happening on the inside, as long as I remain cool and collected on the outside.

Clayton wants to act like Harper's protector, and that's fine with me. He can take the brunt of my anger on her behalf. The dull ache in my chest gives way, finally allowing my pulse to start thrumming with fury again. Harper is far too comfortable questioning my life, mocking everything I've built. But if she wants to declare a war and leave her stoic soldier behind to face the fiery wrath, then I'm more than happy to burn him alive. Not that I've ever needed a reason before.

HARPER

CHAPTER TWELVE

The week is slipping through my fingers faster than I can process, each night spent hunched over library desks doing little more than chasing a finish line that keeps moving further away. My efforts are swallowed whole by the mounting workload that refuses to shrink, no matter how many hours I throw at it.

Rhys has thankfully been a no-show in any of my classes for the past two days, and Clayton has gone back to pretending I don't exist. Both of which have granted me the rare luxury of mental space to be productive. Although I'm starting to wonder if productivity is something I'm even capable anymore. The assignment due tomorrow feels laughably out of reach at this point. I could email Peterson to beg for an extension, but that goes against everything I've been asking for since starting here. No special treatment, no shortcuts.

I've taken over the entire table in the center of the library, covering it with half-open textbooks, aggressively highlighted notes, and the frayed charger of my overheating laptop. Just in case the message *leave me alone* wasn't obvious enough, the navy cotton t-shirt stretched across my chest features seven sets of hands spelling out 'f-u-c-k o-f-f' in neat fingerspelling. I don't expect everyone to be able to read it, but Addy had a good snort about it this morning. Below the table, my legs are folded loosely in worn cream lounge pants, fluffy socks tucked underneath while my sneakers lay forgotten beside the chair. All of the home comforts I could want, aside from the tempting call of Netflix. Instead, the full soundtrack of Hamilton is playing through my implants, driving me to type with rabid focus.

It hasn't stopped pouring all day, so the library is busier than usual. Students loiter around, mingling and waiting for a break in the rain. Several bodies bump into my table and one jean-clad butt even sits on the edge before I shoo them away. I don't think they'll be going anywhere anytime soon. Every time I glance upwards, the clouds above the glass skylight only seem to grow darker and fattened raindrops continue to fall. I'm a firm believer in the weather directly affecting my mood, and this ongoing shitstorm is crushing my spirits. Fuck you precipitation for sabotaging my GPA before I've even had a real chance to prove myself.

Another flicker of movement flashes behind me, this one no different to the countless of others trying to ask if they can take a seat around my table. I point blank ignore them all, muttering to myself, '*God, I love being deaf.*' Except this jostle nudges my seat and causes me to jerk forward over my laptop. Huffing, I pause my music and spin around to look one way, then the other, but everyone nearby seems just as disinterested in me as I am in them.

Slowly returning to sit forwards, I tuck my chair in further, my stomach practically pushed up against the desk, and roll out my neck. On the second roll, my gaze hitches on a steaming paper cup beside my textbook, white with a lilypad logo. Thick black marker has been scrawled across the side with a name that reads more like a social media handle. Beanie26.

Despite my reservations, I lift the drink and inhale the rich scent of roasted coffee. It smells like heaven to a girl whose assignment deadline is closing in as fast as the walls around her. The cup is warm in my hand, batting away the oppressive beat of rain hammering against the skylight. For one simple moment, I just sit and inhale deeply. Not that

I'm going to drink it. Accepting a drink from a stranger would be pure insanity, no matter how much my throat tightens with the promise of just one small sip. On the table, my phone vibrates with a notification from the school app and I lunge for the distraction.

> Beanie26: I didn't know how you take your coffee, but seems like you could use one.

A shudder trickles down my spine. I stare at the message, then cast another searching glance at the tables around me, slower this time. It takes me all of three seconds to find him. Endless pools of black onyx arrest me from across the open space, Clayton's expression open and cautious. He seems panicked, as if he might have overstepped. In one hand is his phone and in the other, a matching coffee cup. After a beat of staring, he ducks his head, his blonde hair poking out from beneath a gray beanie hat.

> Beanie26: It's not poisoned, I assure you.

I swallow, grappling with what to do, with how to respond. The smart thing to do would be the focus on the assignment I came here to finish. To avoid all distractions, yet here one is, steaming in my hand. It's as if Clayton knew I was drowning in pressure and caffeine withdrawals and emotional repression. So I stop kidding myself, lift the cup to my lips and let the sweet caffeinated nectar of a caramel latte soothe my throat. Several heads turn my way, alerting me to the fact that I was moaning, but damn I needed that.

> Readmylips44: It's perfect, thank you.

Not expecting a further reply, I push my phone aside and lift the book on molecular diagnostics I should be reading. My eyes are starting to burn as the words on the page jumble, my face growing itchy the way it does when I'm over-exhausted.

No amount of revision could have prepared me for the speed at which these classes race by, and I'm starting to question why I thought I would be able to do this. Becoming a clinical scientist is the dream. I want to be on the forefront of the modern technology which is constantly changing and improving lives thought to be ruined. But if I don't graduate, all I've done is killed my self-esteem and wasted all of my parent's inheritance. No pressure, Harper.

I sip the latte, hanging onto it like a lifeline while my mind starts to shut down. Doubt creeps in, forcing me to reread the same sentence over and over in the hopes that it will eventually stick. My phone vibrates again, jolting back to the present.

> Beanie26: I find it difficult to open up in person, but I wanted to apologize for what happened in the woods.

Blinking rapidly, I run through the events of that night, wondering why Clayton is apologizing for me being chased by a vicious hog and assaulted by someone with small dick syndrome. Then I remember the kiss, or rather the way I threw myself at him and my lips didn't even make contact. My cheeks burn at the memory.

> Readmylips44: Let's just forget about that whole night, deal?

> Beanie26: Deal.

Across the tables, Clayton lifts his coffee cup in surrender and I do the same. A small smile plays about my lips for my next sip, more than just the coffee blossoming with warmth in my belly. This is good. An ally, someone I can have secret little messages with when my coursework is sending me suicidal. And not to mention, keeping Clayton on side is a good idea for whenever Rhys' next volatile mood swing occurs. I'm adjusting to this small weight being lifted from my shoulders when Clayton messages again.

I stifle a small laugh, but across the way, Clayton is as hard faced as ever. He's leaning on his hand, flicking through a textbook without taking any of it in. There's no sign of mirth, no hint if he intended to be serious or jokey. I watch him openly now, wondering just what it would take to crack Clayton wide open. He can pretend to be indifferent, he can trick people into thinking he has no depth, but I see what others don't. There's a world of trust issues and pain hidden within Clayton's mind. There's a reason he has an impenetrable outer shell, never letting anyone in until he's sure if they are worth his time.

He messages after catching me watching him intently. I don't pretend to have been doing otherwise, leaning back in my chair.

I manage to withhold rolling my eyes at the insinuation that Clayton has already done his assignment. I've barely managed through a third of it, and I'm certain most of that is pointless repetitive waffle.

Sells essays? The casual way he's worded it doesn't make it sound so bad, like it's just a shortcut on a map that everyone's secretly following. But I've always been one to call something as I see it. It's cheating. Am I at such a low already? Then again, I'm exhausted, drowning and dangerously close to giving up. If I keep slipping, I'll never catch up. Like Clayton said, I just need a pass *this time* and then I'll be able to catch up. It'll be a one off.

A small involuntary noise escapes me, which I hide behind downing the rest of my coffee and packing up. I'm careful not to look up, hiding the flush of my cheeks behind the curtain of my wavy hair. Don't overreact, he was just being friendly.

Shouldering my backpack, I scan at the bookshelves bordering the circular seating area. Now that I don't have to stay up all night failing at an assignment anymore, perhaps I could allow myself a respite. A chance to reset back to the girl I was back in Aunt Marg's attic. Casting a glance at Clayton, he gives a small two finger salute as I pass, ending our interaction until next time.

I drift deeper into the quiet solace of the aisles. With closing time creeping closer, no one else has wandered this far in, leaving me to roam freely and trail my fingertips across the spines like I'm greeting old friends.

A familiar warmth swells in my chest. That comforting hum of potential. Each book has a personality tucked between its pages, a voice waiting to be heard. All they ask for is a chance to pull me into their world, to make me care about people who don't exist and problems that aren't mine. A break in the shelves stops me in my tracks. I hesitate, considering my options. Am I in the mood for fantasy or contemp? Slow burn or fast?

I round the corner slowly, scanning the covers with quiet hope, waiting for the one that sings to me from the shelf. The naked bulb overhead gives a tired flicker, a pulse of dim light that casts the shelves in ominous shadow. It's due to this that, when I'm certain there's a flash of movement through the bookshelf gaps, I ignore it. A trick of my mind, that's all. I continue on, dragging my fingers over the paperback spins, occasionally pulling one free of its home to read the blurb. At this rate, I'll be ready to pass out in bed before I've even opened the front cover .

Another quick blur shoots by on the other side of the shelves, this time knocking a few books outward. They topple to the floor by my feet, silently crashing against my private bubble. I spin, casting glances in all areas, suddenly wary of how deep I've strayed. How alone I actually am.

The hairs at the base of my neck rise with instinctive unease. I press my hand flat to the nearest book, now uncaring of the genre, and fight the urge to grab it and get out. My feet begin to move, focused on escaping the maze of shelves. Back to civilization. I'm not too proud to ask Clayton to walk me home, although I won't tell him it's because I've spooked myself with shadows. Perhaps I'm still on edge thanks to Rhys' stupid hog prank and hollow threats.

But when I reach the central seating area, my heart judders. It's empty, and it's dark. There's not a soul in sight. How long was I wandering around? I scan the tables, hunting for something. A clue, a weapon maybe. My eyes settle on the table where I previously sat, one of my textbooks left forgotten on the edge. Despite the unease rippling along my spine, I curse myself for being forgetful and rush to retrieve it. Lifting the heavy weight, swiveling my backpack to shove it inside, I pause long enough to squint at a yellow post-it note stuck to the cover. One that was not there before.

Dread and confusion renders me frozen in place. My first thought is, Clayton? But surely not. Why would he gift me coffee and message with me, just to freak me out like this afterwards? My mind does a full circle back to Rhys. He's fucking with me, as standard. The stupid games of a spoilt, bored man, but even I know not to become comfortable. Rhys is many things, and dangerous is at the top of that list.

A hand lands on my shoulder, making me scream a sound that I can't hear. My eyes adjust as I jerk back, the aged librarian from the front desk clutching her own chest in her fright. Glasses have slipped down the bridge of her nose, hanging on desperately as her chest heaves. I mutter a shaky apology and stuff the textbook, note included, into my backpack.

"*The library has closed,*" I watch her pale lips move, her thin fingers combing the end of silvery locks that rest on her shoulders. I nod eagerly, just relieved to see another person. She escorts me to the exit, but that doesn't ease the feeling that I am indeed being watched. I look around, expecting to see a figure lingering in every darkened crevice. Once we've reached the double doors, the librarian unlocks one of them and pushes it open marginally so I can slip out into the night. I thank her and pretend I'm not stalling as she shuts the door in my face.

It's all on you now Harper, the wind slicing against my cheek seems to say. I rush down the steps, the desire to read myself to sleep tonight forgotten. Simply diving into the covers with the door locked will be enough. I curse myself for not bringing my receivers just in case, relying on my eyesight alone to keep me safe. Silhouettes on the edge of my vision remind me of the kidnapping fiasco on a very similar night, the darkness only broken by streetlamps on each courtyard corner. I check which rooms in the dean's offices still have lights on, mentally planning the route if I should need to find the closest human being.

Am I being watched, like the note states? And if so, why? I slip under the radar on purpose, gliding through life without the validation most crave. That's how I like it. Underestimated, underappreciated. I would be quite happy in a small lab, making small changes so some big-shot scientist can swoop in and make the breakthrough that could change so many lives. No credit needed.

But first, I have to survive this cursed college and the lunatics it seems to attract. First, I need to keep alert, looking over my shoulder, puffing out large clouds of air as I frantically cross the courtyard. When a black cat slinks across my path like a living omen, it's enough to push me over the edge. I break into a full sprint, not stopping until McAl-lister Hall is in sight.

I throw myself into my dorm room, panting and struggling to slow my heartrate. It only accelerates when I find Addy sitting cross legged on her bed, hugging a teddy bear to her pajama-covered chest and sobbing. The tear streaks on her cheeks aren't fresh, her glassy brown eyes staring at the far wall. I close the door and switch my phone's mic on, dropping it between us as I sit on the edge of her bed.

"Addy, what's wrong?" I rush to her side, searching her body for sign of injury. Or perhaps, did she get a note too? "I thought...I thought you were out with Aaron tonight?" I swallow past the lump in my throat. Aaron is in Addy's dance class and she had been so excited when he'd asked her out for a drink tonight. It's another reason why I forced myself to go to the library, as the call of an empty dorm room would have been all too tempting to procrastinate in.

"I was out with Aaron," Addy breathes on a sob. A fresh tear falls from her eye which I instantly wipe away and pull her into a shaky hug. My pulse is still thrashing in my neck and my hands are trembling, but if Addy notices, she doesn't comment.

"Did he hurt you? Try to force you-"

"No, no! Nothing like that. It's just, well, it turns out he just wanted..." Addy hiccups, "wanted..."

I wait on bated breath for her to finish. Did that bastard just want her for sex, bondage, anal?! Tell me woman, what is it?!

"Todd's number." She finally forces out. I sit with a frown tugging at my brows. "My friend Todd in drama. Aaron wants Todd. He thought I could put in a good word for him."

A full beat passes where her words circle around my skull. They settle, sink in, and as much as I know Addy was into Aaron, a strange sensation creeps up my spine. My lips clamp shut in warning, but the pressure builds too fast. *Don't do it, Harper. Don't you dare.*

But the snicker escapes anyway, a bubbling stream at first, cracking the tension wide open. Laughter quickly follows, bursting free, full-bodied and contagious. Addy shrieks, lurching forward to slap my arm, but she's finally smiling. Her whole face lights up as the absurdity hits her, and then she's collapsing beside me on the bed in a heap of hysterics. Tears slip down her cheeks, from mirth this time. We just lie there, laughing and expelling all of the stress from the past few hours. It feels incredible to free my psyche, to just let it all go at last.

When I'm gasping for air, my cheeks aching from the grin stretched across my face, I exhale unevenly. "So this evening, you've managed to turn a man gay while I've been complimented by Clayton and then had the shit scared out of me by some creep. Why do I feel like every day at Waversea is going to be like this?"

Addy suddenly bolts upright, pink hair falling in her eyes as she stares at me. The laughter dies in an instant, replaced by sharp-eyed concern. Despite the puffiness of her eyes, she manages to level me with a serious, no bullshit look.

"Tell me everything."

CLAYTON

CHAPTER THIRTEEN

Lying in bed, I toss a baseball up and down as the sun finally decides to rise. A faded signature spans across the white surface, the red stitching still holding strong after all these years.

Most of my childhood blurs together, fuzzy and fractured, except for the glimmers I hold tight. This one, this day, I remember. Jeremy won game tickets on the radio, desperate to give me a decent present for my tenth birthday. Only four years separated us but he was so much older than his years, having to be the man of the house while mom worked all hours, just like she had to that day too.

Between him and Big Tony from down the road, they'd managed to keep everything a complete surprise, right up until my eyes landed on the stadium. I remember leaning into his solid, muscled frame, too shocked to hold myself upright.

Big Tony had been the most constant male figure we ever had. In his forties, lived alone in a narrow-terraced house with a row of motorbikes out front and tattoos as loud as his laugh. Well, *alone* if you didn't count the sixty-three tarantulas stacked in glass vivarium's in the spare room, an African Grey parrot that only knew curse words, and two chickens he bought in a fit of rage over the rising cost of eggs. Sam and Ella were escape artists, we had to chase them down the street more than once. But we were never short on omelets after that.

When Tony passed a few years later, the whole street felt it. One of the brightest lights in our community, a father figure to many of us boys who were rushing to become men, just gone. I know he would've looked after Mom while I was locked up. Hell, if he'd still been around, maybe the events of that night wouldn't have happened at all.

But right now, safe in the confines of my head, they're both alive and we're back there. The crowd is deafening but it's good energy, filtering through my bones with a lightness I'm not accustomed to. We find our seats, three rows back on the end, but my mind isn't on the baseball. A hot dog the size of my head is in one hand and similarly large lemonade in the other. I haven't had a sip yet, but I'm already bouncing, so excited I feel like I might explode.

Fully invested in my hot dog, Jeremy points outs a group of children running down the aisle between innings, waiting for a ball to be thrown their way. He urges me to join but I shake my head. It's such a big stadium, and as much as I want to put my street instincts aside, my wariness keeps me firmly in my seat. Next thing I know, Jeremy is hollering to a player resting against the railing by the Nats dugout and pointing directly at me.

"Hey yo, Roark! My little brother in your biggest fan!" he yells, much to my embarrassment. After a moment of staring my way, Roark ducks down out of sight, probably to avoid being bothered whilst waiting his turn to bat. But a short while later, he pops back up and beckons me down the steps. The kids all around glare and scowl my way, but I shoulder through with the help of my big brother.

"I know greatness when I see it, kid. You'll do great things one day," he says, tossing me a signed ball and placing a baseball cap over my blonde waves. Jeremy snatches the cap for himself as I marvel at the ball in my hand. Crisp white, red stitching and a scrawled signature across the side. My new prized possession.

"He's right you know," Jeremy nudges me out of my thoughts.

"You're going to be the best of both of us. And I'm keeping this cap." I can't describe the pride that detonates within, looking up into my brother's eyes, wishing I could be just like him. Brave, resilient, humble.

But we weren't in control of our own fates back then, our path had been mapped out long before we were even born. We just didn't know it at the time, nor that Jeremy would be buried with a tattered Nats cap before he had a chance to become the man he was supposed to be.

Kenneth's lumpy shape shudders as he giggles out of nowhere, evidently not asleep beneath his cover like I'd previously thought. I rest on my elbows to watch him roll out of bed, a huge smile spanning across his face.

"What's gotten into you?" I ask raising one eyebrow. His red hair is a tufty mess of curls and cowlicks, sticking out in every direction.

"Had a funny dream is all," he bursts into a fit of laughter like a squeaky maniac. "You were in it too."

"I don't even want to know," I mutter, returning to tossing my ball high into the air. The dorm door closes as he makes his way to the bathrooms, but I can still hear him muttering and chuckling to himself down the hallway. Shaking my head, I swallow past a new lump in my throat.

I can't begin to imagine what it feels like to wake up that happy. To have your brain feed you some nonsense while you sleep and leave you smiling like an idiot. That kind of joy doesn't exist for me anymore. Probably never did, but it's different for Kenneth. He got a normal childhood. I don't need to know the details to know that. I can see it in the way he moves through the world.

Swinging my legs over the side of the bed, I make the most of my time alone. Dressing quickly, I shoot a text over to the Essay Whizz I was telling Harper about last night. Little bastard tried to double his usual fee for the assignment I requested, knowing full well I didn't have the money to pay. I've bargained some self-defence lessons instead, agreeing to work off 'my debt'. As if he doesn't have the file at his fingertips ready to send over.

I grab my hoodie from the floor and pull it on. Kenneth re-enters just as I'm tucking my hair beneath the hood, his eyes still twinkling with leftover amusement.

"Why do you do that?"

"Do what?" I crack my neck side to side and roll my shoulders.

"Hide your hair all the time? If you don't like it, you could just shave it all off."

The idea chills the blood in my veins. My movements pause mid-stretch, a tightness pressing into my chest, making it hard to breathe. I manage a head shake, but no words follow. Just a noise caught somewhere between a grunt and a sob. He doesn't get it, and I don't want him to. This isn't my life I'm living and these choices aren't mine to make. Weren't mine to make. Fuck.

Tension knots in my shoulders as I shoot to my feet and storm out of the room. Kenneth jumps out of the way just in time. I slam the door, not stopping until I'm standing in front of the bathroom mirror. I lean over the sink, splashing water on my face until the sting behind my eyes starts to ease.

I know what's waiting when I look up. I do it anyway. Pulling down my hood, Jeremy stares back from the mirror. His blond waves. His black eyes. That wide, steady stance. My body has filled out to match his perfectly. Externally, we're the same person, if only my mind would catch up. Jeremy wouldn't beat himself down, he'd dust himself off and keep pushing forward.

Yet, I keep doing this to myself like it's a punishment I deserve. Maybe it is. If this is what it takes to remind me that he existed, then I'll take it. I'll keep looking, I'll keep hurting. I'll take it every day for the rest of my life.

I emerge, the pent-up energy I've been trying to set aside all morning returning with a vengeance. Luckily, Kenneth has already left for his morning shift at the veterinary student's coffee shop, 'Toadfully Caffeinated'.

I tap my phone, waiting for that particular file to hit my inbox, struck with restlessness. Since when do I sit around twiddling my thumbs, waiting to help out a girl in need rather than hitting the gym before class? I even debate dropping into the morning basketball drill to let Rhys dial up my fury a notch, but that I decide not to choose violence today.

Instead, I pull the acoustic guitar from the bottom of the wardrobe and settle back on my bed. Most people will have headed out for breakfast before class by now, not that I give a shit either way.

I strum my fingers across the strings, the soft harmony reaching my ears and offering a kind of relief that nothing else can. I shift through a range of chords until one sticks, my hands choosing the song that matches the ache in my chest without needing my permission. *Photograph* by Ed Sheeran spills into the quiet, not aloud, just inside my head, the lyrics threading through my thoughts until everything else fades away.

Every time I visit my mom, I take Jeremy's guitar and work through the long list of songs she always has ready for me. Her full-faced smile and glassy eyes are worth every ounce of self-hate that crashes over me the second I walk out of that place again.

The chorus lifts me, pulling me into a pocket of sound where nothing else matters. A space where the noise in my head finally shuts up. The grief I can never escape drains from my skin, like it's searching for a new host while I'm too wrapped up in the moment to stop it. I barely register the tears until they're already there, slipping silently down my face. I make no effort to wipe them. Wouldn't matter if I did. This part of me is too loud to ignore. Pain is stitched into every inch of who I am, and sorrow is the thread that keeps me standing.

My stomach growls and breaks the spell, tugging me out of the fog. With a quiet sigh, I slide the guitar back into its hiding place and look around the room. I shove my feet into battered sneakers and grab my backpack on the way out.

The second I enter the cafeteria, I regret it. Every table is taken. Loud voices, messy chewing, mouth breathers at every angle. A full room of people existing without thought. And I just stand there, trying not to lose whatever calm I had managed to steal.

Shifting towards the buffet line, my back shields me from everyone else's presence as I grab a tray and eye up the potential breakfast options. I know my prepaid card balance is running low, but hopefully I've got just enough to scrape by until the next round of weekly funds drops in. Grabbing a baguette and pushing a miniature takeaway cup beneath the dispenser, I press for a double shot espresso to carry me through the morning.

"Not much of a sweet tooth?" a feminine voice asks. It takes me a second to realize she's talking to me. Among the mass of bodies in the room, a petite frame leans against the counter beside me. Harper's wide, doe-like eyes are locked on mine, a small smile tugging at the corners of her full lips. I glance side to side, but she is definitely speaking to me.

"I'm too bitter, I suppose," I reply directly, assuming she isn't wearing her receivers. There's no way she could look so calm while someone across the cafeteria yells and launches their tray to the floor. I don't turn to look. I don't want to. Not when Harper is here, watching me like I'm worth paying attention to. I place the lid on my coffee and add it to my tray, moving along in the queue. I can feel her behind me, not touching but close enough to register her warmth. Like she exists on another frequency that part of me is desperate to tune into.

Reaching the counter, I scan my ID, and the screen flashes red. Of course. *Fuck*.

"Add it onto mine," Harper says to the assistant, her hand brushing my arm and pulling me back a step. "I owe you one anyway," she adds. I freeze as she taps her own card and the scanner lights up bright fucking green. Harper's smile hits me full-force, not mocking or cruel, but she doesn't understand my inner working. The shame it triggers in me is sharp enough to cut bone.

Starting as a mild discomfort, it festers and rages until I'm left utterly consumed by its humiliation. This pain is different to the one I bring upon myself each day, this one cuts a little deeper. Feels fresher than the dulled anguish I've grown accustomed to. Without another word, I take my breakfast, preparing to leave when Harper's hand touches my arm. It's tentative, unsure, but I still anyway.

"Did you... shall we sit?" she nods toward a table that's just been vacated. My cheeks are burning as the eyes of half the cafeteria shift toward us. To Harper, I'm the jock who offered her a favor. But to everyone else, I'm the guy who couldn't pay for his own damn breakfast.

I sit down before I can think better of it. Harper places her tray opposite mine, unbothered by the stares. She's got a calm defiance in her posture, like she's already made peace with people misunderstanding her. She takes a sip of her coffee and doesn't flinch at the heat streaming from it. Her gaze holds mine steadily.

"So," she says, picking up a fork, "do you always brood this early or is today special?" I snort softly, chewing through a nibble of my baguette.

"Depends who you ask." I keep my eyes on my food, focusing on the simplest task in front of me. Eat. Don't say anything stupid. Don't look at her too long. But Harper is all about eye contact, a subtle smile on her mouth. She doesn't fill the silence with mindless chatter. She eats opposite me, content with the quiet, oblivious to the social pressure to make small talk.

"You don't have to sit with me, you know," I say after a while, practically mouthing the words without needing to voice them.

"I know," she says easily, a half shrug on her shoulder. "But I wanted to."

I cling onto the weight that tries to lift from my shoulders. Grapple with the guarded wall I've built around myself. One small confession and a pair of green eyes can't undo all of that in four words. Instead, I nod once and swallow the last of my breakfast. The air feels thick now, loaded with things I'm not ready to acknowledge. I glance around and catch a few eyes lingering too long. Whispers moving like smoke between tables. I push back my chair.

"You should stay," she says immediately, as if she was anticipating I would bolt. I consider it for one brief second, but my mind is already set. She's the new girl. She still has a shot at surviving this place without a scarlet letter burned onto her reputation. The best way to do that is to stay as far away from me as possible.

Just as I'm about to get up, my phone buzzes. At last. I open the file from the Essay Whizz, checking that he's made the relevant changes so Harper won't be picked up for plagiarism. It looks good, and luckily she's right here for me to lean across the table and tap my phone against hers. The file is airdropped over by the time I've stood. I leave before she can thank me, sliding my tray into the collection rack and walking out.

Pulling a black beanie from my backpack, I tug it low over my ears, shutting out the world for just a little longer. If I stay, I'll do something reckless. Like sit back down. Like ask her to look at me the way she did, without judgement. Harper is untouched by this place. She's clean. She still has time to carve out her path, and she doesn't need me staining it before she even gets the chance.

CHAPTER FOURTEEN

Despite his usual hot-and-cold routine this morning, Clay's tip-off came through. Clutching the assignment in my hand, I pause outside Peterson's room, steadying my breath. It isn't just the cheating that has me twisted up inside, but the idea of facing the cocky bastard who's no doubt already perched at his stool in the front of class. I have many thoughts evolving around Rhys and the stalker moment I had in the library. There's no doubt he orchestrated it, I just don't understand what he gets out of it.

Switching on my microphone app, I stride into the room and place both the booklet and my phone on the front desk. When I turn, my eyes are drawn straight to Clayton in the back row, watching me carefully. Rhys is, thankfully, nowhere in sight, which means I don't have to shield myself behind Clay's brooding presence. Sitting next to him now would be a decision made freely, and judging by the way he responded to me this morning, I don't think it's one he wants me to make.

Swallowing thickly, I settle into a stool in the second row to stay out of his eyeline, pulling a stack of textbooks from my bag.

"Good morning, everyone. Before we begin, a quick reminder to return your consent forms by the end of today for our trip to the

Grayson Laboratory next week." Peterson's voice echoes in my mind as I set down my notepad and pen, eyes drifting over the equipment arranged neatly around me.

Each table, raised and spanning six rows back, is lined with a tray of glass beakers, test tubes, pipettes, and the Bunsen burners fixed permanently at the far end. The furniture is all metallic and grey, stools matching the tall cupboards lining the white walls. Long, exposed bulbs stretch across the ceiling, their glare bouncing off the pages of my notepad and nearly blinding me as I begin to write.

I'm mid-sentence when the atmosphere shifts, thickening around me. I don't need to look up to know exactly who just walked in.

"Ahh, Master Waversea. Nice of you to join us."

Rhys enters in a full navy tracksuit, the ink on his hands and neck blending into the soft fabric. His hair is swept back with effortless style, but the shine from product betrays how long he must've spent getting it just right. His bright eyes land on the empty stool beside me, a smug smile forming as I scramble to block it with my backpack. Tossing his assignment onto the growing pile, he strolls over and knocks my bag to the floor with the back of his hand before dropping into the seat.

"Asshole," I mutter, scooping up my things from the floor. Peterson waits until I'm settled again before continuing, drawing attention back to the opening slide with a chrome pointer.

Rhys leans on one elbow across the table, his smirk dominating my vision.

"How am I supposed to work with a lab partner who can't hear me?" he mouths, the metal ring in his bottom lip catching the light more than his words do.

"I can read lips better than you can spread legs," I fire back under my breath. "The better question is how am I supposed to work with a lab partner who never shows up?"

His resulting smile would be dazzling on anyone else. Straight, white teeth that scream private orthodontics. But on him, it's something else entirely. It's a cocktail of arrogance and temptation, dangerous in a way that feels deliberate. A trap I have no intention of falling into.

"What about him? You can't see his mouth when he's turned around." Rhys tilts his chin toward Peterson, who's currently filling my head with ways to tell plasma and serum apart. I raise a hand in front of Rhys's face to block him out, trying to scribble down a few notes before the slide changes. A sudden wet heat against my palm startles me. His tongue curls around my middle finger.

Yanking my hand back in disgust, or at least what I tell myself is disgust, I catch his eyes waiting for my reaction. With a sigh and a roll of my eyes, I jab a finger toward my phone on the front desk and return to ignoring him. The lessons are fast-paced, and I'm determined to keep up from now on. Not that my partner has any intention of letting that happen. Rhys leans in and grips my thighs with both hands, spinning me on the stool until I'm facing him.

"How does it all work?" His hands remain on my legs, warmth bleeding through the denim. I try to loosen his grip, but he's deceptively strong for someone with such a lean frame. I give up. For once, his cocky smile is absent, and there's a flicker of something real in his eyes.

"Microphones transmit sound via Bluetooth directly into my inner ear through an implanted disc. Same with music," I say, shrugging like it's nothing. Turning back toward the front, his hands shift fast enough to make me flinch. One cradles my jaw, the other pushes my hair aside, his thumb dragging across the metal disc beneath the skin behind my ear. A shiver rolls through me. I've never shown anyone before, let alone had someone touch it with inked fingers and quiet curiosity.

I stay still while he explores it, not entirely comfortable, but enjoying the attention far more than I should. Around us, no one seems to notice. The class goes on like this is just Rhys being Rhys. Eventually, his hands fall away, and he studies me with a tilted head.

"That's actually pretty awesome." His voice carries a genuine note,

and the surprise in his own expression confirms it. I shrug again. Maybe it sounds cool to others, but for me, it was just survival.

"I don't like to wear the aids. This way makes me feel a bit more—" I stop myself. His blue eyes wait for me to finish. "—normal." Clearing my throat, I pull my notepad closer and try to catch up on what I've missed. Most of it doesn't make sense, but I jot it all down anyway. If Rhys keeps this up, I'll be in the library for the fourth night this week.

"So for today, you'll be investigating the components of plasma and how we can isolate the fibrinogen using real blood samples, essentially turning it into serum. Make sure to include in your findings how this could be applied in a case study situation." Peterson smiles like it's all straightforward and starts handing out sealed vials of blood to each table.

"Is this human blood?" I ask, holding the tube up and squinting at the thick red liquid inside.

"No. We were able to trade some equipment with the veterinary medicine department for rodent samples," Peterson replies, already moving back to the front of the room. Rhys nudges me with the back of his hand.

"Yeah, we've got our very own rat expert in the house," he says, bobbing his eyebrows in the direction of the red-haired boy in the row behind. "Dickerson knows 'em inside and out." Rhys winks as I cringe at what he's implying. I glance at poor Kenneth, who looks like he might cry, then shove Rhys hard enough to knock him sideways on his stool before going back to work.

With my head down, I jot down every fact I can remember about blood before twisting off the cap and pouring the sample into a test tube on the wooden rack. Rhys leans close enough that I can feel his breath against my cheek, but I ignore him. Grabbing a second vial, I repeat the process, lifting a pipette to collect a drop for the glass slide. That's when Rhys knocks the entire rack over.

I jerk back as blood spills across the table, soaking my notepad and dripping onto the floor in syrupy red lines. Rhys stays perfectly calm, dragging his middle finger through the mess to draw a lazy figure of eight before finally looking at me.

"Don't ever ignore me again."

Finding my resolve, I pout and give him my most lethal puppy-dog eyes.

"Aww, did the wittle wich boy not get enough attention growing up?" I mock, laying it on thick with a baby voice before straightening up, sharpening my expression. Rhys might not have met his match before, but he's met it now. He'll learn soon enough that I'm not someone he can intimidate.

I don't even see Rhys move, I only feel his bloodied hand slide around my throat, his long fingers tightening at my pulse. His eyes, blue and ice cold, bore into mine with a solid resolve. Peterson has gone strangely silent, and for a second, everything seems to freeze. Then, in a blur of motion, Rhys is wrenched from his seat and collides with the solid chest of Clayton, who is suddenly standing between us.

I peek around his wide frame to see, but I didn't need to. Clay slams Rhys down onto the blood-covered work surface like a ragdoll. The glass beakers shatter beneath Rhys' back, not that he appears to have felt it. An easy smile spreads across his face, despite the thickly corded, veined arm pinning him in place.

Clayton bends low, speaking words I can't hear, but whatever they are makes Rhys' smile slip. He releases him with a final shove into the tabletop and walks away without so much as a glance in my direction. Rhys slips off the desk, grabs my stool from where it must have landed, and slides back into his seat like nothing happened, swinging a look my way.

"Sit down, Babygirl, we have work to do." I gape, not realizing I was out of my seat. Rhys snaps his fingers high in the air, and a group of students—mostly girls—swarm in to clean up the mess and replace our equipment. Peterson arrives with a fresh set of vials, casting a wary glance at me while Rhys is distracted. I watch him closely, signaling with my expression, *'where the fuck were you three minutes ago?'*.

Regardless, Peterson retreats, and I'm left beside a madman, pretending my fingers aren't trembling as I open a brand-new notepad and begin to write again.

This time, Rhys is the perfect lab partner, calmly dividing the vials into test tubes and pushing the microscope over so I can examine his first sample. He doesn't speak again, at least not that I can hear, only pointing out my incorrect notes or signaling when I should record our findings. The curiosity is eating at me, gnawing beneath my skin like an itch I can't reach, needing to know what changed everything so suddenly.

"What did Clayton say to you?" I finally cave. If there's a magic spell or a safe word or a voodoo combination that unlocks the cooperative side of Rhys Waversea, I need it. Rhys chews on his lip ring, considering his answer but when he opens his mouth, Peterson's voice cuts into my head.

"Harper, Rhys, can I see you both at the front?" I glance up to see the professor holding two assignments, his brows pulling together as he looks between the pages and then directly at us. "Seems like I've got the same essay from the both of you."

My stomach flips and my jaw goes slack, heat crawling up my neck. *Oh no.* The first time I've ever cheated in my life, and I've already been caught. Rhys will be fine, but I won't. A mark on my record, a formal reprimand maybe? Panic spreads like wildfire, tightening my chest with shame and dread.

I glance toward Clayton, hoping for something, anything, but he just stares back blankly. After a beat, he turns to his beakers and resumes his work. I have to stop my mouth from dropping open. So much for his protection. Flames lick at my cheeks as I face forward, inhaling deeply and bracing myself to get up and walk to the Dean's office.

"That's on me, I'm afraid." Rhys suddenly stands, his voice clear enough to be picked up by my mic. I whip my head toward him as he strides up and plucks one of the assignments from Peterson's hand. "I cornered the new girl and made her print me a second copy. Didn't think you'd actually notice, so props to you."

He pats Peterson's shoulder with mock praise before turning to me with a wicked smirk. I figured Rhys would return to the table, but he opts for a dramatic exit instead. His gaze pins me on the way out, the classroom fading around us. Only his sharp grin and the threat in his eyes remain. Those slanted lips move and even from here I can tell, it's only for my benefit.

"Now you owe me."

CHAPTER FIFTEEN

I was murder-level pissed about Clayton ruining my Hugo Boss polo today, until a sweet little prize landed in my lap. Or rather, was swiped by my hand.

Striding out of the bathroom with nothing but a towel around my waist, I snigger again at the ridiculous stream of messages lighting up Harper's phone. The nonstop vibrating is edging into harassment territory. Dropping onto the edge of the bed, I scoff with a mix of humor and disgust, marveling once again at Harper's lack in security.

> Beanie26: Are you okay?
>
> Beanie26: Let me know if you need anything.
>
> Beanie26: I'm starting to get worried, let me know you're safe.
>
> Beanie26: Maybe I'll see you in the library later?

Pathetic. Looking through her inbox, I see it's only Clayton who messages her *constantly*. It also doesn't escape my notice that he's the one who suggested she bought her essay like I did. I honestly didn't know Mr. High and Mighty had it in him, but the irony is too sweet. He led her down the wrong path and I'm the one who heroically took the fall.

I can imagine it now. Her, trapped in a tower and guarded by a beanie-wearing mop. Me, the incredibly handsome savior dripping in tattooed armor and hung like a horse. I'll call out, "Stubborn Damsel, let me save your hot ass." Harper's brunette locks will billow in the wind as she leans out of the window to shouts back, "Huh? What? I can't hear you!"

I'm chuckling to myself, water droplets rolling down my body. Scrolling back to the last message from Harper, I swipe every response below and move each one to the trash. When I'd snuck her phone out of class, I figured I would be adding a mild inconvenience to her day and giving her a reason to seek me out. I wasn't prepared for the sheer level of entertainment her personal life would provide me.

Another message comes through, this one promising to hunt Harper down if she doesn't respond. This one gives me pause, just before I delete that one too.

Where does Clayton get off hounding after my current source of amusement? The only person who gets to terrorize students is me, and tormenting Harper is one hell of a thrill. As of this second, I've decided she's mine alone to bully until she flees screaming, and no one else will get a piece of the intimidation pie except me. I won't waste too long thinking on why my focus is centered on her, supposing it's because she's the first one to actually stand up to me.

Throwing on the first pair of jeans and t-shirt I find laundered and folded in the chest of drawers, I make sure to keep Harper's phone with me as I jog down the stairs. The frat house is oddly quiet, only a few guys in the kitchen throwing darts directly into the wall. Ignoring them, I stride out the front door and use a key fob to open the attached garage.

Whipping off a dust sheet, my Kawasaki Ninja comes into view. This machine is a pure beast with its four-cylinder, liquid cooling engine. Gah, I could nerd out for days with the biggest hard-on in history for this beautiful metallic outline. The body is a mix of black matte and shining chrome, deserving of a tender stroke before mounting. I don't think I've ever acted like such a gentleman before, but she deserves it. Nina the Ninja may be the cause of future broken legs and various other bones, but she'll never break my heart.

Settling myself on her leather-encased curves, I rev the engine loudly before shooting out into the street. Heading in the opposite direction of the main campus, the tires eat up the road with all the smoothness of a purring kitten. Swerving around corners and shooting down various streets, the tightening in my chest that comes with residing at Waversea begins to ease.

There are three segments to the college grounds. The main sector where the student bullshit happens, a circular band of buildings around the outside for the admin crap and the town beyond. *"All the amenities a student could need,"* the brochure says. Huh, so where the fuck is the strip club and casino, Dad? A couple bars, restaurants, a rec center and movie theatre aren't enough to keep me contained in this hellhole any longer than necessary.

I spend a while riding around, chasing the taste of freedom I've never actually felt, and scaring more than one old lady taking her sweet-ass time crossing the road. Begrudgingly, I head back toward a row of depressingly gray office buildings and park around the back in a narrow alley. I made it my business to know the layout of the admin segment, exploring every hidden nook and figuring out what happens behind each locked door.

Walking the rest of the way, I pass the treasury and admissions offices, with a bunch of staff residences visible at the far end of the street. A red door comes into view at the top of some stone steps, still wrapped in a half-dead string of Christmas lights. Pushing inside unannounced, my eyes fall on Mitch reclining behind the desk.

"Master Waversea, so good to see you," he jumps up, flashing a too-wide grin. Mitch is a short, rounded guy with a perfect bald patch like someone scrubbed the top of his head clean. He's got that jolly, approachable vibe most people fall for, but behind the curtain he's got nine kids by eight different women to support and he's crooked as they come. Not that it matters. Even if he were squeaky clean, everyone's got a price.

"How's it going, Mitch?"

"Oh, you know, same old. Something tells me we're about to have another glitch," he winks. Funny how the finance system's glitched more than a few times since I enrolled, but stranger shit's happened. Tossing him a roll of cash, I stroll down the corridor to a single elevator at the far end. The doors take forever, so I jab the button repeatedly until they finally slide open with a ding.

Stepping out on Floor Four, the stale warmth hits me in the face. The heaters crank year-round in here. Unlike the sad concrete outside, the interior is light and glassy. Offices are divided by panes instead of walls, with oversized plant pots scattered around like they're gonna fix anyone's soul-sucking job.

No wonder a few pairs of eyes lift when I walk through. I'm probably the most exciting thing they've seen all month. Aside from a few breaks in keyboard tapping, no one bothers me as I slide into an empty desk.

This level deals specifically with student loans and scholarship grants, including weekly allowances for the totally broke. I punch in the password I memorized while getting head from an intern down the hall. Honestly, I can't even remember which one. The screen unlocks to reveal a sea of virtual files. Navigating through the maze where I buried Clayton's records so nobody else could touch them, I open the BACS account and cancel his next weekly payment, which was set to drop at midnight.

Stalking isn't cool, even by my standards. So that prick can skip a few meals. I double check that his gym membership is still flagged as pending, then log out with a satisfied smirk. Reclining in the chair, the grin fades as the weight of what I just did settles in.

Was that... a good deed? I've never jumped in to fight someone else's battles. People need to take care of their own mess because I'm too busy planning the takedown of the century. Dismantling a billionaire's pride and joy doesn't happen overnight, but I've got years of simmering hate to keep the engine running. And I'm the only one twisted enough to finish the job.

After stopping by Floor Three to tweak a few payroll numbers, because screw you for calling me out Peterson, I head back down, give Mitch a lazy nod, and return to my bike. I tear across campus toward the back of the basketball court, duck into the rear entrance of the locker room, and take my time changing even though I'm stupid late for practice. Coach scheduled extra sessions ahead of a big game on Friday, but I don't take orders. He's lucky I bothered to show up at all.

Scrubbing a hand down my face, I roll my shoulders and step out onto the court. The entirety of the team are sitting in the first row of the bleachers, watching the two sophomores go head-to-head in a private game of one v one. Huxley and Garrett don't even look my way, locked in on whatever bromance rivalry they've got going on.

"What the fuck?" I mutter, my hackles rising beneath the surface. These guys may have been the shit last year, but they stepped back this semester to make way for new talent, AKA, me and anyone I deem worthy. Not that it stops them from loitering around, hanging in the back like uninvited guests. Noticing me with my arms crossed and eyebrow cocked, Coach jumps up from the bench and rushes over, stumbling in his haste.

"The returning players thought it would be a good idea to demonstrate some offense and defense tactics for the team to work on," he fumbles out. For a coach, he's more than a little overweight and sweats like a hooker awaiting STD results. Apparently, he was a star player in his day, but if that was so, I doubt he's standing here quivering under the rule of a nineteen-year-old. Knowing the team will need as much help as they can get before next Saturday, I drop on the edge of the bench without another word.

Huxley has his blond waves tied back, his concentration on the ball in his hands, stalling with a few bounces whilst looking for an opening. Faking left, he spins on his heel to dart right but his teammate is a step ahead of his tricks. Garrett crouches low to steal the ball mid-bounce, twisting his body in the opposite direction. He jumps to shoot from the arc line to make a clean basket.

The team beside me applaud eagerly like a bunch of seals clapping for fish. Rolling my eyes, I lean back against the bleacher's railing. There's nothing they can show me that a personal tutor back home hasn't done a thousand times. A shudder rolls through me at the thought of that dark and depressing mansion being a *home*.

Luckily, I missed most of practice because the sophomores are clasping each other on the back before announcing it's time to head out. An excited murmur passes through the team, many with an inspired glint in their eyes. Remaining in place until everyone has left, I hope to get some time alone on the court until one person in particular notices me not following.

"You're always late for practice," Garrett states the obvious, dropping down beside me. Leaning forward with his tattooed forearms on his thighs, he blows the long fringe from his eyes and glances at me.

"I decide when practice starts. Everyone else is too early," I shrug, much to his amusement.

"I used to be a lot like you," he muses. I purse my lips, looking across the empty court. There have been many comparisons between Garrett and myself over the year. Just because we both have dark hair, tattoos and reek of sarcasm, doesn't mean we're the same on the inside. No one is like me, practiced in the art of concealing rage behind a perfectly placid mask. Garrett watches me out of the corner of his eye.

"Trust me, I've seen how quickly life can change. One day, you're going to want somewhere to turn and find there's nowhere willing to take you. Food for thought." I laugh at his ridiculousness, because what he fails to realize is I don't need anyone. I'm enough company for myself. That way I will never fall victim to the melancholy emotions which tear others down.

Snatching up the ball by his feet, I dribble across the room to end the chitchat I have no interest in being a part of. After a beat, Garrett stands on a sigh and exits in my peripheral vision. Running to the far end of the court, I slam the ball into the basket before doing the same on the other side.

Not for the first time, I wonder why I am actually on this team. For someone who has decided to remain isolated, I've entered a sport which means I must depend on others. It was an average day of torturing freshmen and bribing the staff when I noticed Clay's name scribbled on the sign-up list and something inside me sorta snapped.

Clayton's a funny fish. He doesn't speak, doesn't participate in anything. From what I understand via my sources, he's already got a record and his own mother can't even remember him. But he continues to call her weekly, and then decided to join a team sport. I joked that I had wanted to terrorize him further, but secretly, I was fascinated. I had to see with my own eyes if he managed to find a shred of happiness despite the life he previously led. But he hasn't, which means there's no hope for me either.

Bouncing the ball between my legs as I walk, I allow each thud to resonate with my being. Like a chime passing through me until I'm able to block out unwanted thoughts. Throwing the ball from the center of the court, it hits the back board before dropping into the net. Running after it, I circle back and do it over and over again, each time taking a step back to see how far I can shoot from. It's evident I'm lacking a challenge in my life if this is what the height of my excitement has come to.

My thoughts turn to the girl who has invertedly dug up all of these unwanted questions. Who has stirred unwanted emotions within me. The one who's managed to cut through my bullshit, making me re-evaluate everything I stand for. The only girl I can't have.

I stop so quickly, I almost topple over. What the fuck am I thinking? There is no girl on earth I *can't* have, and just like that, I see what the issue is. I drop the ball, its small bounces pounding across the wood as clarity clears my jumbled mind. The allure, the appeal, the attraction. It's all because she isn't pawing at my feet, begging for a scrap of notice.

By refusing me, she's only enticed me. There's appeal in the unknown, and now I realize that, I'm determined to know her inside and out by the end of next week. A smile grows across my face, a light giddiness filling my chest. She will put up a good chase, but I have eyes on my prey now. To rid her from my system, I'll have to revert to my base instincts.

Fuck and forget, then I can focus on casting her out quicker than she can scream, *"More, Rhys, more!"*

CHAPTER SIXTEEN

"Give me my phone back." I glare, planting my hands on my hips just to stop myself from punching Rhys in his smug face the second he steps into the locker room. I had to run back to my dorm for my damn receivers before spending two full hours hunting this tattooed asshole down.

In hindsight, I probably should have started with the basketball court instead of the gym, the pool, the girls' locker room, and definitely before spying through the window of the cesspit he calls home. But whatever. I found him.

Rhys stands in the doorway and looks me over, a strange sense of happiness settling over him. I refuse to let my confusion show, entering a stare-off until I hold my hand out expectantly.

"Phone. Now."

Chuckling to himself, Rhys peels off his jersey like he's auditioning for a slow-motion shampoo commercial, dragging it up his chest with a casual flick of his wrist. My eyes roll so hard I almost sprain something. He strolls to his locker and punches in the code. After a full minute of unnecessary flexing, he finally slams the door shut and struts over with his usual shit-eating grin.

"You really should have a passcode, Babygirl."

I snatch the phone out of his hand and immediately open all the apps I use daily, half-expecting to find everything rearranged or worse. Surprisingly, there isn't a single fake text. No new photos, namely no dick pics. Weird. I open the college messenger and see there's also nothing new from Clay. I suppose that's the end of that.

"I wouldn't waste my time with him if I were you." Rhys peers at my screen, before reaching across and tapping the block button. I cancel it right away, though I don't know why I even care. Rhys shrugs, his smile lopsided as he kicks off his sneakers and drops his shorts to the floor right in front of me.

"What the hell are you doing?" I start to turn away, until something shiny catches my eye. In fact, many shiny things. Rhys is pierced with a singular stud in the head of his dick, and a hint of a Jacob's ladder trailing the underside of his shaft. His tattoos trail all the way down to the base, swirling black lines that enhance his generous size. Holy hell. I stare, horrified and slightly fascinated, as his long cock twitches like it's glad for the attention. My face heats and I whip around instantly.

"No need to be shy. Next time you're horny, save your batteries and come find me instead."

"My vibrator's rechargeable," I shoot back, flipping him off over my shoulder and walking away. I got what I came for. The showers start up to my right, an instantaneous billow of steam thickening the air. Halfway out of the door, Rhys' voice stops my feet in their tracks.

"Oh, before you go," he calls out, humor lifting his tone, "I figured out what your payback can be." I still with one hand pressed against the door. Everything in my head screams not to engage but my mouth moves regardless.

"Payback for what?" I play dumb. Rhys just laughs, and I lower my forehead against the cool door. Whatever is about to happen, I know I should have just owned up to cheating on Peterson's essay and taken the punishment. Instead, I'm here, turning back and make my way toward the showers. I lean against a metal door marked *Coach's Office,* arms crossed, silently waiting for whatever nonsense Rhys is about to drop.

From this angle, I can see the back of Rhys. His back ripples, the creamy skin untouched by ink. It's a stark contrast to his front, and my eyes trail south. I'm headstrong to a fault, but even I can appreciate a cute butt when I see one. It's a refreshing side to Rhys, pun intended, to see him all soft edges and carefree without putting on an act.

Probably because he's sensed I'm watching, Rhys takes his sweet time. He lathers gel in his hands, spreads it across that artwork of a body, and lets the bubbles slide down until they swirl around the drain. When he finally speaks again, it's under the roar of the water, and I have to step closer just to hear him properly.

"I'm having my usual party after the game Friday. You're going to be there."

I scoff, shaking my head even though he's not looking my way. I've been chasing him around campus for hours, bracing myself for the worst-case scenario, and he's talking about his parties again? I can't grasp why this is so important to him, why he cares if I attend or not.

"I hate parties," I call back. Rhys is ready for my argument.

"Then your other option is to dress up like a cheerleader and chant my name during the game. Between you and me, I can't stand cheer-leaders." He runs his hands through his wet hair, pushing it back from his face. Catching his side eye, I force myself to keep my eyes in an appropriate place.

"Why do you even want me there?" I throw up my hands. "Another way to humiliate me? The poor little deaf girl who can't hear the music." My jaw tightens, an insecurity coming to the surface before I can wrangle it back down. Thankfully, Rhys is in his own little dream world as he shuts off the faucet.

"Maybe I want you close to my bed," he says, smirking with that same arrogance that dares me to back out.

"Maybe I'll bring a date," I shoot back. He crosses the space in an instant. Suddenly towering over me, close enough that I have to tip my chin up, a dare gleams in Rhys' eyes. The light fades into something darker. For a depraved second, I wonder what it'd feel like if he ever really let himself go. Would he kiss me or strangle me? Why does either option intrigue me? His chest rises and falls with tension, and I can see the war playing out across his face.

"Don't. You. Dare," he breathes. Droplets from his soaked hair hit my skin but I don't flinch. I lock onto those icy blue eyes, refusing to look anywhere else, especially not at the ink stretched across his bare chest or the ring in his lip he just teased with his tongue. "I would be your date, and you will be mine. That's my condition of saving your ass earlier."

"Why would you even want that? I'm literally nobody." Somehow my voice remains strong, but a small tremor threatens to rise at that last part. For someone who has spent every waking minute of the past ten years trying to disappear, my psyche did not like professing that to Rhys. His smirk is ever present, as if he's withholding a dark secret.

"Harper Addams," he chuckles, lifting a hand to tuck my hair behind my receiver. "I think you might be the most somebody I've ever met."

Consider my brain short-circuited. A shudder rolls through me at his admission, my tongue darting out to touch a droplet that lands on my lip. Rhys tracks the movement like an eagle, zeroed in on his prey. My lashes flutter, the stretch of my neck putting me in prime position for Rhys to dip his head and close the few inches between us.

A shrill voice cuts through the room, slicing through my skull. I wince, my hands flying up to my receivers. Rhys catches them by the wrist, holding my hands softly against his damp chest. Klara storms straight up to her naked boyfriend like a blonde hurricane of fury. Her black and yellow pom-poms lie abandoned on the floor, her cheer top printed with *Rhys's #1.*

Rhys doesn't seem to care for her presence, raising my hands to his mouth. He places slanted kisses on my knuckles, time freezing in place.

Both Klara and I are stunned, playing along with Rhys' whims. He drops his face to my hearing aid, his wet fingers easing my hair aside.

"I'll see you at the party," he whispers before slinking back into the shower and turning the water on once more. From the brief glance I couldn't resist, it appears he'll be having a cold shower this time.

Also ignoring Klara, because what the fuck am I supposed to say about anything that just happened, I stride away and successfully walk through the fire exit this time. The sun momentarily blinds me, the freshness of the air almost sending my lungs into shock. Making my way to the bottom on the hill, I pass a group of girls cackling like witches whilst admiring each other's hair and nails with fake smiles. I register their cheer outfits, deciding to give them a wide berth, when Klara strikes once again.

"Get that whore!" Klara's scream travels from the locker room doorway, pointing my way. All heads turn her way at once, mine included. I barely have time for my mouth to part before the band of cheerleaders turn as a unit, their faces twisted like dried up prunes. They lunge forward to grab at me, but I jerk back, quickly sizing up their inappropriate footwear for the winter. I salute them a *good luck catching me in kitten heels,* and take off in the direction of the science block.

Their angry cries echo behind me as they give chase. I yank my backpack straps tighter and dodge through the crowd of students milling around without a care. Skirting the edge of the courtyard, I duck behind planters and weave between stragglers, aiming for the white building up ahead. Not because I think they could actually hurt me, but because getting dog-piled by a swarm of petty Barbie clones isn't high on my bucket list.

Jumping through the open doorway as a guy opens it, I skid around the corner and slow to a walk passing the lockers. At the far end, a living barbie doll appears with clenched teeth and a scowl that could melt iron. Clearly my advantage in speed is overshadowed by their knowledge of the campus. A group of students appear at my back, blocking me in and leaving me no choice but to race up the staircase on my left. Further away from the dorms I wish I was heading toward, but I didn't want to lead these psychos directly to mine and Addy's door.

I don't know the layout up here, but I figure the halls will form a rectangle like the floor below. My moment's hesitation costs me as several pairs of heels click against the stairs. Fuck, these girls are delusional and relentless.

Darting to the right, I ignore the closed doors lining each side, anticipating each one will be locked. The professors are long gone. A row of blue lockers sits against the wall opposite huge windows. I scowl at the stadium visible through the glass, the image of Rhys carefree and naked in the shower definitely not filling my mind.

Not letting up my speed, the squeak of my boots on the shiny flooring makes me wince. The overhead lights buzz faintly, casting too-bright reflections on the floor that make it feel like I'm running through a fishbowl. I tear around the corner that should mark the halfway point in the circuit and slam straight into a closed door. Dammit, a dead end.

Pain blooms across my chest and forearms but luckily I manage to avoid hitting my face. I rest my palms on the wood, taking a breather. Surely there's a way we can talk through this. I didn't even do anything with Rhys...except stand before his naked body with my face angled upwards for a kiss when his girlfriend walked in. Yeah okay, not my finest moment. The hallway behind me stretches empty for a moment, and then I hear them. Multiple pairs of heels click against the tile, the shrill sound of laughter not far behind.

"Harper," one of them sings overly sweet. "We just want to talk."

I dart to the nearest classroom and twist the handle, finding it locked like I knew it would be. The rhythmic slam of locker doors opening and closing echoes down the corridor, as if they're searching every possible hiding spot they can reach. Another voice joins the first, this one tinged with amusement.

"She ran this way, I swear. You check left. I'll check this hall." My pulse hammers against my neck. These crazy bitches are going to tear my face off up here and there's nothing I can do about it. There's a short distance between me and the opposite hallway which will leave me exposed, but standing here is as good as admitting defeat, so I bolt.

One of them shouts that she saw movement, and their footsteps grow louder. I reach another junction and choose right again, running blindly now, my eyes skimming the wall for something, anything. Online yoga has done nothing to prepare me for this kind of exertion. My legs burn with desperation, threatening to be my downfall. My lungs tighten with each breath, the corners of my vision slightly graying from the effort and the rising panic.

For the hundredth time since Rhys steamrolled into my life, I'm wondering what the hell I'm doing. Running from aggressive cheer-leaders, and apparently attending a Friday night party as his date, where said cheerleaders will most likely be. So much for a low profile.

The second floor is beginning to feel like a maze with no exit. My legs are slowing. I swipe sweat from my brow and focus on the sliver of hope up ahead, a narrow alcove or doorway. I stumble toward it, praying it's more than another locked janitor's closet. Just as my fingers grace the handle, a whisper of a shadow from behind startles me. Before I can scream, a hand clamps over my mouth, the door is torn open and I'm yanked into the dark.

The girth and strength of the arm snaking around my middle is undeniable, pinning my back against a firm torso that can't possibly belong to a female. My struggles are fruitless, but that doesn't stop me from twisting and kicking out. I'm caged in a hold like steel, the hand remaining tightly closed over my mouth.

After a beat, his other hand raises to my hair and feels for the receiver clinging behind my ear. A relieved sigh sinks in his chest.

"It's me, it's Clayton," he whispers when he realizes I can hear him. With that knowledge, the atmosphere in the closet suddenly changes. The panic doesn't vanish, but it shifts. My heart continues to pound like a war drum in my chest, yet something in me goes slack at the sound of his voice. I stop kicking. I stop writhing. Every muscle holds rigid as the reality of who is holding me begins to settle. Another man who is turning my world on its axis.

It's impossible not to compare Clay and Rhys, considering they've both had hands on me in the past half hour. Where Rhys' touch was teasing, trying to evoke a reaction, Clayton holds me firm. Protectively. His instincts override his desire to be solitary. His hero complex can't seem to leave me be.

Clay's breath brushes the shell of my ear, warm and quick, his chest rising and falling in short bursts against my back. The closet is so tight I can feel the thump of his pulse where his wrist presses against my ribcage. Darkness stretches in every direction, and the feeling of safety envelopes me thoroughly.

Outside, footsteps drag past the door. One of the cheerleaders mutters something about splitting up again. Another whines about catching her heel on the stairs. The tension in Clay's body tightens, seeking to cover every inch of me as if we're on a battlefield. I focus on the rhythm of his breathing, acutely aware of every place our bodies are touching, and quickly become less concerned about the girls outside. They can find us for all I care, I know I won't be taking the brunt of their outrage and gossip alone.

We wait a minute. Maybe two. The voices grow distant. The click of heels fade. Clay's fingers drift, pushing down on my shoulder as he leans over just enough to peer through the crack between the door and the frame. I can no longer hear anything beyond the wood, yet I don't breathe. I don't move. For whatever reason of being too headstrong for too long, I don't want Clay to stop holding me like this.

Butterflies flutter in my stomach, Clay's warmth seeping through my back. I breathe in his woodsy scent, rest about his tightly corded muscles. Turning my head ever so slightly, the stubble on his jaw grazes my cheek. My veins set alight with a newfound energy.

"Clay." I clear my throat as quietly as possible, hoping the flush in my cheeks will die down before I have to face him properly. "What are you doing here? How did you find me?"

He doesn't answer right away. Then his mouth shifts to brush the edge of my hair.

"I use one of the chemistry labs for extra study, Peterson gave me a key. When you jostled the door handle, I saw you were being chased so I sent them the wrong way and waited here in case you realized it was a dead end. I didn't think they'd come back around so quickly."

I turn my head further, enough to catch the outline of his jaw and the fabric curve of his beanie. The tension between us shifts again, less from danger and more from awareness. I feel it in the way my spine arches as his hand drops to my hip, lingering a little longer than it needs to. The shift has brought another sensation to life, one that is now pressing against the curve of my ass. Oopsie.

Twisting to put an inch of distance between us, I turn the handle and half spill out into the hallway. The light spills over us in a harsh flood. My eyes instantly fly south, checking out Clayton's gray sweatpants and a curtain of warmth covers my face. "Oh, um, sorry. I didn't mean to..."

Blinking downwards, Clay flinches and gasps at the same time.

"Oh god, no. No. No, it's a banana. I skipped lunch." Completely avoiding my eye line, he pulls the offensive fruit from his sweatpants pocket. The peel is squashed and bruised, a sad sight from my ass grinding all over it. "Not to say...no, just not...this time? Gah." Clay rubs the back of his beanie while his face reddens. I press my lips together to hold in the trickle of laughter that wants to break free.

I don't know which one of us wants the ground to open up and swallow us more. Tugging his beanie further down, Clayton turns to leave, probably to go rethink his entire existence, and I almost let him. Almost. But beneath the crushing embarrassment we're both feeling, a flicker of clarity cuts through.

I need to stop this. Not just *this* moment, but *all* of it. The close calls, the cramped hiding spaces, the ridiculously charged silences with the two guys I should be running from, not flirting with in dark cupboards.

"Sorry for ruining your study time, and thanks for the rescue," I offer weakly. "I'm sure I won't need any more." An attempt at a smile pulls at the corners of my mouth. Halting his stride, Clay looks over his shoulder at me, a strange sort of misery in his eyes.

"Yes you will," he nods. I tilt my head, straining my receiver. Is that disappointment in his voice? "As long as you keep humoring Wavershit, you're always going to need rescuing."

The breath is knocked out of me, a fresh flame of embarrassment rising within. I suppose it doesn't take a genius to figure out why the cheerleaders were chasing me around campus, but the dejected way Clayton says it adds a new layer to the mix. Am I so easy to read? Or am I a walking cliché? The new girl catching the attention of the bully.

Clay walks away, leaving me questioning my life choices but he's right. I will continue to need saving and there's nothing I can do about it. I'm going to be Rhys' date on Friday after all.

CLAYTON

CHAPTER SEVENTEEN

Lying back on my bed, I gave up trying to play Jeremy's guitar a while ago and now it just rests across my chest while I stare at the ceiling. Kenneth picked up an extra shift and said he was going to study hall afterward, which gave me some much-needed time alone. Though now that I actually have it, I'm starting to realize solitude might be the exact opposite of what I really want. Take away the window and shove five psychopaths-in-the-making into my shower and I could be back in the JDC for all I know.

Moments like this make me feel like I'd take just about any job that would have me, mostly for the distraction of doing something other than memorizing every crack in these walls. The extra cash wouldn't hurt either. But thanks to the permanent shadow of my record, I'm pretty much unhireable until I've earned some kind of qualification to prove I'm not a walking liability.

I'd considered calling my mom again, which would make it the second time this week, but there's only so much of the act I can stomach. At first, pretending to be Jeremy felt like I was doing her a kindness, trying to protect what's left of her mental stability. But lately, each phone call feels less like protection and more like a mask I can't seem to take off. It's not pretending anymore. It's hiding.

And then there's *her*. I can't close my eyes without her fabricating in my mind. Harper's soft skin, her curves, the whisp of her hair against my face, I'm convinced I can still feel it all. She is so small compared to me, yet not fragile in the slightest. I know she doesn't need my help, but I can't seem to stop myself. I'm drawn to her like a drug, getting high on being there when she needs me most. I'm surprised I'm not loitering outside her building, on high alert for the next stunt Waver-shit pulls. No, I'll stay right here, holding Jeremy's guitar and telling myself I'm better alone. I deserve to be alone.

A knock sounds at my door and I sit up bolt upright. Is it Harper, does she need me?

Fuck's sake Clayton, get a grip. No one besides Kenneth knows what dorm I'm in, and I've worked hard to keep it that way. My privacy is one of the only things I still have any real control over. Assuming the knock must've come from further down the hall, I wait, but then it comes again, louder this time.

I don't hesitate now. I cross the room in a few strides and swing the door open, not sure who or what to expect. For a fraction of a second, my heart kicks hard at the sight of shabby blonde hair and a wide-set frame standing just outside, the ghost of someone I wish more than anything I could see again. But I blink twice, and the illusion breaks.

The eyes staring back at me are warm brown, not endless black. The jawline is too square, and the clothes are all wrong. Jeremy would never wear unlaced tan boots with baggy jeans and a plaid jacket with sheepskin lining. Reality settles in with a quiet thud, dragging the hope inside of me back down where it should stay buried.

"Clayton," Huxley says with a casual nod in greeting. I eye the sophomore warily, not bothering to hide my skepticism.

"What do you want?"

If Huxley is surprised by my hostility, he doesn't show it. Instead, he grins.

"A friend of mine is studying psychology this year. Remote learning setup. He needed to take some time off." Huxley pauses, adjusting the sleeve of his hoodie. I sense a hidden meaning to his words but I also don't give a shit. "Part of his course includes offering free life coaching sessions to students on scholarship, and according to him, you haven't taken him up on the offer."

I recollect a series of unread emails from a couple months ago. I'd scoffed at them then, the same way I'm scoffing now.

"Nice to know you've been talking about me behind my back." I roll my eyes, already retreating back into my room. Huxley takes this as an invitation to follow me inside.

"Loosen up, Clayton. You might pull something." He drops onto Kenneth's bed, crossing his ankles. I take my time, putting Jeremy's guitar away, not caring for the eyes watching my every move. I close the closet on the guitar and the shoe box of memories I leave stashed there, finally turning back to face the man relaxing back on his hands.

"I'm not interested." I declare. In fact, the last thing I want to do is sit around and talk about my feelings. I'm going to internalize them like a big boy. Moving to the door, I gesture for Huxley to get the fuck out. He glances over his shoulder at the window, weighing up his options.

"The sun's finally out. Take a walk with me."

Huxley doesn't wait for a response. He stands and strolls out, stopping by the stairwell. I watch him from the doorway as he leans against the railing, props one leg up, and folds his arms patiently. He's really not going away, is he?

I drag on a pair of worn sneakers, grab my beanie, and head out, catching up as Huxley leads the way down the staircases without saying a word. We push through the doors and step outside into a burst of sunlight.

Against my better judgement, I must admit Huxley was right. The break in the rain and dark clouds would have been a shame to miss, but I'm careful not to look like I'm enjoying myself. I tug the beanie low over my hair and squint against the glare. My hands disappear into the pockets of my gray sweatpants, the same shade as the hoodie I'm wearing, as we walk side by side toward the courtyard.

If I keep my gaze straight ahead and avoid looking too closely at him, I can almost convince myself I'm walking with Jeremy through the campus he once dreamed about. I brace for the usual twisting knot in my chest, maybe even a wave of nausea at the lie I'm living, but neither comes. Instead, there's a numbness deep-rooted in my chest, as if I've come to terms with my reality. I know he's not coming back. I know I need to start living for myself.

Huxley and I pass the stone fountain and drift by the main hall, where auditions for some end-of-semester talent show are in full swing. Judging by the voice currently massacring what sounds like an opera ballad, I make a mental note to avoid being anywhere near here that evening for the sake of my ears.

Students sprawl across the lawn, soaking up the rare sun like plants finally being given light. A fresh wave of posters featuring Rhys line the path through the open greens, each one plastered with his smug face above the black and yellow basketball jersey he doesn't deserve to wear. Huxley lifts his head, taking in the sight and muttering under his breath about spoiled assholes. I smile on the inside, wondering if I initially misjudged the sophomore.

Veering left, heading in the opposite direction to the gymnasium, Huxley leads me around buildings I've not bothered to explore before. There's another five sets of dorm halls over this end of campus, each one having a coffee house next door. Alcoves have benches hidden beneath overhanging foliage, creating small retreats away from the hustle and bustle of classes and the stress of having a roommate in your space constantly.

We walk for far longer than I originally anticipated, and I find myself content to match the slow, steady pace Huxley has set. There's no urgency in his steps and apparently no real destination in mind, which suits me just fine. It beats laying around in bed, wasting my free periods contemplating why I care about being lonely when I actively avoid socializing at all costs. For once, I'm going to let someone else take the reins and allow my mind to switch off for a while.

At some point, we wander off campus completely, threading our way through the outskirts of the town that borders Waversea. The buildings grow taller with each block, yet the noise steadily diminishes. People here are too absorbed in their errands to notice much of anything, including each other. The shift in atmosphere offers a strange relief, as if all my usual problems have been left behind with the dorms and lecture halls, making it easier to take in a full breath for once.

As Huxley guide us down a narrow alleyway tucked behind a string of storefronts, suspicion starts to rise. There's a Chinese restaurant on the corner, the scent of ginger, soy, and something sizzling reaching us as the kitchen prepares for the lunch crowd. My stomach cramps at the smell, sick of surviving on leftover sandwiches that Kenneth brings back from work. He always insists they were going to be thrown out and that I'm doing him a favor in eating them. I don't thank him the way I should for his blatant lie to make me feel better.

We don't hang around, Huxley heading straight for the rusted fire escape attached to the side of the building. He starts climbing, the groan of metal beneath his weight echoing faintly. I look back towards the street, debating what I'm doing here after all but I've come this far. The railing rattles as I follow.

I don't know what I was expecting once I reached the rooftop, but it wasn't as unremarkable as this. A flat concrete expanse dotted with feathers and bird shit, a metal vent unit, and an aging generator that hums in a constant low vibration. All around us, rooftops stretch out like the tops of neatly stacked boxes, their shapes and sizes varying in a tight, organized grid. Traffic lights blink at intersections, while the distant whir of a drill carries over if I strain to hear it. Above it all, a flawless blue sky spreads endlessly, the kind of sky that makes you think there might be something bigger out there, even if you're not sure what it is. At moments like this, I can take a step outside myself and see how small my world really is, how temporary every problem becomes when placed against the sheer vastness of everything else.

Huxley steps up onto the short ledge that borders the roof's edge and lowers himself to sit, legs dangling freely over the side. I join him, resting my arms on my knees while casting a glance over the drop below. The air is unnaturally still today, the kind of stillness that makes every sound more noticeable. I let it settle over me. The generator drowns out the scattered conversations down on the street, the odd coo from a pigeon and the flapping of wings slicing through the drone. I should be disgusted but weirdly, this reminds me of home. Of climbing fire escapes with a spray can in hand. For the first time in what feels like weeks, maybe months, I feel something close to peace sitting above the world rather than being a part of it.

Without speaking, Huxley nudges my arm and tips his chin further down the street below. I wait until he leans forward to follow my line of sight. There's a McDonald's drive-thru across the road, and a long line of cars has backed up into the street. As they inch forward, one person in particular grabs my attention. It's not just anyone, but Garrett, with his messy brown hair and unmistakable swagger. I squint and tilt my head.

"What the hell is he doing?" I mutter mostly to myself, but Huxley answers anyway.

"Our brother Dax is back in town for the week. He wanted some time alone with Avery, so he's dared Garrett to get him out of the way for a while. Garrett never backs down from a dare." Huxley lifts his brow knowingly. This just confuses me more. Not just because their set-up is strange, a group of grown-ass men who call each other brothers and share the same girlfriend, but also by the simpleness of it. Pranks, dares, it's all pointless, yet Huxley is smiling. He looks like a man who has carved out a piece of life just for those he deems worthy. He looks like he knows the answers to all of the important questions.

Shaking myself, I return to the scene before me. At the front of the drive-thru, Garrett is wearing a cardboard car strapped around his waist by ropes hooked over his shoulders. It's been painted and taped to resemble a racecar with apparent sponsorship, complete with a hood, side panels, and a trunk. A hell of a lot of time and effort has gone into the craft project. Tin foil rims and mirrors catch the light, while cut out windows allow him to barter with the server. Even from this distance, she appears exasperated by the animated, colorfully inked man before her.

Successfully receiving his order, Garrett lets out a whoop and starts revving his imaginary engine, zipping around the idling vehicles and screeching to a halt with his own mouth-made tire sounds. He pauses dramatically for a mother and her kid to cross at the zebra crossing before tearing off on his legs again, vanishing around the corner to a chorus of angry horns.

"What a dick," I roll my eyes before I can catch myself. A smile tugs at the edge of Huxley's mouth.

"That he is." Huxley nods knowingly. "Trust me, when I heard it was just me and Garrett returning to Waversea with Avery, I wasn't exactly jumping for joy. Life with Gare can be infuriating, definitely unpredictable, but never boring. He's family to me." Huxley stares off into the distance, the faint humor in his features suggesting he's reminiscing. I leave him to it, burrowing further into my own confusion. I could never live with someone as erratic as that, never mind share a girlfriend with them. It would be like moving in with Rhys and Harper. Now that is a laughable scenario.

Huxley's smart watch buzzes with some sort of reminder, bringing our sort reprieve to an end. His attention is back on me after he silences it and fishes out a protein bar from his pocket. "Here, eat." He tosses it at me. I try to argue but he won't have it, pulling out his own and taking a few lazy bites while watching the world unfold below. I sigh, and eat the damn thing anyway.

From up here, it's like watching a chaotic performance on a stage. People crash into each other without looking up from their phones, some barreling through the crowd like they're on a mission. A pair of women in workout gear strut by, gossiping while speed-walking in sync, and more than one guy turns to check them out as they pass. A rottweiler drags its frazzled owner down the street, straining to catch up to a chihuahua being pampered inside a designer handbag. After the longest time, Huxley finishes his snack and pushes the wrapper into his pocket.

"We're not so different, you know," he finally speaks. I look up to the sky, wanting to snip back with, *'there it is.'* I knew there was a reason he brought me up here, and it wasn't to watch the perplexing spectacle that is Garrett. "I've experienced a trauma in my past too. I might not know yours, but I see the haunted look in your eyes. For a time there, I stopped eating, stopped caring if I woke up the next day. I kept waiting for something or someone to pull me out of it, but it doesn't work that way. Even if you're surrounded by people who want to help, you have to be your own reason to keep going. You have to *want* to keep going. Otherwise, we might as well jump and let fate have its way with us."

Huxley's eyes lower to the steep drop between our feet and the sidewalk. His legs shift slightly, a ripple of tension passing through his shoulders. There's no barrier on this ledge, no fence to stop either of us if we truly wanted to push off the edge.

Sadly, the only reason I can think of not to is the fact that my grant money will stop and my mom's state pension won't cover her care home costs. Other than her occasional moments of clarity, she wouldn't even realize she'd lost both sons and could continue living blissfully unaware inside her mind.

"I'm telling you this because there is no quick fix," Huxley contin-ues. "Only small steps that start to nudge us in the right direction." Reaching into his other pocket, he pulls a few hundred-dollar bills and pushes them towards me. I rear back, lurching away as if his offer is an insult that has physically burned me. Heat pulses through my cheeks, pride setting my jaw on edge.

"I don't accept charity," I growl harshly. Huxley is unaffected, most likely expecting my reaction.

"And I don't accept someone punishing themselves to the point of starvation for the past. I don't need to know your story. Everyone makes mistakes. I can tell you've paid for yours, it's time to start forgiving yourself." He pushes the money my way again and I cross my arms like a child.

"I've not nearly suffered enough," I grumble, pity lacing my tone. Shrugging, Huxley places the bills under a rock between us and returns to stare at the horizon.

"Suit yourself."

In the next second, Huxley's hands are on me, shoving me off the ledge by my hoodie. I gasp, twisting in shock as my body slips off the ledge. My hands catch the wall just in time, the brick cutting into my palms and panic floods my vision. The handfuls of cotton Huxley still has in his grip strain as he yanks me back up. As soon as my forearms brace the ledge, I scramble onto the rooftop, rolling in the pigeon shit with my chest heaving and eyes wide.

"What the fuck is your problem?!" I yell, disturbing a nearby nest. I kick away from the ledge, putting a distance between myself and the psychopath who coolly turns to face me. Huxley lifts the rock, adds a folded piece of paper to the pile of cash and slides it towards me once more.

"This isn't charity, it's a loan, and it comes with a condition. You have to take part in the life coaching sessions from my friend, he needs them for his coursework." When I don't immediately move, Huxley reaches over and tucks the money into my hoodie pocket. "Top up your restaurant card, replace those god-awful sneakers. My number is there, message me when you're ready to pay me back."

Rising, Huxley walks to the rusty fire escape. I lie still, trying to still the pounding beat of my heart, watching him descend. Just before he disappears from view, Huxley stops and lifts a brow,

"Oh, and Clayton? Hold onto whatever reason that just made you cling onto that ledge." He disappears then and my hand sinks into my pocket. I crease the money in my fist and fall flat onto my back, focusing on shallowing my breathing. My limbs tingle with aftershocks, my brain catching up with the possibility that it was nearly cracked open on the sidewalk. That my mom was almost left childless.

No longer lulled into a false sense of security, clarity breaks free. Huxley is a fucking lunatic. In fact, I'm certain there are no sane people left in the world, the disjointed reality provided in video games and movies distorting people's rationality. But, crazy as he is, Huxley is right. Something forced me to latch onto the ledge, and now I have the burning need to find out what it was.

CHAPTER EIGHTEEN

Slouched in one of the many oversized armchairs tucked away in the silent zone of the library, I give up pretending to read and shut my book with a defeated sigh. Things must really be spiraling if even a pitch black, twisted romance can't pull me into another world. I let my head loll to the side, the patch behind my ear free from my receivers. My chest sinks beneath my cream-colored sweatshirt that declares, *There's not enough coffee in the world for me to talk to you today.* It's one of my favorites, soft and fluffy on the inside, with sleeves long enough to hide my hands completely.

The week is crawling by with the sluggish determination of a depressed sloth, each day dragging me through the same cycle of gray skies, dull conversations, and a sense of unease that never quite fades. Classes have been intense, but I've forced myself to carve out at least one solid hour of revision every day. Whatever it takes to not be caught off guard again. To not be left at the mercy of a wolf in human form again. I guess that makes me Little Red Riding Hood, except this time, getting eaten—in any sense of the word—will have to stay a fantasy.

With each passing day, Friday looms closer. I don't even want to think about what Rhys has been planning for this ridiculous party of his whilst skipping out on classes all week. At first, the arrangement had seemed simple enough, even if the thought of being paraded around made my skin crawl. I'll probably flounder in a cramped room filled with strangers, harsh music, and the kind of loud energy I spend most of my life avoiding, but at least I'll be living. I'll be a fully-fledged student with the regret and shame to match.

The faint buzz of my phone vibrating between my crossed legs barely registers until I glance down and see a certain username light up the screen. The man attached to said username has been giving me the cold shoulder all week, and I'm bored of it. Especially as the message he's sent has come out of left field, once again.

> Beanie26: Where's your spark gone, Beautiful?

I jolt upright and immediately glance around the library, hating that my heart skips a beat. Every chair is occupied, students buried in books or silently mouthing words as they study. The towering shelves create blind spots where shadows flicker in the periphery, and for a moment, I feel eyes on me from every direction. Leaning cautiously over the armrest, I peer down the central aisle and spot Clay sitting at one of the main tables, papers and textbooks spread out in front of him as he works.

First thought, fuck that guy. Second thought, are we sending compliments now?

Sinking back into the chair, I stare at the message for a long moment, weighing up my options. I could humor him, or I can admit I'm tired of this game. I guess we will see what I decide in the moment. Pushing myself up, I storm through the library, defiance driving me forward. I reach his table and slam my book down hard enough to make his pen pause mid-sentence. The heat of attention floods in from all angles, but I keep my focus narrowed on Clay.

"Do you want me or not?"

From beneath his blond swoop of hair, Clayton's dark eyes meet mine with infuriating calm. Nothing flickers in his features. Around us, I sense the whispers spreading like wildfire, but I don't care. All that matters is putting an end to this loop of wanting and waiting while he keeps his cards pressed to his chest. "I don't care which it is, but at least be man enough to own how you feel."

I only wait for a few seconds, but that's enough to realize he isn't going answer. Clay doesn't speak openly in public, whether being confronted or not. I snatch my book off the table and turn on my heel, my hips swaying in oversized sweatpants as I walk away. Indecisive asshole.

Winding through the stacks, I head toward aisle thirteen, intent on putting my book back and leaving. The overhead bulbs dangle on cords that sway slightly, casting patches of soft light that stretch and shift as I pass beneath them. A fitting atmosphere for the kind of romance that should be read in the dark by flashlight. Reaching the gap I left earlier, I slide the book back into place . Until next time my fictional lover. Letting my hand linger for a moment, I stroke the edge of the spine, debating whether I check it out and give it a second chance in the comfort of my bed. No, I don't have the focus tonight.

Broad shoulders and a wide chest in white cotton closes in on me, the sudden nearness making me jolt as if caught doing something illicit. Clay's face is half-shadowed by his gray beanie, the tic jumping in his jawline making it appear sharper. I've been close to Clay before, but he's standing over me now, the sheer height of him makes me feel simultaneously cornered and oddly safe. His hand clamps around my arm with a grip that is neither careless nor gentle, and in that single touch there is an entire conversation I cannot quite translate.

"Am I not man enough?" Clay's lips say and I don't have to hear him to feel the guttural frustration in his tone. I force myself to keep my gaze level with his, although my breath feels caught somewhere between my lungs and my throat. There's a heated fury in his black eyes, the quiet simmer of a man wrestling with something he does not want to admit.

My hand slips into the pocket of my sweatshirt, finding the small microphone clip I pushed in there earlier. Without breaking his stare, I attach it to the rounded neckline of his T-shirt. My knuckles brush against his throat, sliding for a fraction of a second over the powerful beat of his pulse. It thrums against me, impossibly fast, as though my touch has unbalanced him.

His hand knocks mine aside, and in the next instant, my back hits the bookcase. I gasp at the spread of fingers slipping beneath my thighs as Clay effortlessly lifts me to match his height. My legs wrap around his waist, instinct taking over in a way that makes my cheeks burn. The solid pressure of him pins me in place and the wooden shelf digs into my spine, but the discomfort only sharpens my awareness of where his body meets mine. The hard press of his jeans against my center has my skin flushing hot enough to chase away every coherent thought.

"Clay," I breathe, not able to form an end to that sentence. Managing to free my phone, I open the app over his shoulder to activate the Bluetooth between the mic and my implants. As if waiting for that precise moment, Clay growls against the mic.

"Is it not man enough that the urge to protect you keeps me awake at night?" His chest heaves. Oh, he's pissed. "Or that when I eventually fall asleep, your green eyes haunt me there? Maybe I'm not man enough," Clay pushes his jeans harder against my core, which carves through me deliciously, "because I push you away, knowing I'm not worthy of your attention."

His head dips until I feel his breath on my skin, and then the ghost of his lips brushes my jaw. I lock up, overcome with revelation and lust. I broke Clay, I broke him wide open and now I'm going to see exactly how he feels. At freaking last.

His lips move again, traveling in slow, deliberate strokes from beneath my ear to the hollow between my collarbones. My head tips back against the shelf, and my eyes slide shut without my permission. His voice is in my head, reverberating, undoing my defenses thread by thread.

"Perhaps if I was man enough, I would be able to stop confusing chivalry with obsession and get you out of my head once and for all."

I barely have time to open my eyes before his mouth covers mine. My toes curl, a surprised inhale passing between us. Unlike what I would have imagined, there is no hesitation in his kiss, no careful testing of boundaries. Only an immediate and all-consuming claim. Clay's lips taste of coffee and desire, a layers of tension between us unraveling in an instant.

My hands slide up the back of his neck, fingers threading into his hair beneath the beanie, pulling him closer because whatever this is, it is not enough. I want more. I need everything he's willing to give before he decides to rip it all away again. Every point where our bodies meet feels like a spark catching dry tinder, small fires spreading with reckless speed. His grip tightens at my hips, his fingertips digging in as though he needs to anchor himself, and I realize I am clinging to him just as desperately.

The kiss deepens, and his tongue parts my lips without asking, taking what he wants. I give it willingly, my own need tangling with his until I cannot tell whose hunger I am feeding. The rhythm of our bodies shifts and I am grinding against him before I have even thought about it, the friction pulling a soft, unguarded sound from my throat. It makes him groan, the air between us thick enough to drown in.

I am on the edge of doing something reckless, something I will not be able to take back, when the world tips. Suddenly I am lifted higher, thrown aside, the warmth of him gone. A startled cry tears from me as I hit the ground hard enough to jar my teeth. My limbs sprawl across the cold floor and my head spins, the rush of the kiss ripped away so fast my body almost aches from the loss.

I have barely caught my breath when a deafening crash fills my skull. I scream against it, grabbing the sides of my head but there's nothing I can do. The sound is coming from the mini microphone that I'm hooked up to. I blink up, strain forcing me to squint, just in time to see the bookcase opposite slamming into the one I was just pressed against. A waterfall of books rains down, a stampede of hardcovers and paperbacks tumbling with bone-rattling force.

And Clay is buried beneath it. My heart judders as I take in the scene and realize what happened. He threw me out of range, out of harm's way. I cannot move, my eyes locked on the shifting pile where he disappeared. My cries are raw, scraping their way out of me, and even through the ringing in my ears I can hear the muffled grunts from the microphone still clipped to his shirt. Each short, uneven breath he makes filters directly into my head and freezes the blood in my veins.

Feet pound past me, scattering fallen books as others rush to pull him free. A girl I do not know kneels beside me, her hands checking for injuries, her mouth moving in questions I cannot process. My eyes are fixed on the moment Clay emerges, hunched and bruised, blood pouring from his nose. His lips, the same ones that had just been on mine, are split and red, and yet his gaze finds me first. The tension in his face softens and he exhales as though relieved simply to see me standing.

"Holy shit, are you okay? What happened?" My voice is sharper than I mean for it to be, my hands hovering inches from his chest, desperate to check him over but afraid to cause more pain. I can already imagine the bruises spreading beneath his shirt.

"I am fine. I've had worse," Clay responds, dejection in his voice. The hollowness resonates in my own chest. We couldn't simply have one moment. I take his hand before I can stop myself, our fingers fitting together as if they have been doing so for years. I pull him through the wreckage, heading towards the main part of the library. The girl who helped me is still at my side and several others shadow Clay like guards. Ironically, this is the most support I've seen come to Clay's aid, and it only took him being battered by books to earn it.

Stepping into the central space, my eyes land on Rhys instantly. Dots connect in my mind, the actions of a jealous bully flaring to life. Motherfucker.

Rhys is seated in the chair Clay had been using, his ankles crossed lazily on the table as a flock of girls drape themselves over him. Clay's books are in a careless heap at his feet. His blue eyes meet mine, full of a challenge and my shoulders draw tight. I step forward, ignoring the way Clay's hand tugs against mine in a silent warning. There's not a chance in hell I'm letting this go. Holding Rhys' gaze, I let every ounce of determination show in my expression, and I drop Clayton's hand.

"Harper, don't," Clay tries to say as I turn and pluck the microphone from his shirt. He catches my face, giving a slight shake of his head but the burn in my chest will not let me walk away. Not this time. I walk directly into the center of the library, taking everyone's attention with me.

Klara is perched beside Rhys, idly swinging on the back legs of her chair like a child who has never been told no, her manicured nails twirling a strand of hair. My boot finds the side of her chair and sends it tipping, the motion controlled yet forceful enough to spill her onto the floor in an ungraceful heap. Her skirt flies up, revealing a hot pink thong that would have made me laugh in another lifetime, but now I am focused entirely on the man who has been pestering me from the shadows for far too long.

My hand fists the collar of Rhys's cashmere sweater, the soft luxury of the fabric at odds with the sharp flex of my fingers. I shove the microphone into place against his chest and push him back into the chair with a satisfying thud. His chuckle is low and shameless, his gaze skating over me in a way that feels like both a taunt and a claim.

"I didn't realize public foreplay was your thing, Babygirl," he murmurs, and the sound of it seems to scrape against something raw inside me. My free hand tangles in his hair, tugging hard enough to tilt his head back so he has no choice but to meet the fury in my expression. He only looks more intrigued, his smirk deepening as if he has discovered a game he fully intends to win.

"It was you, wasn't it?" I hiss, ignoring Klara scrambling to her feet. Despite Rhys' lack of fucks in helping her, she stands tall and crosses her arms behind him. Rhys either doesn't realize or doesn't care.

"Sure. Whatever you are referring to, it was me." He says it without flinching, appearing thoroughly entertained. Curling his fingers around my wrist and peeling it free from his hair, Rhys drags my knuckles over his cheek and lips. A chaste kiss is placed there, vibrating with his low laughter.

A weight settles on my shoulder, but I barely register it. I'm too busy trying to decide that, should I rear back and punch Rhys in the mouth, if he'd get off or get angry. Most likely the former.

"That is not an answer," I tell him, yanking my hand free. Rhys tuts, apparently disappointed but nevertheless entertained.

"Everyone blames me for everything that happens around here. Since most of the time it's true, I just agree." He leans back, all arrogance and infuriating calm. Rage flares through me, the image of Clay being pummeled too fresh in my mind. More than that, his nonchalance afterwards as if this is a common occurrence has sent me over the edge. Perhaps it's my turn to protect him for a change.

But hurting Rhys will only pleasure him, so I need to change tactics. I need to dismantle the pedestal he's placed himself upon. A slow smile curls across my face, and I watch the subtle slip in his smirk with the kind of satisfaction that tastes sweeter than revenge.

"What is so funny?" Rhys finally cracks his stoic surface of amusement, and he rises to his feet, trying to loom over me with height alone. I yank the microphone back and press my palm flat to his chest, shoving him with enough force to catch him off guard and send him falling back into the seat. Leaning in so close that his breath skims my mouth, I let the venom in my voice coil between us.

"It just occurred to me that the second you step off this campus, you're no one. Just another overconfident dick without any real power or worth. One day you will find yourself bitterly alone, and I will savor every second of watching it happen."

Rhys's pupils blow out, my words finally striking a chord. His hand moves so fast that both Clay and I think he's going to hit me. Clay's arm comes around my middle as Rhys tucks my hair behind my ear, searching for my implant. Failing to find it, he speaks slow and clearly for me to read.

"I'd better enjoy Friday night then, before my bitter loneliness sets in." Rhys gives a sultry wink as Clay tugs me away, the strength of his body pulling me from the tension-charged air and steering me into the cold night. His pace is steady and sure as he keeps me tucked close, as if he believes distance is the only thing that will keep me from going back for more. The quiet between us hums with the residue of everything unsaid, and I let him guide me all the way back to my dorm without resisting.

At the base of the staircase, I take the lead until we stop before my door. I have no doubt Addy will be inside, peering through the spyhole to watch our interaction. I stall, allowing Clay to turn me gently to face him, his blood-darkened lips moving slowly as he speaks.

"Promise me you will not continue to provoke Rhys. If he keeps fixating on you, I will have to deal with him, but for as long as I can, I need to keep a low profile. I have to finish my degree. It is... important to me."

A twinge of vulnerability lingers in the air, heavy with something that feels almost like pleading, though Clay is not the kind of man who pleads for anything. His gaze holds mine steadily, consuming any argument I may have had.

I nod, lifting my hand to cradle his cheek, my thumb brushing along the coarse line of stubble. His skin is warm under my touch, the heat radiating into my palm in a way that makes me want to hold on longer than I should. There is a sorrow in his eyes, a quiet ache in his features. Seeing him like this, bared and bloodied, stirs something deep inside me that I'm not prepared to face right now.

I watch as his lips shape words too soft for me to hear, as if they were not meant to be spoken aloud. Before I can ask him to repeat them, he steps back, securing his beanie back in place on his blond hair, then he turns and walks away without looking back.

I stand there a moment longer, the echo of his warmth still on my skin, my breath clouding slightly in the hallway's chill. He's right. I am getting too entangled in my need to give Rhys the comeuppance no one else seems willing or able to deliver. As if it's my duty. As if I'm the only person that can. Although, if I keep being drawn into his games, Clay's focus will begin to fracture. I know this, yet I can't seem to help myself. I yearn for the adrenaline rush that comes from going toe to toe with Rhys.

Another rational thought reminds me that I should push Clay from my thoughts too, to bury the way his presence feels like a shield I did not know I wanted. I won't be doing that either. This evening gave me startling clarity. Clayton feels something for me. He probably doesn't want to acknowledge it, but I won't let him retreat back into himself. We're finally getting somewhere and I want to see where it leads.

Stepping into my dorm and closing the door behind me, I'm suddenly assaulted by the speedy hands of Addy signing a million questions I don't have answers for. Instead, as my phone vibrates in my pocket, the screen lighting up with a message, my mouth curves into a smile I can't contain.

Beanie26: Thank you for defending me, Beautiful.

RHYS

CHAPTER NINETEEN

Chants flood the stadium beyond the closed locker room door, the cheer squad spreading hype through the packed stands. All twelve players for our team are standing in a semicircle while last year's star players spew the usual garbage about being a family and putting faith in one another. I have zero interest in their sermon.

Rolling my neck, the silk of my jersey shifts against my inked skin. A black number one sits in the center of the yellow material, clearly meant for me. Well, technically it was Bucktooth Bill's, probably not his real name, who's staring at the floor from the far end of the bench. He's avoided all contact with me since I beat the crap out of him for taking this jersey first. I got the number I wanted and my knuckles sung with glory that day. Win-win.

Clayton is here for appearances only, also ready to take his spot on the bench and watch the game from the sidelines. Coach suggested we take turns and each play a half, to make it *fair*. There is no fairness in the real world. It is ugly and poisonous, where people with money thrive and those without take bribes, just like Coach did. Offering to either double or cancel his paycheck this month was definitely a bribe, not a threat. I am not a complete monster.

The stadium is at full capacity tonight, evident from the split of cheers and boos as the team from Armitage State enters. I pace back and forth across the locker room, ready to get tonight over with. Whatever reason I joined the team for in the first place still escapes me. I enjoy having an excuse to leave the house in the morning, to get some exercise and flood myself with the adrenaline I had been missing. But now, with the noise of the crowd pressing in, I can't summon a shred of enthusiasm. Maybe today is the day everyone realizes I am nothing but a walking legacy and a superficial last name.

The fuck? I freeze and frown at the thought, wondering where on earth that came from. The answer comes in the form of glaring green eyes in my mind. Ever since Harper insulted me the other night, I've been playing it over and over. Evidently, her words have sunk in, rooting themselves in places I can't reach. Shaking myself off, I start jumping in place, and stretching my arms. Just wait until the after-party, where I will finally have little Harper at my mercy. That will free me from whatever binds she's created.

The team does an immature hands-in cheer before joining me by the door. "Look after one another out there," Coach finally pipes up as he pushes his way to the front. He glances at me before stepping out into the central arena, and the crowd on our side erupts. The noise is deafening, and through the discomfort, a sense of ease settles within. My smug mask falls effortlessly into place, a smirk hitching my mouth. Praise rains down and seeps into my inked skin, lifting the pre-game stress from my limbs.

Ahh yes, that's why I'm in this team. That's my name being chanted. This is still my playground. The cheerleaders shake their pompoms and hips with energy on the sidelines. Girls scream and blow kisses, leaning over the railing for my attention, but none of them have the green eyes I keep subconsciously scanning for.

Stepping onto the court, I size up the Armitage players in green and white. And by sizing up, I mean holy hell. Their center has to be seven feet tall, all legs and wiry muscle. I am not short at five eleven, but there is not a single player on their team my height or shorter. Fuck, we are completely screwed.

A few Armitage players shake hands with my NBA wannabes, drawing a snarl from me. There's no point acting like this healthy competition is going to be any less than a bloodbath. We're not coordinated enough to beat guys whose statures alone take up most of the court.

The appointed referee strolls between us, whistle in his mouth, and sends the benched players off. I let Justin take the jump for us at center, preferring to fall back and make sure the crowd stays riled up. My name is chanted over and over, a comfortable pressure settling on my shoulders. For once, people are depending on me. Hell, my team is depending on me to keep the atmosphere alive, and I give our audience the show they came for.

The scoreboard timer lights up for the first quarter, the whistle blows, and the ball is launched into the air. The acne-ridden giant wins it easily, slapping it to his own guard. He dribbles toward our basket in long strides, his shadow swallowing up the paint. We all leap to block his shot, but at the last second he drops to a crouch and passes to an open shooter at the three-point arc. The ball leaves the guy's hands like it was born to fly and swishes through the net. Three points to them.

Chris grabs the ball next, taking off for the other end, passing to Lance, then to Chase, who shoots from inside the arc. The ball clangs off the rim and straight into that same giant's hands. I hang back this time, betting he will go for the same play. Sure enough, while my guys try to block him, he swings the ball to a frizzy-haired guard near me. I leap the same second he does, waving a hand across his eyes to ruin his sightline. The shot falls short, and I toy with my lip ring cockily. His red-faced frustration is almost better than the rebound I snatch for myself.

I push my legs to full speed as I cross the court, the pounding of sneakers on hardwood filling my head. The chants blur into static, my vision tunneling on the rim. My first shot drops cleanly through the net, a faint whoosh catching my ears before the crowd roars. Punching my fist into the air, I step-side around the sidelines, whooping and drinking in the applause. That's right fuckers, I own this place, inside and out.

The game grinds forward into a fully-fledged battle. Armitage are relentless, but we keep clawing back, just about. Sweat pools at the base of my neck, the sting of old bruises resurfacing each time I drive through my practiced play. The giant keeps smiling at me like he knows exactly how far he can push before I snap. My mouth tastes like adrenaline and spite.

By the second quarter, my breathing is heavier than it should be. Every time I glance at the scoreboard, the points are too close for comfort. The crowd cheers, but now it sounds warped and stretched out. Almost as if they're losing faith in me as quickly as I'm losing it in myself. Regardless, I keep my face blank, my hands poised, my legs moving. When the giant blocks my layup with one massive hand, I hear the laughter from the Armitage bench before I even hit the floor. My palms sting, my pride takes a temporary dip, and the ball is already at the other end being slammed through the hoop. I shove myself back into the game, a tightness clenching my jaw.

Coach calls for a time-out and we all jog over to hear what he has to say. Hopefully, he's going to do his job for once.

"I think we should put Clayton into play," he states as soon as we're huddled up and I resist the urge to face palm myself. It was far too hopeful of me to think this idiot would offer some real pointers.

"No fucking way," I bat my hand through the air as if I can knock that stupid notion out of my atmosphere. Coach levels me with a hard stare.

"I'm serious. He's the only one we've got that remotely resembles their size." We all look over our shoulders at the Armitage boys drinking water and patting each other on the backs.

"I can handle it," I growl, narrowing my eyes to the sad sap still sitting on the bench. His black eyes are hollow and staring at a rogue spot on the floor, his hair flopping in all directions. Something is up with him today, and I don't care what it is. "If Clayton wants to be on the court for matches, he needs to show up for practice. We can't count on someone who doesn't know how to be a team player." Yeah, yeah I know. I hear the irony too, but it sounds convincing. "Leave this to me."

Clayton doesn't get to stroll in and take the win, not when I know Harper is looming somewhere in the crowd. Not just because I'm an arrogant asshole, but because I will not give him the satisfaction. We don't need him. No one needs him for that matter.

No longer bothering with this huddle bullshit, the whistle is blown and I'm straight back to it. I skid and duck away from the opposition whilst gunning across the wooden floor. Sweat slicks my palms around the ball, my sneakers screaming against the varnish as the air fills with the sharp tang of polish and body heat. A blended roar of jeers and applause assaults my ears, some voices cutting sharp like glass, others swelling into a low, hungry chant.

I catch sight of the twenty-four-second shot clock bleeding down to the last five seconds. No time to set up, no time to think. My teeth are grinding together, aching from my jaw up to my ears. Since when did I give this much of a shit about anything?

Not having a choice, I shoot the second my foot kisses the arc line, my wrist snapping clean. The entire stadium seems to stall to watch the ball slide through the net, the rope swaying silently in its wake. Beautiful. I would clap for myself if half of the arena wasn't doing it for me.

Undeterred, Armitage's star player bounces the ball a few times on the spot, shoulders loose like he's got all night to watch us stumble and shuffle into place. The formation of our team is wrong, scattered like they've just about given up. Trash, the lot of them.

I spot an opening straight down the middle the same second the Giant does. Watching his feet, noting the slight roll of his ankle and the lazy confidence in his stance, I brace myself. He catches my eye, igniting a one-on-

one challenge between just us two. On an exhale, I sharpen my focus until the edges of my vision blur, my entire body tuned to his rhythm. He turns his left foot in for some unnecessary spin, pure show-off bullshit. The second the ball hits the floor and bounces back up, I'm there. Snatching it clean, I drive it back the way it came, my heartbeat thundering in my ears.

A shout breaks behind me and my grin widens. The court opens ahead as if everyone here knows it's mine by birthright. I leap, slam the ball through the hoop, and hang on the rim for a few seconds, letting gravity pull at me before I drop. The buzz in my veins spikes, and that's the moment I see her.

Widened doe eyes, slightly upturned nose, liquid chocolate hair pooling around delicate shoulders. Front row and center where she should be, gaze locked on me like I'm the only thing in the room. My chest tightens. Desire flares through me at the same instant the beeper cuts in to announce another Armitage score. Dammit, focus. By the end of the night, she'll be at my mercy, but right now I need to keep my head and my cock in check.

I hold my hand up for Joey to pass the ball, as I always do. If I want that ball, it has less then three seconds to land in my grasp. This time, however, a flicker of panic flares in his eyes, chased by a look of regret just before the ball leaves his hand and lands in Chase's instead. My mouth drops open before I can catch myself. Catching myself, I glare daggers at Joey, watching him swallow hard and jog away. He knows he'll pay for that.

Chase dribbles with the grace of a drowning duck, his sneakers slapping like he's never ran a day in his life, then lobs it to Justin, who manages to miss yet another shot. What are these useless fucks doing?! They never play this badly in practice.

Other than one more basket from yours truly, the rest of the first half is a slow bleed. We're getting slaughtered out here. Gutted and dragged through the dirt while the cheer squad keeps screaming Waversea chants like a stuck record. The next time I'm near, I turn on them with a low growl that makes them jump back and, thankfully, shut the hell up.

The claxon finally sounds for halftime, our team trudging toward the locker rooms with their heads down, sweat dripping like they've been beaten into the floor. I'm equally drained and exhausted, since I'm carrying us all, but my pulse remains sharp and restless. Pure stubbornness will pull me through, although a little sugar wouldn't hurt too. Passing Klara's sulky face without a glance, I lean against the railing in front of Harper, smirk back in place.

"It's hard work carrying the team here, Babygirl. You'd best grab me a coffee on your way over tonight. I have a feeling I'm going to need all the energy I can get." Her eyes track my mouth. No receivers today, got it. I drag my tongue across my bottom lip, all slow and sensual just to see if she'll react. She does not.

"If it's such hard work, maybe you should let Clay cover you for a while."

I rear back as if I've been slapped. Maybe I misheard her, but the serious set of her delicate features leaves no room for confusion. Then, I burst out laughing. It echoes loudly and is quickly mimicked by everyone nearby, even though they don't know what I'm laughing at. In the center of it all, Harper remains still as a statue, oblivious to it all. Eventually, I sober too.

"Let's pretend I've lost my mind and I do let Clay on the court. What's it going to earn me?"

"Other than a win?" Harper raises a brow. I stare at her as if she's lost her mind but let the cogs in her brain work. Finally, she sighs. "What do you want?" The smile that grows across my face stretches almost painfully, and just like that, I'm back on top.

"Coffee." Harper's green eyes narrow, her hip popping out as she waits for the catch. Boosted by self-assurance, I lean over the railing and stop just short of entering Harper's personal space. Even though she can't hear me currently, I lower my voice for her only. "I want you waiting for me outside with a coffee that tastes just like you. Wet, warm, slightly bitter with the sweetest aftertaste."

I seriously hope Harper got all of that before I lunge forward and lick her cheek with the flat of my tongue. She shoves me away and I drop onto the court in time with the players returning. Clayton attempts to sink onto the bench, his eyes just as sunken, until I grab the back of his shirt and drag him back upright.

"You're in, Joey's out." Pushing Clayton's sorry ass away, I catch Joey's eye and draw a singular line across my throat with my finger. I haven't forgotten how he refused me a pass earlier, and he won't anytime soon either. Coach appears relieved at the change of events, giving me a cheesy thumbs up. I roll my eyes and get into stance beside an Armitage player I'm going to call Weasel Features. I stand uncomfortably close, gearing up to become his worst nightmare for the next twenty minutes.

Just before the ball is thrown into play, with Clayton up front and fully absorbed, I brave one more look to Harper, and regret it instantly. A smug, satisfied smile lifts on her full lips. What was previously a bored, flat glaze to her green eyes has now ignited with interest. They flick my way for less than a second before returning to Clayton, effectively baiting and dismissing me in one move.

Murderous intent swells within my veins. If there ever was a day I was going to kill Clayton for real, this would be it. Instead, for some unexplainable reason, I give Clayton yet another free pass and turn my attention to Weasel Features instead. Since it's not on me to carry the game anymore, I choose to ignore the scoreboard and create a game of my own. Simultaneously drive Weasel Features to the brink of madness and the ledge of suicide.

Gluing myself to his side, I refuse to give him an inch of breathing space. When he pivots, I match him step for step. When he goes for a shot, I am already in his face, my hand waving inches from his eyes, my laugh dragging across his ear until frustration radiates from him in waves. Each step is a taunt, my sneakers squeaking over the ball bouncing on by. I pay it no attention, planting myself in front of my chosen foe with a smirk I'm sure he wants to rip off my face. However, it seems like I'm not the only one who's changing tactics.

"Seems like your girl has eyes for someone else," he grunts with a heavy dose of halitosis. His bleak gaze slides to Harper beyond my head and that riles me more than his attempt at a taunt. He's about to lose those eyes into the back of his skull.

"She's not my girl," I grind out in a weak attempt to divert attention away from Harper. It doesn't work. Weasel Features smiles wide, the yellow stain of his teeth matching the scent of his breath.

"Oh, good to know. I'll make sure to introduce myself on the way out. Give her my winning jersey. There's nothing I love more than a hot babe wearing absolutely nothing except my jer—"

My fist connects with his cheekbone before my brain even finishes processing that sentence. The impact sends a jolt up my arm, satisfying the darkened parts of me in a way that only real violence delivers. The whistle screams overhead, ref's voice booming "Ejection!" but I couldn't give less of shit. My fists are singing with pent-up rage, landing again and again in Weasel's pinched, pointy features until I don't know where his blood stops and mine starts. All I know is there's a burning itch where my the skin across my knuckles has split and if it leaves a scar in my ink, I'm going to hunt this fucker down and finish the job.

Hands clamp onto me, trying to drag me back, but I twist, my chest heaving, every muscle coiled for another strike. Weasel gets in two swings of his own, one splitting my lip. His smile is consistent despite the crimson smeared across his face, and I catch a glimpse of what riles Clayton up so much. Smiling in the face of a beating really is annoying.

The team manages to haul me toward the locker room like a rabid animal needing a fix. The second the door closes, effectively shutting me off from the stadium, a red haze devours my restraint. My fists slam into metal locker doors, one after the other, the hollow clang echoing off the tiles until blood streaks across the silver. It's been too long since I've lost control like this, letting the mask slip and the shadows slip free.

I'm no longer seeing the room around me but the face of the man I loathe. My father appears behind every blink, mocking me for revealing my weakness. Hell, for having weakness at all. The thought brings me up short, cutting through my fury, but it doesn't erase it.

Somewhere beyond the walls, the whistle shrills again, and I am done. Jacket on, I push through the back door, gulping in air that is mercifully free of sweat and failure. I can't believe I let some asshole stranger pull me in so easily. I can't believe my trigger point is that easy to reach. My hand clenches again, ready to leave a dent in the Armitage minibus, when a lithe figure peels herself from the side of the building.

I glare at Harper before catching myself, and don't pay any attention to the way my anger melts a fraction at the sight of her brown hair spilling over one shoulder. Her bare neck catches the low light from the lamppost, a lickable column stretching from collar bone to ear. Her leather jacket is zipped halfway to reveal the edge of a black lace camisole. The rest of her outfit is a blur because my eyes keep dragging back to the soft bow of her lips. She extends a hand, offering me a steaming takeaway cup, the scent of cheap coffee curling between us.

"Thank you," she breathes and offers me a genuine smile. My thoughts stall, not entirely sure how I have earned her gratitude, but I'll take it every day of the week. Then she speaks again. "For giving Clay a chance."

The flare in my nostrils is instinctive. I take the coffee from her hand and burn my tongue on the first sip, but at least the heat covers the metallic taste of blood still pooling at the corner of my mouth.

"Don't thank me yet. I have plans for you later," I reply gruffly. Harper doesn't show any reaction, most likely because she can't hear the threat in my tone. I haven't fully decided what those plans are, but I'm certain Harper won't like any of it. Whether I like it or not, Harper stirs something dangerous in me, something possessive that does not just want to win, but to take. To overcome. To own.

Turning to leave, I stop her by grabbing her wrist and pushing the coffee back into her hand.

"Wait." Reaching behind my neck, I pull the collar of my jersey over my head in one motion, cool air skating across the sweat covering my chest and abs. I fight a shiver, soaking in the blessing of an early winter evening. Shoving my jersey between us, I exchange it for the cup.

"You're wearing this tonight. Nothing underneath." Harper's gaze drops to the jersey and she turns it over in her hand.

"There's blood on it."

"Then wash it, but that is your outfit. Got it?" A beat passes between us, my heckles raised and ready for this fight. However, for once, she doesn't argue. I must look deadly serious. Harper disappears around the building with my jersey in hand whilst I'm left grappling with warm fuzzies spreading through my insides. That heat gives me a false sense of reality, the need for power overriding my brain. I don't even realize I'm shivering until Klara bursts out of the rear door and asks me if I've fallen ill. I believe I have, fallen victim to a virus that smiles sweetly and then whips the world out from beneath my feet.

Running a hand through my sweat ridden hair, I head in the direction of my house. Klara rushes to keep up. "Where's your shirt?!" she continues to badger me with questions that I continue to ignore. My steps are clipped, the shower calling my name. Specifically, an ice cold one to rid me of the lasting tension riding my dick.

Just a few more hours, I tell myself. Then I will be done with Harper. My attention has never lasted long enough to enjoy the same girl more than twice. I just need to cut off this game of cat and mouse and take back the reins Harper has stolen from me. Steal back the control she's somehow gained.

HARPER

CHAPTER TWENTY

I stare down at the message on my phone with one eyebrow raised. Rhys must have added his number to my contacts when he stole my phone, adding a profile picture of his tongue toying with his lip ring. I thought I'd broken through a barrier earlier, somehow managing to bend his will and then reward him like a pup with a treat. Although, now I'm becoming more than fashionably late to his party, the beast seems to be rising back to the surface.

I toss my phone onto the dresser beside my receivers, not about to let him boss me around like he does with the rest of this school. After the disaster that was today's game, I had anticipated his mood, but he's going to learn that no matter the circumstances, I am not one of his subjects.

My fingers drum against my thigh as I turn in a slow circle. I'm stalling, waiting for Addy to return from drama club and talk me out of wearing the jersey that is now air-drying over my headboard. Call me weak but the breakthrough with Rhys this afternoon doesn't fill me the same stubbornness to fight his every whim. For tonight at least. I'm generous like that. A flash of white catches my eye, a piece of paper slipping beneath the door. I bend to pick it up, reading the scrawled message.

'Have fun at the party.'

I open the door, finding no one in sight. Leaning forward, my toe nudges a small pink gift bag on the doorstep, a big bow tying the handles together. I return inside, planting the gift bag on my dresser to consider it.

So much for Addy being my last line of defense. She must be running really late and feeling extremely guilty to have someone run this up to me. We'd planned to get ready and head over to the party together. I suppose I'll have to dig deep and find the resolve to go on my own.

Untying the bow, I pull out a tub labeled 'Hair Mask' along with a spotty shower cap. The directions say, 'Apply generously and leave for fifteen minutes for a luxurious shine.' I glance at the time on my phone, deciding I'm already late so there's no reason not to squeeze in a quick shower since Addy went to this much effort.

In the communal bathroom, where the mirror is fogged over and steam is curling around my shoulders, I smooth the mask from root to tip, applying generously as instructed, and twist up into the shower cap. The heat from the cubicles makes the clinical scent bloom and my nose itch, but that must mean it's working. Everyone is in full pre-party prep mode, so I patiently wait my turn. Setting a timer, I sit on the countertop by the basin, shaving my legs while a R&B mix plays in my inner ears. My timer goes off by the time I finish both legs and my underarms, and still none of the showers are free. I suppose a few extra minutes won't hurt, I'll just be extra silky smooth. My mind runs away with me, the thought of Rhys' tattooed fingers rubbing the strands of my hair seeming all too appealing until a cubicle door opens.

Finally. I wash and rinse until the water runs clear, wrap my hair in a towel, and hum softly as I pad back into the room. The music in my ears is louder now, the bass thumping through my skull. My scalp is tingling and the smell isn't as pleasant as I'd hoped, but I'm not going to complain. Swinging the dorm room door open, I smile to find Addy is back. Flushed from the cold with a scarf around her neck, she quickly finger signs and apology for being so late. I wave her off and drag the towel from my head. Her fingers freeze in mid-air.

What happened to your hair? Addy slowly asks, her eyes wide. I frown.

"I used the mask you left me," I say, my voice faltering as I glance down. The strands are... lighter. Not just lighter. Patchy. My dark brown is now a mix of uneven caramel streaks and brassy orange chunks, the kind of color you'd get from a box left too long in the sun.

Addy's brows furrow, her head turning to the pink gift bag on the dresser. She shakes her head hard and signs, *That is not from me.*

The sound of the music filtering into my ears becomes too much so I grab my phone and shut off the background noise, turning on my mic app instead. My pulse races as I turn toward the mirror. Addy comes up behind me, unable to hide her uneasy expression.

"You didn't happen to piss off Klara Kavanagh, did you? Bleach in a hair mask tub is her calling card. She nearly sent one of her cheer-leaders bald once for hooking up with Rhys after a cheer rally."

The streaks catch the overhead light in ugly flashes, my hands curling into the towel still damp with bleach-scented water. I knew it didn't smell right, but I've never dyed my hair before. Damn home-schooled naivety.

"Klara," I grit out. My eyes fall on the jersey strewn across my head-board. The party is happening right now, and I bet Klara's smug smile is probably somewhere in that crowd, making a fool of herself for Rhys' attention. She thought she could trick me into missing the party, or push me out of Rhys' life. I'm afraid to say that stubborn streak is back in full force and I won't be doing either of those things. Quite the opposite actually.

Climbing the steps of Rhys' frat house, I flick my hair over my shoulder and straighten my spine. Beneath my leather jacket, the jersey clings to me. Transformed into something closer to a dress thanks to the belt cinched at my waist, its hem brushes my thighs. The chestnut cowboy boots Addy lent me hit the floor with a confident knock of the wedge heel. My entire look and posture strikes out with a level of conviction that I hope slaps Klara across the face. She meant to drag me down, but Addy has worked her magic and elevated me to another level instead.

Her pink hair dye now runs from my roots to the gentle curls sitting on my chest, soft rose ribbons blending through the hot pink strands like highlights. To anyone who didn't see the disaster an hour ago, it looks intentional. Addy links her arm through mine, her smile giving me an extra boost of courage.

Crowds spill across the front lawn, making out or dancing to the silent music I assume is blasting through the open windows. The porch is crammed with bodies shoving in and out of the doorway, red cups in hand. I sign to Addy, *Drink first*, and we push our way inside.

The floorboards thump beneath my boots, either from the press of people jammed into every inch of the place or the bass pounding from the DJ booth set up in the living room to the left. A staircase runs along the right wall, with the faint glow of the kitchen at the end of the hallway.

I don't know what I expected from Rhys' house, but it was something extravagant. Unnecessarily vulgar. A life-size portrait of him dripping in jewels and blood, or a diamond-studded chandelier. Instead, I'm met with plain gray walls, no photographs, not a single personal touch. This place feels cold and calculated, an ideal space for a dark entity to fester.

Glass bottles cover every inch of the kitchen counter. A keg and a tower of plastic cups crowd the central island. Addy makes a beeline for the vodka, pouring herself a heavy measure and knocking it back in one go. Grinning, she pushes a cup toward me, but I don't get the chance to take it.

Rhys appears as if out of nowhere, plucking the cup from her hand and passing it to a random stranger. He wears an open black shirt with the sleeves rolled to his elbows, his torso on display above dark fitted jeans. Whilst eyeing his tattoos and abs, I unclip the mini microphone from my belt and attach it to his collar. His blue eyes are on fire, dangerous energy circling within as he places a prosecco glass in my hand, pale liquid fizzing with a strawberry floating on the surface.

"She's not drinking that shit," he says to Addy without looking her way. Beyond his shoulder, Addy shrugs, squashing her cleavage together in a punky black dress trimmed with pink lace, happily reclaiming the vodka and drinking straight from the bottle.

"You're lucky," Rhys licks his lips, his heated gaze raking over his jersey covering my body, "I normally lose interest when girls try to play hard to get." He lifts the newly colored ends of my hair, deep rose-pink sliding through his tattooed fingers like silk. A smile curves across my lips, bathing in his fascination.

"Who said I'm playing? I *am* hard to get."

Following the flare of his nostrils, I swear his pupils dilate slightly. I lift the glass to my lips and drink in slow sips, Rhys tracks the hollow of my throat. Bubbles pop on my tongue, taking off the edge enough to just enjoy Rhys' attention. The desire oozing from him right now makes it hard to remember this is the same guy who chased me through the woods in a pig mask and assaulted me. But I haven't forgotten, and I fully intend on making him pay when I've had my fun.

Finishing my drink, I place it on the counter and I take a step back from his overpowering presence.

"Where's Klara?"

"How the fuck should I know?" Rhys barely reacts, his fingers back in my hair. I wonder if he knows his head tilts to the side when he's in deep thought, his eyes roaming over me like he's trying to memorize this moment. Maybe I'll allow him to continue his soul searching in my hair later, but right now, I have a mission in mind.

A gorgeous jock with ebony skin and dreadlocks is finishing mixing up a cocktail for the brunette hanging on his arm when I gesture for the shaker. He passes it over with the pink gin, but I shake out of my jacket, laying it over a stool and head straight for the fridge instead. Two eggs, a tub of cottage cheese, whipped cream, and an expired pack of prawns later, I dump my finds on the table and start assembling the vilest concoction imaginable.

"Care to explain?" he wrinkles his nose at the smell. I have to admit, it's gag-worthy, and it's perfect. I shake my head, keeping my eye out for a shine of blonde hair amongst the crowd. I can sense her nearby. She never strays far from Rhys. A small crowd gathers, their voices leaking through Rhys' mic through holding their noses.

"Is she going to drink that?"

"What is she doing?"

"I'm gonna throw up."

I scrape everything into the shaker, add a pour of tequila—because I'm classy—and lock the lid. Rhys remains by my side, watching on and making no move to stop me. Blinking up, I spot her leaning against the staircase, not so suitably curious about the gathered crowd. I have to tilt my head down to contain my grin. Satisfied it's as smooth as it's going to get, I pour the pale, lumpy mixture into two cups and hand one to Addy. It smells as bad as it looks.

The crowd lurches back to create a path as we cut through, my gaze locked on my target. To her credit, I suppose, Klara holds her ground. Arms crossed with a rally of cheerleaders at her back, all glaring at my hair with equal distain. They didn't think I'd be here, never mind looking like I own the room. Addy catches my eye, winks, and darts up the stairs without a word. I clear my throat, the rancid tang of stale beer and sweat coating the back of my tongue, and the cheerleaders behind her immediately back off, their faces twisting at the smell.

I close the distance between Klara and me until our noses are almost touching, and even without hearing it, I can feel the hush ripple through the house.

"Apply generously and leave for fifteen minutes for a luxurious shine," I grit through my teeth as I tip the contents of my cup over her head, watching the thick liquid cascade down her face in slow rivulets, while above us Addy attacks from the rear with her own. When the last gloopy drop has slid from the cup, I crush the flimsy plastic in my hand and let it fall onto her glittering gold heels. Klara gags and chokes beneath the gloop, her make-up running in equally thick streams.

I pivot sharply, flicking my cotton-candy hair over my shoulder, and stride through the circle of applause to find Rhys. A jock is at his side, leaning in to murmur something I can't hear through the mic. Rhys's expression darkens with every word, his gaze sharp and unreadable. Replying with a clipped order, the jock rushes out of the back-door. Rhys waits for me to reach him, carefully lifting my wrists and dragging me towards the basin. He flicks on the water and pumps soap into his own hands to wash mine.

"I feel like I'm missing something." He tentatively scrubs any gloopy residue left between my fingers, turning my hands back and forth in his before washing them off. His own knuckles are red and swollen, thin slices tearing across his hands but he pays them no mind. I lift one shoulder in a shrug, unwilling to admit that I've entered myself into some bitchy rivalry on his behalf. I won't give him the satisfaction.

"You're missing a lot of things, Rhys." Sharp, blue eyes slide to me and he doesn't say anymore. Grabbing a towel, he pats me dry and hooks my arm into his. His grip is tight, as if I'm a wild animal he is trying to wrangle. Pushing through the backdoor, where the jock jogged out, I catch the tail-end of a speedy clean up. The jock ushers naked people from an adult-size bounce house, while another breaks up an orgy in an equally-nudist boxing ring.

Rhys turns me right, using his body to block my view. At the end of the porch, a junior is swiftly scooting empty cups into a trash bag around the hot tub. He keeps his eyes low, not addressing Rhys and sneaking away as we approach. A minute later and we're alone, the slam of the back door echoing in Rhys' mic. The kitchen blinds are pulled down just after.

Rhys doesn't say anything at first. I watch him unclip the mic and attach it to a thin chain hanging around his neck. Shimmying out of his shirt, he pulls a cigarette from his jeans pocket and lights it before shedding those too. Between lighting the cherry, he slips out of his shoes and jeans, and leans against the railing in just his boxers.

"If you're expecting me to-" I instinctively wrap my arms around myself, but Rhys waves me off.

"Seeing you wearing my number is..." he inhales on his cigarette and exhales a cloud of smoke through his nose, "intoxicating." Balancing the stick between his lips, he crooks his index finger in my direction. Despite hating the smell, I inch closer and Rhys' hand falls to my belt. Deftly, he unhooks the buckle, letting it crash to the floor and then points at my boots. I play along, thoroughly enjoying the way his breath quickens when I obey him so easily. My submission must be something he's been waiting for. Standing bare foot, I wait for my next instruction. Rhys swivels his finger in the air and I turn around.

"I think you like being a good girl for me," he mumbles, sinking his hands into my hair. I don't respond, surprised when his fingers find my scalp and start to softly massage. "I think you like being the good girl for the villain that everyone fears."

Rhys kneads and rubs, dragging his fingertips over my scalp, lingering until I shiver. Not from the cold, but from the unexpected pleasure of simply being touched. Of being cared for. His thumbs sweep over my temples, gentle and reverent, making it difficult to stand still in the winter's air. The low hum that slips from my throat betrays me, and I feel his chest expand with satisfaction against my back.

Guiding my newly-pink hair on top of my head, he secures it with something to give him full access to my neck. His hands slide over my throat, lingering for a moment before continuing over my shoulders. Brushing over the neckline of the jersey, my nipples harden against my will and my breath stutters. Rhys takes one more pull on his cigarette before flicking the ash lazily over the railing, the ember glowing faintly in the dark.

"Get in the tub, Babygirl." He eases me forward by the waist, holding my weight as I step into the hot tub in his jersey and the black lace underwear Addy insisted I wore underneath. He's right behind me, mirroring my actions as he glides into the water and when I attempt to move away, he drags me down into his lap. I tense slightly but his hands are on me again, massaging my shoulders this time.

Bubbles lap around me, the heat seeping into my skin. Of all the things I expected to feel tonight, this wasn't it. Pain was at the top of the list, probably possessive throat holding and having my face slammed into a wall whilst Rhys attempted to take me from behind. I'd fully planned on waiting until the last moment before snapping his dick off, but he's decided to come at me from left field. Easing the knots from my shoulder blades, attempting to convince me that I'm discovering a side of him no one else gets to see. A power move, I'm sure.

Movement appears at our side and I flinch, catching the delayed beat of music through the closing back door. The junior that helped with clearing up kneels to balance a tray of drinks on the edge of the tub and whisks away again, keeping his eyes diverted at all times. Rhys only moves once he's disappeared back inside. He keeps me pressed against him, leaning forward to hand me another prosecco and retrieve himself one of the whiskeys.

"Drink," Rhys orders. "And relax. We're going to be here for a while."

"Doing what?" I raise a brow over my shoulder. I jolt for a second, not spotting his chain or my mic, until I hear the faint static of my hair rustling with the movement and realise just what he's secured my ponytail with.

He reaches around to lift the glass in my hand and tip it against my lips as the water swirls around us. I hold his gaze, unblinking as I drink. Rhys sips his whiskey too, smirking behind his glass. For a second, the night feels suspended, the party noise a dull echo in the background. My pulse thrums in my ears, not from fear but from the dizzying rush of being seen, chosen, and dared.

"You are nothing like what I expected," he says almost too quietly to catch. I hold back a sarcastic comment along the lines of, *well yeah – you expected me to be blind and helpless.* There's no point bringing up the past now, not when I'm too interested in what's happening in the present. Tonight is a one-time deal, might as well let my inhibitions go.

Finally giving in to temptation, I twist, swiveling until I'm straddling his lap. Rhys lets out a sound of pure approval, his arms spreading to lean against the wood-lined tub. Setting my glass down, I let my fingers wander across the elaborate tattoos etched into his chest and shoulders.

They remind me of Rodin's Gates of Hell, an intricate masterpiece of angels and demons, men and skeletons locked in a desperate climb. My touch follows the curve of an angel with white-feathered wings lifting a crying woman upward, then drifts to a demon crouched over the severed head of his victim. Every figure is unique, yet all are drained of color, their stories told only through line and shadow.

Before my fingers reach the ink at his neck, he catches my hand and presses it firmly to the center of his chest, the steady beat of his heart drumming against my palm. His skin is hot beneath my touch, slick with the steam curling from the water, and when he leans in, his tongue traces a slow, deliberate line along my jaw from chin to ear.

My breath hitches as his intoxicating scent floods my senses, the smoke from his earlier cigarette clinging to him, threaded through with something darker, sharper, and undeniably Rhys. The heat of the water merges with the heat of his touch until it feels as though every nerve in my body is on high alert, every part of me pulled taut like a string about to snap.

"Since when have you been anything except a scheming asshole?" I ask, not really expecting an answer, my voice coming out rougher than I intended. My mouth takes on a life of its own, brushing against his temple. "I figured you would have your way with me and kick me out." Rhys' lips graze my earlobe, creating a dance of movements that clearly avoids our mouths touching, until he pauses.

"Is that what you came here for?" His voice is infuriatingly calm, each word vibrating against my skin.

"Maybe." I swallow, hating how unsteady I sound. My hands dip beneath the water, trailing over his abdomen. "I figured we could burn through this attraction and get back to our lives." Rhys chuckles, his hand sliding to my thigh in an attempt to anchor me more securely on his lap.

"We have a lot more in common than I thought. It may have started that way, but when I saw you in my jersey, looking like a pink-wrapped package just for me, I changed my mind." He tilts his head back slightly, meeting my gaze with a smirk that is softer than his usual dangerous vibe. "I'll go back to being the asshole you hate tomorrow. Just give me tonight."

Something inside me twists hard, my stomach coiling as the heat seeps all the way to my core. I clench my thighs out of habit, and Rhys' cock pulses right back. He's growing harder, pressing firmly against my center. The warning bells in my skull clash with the thrill of surrender.

"Okay. I'll give you tonight."

Rhys' thumb strokes slow circles against my waist, the touch maddeningly tender compared to the way my nails are digging into his skin. I need to calm down. I can't be the one who is out of control here. Wetting my lips, which was instantly a bad idea as it brings Rhys' attention back to them, I exhale deliberately.

"You're wrong by the way. I don't like being the good girl for the villain everyone fears." Rhys' brow arches, interest sparking in his blue eyes, the lip ring at the corner of his mouth curving. He leans forward, finally crossing the boundary we've been dancing around and brushing his lips over mine.

"Oh no? What do you enjoy then?"

I smile, pulling back and taking great satisfaction in the way his mouth follows me. The way his body leans over mine and an arm snakes around my back as if I might push off and disappear any moment. Toying with my tongue between my teeth, I bathe in his full attention before offering my confession and challenge all at once.

"I like being the villain's weakness."

CLAYTON

CHAPTER TWENTY ONE

I can't watch any longer. Whatever excuse I told myself for coming here, that I was checking Harper was safe, disintegrated the second I saw her with him. Now I'm standing half-hidden behind a thick tree trunk on the edge of Wavershit's yard, drunk enough to feel it in my legs, sober enough to know I look like a fucking creep. My fury's rotting inside me, turning into something feral, but still I can't move.

In the hot tub, Harper's plastered to his chest like she belongs there, fingers sliding over his tattoos, eyes dark with want. I'd pictured her dangling upside down from the banister again, or drunk out of her mind and shoved into the woods as some cruel joke. Instead she's perfectly fine. More than fine. She's a college girl at a party on a Friday night. And me? I'm the lunatic in the trees, watching. *Fuck.*

I'll never trust Rhys Waversea as far as I can throw him, but Harper, she doesn't look like she needs saving. Not from him. Not tonight at least.

I peel away into the shadows, tugging my beanie lower and striding out into the empty campus. The music is still thumping behind me, carrying for miles, but everywhere else is dead quiet. Either everyone's at the party or hiding in their rooms wishing they were. I try to map out how I'll waste the rest of the night. Hit the library, shoot hoops, maybe grind out the anger in the gym. Anything but picture Harper wrapped around *him.*

Truth is, I don't even know why I came. My feet dragged me here before my brain could object. And now, after seeing them together, every excuse rings hollow. *She's not yours to save.* She never was. I can't even save myself. Christ, I've proven that a dozen times, but some warped part of me still wants to try. If Harper ever looked at me like I was worth something, maybe one of the million broken cracks inside me might finally snap back into place. Which is pathetic, because that makes me no better than Wavershit, using her to prove a fucking point.

Yanking off my beanie, I claw a hand through my hair and give a tight tug to the ends. Life was simple up to a few weeks ago – shit yes, but simple. Now I'm questioning every move I make and toying with impossible fantasies which are not meant for me. The night is as cold as any other this time of year, but my blood is pumping hot enough to warm me through in my thin, military jacket. A pair of young ladies in thigh high boots and not much else huddle into each other, barging passed me in the direction of their dorms.

"I heard that deaf girl is Rhys's date tonight."

"Don't be stupid. Rhys doesn't date, and he sure as hell doesn't fuck rejects."

Their laughter travels to me as they walk away, forcing me to stop still in my tracks. My body shakes against the strain of my mind, trying to pull me backwards against my own will. My fists clench, my vision swimming with ways to make them choke on their words. Harper is everything they could ever hope to be.

After a moment of tensing hard enough to cause the start of several cramps, I manage to step forward on a long exhale. I can't defend Harper's name every time, especially not when she insists on walking directly into the line of fire. She's not my problem. Thankfully, I don't pass anyone else for the rest of the walk and I finally arrive back at my dorm. Twisting the key in the lock, I push open the door to see a peculiar sight. Even more peculiar than Kenneth's usual standards.

My roommate is hunched over the desk we share, inspecting a pigeon whose neck has clearly been snapped. There's no blood or smell yet, just a lifeless pile of feathers sprawled across the first draft of my thesis.

"What the hell are you doing?" I slam the door shut, making him jump. Kenneth's red hair is particularly wild tonight, shock paling his features but I'm sure I see a hint of excitement in the depths of his brown eyes. Pushing his glasses up, he bobs towards me like a puppy which I won't let get too close.

"Clayton! I found this pigeon outside and I think someone must have killed it but guess what! This will be a perfect dissection for the project I'm working on about the differences in manifestations of diseases carried by rodents and birds!" Shoving him aside, I move to try and save my work since it's the only copy I have.

"Fuck's sake Kenneth, stop bringing dead animals home! You have a key to the veterinary lab, just take them straight there." Nudging the paper out from underneath, the pigeon rolls and falls onto the floor with a hollow thud. Nope, I'm not staying in here all evening while Kenneth gets hard over roadkill. He rushes to pick up the bird with his gloved hands and roll it into a cloth.

"I'm done for tonight, pinkie swear." Kenneth holds up his pinkie and I just stare at him like I'm considering how to dispose of his body. He promptly lowers his hand. "I wasn't supposed to be home this long anyway. I have two tickets for the special midnight screening of 'Iron Man 2.0', but Samuel heard from Donna that Rachel was going to the afterparty and she's a real light weight so he's going to finally tell her how she feels and hence.....he ditched me."

There's a wobble to Kenneth's bottom lip as something has finally managed to shut him up, a glistening in his eyes that has me ready to bolt through the door if a single tear falls. But all at once, the misery vanishes and is replaced with a buzzing excitement that has his mouth dropping open on a high-pitched squeal.

"Oh! You could come with me!"

Shaking my head, I start rooting through my drawers for some shorts. Gym it is. I can't imagine a worse way to die than for Kenneth to drag me to a movie he'll probably talk though and bore me to a vegetated, non-breathing state.

"Please Clayton, pleeeeeease. Don't make me go alone, the ticket is paid for and I'll get you popcorn and I promise I won't say a word the entire time." I still and quirk my eyebrow in disbelief, but Kenneth starts doing that nod again where his head just might fly off.

"There's no way in hell you can stay quiet for an entire night."

"Cross my heart, from the time we leave this room, I will be silent. Come on, help me out here. Everyone already thinks I'm a creepy weirdo. What would they say if I went to a movie all by myself?"

I stare at him unblinking, not understanding how my presence would change that fact. But dammit, I kinda get it. I was just downing my sorrows in a bottle of rum behind a tree. Being a loner gets you into strange situations where the world seems to keep going on without you. I do need a distraction tonight, and hell, I might just need a friend. Besides, I haven't been to the movies in years, if the run-down cinema with one screen at the end of my childhood block counts. If not, then I've never been to the movies.

"If you manage to go all night without saying one word, I'll let you be my partner for the Grayson lab trip," I snort against my better judgement. Again, maybe a friend isn't the worst idea, even if there's no way he'll manage to stay quiet. I'll most likely team up with him anyway, and this way, I feel better about taking his free ticket. Accepting charity isn't in my nature.

Kenneth squeals like a three-year-old girl on Christmas and flies around the room grabbing items for his backpack. I'm more than a little concerned to see two pairs of socks and a blanket go in there.

Swapping the shorts in my hand for jeans, I head into the bathroom to freshen up and change. When I emerge, thankfully the soon-to-be dissected disease-potato is nowhere in sight and Kenneth is vibrating with excitement. His carroty plaid shirt matches his slicked back hair, with black slacks over his trainers and I briefly worry why he's dressed as if this were a date.

Grabbing my military jacket, I shove out the door before he does something stupid like hug me. Once in the hallway, Kenneth mimes zipping his mouth closed and then counter-productively swallows the imaginary key. Swiping the tickets from his free hand, I examine the cinema logo with a nod and pull my keys from my pocket.

"I'll drive."

Sure as shit, Kenneth is yet to mumble one word. I didn't know he had so much restraint. Exiting my beat-up truck, he sprints ahead of me to the cinema entrance. Tonight, it seems, I am the owner of an over-excited puppy as I push through the glass doors and find myself immersed in an alternative universe where cinemas apparently resemble swanky hotels.

Gold bollards with red ropes frame the walkway, the ceiling a mass of golden LED lights. The foyer floor sparkles as I walk over it, a black swirl cutting through the smooth vinyl and leading to the kiosks. Along the walls, huge TV's flash with movie trailers amongst vintage movie memorabilia and artwork. Kenneth darts in the opposite direc-tion as I'm pulled towards a wooden stick hanging above a scene from Lord of the Rings, the prop apparently the real staff used through all three movies.

After reading the lengthy description, Kenneth nudges me to signal his return and plants a tray into my hands which he was struggling to hold. Beside two jumbo sized sodas sits hotdogs with crispy onions, cheesy nachos, a salty-scented tub of popcorn and pack of caramel chocolate bites. On the edge of the tray, *'I didn't know what you liked...'* has been scrawled into a napkin, although strangely the items are all exactly what I would have chosen for myself.

I attempt to form some sort of thank you, not expecting Kenneth to feed me as well, but he's already moved on. Putting up six fingers, he points at an overhead sign which shows the direction of the screens. The huge grin on his face shows how proud he is of his miming skills, leading the way for me to follow behind. Even when the assistant checking tickets asks how he's doing tonight, he replies with a cheery thumbs up.

Just like the foyer, the auditorium does not disappoint. And by "does not disappoint," I mean it's the kind of over-the-top bougie bull-shit that makes you feel like you should've worn a tux just to eat nachos. Maybe I should have followed Kenneth's lead and put on a shirt. I don't have much experience with movie theaters, *thank you tragic backstory*, but the red velvet curtain-framed screen filling an entire wall isn't what I was expecting. Instead of neat rows of seats, there are small sofas with side trays. As if Netflix and Chill needed to be franchised.

I trail after Kenneth like a reluctant date, my boots sinking into the plush grey carpet that feels expensive enough to sue me if I spill soda on it. A couple guys glance at me on the way, their eyes flicking between my scowl and Kenneth's bouncing ginger mop. Fantastic. Nothing like walking into a midnight nerd nest looking like the bodyguard for Ronald McDonald's estranged nephew.

We settle onto our assigned sofa. Everyone in attendance seems to be male but I suppose it's cliché for men to venture out at midnight for the latest comic book action flick. Sitting beside Kenneth, he gives me a secretive smile, his usually dull eyes alight with mischief. I barely have time to frown before the lights go dim.

Using the glow from the LEDs down the central aisle, I place my chosen snacks on the moveable tray and pass the rest to Kenneth. The popcorn goes between us as there's only one tub, but there is no way I'm risking an accidental hand touch. He's welcome to the popcorn.

The trailers begin to roll, an odd mix of romantic comedies and musical theatre recordings. My suspicions only grow when the couple behind start to giggle excitedly, pulling out a blanket to spread across their laps. By the time the opening credits flash upon the screen, it's a good thing I'd stopped slurping my soda otherwise I would have sprayed it all over the floor.

'*Iron man 2.0. The Return of Tony Starkers*' appears in an amateur red lettering, my jaw dropping into my lap. Where I expected to see a metallic suited hero, instead stands a stubbled middle-aged man in a red and gold thong. A tinfoil crafted 'jetpack' sits on his back, a light in the shape of testicles stuck to the center of his chest. Aside from that, he's not wearing any clothes.

"Kenneth," I murmur, "What the f- "

"*Ahh, Jack Hammer, my old nemesis.*" Thong-man proclaims, throwing his arms wide. "*Have you finally decided to surrender to me?*" Another actor struts on screen in a wrinkled bodysuit, glasses perched on his nose, and the world's most obvious boner straining the latex.

Prickling shoots up my spine. Not the good kind. The kind you get right before a mugger pulls out a knife. Only here, the mugger's weapon is a raging erection and I'm about to see a lot more than I bargained for.

Turning to throttle Kenneth, a vibration pulses through the seat and he rushes to remove his phone from his pocket. He's lucky that was his phone. The brightness of the screen highlights his shock of red hair and freckles against the dark. He looks at me and back to his screen a few times, rushing to type a message into his notes.

I have to go! So sorry, enjoy the movie and help yourself to my spare sock.

Before I can process the words *spare sock*, Kenneth launches a wadded ball of fabric at my chest and bolts before I have time to catch the slimy bastard, his blanket trailing from his backpack like a cape.

"*It's Hammertime,*" says the suited character on screen as he starts to undo his belt. Nope, no, nada, uh huh. Catapulting from my seat, I abandon the food, the socks and my dignity, running for the exit. A guttural moan from Tony Starkers escapes before the door closes at my back and I know that I'm never going to unhear it. That sound is now part of my damage.

That little bastard knowingly took me to a midnight screening of a gay porno, and thought I wouldn't wring his scrawny neck with his spare sock? If Kenneth knows what's good for him, he won't come home tonight, but I'll be waiting for when he does. Fuck having friends, I'm better off alone.

HARPER

CHAPTER TWENTY TWO

I'm going to do it. I'm going to fuck him, and let myself regret it in the morning.

Maybe I shouldn't have had a fifth prosecco, or maybe the sexual tension Rhys massaged into my body is winning through, but I don't currently care. I'm a student. This is what students do. Make bad decisions and spend the rest of the semester running from them. Yes girl, be a cliché, and enjoy every hard inch of it. I mean minute. Every veiny, throbbing minute.

I hiccup a laugh, stumbling slightly on the stairs. It must be late, because mostly everyone who doesn't live here has either left or passed out. Either that, or Rhys has had them all kicked out again. Less people to watch me navigate my way up the stairs, dripping wet and hugging the railing like a lifetime. I only slip twice, to my credit, and manage to remember Rhys' directions. *Left at the top of the stairs, last room on the end.*

There was also something about preparing for a night I'll never forget as Rhys pushed me from his lap to stand in all his tattooed glory. I kind of stopped listening when I saw the outline of his erection touching the inside of his waistband. He left me to finish my drink, which was inevitably the one to push me over the edge of sanity.

Turning left at the hallway, the jersey clings to me like a second skin, restricting my movements as if it's trying to drag me backwards. '*No, don't do it*," the material seems to say, so I drag it over my head and slap it down onto the tiled floor. I then proceed to trip over the heap of sodden material like a final kick from karma, but I'm still undeterred with no fucks given.

I'm a big girl. I can handle this. Squaring my shoulders, I reach the final door at the end and push it wide open. The room is dark, only lit by a bedside lamp with an ominous red bulb. Sturdy, wooden furniture sits around the edge of a huge bed in the middle, various curiously shaped objects spread across the covers.

"You sure love making me wait." Rhys's voice echoing inside my head makes me jump as I step inside, the door slamming closed behind me. He steps into sight from his spot against the wall, crackling his knuckles one at a time. His eyes are churning with a such ferocity, I can't tell it's from desire or impatience. Probably a mixture of both.

Looking at him over my shoulder, I cock an eyebrow with a slanted smile and head towards the bed. What do we have here then? There's an array of objects from every sadist's dreams, all in black and most in leather. Handcuffs, blindfolds, vibrators and butt plugs in multiple sizes, and a paddle. That one I quickly discard, flashbacks of the hog chase filtering through my drunken mind. Rhys doesn't react to me flinging the paddle across the room, most likely realizing his fuck up.

Moving on, I trail my finger over a thick leash and lift the surprisingly heavy collar attached. Rhys's initials have been engraved in the center above a black metal ring.

"Do you need a safe word?" Rhys presses his body against my back so he can trail his lips along my exposed neck. His fingers follow, appreciating the lace underwear he's seeing for the first time. Plucking the string of my thong, a low sound vibrates through his chest and his teeth lightly sink into the space between my neck and shoulder.

"No," I breathe, unhooking the collar's buckle. "But you do." I twist in his arms before he can anticipate the shift in power, looping the leather snug around his throat. His eyes flicker with surprise, but he's too late to catch me. Maybe I'm not the only one a tad too drunk, or maybe he's just drunk on me. His hooded eyes blink lazily, a delay in the tightening of his jaw. Toying with the leash, I curl it around my hand and give it a hard yank so he's eye level with me. Unclipping the mic from the chain in my hair, I attach it on the side of the collar with a mischievous smirk.

"I don't think so, Babygirl," he practically growls. Delayed fury blazes in his blue irises but it only boosts my actions. I tilt my head the way he does, thrumming with dominance.

"Your safe word can be *jacuzzi*. I hope you're prepared for a night *you'll* never forget Rhys Waversea." Sliding my fingers beneath the leather, I pull him closer for our lips to brush. A mockingly light touch before I bite down on his bottom lip hard. Talking about hard, Rhys' cock jolts against my stomach, a deep rumbling continues to passing through his throat. Licking a path across the bite, savoring his taste of smoke and whiskey, I drag the pad of my tongue across his piercing, and Rhys snaps. Lunging forward, he devours me. My tongue, my mouth, my jaw. He returns the bites all over my skin, shaking with the need to cause pain and bring pleasure.

I tug on the collar, dragging him back to my mouth. Heat bursts throughout my body like molten lava seeping down my throat, his tongue coiling and battling with mine for the control I refuse to let him have. Every part of me feels too warm, my skin too tight. His hard length is pushing against my stomach, my thighs clenching together with need.

Pushing him back a step, my chest heaves and I fight to regain focus. Moving the rest of the items aside, I point for him to sit on the edge of the bed. He looks like he's going to refuse me, so I release my hair from his chain, letting the pink strands tumble down either side of my breasts and I pout.

"Sit for me?" After a beat, Rhys reluctantly complies, sitting so his mouth is a breath away from my chest. Yep, defiantly drunk on me.

"Now, don't move," I order. I unfasten my bra and peel the wet material from my body as Rhys watches on hungrily. My nipples are painfully hard from a mixture of the damp and cold, Rhys's fists clenching as he spots the small, metal bar through my left nipple. I hear his frustration vibrate through my skull. I laugh internally while easing my thong down my legs and stepping out of them.

Sensing he won't stay seated much longer, I saunter towards him slowly and use his jaw to guide him onto my breast. He latches on so quickly, I gasp loud enough to hear myself through the microphone. I tease the length of the leash through my fingers whilst bathing in his attention, his raw power.

Sucking, licking, biting. Pleasure and pain zip straight to my core which he increases by slipping a hand between my legs. He groans against my skin at how wet he finds me, pushing two fingers inside instantly. Light bursts behind my eyes. All of the teasing and touching and waiting up to now has been foreplay. There's no need to wait anymore. Propping my foot beside him on the bed, I hold onto his shoulders as he pumps his fingers vigorously and moves to draw my pierced nipple into his mouth.

Every internal stroke mirrors a powerful suck on my breast, need building into a quickened crescendo. I've got the devil between my legs, fixated on playing my body like an instrument. Pushing his thumb roughly against my clit, I can't stop myself from coming apart on a strangled moan. My free hand finds his hair, gripping it tightly so I can ride the waves of ecstasy without him pulling away.

Biting my lip, I pick up my resolve and take a step back out of Rhys's reach. Maintaining my eye contact, he lifts his fingers into his mouth and sucks them clean. A shudder races down my spine, a level of lust I've never experienced before banishing all of my reservations and spurring my actions here on out.

Dropping to my knees, I reach across to grab the handcuffs and shackle each of his wrists to the bed's base either side of his thighs. He doesn't resist, watching me intently and curiously. Once secure, I scrape the tips of my nails along the inside of his legs making him buck and hiss.

"I could break out of these easily, you know." He growls whilst tugging against the restraints, but I simply sit back on my heels.

"Each time you try, I'll stop." His chest is rising and falling quickly, the inked angels and demons coming to life as they are stretched and twisted. Rhys grits his teeth and relaxes, signaling that I can continue. That he'll behave. A different kind of beast swells in my chest, instinctively knowing that I have Rhys in a way no one else has. I have him submitting.

Kneeling upwards and starting at his neck, I kiss my way down his tattooed skin and lean muscles. Several hidden scars pass beneath my lips but I'm too distracted to question them, turning my attention to Rhys' boxers. He's rock hard inside, bobbing free when I peel his waistband off and down his legs. What a beautiful cock. I've avoided appreciating it until now, both to annoy Rhys and to gear myself up. He's as big as I knew he'd be, having caught a glimpse in the locker room showers, those small silver balls gleaming.

My gaze flicks up and Rhys smirks at me knowingly. He's far too cocky for someone who's tied up and supposed to be at my mercy, so I don't hold off wiping that smile off his face. Taking his length into the back of my throat in one swift thrust, Rhys' shocked grunt reverberates through my head. I beam around his shaft. The rounded ends of his piercing take a moment to adjust to, but soon become my new favorite obsession.

Licking his smooth head, taking him deep for few seconds and sucking the tip on the way up, I find a rhythm that has him bucking beneath me. He groans and grinds, trying to relieve the pressure that has his balls tightening. Using my nails, I claw up the inside of his thighs and over his balls, enjoying myself far too much.

"That's enough," Rhys tries to bark but there's a desperation to his voice that has me grinning with satisfaction. Unhooking the clasp of his cuffs so they remain attached to his wrists, I push him down onto the bed and straddle his stomach. Leaning forward, I link the cuffs together above his head which he takes as a chance to bite my nipple.

Jerking back, I give his leash a hard yank. "You're so lucky I don't decide it's your turn to be battered with the paddle," I murmur, gripping his jaw tightly with my other hand. He opens his mouth to respond but I swallow his words with a kiss, not wanting to hear his excuses. He's an asshole, he knows it, everyone knows it. But for tonight, he's mine to play with. Our mouths crash and collide, a battle of will with our tongues.

Shifting slightly, Rhys's hands slip beneath his pillow to retrieve a condom he must have stashed there. I take it from his grip, ripping it open with my teeth and sitting back to slide it down his veiny length. That touch alone has Rhys groaning and thrusting into my hand, biting on his lip ring and enticing me to come back for more.

Pure sin coils around my tongue as I drive it into his mouth again, tempting me to overpower the beast beneath my hands. Lifting my hips, I lower myself onto his cock as I gasp into his mouth. His girth stretches me to the point of pain, stars bursting behind my eyes. His piercing smooths against my g-spot with enough pressure to have my walls tightening before we've even started. Pushing myself upright on his chest, I become fully seated and rock my hips to adjust.

Rhys waits and watches, drinking in my tiny moans and staring the point where our bodies meet. Starting slow, I lift and ease myself up and down his length, a climax already threatening to explode if I move any faster. Every time I sink down, Rhys jolts upwards to meet me and I groan loudly, scratching his chest and abs deeply. Building up to a faster pace, I ride him hard enough for us both to be panting. My thighs are burning from exertion but I don't let up, grinding against his groin for the metal inside to brush my g-spot over and over. A tightening starts to pulse within my core, a release I need more than my next breath coiling around his shaft.

"Release me, Babygirl. Let me show you what I've been dreaming to do to you." His pleas are cute but I narrow my eyes and tug his leash hard.

"You don't have dreams, Rhys. You're a thing of nightmares." A smile grows across Rhys' face, that manic razor-edged look igniting in his eyes.

"Oh yeah, you're right." Thrusting his hands upwards, he snaps the chains and lunges upright. I scream, shoving at his chest to get away. I meant what I said, if he broke the restraints I would stop, but he doesn't give me an inch. Well, to be literal, he gives me nine.

Wrapping my legs around his hips, Rhys hands grab my ass, lifting and slamming me back down whilst thrusting from underneath. I lose all fight and give into him. His body, his aura, his desires. The world falls away until only Rhys' toxic recipe of irresistible lust and bad judgement remain. He doesn't hold back, slamming into me while his fingers grip my ass, holding me firmly in place. The darkness of his soul latches onto mine, pulling me down a path I won't be able to come back from.

Shamelessly grinding me against him, Rhys's mouth clasps onto my neck and sucks hard. I hiss in pain but don't want it to stop either and on the next deep thrust, my walls crash with a rush of ecstasy. My nails claw his back and I bite down hard on his shoulder, the taste of blood tainting my mouth but it only seems to make him fuck me harder.

Pounding relentlessly while I continue to moan, Rhys crushes me against his body to hold me in place. He flips me at the last minute, sharp snaps of his hips driving me further into the mattress. All I can do is hold on and scream every curse I can think of. Anything, as long as it isn't his name. I'm drunk, not stupid enough to let him hold that over my head. Hiking my hips up, Rhys explodes with a flood of heat against the latex separating us, unrelenting until he's full spent.

We remain connected for too long whilst regaining our steady heartbeats and even breathing. Long enough to probably be considered cuddling if it weren't for the swelling of our lips, blood dripping from his shoulder or skin beneath my fingernails. No, this is more like the aftermath of a psychotic ritual or an exorcism.

Sitting upright, Rhys unclips the collar and flicks off my mic, tossing them aside. Plunged back into the silence that's only interrupted by the pounding of my own pulse, the regret settles in faster than I expected. I thought I had at least until morning, but now I'm taking in my surroundings, I can't help but feel defeated. Rhys got what he wanted. Another notch on his bedpost.

I take that as my cue to roll out from beneath him but his hand catches my throat and his lips crash back down on mine. The kiss doesn't even deserve to be called that. It's just as depraved, just as possessive and bruising. Just as delicious. My back arches, pushing my nipples against Rhys' chest, chasing the pleasure he ignites within me so easily. Squeezing my throat tighter, he leans back just enough for me to read his lips moving.

"Where do you think you're going? You promised me tonight." My brows raise slightly, a tightening happening within my core.

"To freshen up," I quickly recover. After a beat, Rhys nods and releases me, jerking his chin toward the corner. There's an open doorway, dark beyond the frame.

I slide out from beneath him, my legs shaky but determined, and slip inside. The door clicks closed with my back pressed against it, and I let out a shaky laugh. *Holy hell... that was just the beginning?* My old flings were all reckless quickies, squeezed in between stolen moments before someone's parents or guardians came barging through a door. Fast, dirty, and forgettable. But here? There are no rules or witnesses. Here, it's just me and Rhys. Me and the monster I've provoked.

Finding the light switch, I cross the room of slate grey tiles and white porcelain amenities. Just as bland as the rest of the house. The shower, however, that thing is a work of art with a square head in shining chrome and a drain built into the floor.

I twist the dial to near-scalding, stepping beneath the heavy spray. The water pounds against my skin, washing away the haze of alcohol and replacing it with raw awareness. My head tips back, eyes fluttering shut.

"Oh, *God*," I moan, not even faking it. "I don't know what's more pleasurable, you or your power shower," I call toward the bedroom. He's probably not even listening but that's fine. I'm quite happy in here, leaning back to keep my dyed hair dry and my nipples thoroughly entertained.

The water beats down, soothing, until heat flares across my stomach. I gasp, jerking at the unexpected hand smoothing across my skin. A teasing nip at my earlobe follows, then the ghost of a kiss against my cheek.

"Jesus, you scared me," I spin, finding him right behind me. Still rock-hard, tattoos slicked black from the water, one hand lazily stroking his cock like he's got all the time in the world.

"You've praised God and Jesus in this shower. Where's my praise?" His lips curl around the words, one brow raised. I tilt my head defiantly. I really should learn to quit while I'm ahead.

"You have to earn it."

Rhys licks his lip ring, the grin splitting his face in two. He reaches past me, switching the spray to a smaller handheld head that he's unhooked from the wall. The blast of hot water hits my nipple at close range, a sharp sting of sensation making me yelp, then moan through gritted teeth. Every nerve ending sings, sounds tearing out of me without permission. None of which are Rhys' name.

His grin only grows, wicked and dangerous, lit with blue-eyed hunger. He drags me closer, wet skin slapping against wet skin, until my chest is pressed flush to his. The shower head is moved south between us, carving a path towards my pussy. My hands splay across his shoulders, trying to ground myself, but it's useless. Rhys Waversea is a live wire, and I'm stepping straight into the current. The jet touches my already sensitive clit and I forget how to see, the world going dark around me.

"Fuuuuuck, Rhyssssss."

RHYS

CHAPTER TWENTY THREE

My hand tremors as I lift the phone to my ear. I can't believe I'm doing this, but I don't see any other way. The ring through the receiver is like a gong, clanging against my better judgement. Rhys Waversea doesn't ask for help, he gives orders. However, this time, I don't think that's going to work.

"Who the fuck is this?" A voice grumbles, thick with sleep. Perhaps a five a.m. wake up wasn't on Clayton's agenda for today, but the big lug should be up and putting in all the ball practice he can get. Sure, he may have single handily won the game against Armitage yesterday, but it was sloppy AF. He has all the grace of a fumbling hippo. *"I said,* who the fuck is this?!"

Oh yeah, words.

"I need you to get here right now!" I bark into the phone way too loud, my voice cracking like a teenage choirboy on his first solo. Great start, Rhys. Real commanding. On the other end, there's a groggy snarl.

"Kenneth, I spent all night searching for you. I swear on anything I am, I'm going to find you and I'm going to tear you limb from limb for leaving me alone in that damn porno." His voice rises, cancelling out everything I wanted to say. As in, my mind has gone completely blank as I sink onto the edge of the mattress, sniggering into my hand. What in the sweet juicy tea have I just stumbled into? There's a shift beneath the covers and I remember myself, shooting back upright. "Seriously, what kind of psycho—"

"It's Rhys," I hiss, stalking into the bathroom and easing the door closed.

"Rhys who?" Clayton asks, a frown evident in his voice. I roll my eyes.

"The only Rhys in a thirty mile radius." I know that for a fact. Anyone who's started at Waversea and thought their name was Rhys since I arrived here has quickly had second thoughts. There's an intense quiet on the other end of the line, punctuated by sharp huffs of breath. Might as well get this over with. "I need you to get to my place. Something terrible's happened."

"Rhys," he finally grunts my name. I can practically hear him bristling. Figuring I have minus two seconds before he hangs up, I force the words through my teeth.

"Look, you're also the last person on earth I want to be speaking to, but I kinda....well, I might have..." Swallowing past the lump in my throat, as if it's trying to close up on me, I pinch the bridge of my nose. "I just need you to come over. Right now."

The silence stretches, a knife's edge scraping at my nerves. I press my thumb harder into the bridge of my nose, almost wishing the bone would crack so I could focus on something other than the emptiness on the line. I want to check on Harper, but my legs refuse. The memory of what I saw already has me clawing at my open shirt like I can tear the panic straight out of my skin.

"Why would I give a shit about helping you?" Clayton asks whilst clattering in the background. I imagine him kicking a chair or smacking items off the desk, too frustrated to stay still but too intrigued to cut me off. Trust me, I'm just as uncomfortable on this end of the phone, my skin itching with the need to be anybody else right now. "Do you realize how insane you sound, calling me at the crack of dawn? You of all people? What kind of twisted—"

"It's Harper," I snap, my voice tearing itself raw. My chest seizes as I drag in a breath. "Something's wrong with Harper. Just get your ass over here." A soft chuckle sounds, gently mocking me into a worse mood.

"Ask me nicely." I pull the phone from my ear, staring at it like the thing just grew fangs. Is this asshole serious right now? My free hand fists into my hair, tugging hard enough to sting as I pace a tight line across the bathroom tiles.

"Ask you nicely? Do I sound like some sort of little bitch to you?!" My laugh is hollow, sharp, scraping out of my throat like broken glass. I kick the base of the sink, the impact jarring up my leg. A muffled sound comes from my bedroom.

"No," Clayton says after a beat, his voice smug. "You sound desperate. You want my help, so ask for it. In fact, I want you to beg me for it."

I catch sight of myself in the mirror and shake my head, thinking to myself, *get a load of this guy*. I thought Clayton's hero complex would have shoved him out the door before I'd even finished speaking. Maybe I overestimated his connection with Harper, the way he jumps to her defense or how she makes deals with the devil on his behalf.

"I don't beg." A snort escapes me. My jaw ticks so hard it aches. I stare at my reflection in the mirror. Wild eyes, shirt creased, sweat rolling down my neck, and for a flicker of a second, I don't even recognize myself. But the problem is bigger than my ego. Just about. I can't trust one of my lackies with this. It has to be him.

"Will you get your ass over here and help Harper?" My reflection is just as disappointed as I am. Dark shadows circle my eyes, stress wearing on me. There's no response down the line. Nothing. Not even a grunt of acknowledgement. As I wait, my stomach knots so tight I think I might puke right here against the marble basin. For a second I swear I can hear the stubbornness of his jaw locking into place.

Dammit. I turn away from the mirror, unable to look at myself for this part. "Please."

I hear drawers slam, frantic rustling, the sound of him moving like a man possessed. His breath has gone harsh now that my desperation has leaked through. The line goes dead in my ear. I lower the phone, staring at the black screen, unsure if I got the response I wanted.

The walls close in, every tile and polished surface mocking me. I slip out, heading straight into the hallway to pace the length of it, purposely avoiding looking at the bed. I can't bear to look. I'm not easily disturbed but the sight in the center of my bed is beyond horrific. Disastrous. Fuck, I can't stop wringing the ends of my open shirt that I shoved back on over my jeans upon waking.

I refuse to think about last night, the visions of her sweat-slickened body trying to slip beneath my mental shields. I'm always in control of my emotions for a reason; the consequences of being out of control too drastic for anyone to handle. How the fuck did I let this happen?

Clayton arrives in record timing, bursting through the front door with fury ablaze in his eyes. Spotting me, he runs up the stairs in sweatpants and a tank top. His blonde waves shake erratically with each movement, no beanie hat in sight.

"Where is she?" His bunched shoulders and clenched jaw are nothing compared to the worry etched into his features. I point to the closed door with a slight shake, words not making it past my lips.

Resting his fingers on the handle, he takes a visible breath to brace himself and pushes the door open. I scrub a hand down my face, as the panic surfaces again. There she is. Her pink tinted locks spread across my pillow, the naked outline of her hourglass figure pressed into my mattress with the cover pooling low on her ass. *Perfection.* Wait no, fucking disaster!

We both frown at the bed, taking in the view until backtracking into the hallway. Clayton's nostrils flare, his arms crossing over his chest like a solid band.

"I don't understand. Other than her terrible lack in judgement, what's the problem?" I gape at him, gesturing to her sleeping form because the issue is so glaringly obvious.

"She's in my bed?!" I whisper-shout, looking at the dude like the moron he is. His black eyes turn impossibly darker, shadowed by lowered eyebrows.

"Did you call me here just to see her in your bed?" Clayton's jaw ticks, the taste of violence crackling between us. If I weren't vibrating with the kind of panic that makes my bones itch, I'd laugh in his face, because this would be the perfect torture for him, dangling her inches away like raw meat, but the one being tortured right now is me.

"Don't you get it? No one stays the night in my bed. When she wakes up, she'll be hopelessly in love with me like all the other mindless drones around here," I spit the words at him, pacing like a caged wolf, my eyes flicking to the railing where bodies sprawl across every available surface, the debris of my parties consisting of youth and poor life choices. There's even a few slumped across the stairs who will need a chiropractor when they sober up. "I can't believe I've let this happen. I wanted to screw her and move on, not...this?! Everyone becomes obsessed with me after they've experienced Rumpleforeskin."

"Fuck my life," Clayton mutters, attempting to barge past me, but I slam my hand against his chest. For the first time since I woke up, a jolt of exhilaration courses through me as his body tenses under my palm. He growls, a sound that reverberates through his ribcage, but he can't intimidate me. Forget the private martial arts lessons, forget the home-installed boxing ring. I'm a ruthless bastard who strikes to kill and bathes in blood before anyone has the chance to disrespect me.

"I need you to get rid of her. Carry her back to her dorm or slip into the bed and have your way with her, I don't give a shit. But you are leaving this house with her, and no one has to know I took pity on the school's charity case."

He goes for my throat, but we've done this dance so many times I know his every tell. The twitch of his shoulder before he lunges, the way his weight shifts to his right foot, the faint hiss of breath before he commits. Every fight has been a rehearsal, a script I've studied and memorized, every failure feeding me knowledge, sharpening and molding me into his personal nemesis. That's why, on orientation day, I picked the biggest fucker in the room. Ripped muscle never beats a calculated mind.

I duck low and ram my shoulder into his ribs just left of center, the crack of impact sweet in my ear as I slam him into the wall, my fist driving into his gut hard enough to drag a strangled gasp from him. It's not pain, it's surprise, and I revel in it. Sweeping his legs, I crash down with him, straddling his waist and hurling a punch straight into his granite jaw.

The pain that splinters up my knuckles is pure rapture, and each punch after that only feeds the half-formed erection pressing against my zipper. Clayton's hand finds my throat, clamping down, and the noise that breaks out of me is dangerously close to a groan.

"Tighter," I rasp, slamming my fist into his temple to encourage him. His legs snap around my waist, bucking me off in a violent spin, and in one smooth movement I'm pinned, his grip even tighter around my throat. Black dots creep into the corners of my vision as his fist pounds into my face, each strike a violent and brutal. The split in my lip from yesterday reopens, the slice of pain almost getting me off quicker than Harper did. Almost.

"Fuck yeah. Give me more, Big Boy." Clayton tears himself off me as if I've burned him, leaving me splayed on the floor with blood dripping down my lips, copper sweet and addictive on my tongue.

"You're so fucking twisted. I'll never understand why she let you near her," Clayton growls, stalking away with his fists still balled. "Is that why you called me here, you sick bastard? To goad and then fight me?"

I open my mouth to reply that actually, I called him here because I can't trust my lackies to carry a hot, naked woman out of my house and not be tempted. I may not want Harper maddeningly in love with me, because clingy girls give me the biggest ick, but that doesn't mean I want her at anyone's mercy. At least I know Clayton is too noble to touch her. And yeah, maybe a little bit, I wanted to goad him into a fight. But I don't get to say any of that.

The door beside me flies open and a lithe half-dressed nymph bursts into the hall, hurdling over my body without pause. The shirt, *my shirt*, rides high as she vaults, flashing a glimpse of rounded perfection, her bed-tangled hair messed up divinely in a way that appears freshly fucked. My brain stutters.

"Oh Clay, thank God! Get me out of here before anyone sees me here!"

Hold up, what did she say? I shove myself upright, grabbing Harper's shoulder and spinning her back to face me. Clayton's chest rumbles when his eyes catch the hickey blooming on her neck. If only he knew there are bite marks all over her breasts and thighs, branding her as mine. Wait, no, *fuck*.

Harper's gaze holds mine, not even tempted to dip to where my shirt is loosely buttoned over my stomach. To where her claw marks bled me dry beneath my tattoos. Her lips are beautifully bruised, their deepened red and slightly puffy appearance sending an arrow of lust straight to my dick. Yet, all of the desire from last night has vanished, distaste left in its wake.

"Why are you in such a rush to leave?" I ask harshly, accusation in my tone. Harper reads my lips, not bothering to turn on the mic clutched in her hand.

"I don't want anyone to know that I..." She waves in the air, gesturing to all of me. My left eye twitches.

"You're ashamed? Of me? That's not right," I shake my head. Behind her, Clayton chuckles, tapping her arm for her attention. She blinks up at him with wide, green eyes. Looking at him like he's her damn savior. Yeah, I've really fucked up here.

"This idiot," Clay nudges his chin in my direction but maintains her eye contact, "thought one night would make you fall head over heels in love with him." His grin is wider than I've ever seen, encouraging the same to grow over Harper's face. She giggles, once, twice, and suddenly dies in a fit of hysterics whilst holding her sides. Clayton laughs too, taunting echoes booming around the hallway. Harper raises her hand to rest it on his chest, absorbing his laughter through her fingertips. All the while, I stand there, heat rushing to my cheeks, bile rising in my throat.

"You thought," Harper manages to force through her hysteria, "you have some sort of magical dick." She's wheezing now, tears streaming through the smudged mascara from last night. I narrow my eyes, grinding my teeth. I don't know if Harper has ever heard herself laugh, but it isn't the cute, restrained, hidden behind a hand type that girls usually do. It's full-bodied and loud, grating against my ears, particularly because it's aimed at me.

Clayton winds an arm around her shoulders, making a half-ass attempt to put a finger over his lips to stop her from waking the entire house. Somehow, it doesn't have the same effect when he is also howling, and the house is stirring already. I plaster myself to the wall, watching them leave like I wanted, despite the regret cutting deeper than any blade.

She's walked out on me. Barely looked at me. I'm stuck rooted in place, unable to decide how to react until they've disappeared, finally out of my vicinity. I've never been laughed at before, not behind my back, not right in my face. No one would dare.

I chase after them, even though they're long gone, emotions I don't understand bringing me to the open front door. A bitter icy chill seeps straight through my shirt, freezing over the fire burning in the pit of my stomach. I welcome it, inhaling deeply, standing there until my toes go numb and my chest holds a different kind of burn.

This isn't how tonight was supposed to go. Woo her, fuck her, forget her. That was the plan, and I got what I wanted. I had her screaming my name, clawing at me like I was the last breath in her lungs, begging for the strength only I can give. And somehow, I'm the one standing here furious, and dare I say lusting for her. How do I still want more? Why do I crave her like she didn't just humiliate me? I don't chase seconds. I don't circle back. I'm in a house filled with women I could have at the snap of my fingers. Yet not a single one appeals to me. I didn't ruin Harper. She's ruined me.

Ugh, where is my self-respect? I'm not going to stand here and *pine* for a girl who just left with someone else, regardless of my part in that scenario. Nor am I going to stand here being made to look like a fool. Slamming the door closed, I turn and kick a nearby inflatable ball with all my might. The neon orange sphere bounces off the wall to my left and slams right back into my face. I can't contain my bellow now, grabbing the offensive piece of plastic and marching into the kitchen. Jagged knife in hand, I slaughter the shit out of it until the limp plastic falls to my feet.

"That's it! Everybody out!" I roar, my fists clenched as tight as my jaw. Bodies suddenly jolt up and scurry like rats, most piling out of the door without their clothes. A pounding in my head starts to pulse as I spiral into a depth of rage I haven't stooped to in a while. Now that it's back, I suddenly realize how long it's actually been. Around two or three weeks I reckon, just before a green eyed girl steamrolled into my life and turned my world on its head.

I'll be damned if I'm going to sit stewing in misery all day. I need to purge it from my system, fast, because if I don't, it will spread and consume every thought. I've learnt from experience I make shitty choices when I'm distracted. This morning is case and point.

Grabbing a female with electric blue hair by the arm as she tries to leave, I pull her outside onto the porch. A line of piercings follows the outline of her ears which instantly reminds me of Harper's receivers. I physically slap myself to knock the image from my mind, much to her confusion.

"I need you to hurt me," I rasp. Her brown eyes widen and she tries to step away but I latch onto her wrist to hold her in place. "No catch or repercussions. Just do as I say and I'll make sure you graduate with honors."

Her fear stirs something unpleasant in me, not guilt, but recognition. As if she sees what I am trying to bury, and I cannot allow that. On her hesitant nod, I pull a pack of cigarettes and my zippo from my back-jean pocket, handing them to her and removing my shirt. Tossing it over the balcony railing, I point to the bare patch of skin on my lower back and brace myself. Not for pain but for the clean disconnection it brings, the one thing that stills the anarchy in my being. The pain I can control. When nothing happens, when hesitation clogs the air between us, I growl at her over my shoulder until she sparks up a flame.

The first sting comes and with it the flood, a surge of white static coursing through me, cutting off the noise that has been screaming inside my skull. I hear myself groan, low and guttural, welcoming the release like an addict chasing a fix. "Again," I bark, because once is never enough, because I know what it takes to scrape myself hollow until the emotions can no longer find a place to settle.

No amount of therapy has been able to help me, to stop these urges. They're not urges, not impulses, but survival tactics written into my bones. It is a base need which calls to me like a whisper on the wind, drawing me into a lull of peace others would run from. Long story short, I'm broken, but this is how I keep myself stitched together, as crude and temporary as it may be.

My unwilling torturer grabs a plastic cup from the floor and uses jacuzzi water to throw across my back. Like the damage, my internal agony is extinguished almost instantly, leaving behind the kind of emptiness I crave. She frets about the redness and the scarring until I shoo her away, needing to be alone now with only the afterglow of agony for company. Once the marks have healed, I'll just have them tattooed over and it will be like they never existed, hidden beneath my ink the way everything else in my life is.

Bending to pick up the cigarettes she dropped, I place one between my lips to spark up on a relaxing inhale. Everyone has different routines and quirks, here's mine, a ritual of obliteration and rebirth. Of burying what I don't want to acknowledge beneath layers of loathing. This way,

I'm safe. No one can hurt me, no one can reject me or laugh in my face, and no one dares to walk out on me.

At least one thing has become clear through all of this. I dropped the ball. I gave Harper Addams too much power over me. Every thrust, every broken gasp, every shuddering roll of her hips. The way her skin glowed against mine, the way she rode me with those perfect curves, the way her eyes rolled back every time my piercing hit her sweet spot.

I lost my precious control, and I will do whatever it takes to get it back.

CHAPTER TWENTY FOUR

What was I thinking? Well, I wasn't. At. All. The first party I've ever been to, and I have officially entered into a war with the campus queen bee and then gone ahead and slept with the host, who just so happens to be her on/off boyfriend and sworn enemy to the man currently clutching my arm. Not my brightest strategy.

I allowed myself to be pulled into Rhys's mind games, convincing myself I needed to be a fully fledged student. As if the enrolment papers, long classes, and constant feeling of failure weren't enough. Nope, I figured a hot one-night stand was going to give me a sense of fulfilment. Maybe I thought it would be thrilling to know I conquered the bad boy billionaire.

Instead, I gave him exactly what we wanted. Another faceless body to add to his endless collection. I let myself be used harder than a recyclable condom, and the humiliation burns hotter than the walk of shame I'm currently on.

At least Aunt Marg will have something to gasp about when she calls later today, though I imagine this will send her reaching for her blood pressure tablets. Yeah, I'll keep this one to myself. In fact, I'll keep this from every human being I encounter for the rest of my life. Except myself of course, because as soon as I collapse into bed later, every detail will come back to taunt me in vivid detail. The delicious ache between my thighs, the heat of his mouth on mine, the reckless way he made me forget that I ever swore to hate him.

His eyes devoured me before he even touched me. His hands, soft from never having done a real day's labor, clutched at me like I was the last thing tethering him to earth. Twice last night and once again this morning, he claimed me. Owned me. I was the buffet, and he was the starved man who would not stop eating. Literally. He didn't ask for permission. He took and my body betrayed me by giving, wanting, and begging for more.

It's a little late for a revelation now, but my self-preservation digs deep for one anyway. There isn't much else to do, walking into campus on Clay's arm, ignoring the crushing weight of his judgement. Instead, I use this time and the cold slice of morning wind to compartmentalize. I had one hell of a regrettable night, and it's done now. Rhys will finally be satisfied and leave me alone, and I can move on. I can concentrate on what's important. What I came to Waversea Academy for.

Clay walks slow, matching the smaller strides of my boots to keep us in sync. Most likely to keep himself from flying into the lecture I know is brewing on his tongue. I've clipped my mic onto the belt snatched around my waist, and purposely left it switched off. As far as outfits go, there's no mistaking what I've been up to, but hopefully it's not too obvious where I'm coming from. Although, contrasting against Clay's hand-me-down military jacket with patches covering the worn elbows, the stark-white Gucci shirt is like a beacon of bad decisions.

A frown tugs between my brows. I've yet to question what Clayton was doing at Rhys' house. Why he was hanging around outside Rhys' bedroom in fact, finishing a fight I doubt he started. And more than that, why Clay keeps appearing when I'm in a situation I have no business getting myself into. I'm beginning to notice his pattern, laying low until needed, showing up when I'm at my lowest. Reliable. Dependable. Kissable.

I stop in my tracks, heat rushing to my cheeks as Clay glances back with a questioning look. Holy shit, Harper. What is wrong with you? My brain is clearly running on fumes, a severe lack of sleep and no caffeine stirring inside. A rumble in my stomach confirms it as I catch sight of the cafeteria doors. Might as well give everyone something else to talk about.

"Grab breakfast with me?" I look up into Clay's endlessly black eyes. He glances uncertainly at the building and back to me, a look of regret passing his features. "Please, my treat." Using our linked arms, I look straight ahead so he knows I can't read his lips, and drag him inside.

Even without being able to hear it, the room falls into a stagnant hush. Eyes follow us, wide and shameless, like my life is suddenly the Saturday morning special. My newly-pink hair is a bird's nest, tamed only by my fingers, the make-up around my eyes leans more into panada than smokey, and the oversized shirt I'm wearing does little to hide my black underwear underneath. Standing tall, I cross the room with squared shoulders. Let them look. Let them whisper.

I grab a tray, order him a double espresso since he refuses to choose, and pile high two plates with eggs, bacon, hash browns. For myself, an orange juice and a coffee large enough to resurrect the dead. The perfect hangover cure. While I swipe my ID card, Clay carries our tray to a table tucked into the back, far from the curious stares. I give them a few narrowed-eye glares right back, wondering what weirdos are up and dressed this early on a weekend if they don't need to be. From the table, Clay gives me a small smile, his focus steady as if I am the only person for miles. It's surprisingly grounding as I take my seat and inhale my coffee.

Not prepared to waste my limited energy on lipreading, I switch on my mic and slide it between us. Clay watches me dive into my plate like one of those disgustingly intense nature shows. I forgot to warn him I left my manners at the door. After an awkward minute of lip smacking and aggressive chewing, I glance up to find it's not me that has his attention. His eyes are fixed on the plate before him with a slight crease between his brows. I slow the rate of my knife and fork, wondering when I last saw him in the cafeteria. When I last saw him eat in fact.

"Ugh, please don't make me eat alone," I pout. Eventually, whatever chivalrous mindset Clay was battling with fades away and he picks up his fork. He hesitates, then starts eating with a hunger that breaks something fragile in my chest. He clears the plate in record time, while I become the creep who's staring. My stomach doesn't let me pause for too long, growling for more substance until we're both finished.

We linger, longer than we should, just breathing the same air and pretending the world does not exist. I distract myself with a game of "What's the story" about a sophomore and his boyfriend, until Clay's voice in my head makes me jump.

"Do you ever wish you were like everyone else again?" he asks directly into the mic, which he's lifted to his mouth. I reach over to lower his hand with a sympathetic grin. Let's not deafen me any further.

"Quite the opposite actually," I shrug. Clay doesn't ask me to explain but for some reason, my usual defensiveness falters. I find that I want to give him more, to appease the genuine curiosity in his expression. "I'd prefer if everyone else was like me. Imagine how many arguments wouldn't exist because no one could be bothered to sign them. I get to live in my own bubble, free from lies, free from the noise."

"That must be nice." Clay nods thoughtfully, leaning forward, tongue wetting his lips. I track the movement too closely for someone who's baring the hickeys of another man. What a wild ride this academy is turning out to be. Returning from whatever mental dive Clay just took, he blinks the daze from his eyes and comes back to me. "What sound do you miss the most?"

Now there's a question I don't have a rehearsed answer for. In my bitterness, I've come to see all sounds as a concoction of obnoxious noise. But now I'm running through the catalogue of sounds I remember from my childhood, one in particular sticks out.

"My parents loved the seaside. Every summer we traveled, always to somewhere with a beach. It seems stupid really, paying out so much for the same horizon, but I loved it too. The best part was swimming in the sea on a calm day and sinking beneath the surface with my eyes closed. The muffled beat of my own pulse, the waves lapping against me, the illusion that I could hear a whale somewhere in the deep. Once, it began to rain while I was under. I felt like nature's orchestra was playing just for me."

As the words leave me, they scrape against a place inside I rarely allow myself to touch. I keep my memories of them locked away because once they slip past the surface, they multiply like a sickness I cannot cure. The pang is sharp and cold, a reminder of what has been stolen, of what can never be returned. My chest feels too tight, like grief itself is trying to crawl back in, demanding I let it spread through every vein. I know if I let it, I would drown myself in their absence. But I also know they would never want me to spiral and throw my life away in their name. They would want me to keep moving forward, even if it feels like walking barefoot on glass.

I only realize I am on the verge of tears because my expression is mirrored on Clay's face. Grief is painted all over his sharp features, his eyes sunken and all too understanding. My heart stumbles, tripped by nostalgia and guilt for having forgotten those memories until now. "Oh god, that sounded ridiculous," I force a laugh and shake my head.

Clay reaches out, laying his hand on mine. I stare at our point of touch, where his hand swallows my smaller one, where his commanding warmth settles over me. This is the point when I'm told, it's okay, they'd be proud of you. It's okay, you survived. But it's not okay and it's simply not fair. I clear my throat, banishing the despair back to the pit of my soul.

"What about you? Tell me something interesting about your life."

"There's nothing interesting about my life," Clay replies instantly and evenly. I blink a few times, recognizing that's all I'm going to get and even more depressingly, he believes it. I drop the subject and withdraw my hand to cover a yawn pulling at my mouth.

"Will you walk me back to my room?" I ask cheerily. Clay's out of his seat as if it burnt his ass, offering me the crook of his arm again. Grabbing my mic and using his forearm to pull myself up, I smile with a slight shake of my head.

"Please don't move that fast before my second coffee of the day. Maybe third." A rumble of a chuckle passes from his body to mine, finishing as quickly as it started. More of those bitchy looks are passed around as we leave and I roll my eyes at each one. People really need to get better hobbies. Gently tugging on my arm, Clay draws my attention to the library steps.

"Just so you know, I'm in the library every evening from seven. If you should...I mean, if there's anything I can help with." He swallows uncomfortably and I quirk a brow.

"Clayton Michaels. Are you offering to tutor me?"

"Whatever you need," he half-shrugs but I don't miss the bashful smile as he looks away. A warm feeling spreads beneath my skin despite the chilly breeze curling around my bare legs. We walk the rest of the way in silence, the material of his jacket and my shirt acting as a barrier between our linked arms. His presence is so calming, like a soothing balm to my being with an undercurrent of protectiveness, though I can't quite figure out if I deserve it.

Reaching my dorm block, Clay holds open the door and sees me safely inside. I pause at the stairs, remaining a step higher to be closer to his eye level.

"Um, thanks for ... whatever this was," I tug my hair behind my ear while his black eyes track the movement. I still as his hand raises and untucks the same strand, playing with it in his fingers much like Rhys did. Not a comment I will be making out loud, but the moment stretches on and I find I need to say something. Anything. "You haven't commented on the color change," I settle on, inwardly cringing. Great job fishing for compliments Harper.

"I have not." Clay states clearly. I watch his lips, again hanging on for elaboration and not receiving one. Screw it.

"Do you like it?" I chew on my bottom lip, watching Clay's eyes narrow in thought. He straightens, keeping the pink strands in his hold.

"Did you do it for him?" Finally, the elephant in the room presents itself. Or in this case, the jackass in the stairwell. My nose scrunches up and I scoff.

"Hell no. I only do things that appease me." I'm certain my tone reflects my confidence and betrays none of the incident where I was forced to change my hair color. Clay searches my face before producing a singular nod.

"Then I like it." I bite back my smile, not surprised by all the warm fuzzies that flood my mid-section. In the midst of my bad decisions, no matter how pleasurable they were, I feel like I've made a tiny break-through with Clay. Only cracking of the tip of a mountain, but still more than I thought I ever would. Clay's hand hovers between us and for a second I think he's going to cup my jaw but then he wishes me a peaceful rest and leaves. Le sigh. Ever the gentleman.

Jogging up the stairs two at a time, I can practically hear my bed calling my name. The headache, the soreness and the shame are all teaming up with a plan to keep me nestled beneath my covers all week-end. Not that I'm complaining. Despite my inner complaining, I don't regret last night. Somehow, I managed to have a self-proclaimed king at my mercy and all of his attention honed on my pleasure, as if his entire world revolved around my body for one single night.

And then, the morning after, my self-appointed savior reminds me I won't be facing Rhys' wrath alone. It won't be long before there's some sort of retaliation for running from his frat house with another man. That would be an ego beating for any man, whether the lesson was long overdue or not. But Rhys needs to learn he can't have every-thing his own way all of the time.

Approaching my door, I notice another gift bag identical to yesterday's hanging from the handle. This one has lilac tissue paper poking out and is missing any kind of tag. The audacity of that bitch! I locate the spare key balanced on top of the doorframe and let myself in, promptly chucking the gift bag onto the dresser. The room is still, the curtains still drawn even though the sun has turned them almost transparent. I drop down onto my bed with a groan, causing a lumpy shape in Addy's bed to stir at the same time her fuchsia-covered head appears from behind it.

My brows raise and a smile grows across my face. Tut, tut, naughty girl. For the ease of my eyes, I click my receivers into place to wish the pair a good morning, and then promptly tell them to take it elsewhere before I pass out. I open my mouth as the cover drops down.

A busty brunette with several tattoos and dermals similar to Addy's shoots upright, wide eyed and flustered. Jumping from the bed, she gathers all of her clothes and chunky boots from the floor and scampers into the hallway butt naked. I try to tell her there's no need to be shy but she's gone before I can form a sentence. I gape at Addy, who's face has turned a color to match her hair.

"Well, it didn't take too long to get over Aaron. Should I be worried about you mounting me in my sleep now?" I laugh, dodging the sequined cushion Addy has chucked at my head.

"You'd be so lucky!" She squeaks, wrapping herself in the sheet to hobble over onto my bed. I grumble and shove her aside, trying to lay my head onto the pillow but she's surprisingly strong. "Nah ah! You owe me alllll the juicy details! What happened with Rhys and why can I smell Clayton on you?"

"Later," I groan, shoving her again. My head falls back onto my pillow and I sigh with the biggest smile on my face. Sweet bed, sweet dorm room, and once I tug off my receivers, sweet silence. Addy tucks me in, no doubt demanding that I spill my secrets later. I drift into a blissful sleep before I can ask how she even knows what Clayton smells like.

HARPER

CHAPTER TWENTY FIVE

Peterson's monotone fills both the room and my head, sinking into the background like white noise. He's scrawling some equation across the whiteboard, his sleeve already streaked with black marker, but I'm not hearing a single word. I'm too aware of the two bodies flanking me.

Any hopes of an easy morning were dashed when Rhys materialized in the classroom doorway. He appeared far too alert, as if there was a triple shot of coffee in his protein shake. Instead of taking his usual seat up front, he slouched in the chair to my right, legs spread wide and twisted in my direction. Keeping my back straight, I'm determined to ignore whatever game he's trying to play, even if it's stifling all of my motivation.

Clayton sits to my left, arm stretched along the back of my chair in an act of protection. He's grown bolder as the class stretches on, his fingers subtly brushing against my shoulder. I don't need to look to check if Rhys is watching the movement, and if I wasn't trying so hard to keep them both from blowing up, I would shrug it off. As it stands, Clay is forming a shield around me, his body wound tight with anticipation.

It's suffocating. Every time I glance up at Peterson, Rhys's boot taps against my chair leg, pulsing like a countdown. Clayton leans forward, pencil scratching furiously over his notebook, but the rigid set of his jaw tells me he's seconds from snapping. I can't tell him to knock it off, I've brought this all on myself.

Peterson clears his throat. "Neuroregeneration through protein stimulation. Take notes, you'll need this for the midterm." My pen is poised in place, burning an inky hole through my notepad, but I can't catch a single word, never mind form a sentence.

My mind is hazy from Rhys' undeterred attention at the side of my face, succeeding in making me uncomfortable. I use my hair to block him out, shifting the pink strands between us. Instead of sleeping all weekend, I slipped off campus with Addy to a salon in the local town. The patchy pink is now a blend of dark dusty rose into lighter ends. Now that it appears much more purposeful, I'm falling in love with how the color sets my green eyes alight.

Noticing my poor effort to ignore the tattooed, entitled prince beside me, Clay shifts his notepad in my direction so I can copy from him, a note written in the corner.

Try to concentrate. He'll leave once he's bored.

Noting my small smile and nod, Rhys sits forward too, his breath ghosting over my cheek. His chest rumbles against my shoulder, before he takes my notebook and tears a page clean out. I try to protest but he steals the pen from my hand, since he didn't bring anything to class except himself and his shaker bottle.

I'm always bored. And I'm not leaving.

Narrowing my eyes, I snatch my pen and paper back. I suppose we're doing this, but it's better than sitting here and pretending my temperature isn't hiking higher and higher. That the men closing in on me aren't forcing my thighs to clench harder to try and give my libido some sort of relief.

Save the playground games for the courtyard. We're trying to focus here.

Sliding the paper to Rhys, he holds his hands up in defeat and twists himself away, hunched over the page. I exhale, glad for the reprieve of his attention. Clay rolls his eyes and offers me a pen, since Rhys has apparently now stolen mine, and finally I manage to get some notes down. Assessments are on the horizon and I can't afford to fall behind. I can't keep allowing the distractions to win.

Peterson drones on about cellular pathways, the rest of the students with their heads down in concentration. The redheaded boy a few rows in front has peered back twice, trying to catch Clay's eye but it's clear, to me at least, that he's being ignored. The end of class looms nearer and I'm starting to think we're going to make it out of here unscathed, until Rhys slams his piece of paper over my notes. For a second, I consider not looking, just pushing it away. But curiosity wins, dragging my eyes down.

My stomach plummets.

Rhys has sketched in brutal, vulgar detail. I didn't know he had such an artistic streak. A girl unmistakably drawn with my hair and my curves is kneeling between his thighs, her lips wrapped around his cock. We're both completely naked, my breasts marked with his teeth imprints, tears streaming from my wide eyes. Rhys has given himself no shortage of muscle, ribbed abs and thick veins all heading south to his huge girth. It appears my jaw is dislocated just to take him all the way in, drool seeping out.

His smirk is scribbled perfectly, mocking even on paper, one hand gripping her hair so tight it looks painful. Scrawled in the margin are crude little notes. *Babygirl on her knees. Knows how to beg. Mouth made for me.* The man beside me grins wide, leaning in close to lick the shell of my ear.

I jolt aside, quickly hiding the page beneath the table, but it's too late. Clay has seen it. His face has frozen over, jaw tight as his arm withdraws from the back of my chair. The tendons in his neck strain, his fists curling so tight that his knuckles turn white. The look he throws at Rhys is nothing short of feral, and I shrink back in my seat. There's no use trying to be a barrier between them now, Rhys has gone too far.

"*Outside. Now.*" Clayton states from silent lips, his chest rumbling.

"Clay, it's not worth it," I whisper, wrapping a hand around his thigh. I might as well not exist, his black eyes glimmering with the promise of bloodshed. Shaking his head, Clay nudges my hand free.

"*No one disrespects you.*" Rising to stand, Rhys does the same until the two are towering over me. I hear the screeches of chairs and the following whispers drifting to Peterson's mic, the man himself finally aware of what's happening in the back of his class. He gapes at me, unsure whether to intervene or run for assistance. Every student in the room is looking back, some lifting their phones. I pray for the ground to open up and swallow me whole.

A hand touches my hair and I flinch, blinking up to see Rhys grinning down at me. His fingers curl behind my ear and dip to my jaw, tilting me up to watch him speak.

"*Harper loves being disrespected. Don't you, Babygirl?*" he says, and I slam my eyes closed. Rhys is torn from me a moment later. I feel the vibrations of furniture crashing through the legs of my chair, distantly hearing them through the microphone.

For reasons I don't care to explain, as I rush to grab my stuff, the drawing is also shoved into my backpack. Twisting away, I take the safe route to the front desk and snatch my mic, hooking it on the neckline of my t-shirt. The rest of class have congregated by the white board, deeming that as a safe space. I look up in time to see Clayton throw Rhys through the door and into the hallway.

The crowd rushes to follow whilst I stand there and groan at the ceiling. I take it back, I didn't bring this on myself. I'm just the newest fascination in their lengthy rivalry. Left alone with Peterson and the redheaded boy still sitting at his desk, diligently writing away, I look for an escape. There's no way I'm going into that hallway to separate those two when they are in full dog-pissing mode. They're fully grown men who can make their own choices. I'll just deal with the aftermath later.

"Ah hem, Miss Addams?" Peterson steps closer, his expression closed off. "To put it plainly, Mr. Michaels is one of my top students. I'm afraid to say, if you cannot keep from being a distraction, I may have to suggest some other type of provision for you to the Dean." My mouth drops open.

Me? I'm the distraction?! It's Rhys who is the distraction, doing everything in his power to see me fail before I've even started.

Peterson doesn't wait for a response, lifting his laptop bag and pushing his way through those blocking the doorway. I stand there, dumbfounded, my face blazing. How dare Peterson blame me for the circus happening outside. All I've done is keep my head down whilst struggling to keep up, clinging to every sliver of information I can grasp onto. I cast a glance over the lab, setting my jaw with the wrath of an underestimated woman.

If Peterson thinks I'm a distraction, then I might as well be one.

Beyond the redhead, the counters are lined with glassware and half-used solutions from the last demonstration. I approach the workstation nearest the window, the pulse in my throat kicking up a beat. Without considering the consequences, I dive in, fueled by stubbornness.

My hands move without reservation, uncapping one and pouring another. Silly little dumb deaf girl somehow knows what solutions will react with each other. Which liquid will act as a catalyst. Oh, how stupid it would be of me to tip this vial into that beaker. A hiss sounds through my receivers, the mixture bubbling within the beaker. It would be foolish to uncap the sodium and pour the entire lot in, I think as I do it. Oops, what an air head I am.

There's a moment of quiet around me, the hiss fading out just long enough for me to come to my senses. *Oh shit.* The glass vibrates just before it shatters, shooting glass in all directions. I scream at the small lacerations cutting across my arms and cheeks, not noticing the gloopy liquid trailing along the countertop, directly for the basin. I blink up too late, my heart lurching at the pouring faucet. I'm sure it wasn't on a moment ago. Before I can shout nitric acid, the mixture drips into the basin and I dive for cover as a hollow boom denotes behind me.

Beneath the nearest table, I cower from the chaos I've created.

Light flashes and crackles, liquid hissing where it spits against tile, floor and tabletop. My arms curl tight over my head, lungs burning from the chemical sting in the air. For a second, I am ten years old again, pressed between my parents in the car, sound crashing within my skull, everything breaking and the searing burn of pain consuming me. Unable to draw breath, unable to scream, I wait for the black out.

Instead, two solid walls slam into me from either side. Strong arms wrap around my body, Clay dragging me back against his chest. Rhys shoves in from the other side, swearing under his breath as a second beaker explodes behind him. I've set off a chain reaction, slowly eating its way across the counter and combusting everything in its way. I hide my face in Rhys' shoulder, his hands clasping over my ears as he kneels before me. It's a useless endeavor, but the notion warms me all the same.

Their rivalry dissolves as they cover me, fighting with their own desperation to shield me. Clay's heart hammers against my back, Rhys's breath ragged near my temple.

The table rattles above us, another shard skittering down the slope of the metal leg. My breath saws sharp through my throat, every nerve ending alight with pain old and new. Memories contort the room around me, the edges of the car pressing in, my parents shouting to keep down, stay strong. That's how I know it's not real. They didn't get the chance to mutter anything, the crash too sudden and devastating. Burning tears stream down my face, mixing with the small cuts and stinging slightly.

"The fuck were you thinking," Rhys mutters amongst a string of other curses. I quickly come to the conclusion he doesn't know I can hear him. "You're not allowed to harm what's mine. You're mine, you stupid, beautiful idiot. Only I get to hurt you." The murmuring goes on and on, so much so that Clay ignores it.

Clay's chest cages my back, the steady thud of his heart pulsing against my spine. His fingers are splayed over my arms, gripping me as if I might slip free. Eventually, the raining of explosions settles down and I catch the exact moment Clay and Rhys look at each other and realize what they've just done. They came for me, acting purely on instinct. No glares, no insults, no searing hatred.

Similarly to earlier, I'm caged between them, but it's oh so different. Instead of being suffocated, a stillness settles. Even the images of my past hover outside of our huddle, my focus centered on Rhys' thumb smearing my tears away. He holds me reverently, allowing the three of us a moment free of the cocky bullshit to simply *be*.

If these two stubborn, volatile men can forget their hatred long enough to protect me, possibly there is a chance. A tiny, impossible glimmer of a future that doesn't have to be this endless battlefield. Maybe I am not a prize or a distraction, but something worth shielding.

I clutch to Clayton, Rhys and that thought with trembling fingers, letting it warm the cold pit inside me, even as the fire alarm begins to wail overhead.

CLAYTON

CHAPTER TWENTY SIX

After the demise of Peterson's lab, I hadn't expected Harper to take me up on my offer of study sessions. I actually thought she'd shun me, choosing to sit elsewhere in our classes, thoroughly done with the macho bullshit I can't seem to contain. Yet she's been taking her seat beside me each day and she's been at the library every night all week without fail, seven on the dot like clockwork.

Surprisingly, Rhys took all of the heat for Monday's fight and explosion. Dean O'Sullivan came down on him hard, but apparently not as hard as his father. Demanding Rhys work off his recklessness through manual labor, he's been helping to clear out the lab, one shard of glass and piece of splintered wood at a time. I caught sight of him crossing the quad with a paint can in hand, his usually manicured hands covered in lacerations, and thankfully that's the only time I've seen him. It's been a blissful reprieve for Harper and me to meet up without any interference.

Waiting at the same table as always, Harper has two cups of coffee and a wide smile at the ready, as though she's carved a space in time just for me. I'm getting better at returning that smile without instinctively angling my head downwards, and she has definitely noticed.

Tonight, she's wrapped in a ridiculous wearable blanket that swallows her whole in a mass of fluffy gray sleeves. Her hair is loose, soft waves catching the library lights, deep rose blending into the lighter pink at the ends.

Even if I wanted to tell her how the color suits the frame of her face or makes her features appear much softer, I wouldn't know how to put it into words. I categorically cannot tell her how her hair has become a fixture in my dreams, scattered over my chest or brushing against my cheek, often waking me with painfully-hard morning wood.

Setting in for another evening of caffeine and flicked pages, Harper draws her index finger from her ear to her mouth, signing that she currently can't hear. She holds out her hand and I pass over my textbook. We always start like this, Harper cross-checking her notes with mine, making sure she hasn't missed anything or filling in the blanks when Hargreaves mutters too quietly for her mic to pick up. She dives straight in, her fingers drumming along the edge of the page until it's time to turn it.

I unpack my bag, putting two packs of cookies between us as subtly as I can. Regardless, my cheeks flame when her green eyes flick up, and I shrug it off. My latest scholarship payment actually came through on time, so I figured it's time to repay the endless coffee she's supplying us. No big deal. I absolutely did not spend twenty minutes staring at the shelves, trying to decide if hazelnut or oatmeal raisin would be best. In the end, I just bought both and left the store in a huff. One day, I won't overanalyze simple decisions. Today is not that day.

Opening my folder, I pick up where I left off editing my thesis. These sessions were meant to be me teaching Harper, yet she devoured the first draft I sent over and handed it back marked with notes and corrections. She's smart. Really smart on paper, that is. Some of her life choices are questionable.

Every so often, I glance over, possibly to remind myself she's still there. Still softly humming to herself, still becoming comfortable in my icy presence. I've never been one for small talk, and Harper doesn't care for it. Too many words to decipher from my lips when she's trying to focus on studying.

The library hums around us, packed as usual, students crammed shoulder to shoulder, laptops clattering, groans of defeat leaking into the air like smoke. I'm not sure how Harper always manages to secure this same table, claiming it as our spot right in the middle.

I work through her suggestions, removing post-it notes as I go, swiftly making the necessary changes and finishing up around the same time she thumps the textbook back onto the table. Without asking, she reaches over for my folder, collecting the snacks on the way. Harper nibbles on the oatmeal cookie, reading over my corrections.

The sound is barely audible, just the faintest crunch, but it hits me low in the gut. Her lips curve around the bite, her tongue darting out to swipe a crumb from the corner, and suddenly I'm choking on air. My body tightens, blood rushing south before I can stop it.

I shift in my chair, dragging my thighs wider, rearranging the front of my trousers under the table like I'm some teenage idiot who's never been this close to a girl before. Except this isn't just *a girl*. This is Harper. And she's so utterly oblivious to the mess she's making of me, licking sugar from her fingertip as if it isn't the filthiest thing I've ever seen. Three guesses what tonight's dreams will include. Harper in a tiny pinstripe outfit, standing in the door of a gingerbread house and beckoning me inside.

My cock jumps and I lean my forehead on my closed fist. Stop it Clayton, you're just riling yourself up in public. I force my eyes to chase a scratch on the table over and over, staring at the groove until my rising temperature finally starts to settle. When I'm somewhat under control, I look over to the scrawled notes Harper is making in the margins. She's using my pen, which raises to her mouth and tugs against her bottom lip, drawing it down.

Christ.

She must know what she's doing. No one can be that hot by accident. All I can see in my head is her mouth occupied with something else, and my pulse kicks hard enough to hurt. If she happens to look up right now, she'll see every unholy thought stamped across my pinched face. I tug on my beanie, pulling it further down my forehead.

I shouldn't want her this much. Shouldn't need her attention like a starving man begging for scraps. She's...my friend? Maybe? Or in the very least, she's someone I should be protecting from everything, including myself, but I want more. More of her time, her smiles, the little frown she makes when she concentrates. More of her correcting me, teasing me, scolding me until I earn her approval. More of her sitting across from me, unaware she's the only thing I care to learn anymore.

I want all of her. And that terrifies me more than the hunger clawing through my chest.

"Oh Clay," Harper breathes and I fight against a groan. She really can't say my name like that in public. Placing my folder down, Harper blinks a few times, tears collecting in her eyes. Like a bucket of ice water to my dick, I shoot upright in my seat.

"What's wrong? Was it really that bad?" I frown. Holy crap, my thesis is a complete car crash and she's just been humoring me this whole time. Harper wipes her eye and shakes her head. She digs out a microphone clip and signals for me to clip to my collar.

"It's incredible, Clay, honestly." Harper lowers her voice, cautious of those nearby. She knows I don't like praise, especially out in the open, but she also knows the subject of my thesis is extremely personal. After all, I used my mom's case file to back up my reasoning. Harper passes the folder over and I stare down at the text. *Molecular Insights into Dementia: From Mechanisms to Therapeutic Interventions.*

"Thank you," I mutter back, withholding the rest of what I should have said. I want to thank her, not just for the proofreading, but for not asking questions. For not treating me any different once I'd plucked up the courage to share a part of my past with her. I think I was desperate to let someone in, and here she is. Present, attentive and consistent. Harper opens her laptop, clearing her throat and digging out a small smile.

"You've inspired me to write about something personal too. I started my own thesis last night." Tilting her screen toward me like she expected me to be nosy, I read the title sitting bold at the top of her blank document. *Human stem cell regeneration and the advancement of regenerative medicines.*

"You didn't get very far," I manage to smirk, feeling the weight of the world lift from my shoulders. Harper reaches over and playfully slaps my bicep, and I chuckle. Actually chuckle in a room full of people. A few heads turn our way, just as unfamiliar with the noise as I am.

"The title is the most important part!" She laughs and drags her laptop back. "It takes a lot of procrastination to settle on a topic. And thanks to you, I've picked one particularly close to home." Leaning on her elbows, Harper flies into unpicking her brain, explaining her idea in full, step by step detail as if she needs to work through it out loud. "I found this study about DNA solution sent through cochlear implants with electrical pulses, tricking the cells into producing neurotrophies and regenerating nerves. Do you understand how insane that is?! I may not want my hearing fixed, but this is ground-breaking for everyone else who does."

Excitement bubbles out of her, evident in the way her hands are alive, sketching invisible formulas in the air. She's glowing. I would happily watch her talk about paint drying, but this? Her passion, her brilliance, her inner nerd. It makes my chest ache in a way I don't have a name for.

"Wow," I murmur, because she deserves awe, not my clumsy vocabulary. "And one day, you'll be the one making headlines. Harper the girl who rewired the future." Harper grins smugly.

"Damn straight. And Clayton the biomedical scientist will be right next to me, ridding the world of brain-eating disorders." She winks at me and returns to my notes. I haven't told Harper much of my life yet, but we swapped career goals a few nights ago, so that's a start. I've kept my cards close to my chest for so long, I don't know how to lay them down for her to see, but I want to try. Just not right now.

Flicking through the stack of textbooks she'd already prepared, I find a section on stem cell components that can help her start writing. We swap books, claiming my notepad back so I can continue outlining the next part of my essay. I told Harper I prefer to write on paper so she didn't see the large '*Property of Waversea Academy*' sticker on the front of my borrowed laptop. I have too much pride, even if there's nothing in my life to be proud of. Little does she know, I'll be up half the night typing up my notes in bed.

The library begins to thin, students trickling out with dead-eyed groans. But Harper? She's still at it, occasionally asking me to proofread a paragraph before moving on, alternating between chewing on her bottom lip and the cookies between us.

I, however, have barely managed to make a full page of notes. I scratch my hair beneath the black beanie I'm wearing and scrub my hand over my eyes. Either I'm too distracted or I'm burnt out, but since we have our science lab trip tomorrow, I needed to get as much done tonight as possible.

Yet I can't bring myself to care about doing anything other than staring at her. Call this my procrastination. The wild pink curls spilling over her shoulder, the curve of her mouth, the faint brush of her foot against my leg. She probably doesn't even realize she's doing it, but I feel every pass like a live wire down my spine.

"Everything okay?" Harper asks suddenly, her voice so soft it feels like it's only for me. Her foot presses more deliberately into my calf now, and I swallow hard. That wasn't an accident. I sit straighter, dragging my gaze from her lips to her eyes. For once, I am okay. With her so close by, the loneliness I'm so accustomed to lingers in the background. The shadows don't press in as hard.

"Yeah, actually everything's—"

"Honey, I'm homeeeeeee!"

A voice detonates across the library like a grenade, all swagger and venom. Even Harper hears him through the mic clipped to my shirt, her head lifting in alarm. Around us, panic ripples through the room. Students scramble, packing up half-finished essays, fleeing like rats from a ship they know is about to sink.

Rhys freaking Wavershit.

Just when I start to let my guard down, that bastard barrels back in like a shit storm. Striding from between the stacks, his gaze locks onto Harper instantly. My heckles rise at the possessive, dangerous edge to his smirk. It's like watching a wolf spot prey, and my body moves before my brain does. I push back my chair, step around the table, and plant myself in his path. Arms crossed, jaw set, every muscle screaming for a fight.

"Aww, are we doing this again, Claybake? Has your leash been slackened enough to go toe to toe with me?" He doesn't slow, sauntering over until we're almost chest to chest and leaning into the mic clipped to my collar like he owns the right to speak through me.

"If you needed a tutor, Babygirl, you only had to ask."

"And what exactly would you be able to teach me, Rhys?" Harper responds from her seat, a heavy dose of sarcasm in her tone. She meant to insult him, but his eyes glimmer with a thousand responses that will tip me over the edge.

"Oh, a great many things, but I was offering to get you the best tutor in the state."

I shove him back, readying my fist to break every bone in his face when Harper's hand lands on my arm. I just about restrain myself, although Rhys blows me a kiss and shoves passed my shoulder to tower over her instead. Harper is the image of calm with an amused smirk, and for a second I worry she might take him up on his proposition.

"Throwing your money around doesn't impress me. I'm happy with the tutor I've got." Her hand tightens around my arm and I puff out my chest. We may not have established what kind of friendship we have, if any, but she's standing up for me. She's choosing me.

Something begins to uncoil within, something I thought was long dead. The need to be seen, to be wanted. Usually I would turn back before it becomes too familiar, but there's no point. Without even trying, Harper has made me ache for it all the same.

Returning to packing away her laptop, I join her side to collect my belongings, ready to get her as far from here as possible. A tattooed shadow rounds the table in my peripheral vision, leaning his hands on the wood in an attempt to get her attention. When he doesn't immediately receive it, Rhys swipes everything from the table including the lamp, the cookies and Harper's highlighters.

"You should know by now not to ignore me. Stop acting as if I haven't been plaguing your mind since–" Holding up a hand to cut him off, Harper rounds the table, pressing herself into Rhys' body. His eyes widen a fraction and as much as he tries to smirk like he's got his own way, there is a flicker of fear tightening his expression. I angle my view, discovering Harper's hand is clutched around Rhys' balls through his sweatpants. I don't have time to feel jealous when she twists and pulls, making even me wince.

"And you should know by now, I don't care for your spoiled rich boy bullshit. Mommy and daddy didn't give you enough attention growing up? Boo fucking hoo. We all have our baggage, and I'm bored of yours." Harper releases him roughly and steps away, drawing a small gasp from Rhys' parted lips. A crimson shade is creeping through the tattoos on his neck, merging onto his face. He shakes his head at himself on a low growl, throwing a fist into the table.

"People are talking about how you're just leading this waste of space along, using him to boost your studies. Everyone can see it except for him. So pathetic." Rhys' lip curls back, his eyes blazing as they stare at me and if I'm not mistaken, I could swear he was jealous. Raising a brow, I play on this, digging up a small quirk of my mouth. His knuckles crack against the wood surface. Yep, definitely jealous. Harper is oblivious to it all, slinging her bag onto her back and tilting her head at him condescendingly.

"When you're ready to talk to me without throwing your weight around, I'll listen. Until then," Harper unclips the mic on my collar and switches it off, cancelling out any further arguments. She moves to leave but he steps into her way. I was about to pick up her missed highlighters but I appear at her back, not thinking too much about that leash comment from earlier. Ready to launch into full attack mode, Rhys surprises us both by taking Harper's wrists and guiding her to where he sits on the table.

"Don't leave," he states plainly. I look around, finding us alone in the center of the library. Somehow in a rapid twist of events, I just became the third wheel.

"Why?" Harper asks. Rhys considers her, his fingers idly stroking her inner wrists as if he can't stop himself. I know the feeling all too well, although I seem to have much more restraint. Watching them together now, I don't know why I've bothered holding back at all.

"I want your attention," Rhys admits, keeping his sentences short for her to read. His tongue toys with his lip ring almost nervously. At this point, I take a few steps back and put the table back to rights. The air between them grows thick with sexual tension, clogging my throat.

I've been with Harper both in classes and at this table all week, yet Rhys has managed to get physically closer to her in a few minutes. I can't understand where the regret within me is stemming from, so I zip up my bag and decide to ponder on it later. Either way, it seems my work here is done. Two steps away from the pair, Harper's voice travels to me.

"You can't demand my attention Rhys, but maybe you can earn it. Let's see, shall we?" Removing herself from his vicinity, Harper hunts for me. A sweet smile and a small wave are passed between us before she leaves us alone. Two lions pitting over the same lioness.

I watch for the moment Rhys launches himself at me in a bid to purge himself of the strain causing his chest to rise and fall in quick succession, but it doesn't come. His jaw ticks, his eyes flicking back and forth across the shelves behind me as if he's deep in thought. Or possibly having a pre-life crisis. Then, they snap to me, sharp as daggers.

"She might think you can give her what she wants, but we both know she's wrong. You're not as surface level as you appear." Rhys pushes off the table, pushing his hands into his sweatpants pockets.

"What's that supposed to mean?" I bite, narrowing my eyes.

"That you might *look* like the kind of guy who can give her flowers, candlelit dinners, and gentle kisses. Make sweet, sweet love to her beneath the stars." Rhys slowly prowls around me, clicking his tongue as he goes. "But you have your demons. I actually think yours run deeper than mine." Appearing before me again, his smirk is back, that glint of his eyes that dances between amusement and insanity.

"In fact, I think you're worse than I am. At least I don't pretend to be anything except this," Rhys unpockets his hands to hold his arms wide. The veins in his arms catch the light, the ink on his skin crawling with disjointed demons. "I admit that I want to bend and break her for my own entertainment. I want to see how many times I can make those beautiful eyes stream with tears, and still have her tremble with lust at the slightest touch. I want to ruin her so thoroughly, she won't know pleasure if it's not by me."

By whatever divine power, I manage to hold my ground. I've fought Wavershit so many times lately, it's losing its appeal. He's still there the next day, ready to go again, stuck in this loop of unending hatred with me. He must feel similarly, because instead of swinging for me, he keeps fucking talking.

"You'll never be enough to fulfill her needs. She's quite the minx, you know?" His arrogant laughter echoes through the library, provoking me to act on the clenched fists at my sides. "Oh, you don't know. Maybe next time I'll record it for you. She begs so well." Rhys ambles back towards the bookshelves he appeared from, leaving me with the uncertainties that threaten to creep back in.

Tilting my head back, I stare at the domed skylight overhead. Complete darkness clings to the glass, and I suck in a few harsh breaths.

Rhys means to goad me. He didn't get his way with Harper so he turned his fangs my way, striking where he thought would puncture the deepest. Perhaps a week ago, he might have done just that. But not now. Not when I've seen how Harper looks at me. How she shifts into my space, seeking my comfort. True, she may desire him, but she craves me.

CHAPTER TWENTY SEVEN

A bus pulls up by the sidewalk at our designated meeting point in the neighboring town. After Rhys' appearance last night, the only sleep I managed to catch was restless, filled with tossing and turning, wondering and worrying.

The moment I stepped out of the library door, I felt the urge to rush back and make sure they weren't tearing each other limb from limb. Then I reminded myself that I'm not their mothers, and I can't always decide the narrative between them. Sometimes removing the source of the issue is best for all involved.

Running on autopilot, I'd automatically gone to a lecture hall before remembering I was supposed to be heading to Grayson Laboratory today. I'm underprepared, underfed and now standing at the back of a line where everyone has already partnered up. The bags under my eyes have paid for extra luggage that not even my fourth coffee of the morning can shift.

Clay is up front with the red-headed boy talking to the side of his face. He peers back, evidently looking for me. Upon finding what he's looking for, he attempts to shove past his companion. I wave him off, seriously lacking the energy to smile and not in the mood for small talk. There's no sign of Rhys amongst the groups chattering excitedly, which I'm extremely thankful for. I shuffle forward and find a quiet corner at the back of the bus, using my bag as a pillow and hoodie as a blanket. I'm asleep before we've even set off.

Amongst the rumbling, a disjointed dream filters to me. Clay and Rhys are seated either side of me at a ridiculously long dining table, like something out of a medieval banquet. Clay is slicing steak into perfect, uniform cubes and placing them neatly on my plate, while Rhys is pouring me an entire goblet of wine and smirking as if he plans on watching me down the whole thing. Their insults fly across me like arrows, but every time one of them lands too close, the other bats it away. At some point, Clay's tie has loosened and Rhys's shirt is missing altogether, though neither seem to notice as they bicker over who gets to peel the grapes for me.

My head jolts forward as the bus comes to a harsh stop, the pounding behind my eyes worsening into a full headache. It's confirmed. I need a hobby and a new set of friends. Groaning, I stretch and sit upright to see what caused our driver to brake so hard. Rhys' Porsche is sprawled across the road, hazard lights blinking on repeat. He strolls towards the Grayson Laboratory's entrance as if the building belongs to him, tossing his keys to a confused lab assistant without breaking stride.

I toy with the idea of staying hidden at the back of the bus. But this is the kind of place I hope to work one day, the kind of building whose glass walls promise to give me everything I keep telling myself I want. This is about refocusing on my future. So I pull my hoodie over my *'Deaf-inatley Too Good For You'* t-shirt and force myself out onto the sidewalk. Regret crashes over me instantly. The sun burns far too bright, bouncing off the glass tower and causing me to squint. The noise from the crowd of students swells like a hive, buzzing with excitement, and my stomach twists with nausea. Or maybe that is just hunger gnawing through me.

Edging closer to the revolving chrome doors, I take in the reflection of a stranger in the glass. Hollow eyes, hoodie slouched, shadows under my cheekbones. I don't linger long. Inside, the reception area stretches open and cold, the chemical tang clinging to every breath. To the right, a metal scanner looms with a guard in black stationed beside it. Straight ahead stands a woman in a fitted lab coat, clipboard tucked beneath manicured fingers, red glasses softening her sharp presence.

"Welcome everyone. I'm Vikki and I'll be your guide today."

Peterson sidles up beside her, looking strangely misplaced in a pressed suit. When I note the way he smiles giddily and stares at Vikki a beat too long, I understand his need to dress up. He hands out blue visitor lanyards and ushers us through the scanner. Hanging back, I rummage for my ID and hold it out.

"I have cochlear implants, I'll set off your metal detector."

The guard studies my card, nods, and sweeps a handheld sensor across my front instead. Satisfied, he waves me forward where Peterson is waiting with a hearing loop, no doubt connected to the mic already clipped to Vikki's breast pocket. Resigned, I tug it over my head and follow the group into the elevator.

Being the last one in means I am the first one out, stepping into a pristinely white hallway. Vikki directs us into a lecture room lined with rows of seats before a large screen. I slip into the back, hoping for anonymity, but of course Rhys claims the chair right next to me. He drapes his arm around the back of my seat, and I bite the inside of my cheek.

I'm not going to let him distract me today, and I'm not going to give him the attention he's so desperate for until he's earned it. I have no idea how he might earn it, but that's not a problem for me to solve. I'm more interested in the solutions he comes up with all by himself.

"I thought we could start with a quick introduction to the lab and its history before you find out what it is we really do here," Vikki begins. Her cheerful voice hums clearly through my implants as the lights dim. The projector flickers to life and casts long shadows over the room.

The quick introduction drags for nearly forty minutes, recounting the empire of Thomas Grayson and his prophetic visions for data analysis long before the world was ready. His grandchildren inherited not only his fortune but his ambition, polishing it into a future that pulses in the walls around us. By the time the presentation ends, my body has sagged into the chair, head tipped back against Rhys' arm.

Just before I get too comfortable and nod back off, we're ushered back out of the room like cattle and ride up to the second floor. "We offer two apprenticeships to Waversea graduates each year." Vikki's words ripple through the elevator as we step into a functioning laboratory. Finally, the anticipation begins to ripple in my being. This is where I envision myself one day, if I manage to survive Waversea that is.

The room spreads wide, every station manned with experiments I ache to get my hands on. Glass beakers bubble with chemical reactions, flasks glinting under strips of clinical light. Against the right wall, fume extraction hoods tower larger than anything I have seen, their windows glowing with shifting colors. Behind one glass pane, two scientists tug hazmat suits over their shoulders before disappearing into a chamber labeled *authorized access only*.

I wander behind the group at a slower pace while they rush from table to table. They move like tourists desperate to collect snapshots while I want to stand still and drink in the details. Engineers move through the room with a quiet rhythm, their hands confident on equipment I can only dream of using. For all their brilliance, they are ordinary people trying to change the world one calculation at a time. Once, they would have been students like me.

I have never been someone who looks too far into the future. Living in the present feels safer, knowing the ground can be pulled out from under me without warning. Tragedy does that to a person. Yet here, I can almost see it. A version of myself hidden away in this labyrinth of white walls, quietly shaping something that matters, not for recognition but for impact.

Vikki's voice filters through my hearing loop even though she is already leading the class toward the back of the lab. "And over here, a group of our scientists are working on creating compounds to tackle antibiotic-resistant viruses such as pneumonia and bloodstream infections."

Her voice keeps me tethered while I investigate on my own. On the opposite side of the room, a cluster of men are hunched over a raised table, the edges of a blueprint spread wide between them. Curiosity tugs me closer. One of them, with short brown hair and freckles scattered across his nose, notices me and waves me over. His lips shape words I can catch.

"Hey, want to take a look?" I nod and they part to let me in. The blueprint is a design for a microscope, but it is stripped back, almost primitive compared to the sleek instruments I have seen. Confused, I wonder why they are wasting their time. "We've simplified the stereo-scopic microscope so we can sell the parts and plans to local universi-ties. They can build it themselves for a fraction of the cost."

He beams, his smile full of straight white teeth and I return it as if that didn't worsen my headache to lipread. Beginning to gush about the brilliance of the idea, a harsh grip clamps around my arm and drags me backwards. My vision fills with Rhys' pale blue eyes, fury swirling within.

"The entire class moved on without you. Don't fall behind."

Every scientist's head turns at the sudden interruption, finding me being manhandled by a guy who thought wearing a Louis Vuitton tracksuit to a lab would impress anyone. Heat floods my cheeks and embarrassment burns into anger. My hand finds the collar of his shirt and I yank him down to whisper in Rhys' ear.

"When I want your hands on me, you'll know about it." I shove him back, ignoring the flare of desire in his eyes, and stride toward the rest of the group. Clay reaches a hand out as I pass, his eyes narrowed on Rhys, but I raise my middle finger and keep walking. I don't need saving today. I need it to be lunchtime. Peterson frowns as I fall into step beside him, but I keep my face forward.

The next room is dedicated to radiochemical analysis. This time we are kept behind a barrier, only able to watch the scientist's through reinforced glass. Their movements are methodical, their focus unshakable. I cling to Vikki's words but my body betrays me, every nerve alert to the weight of a masculine presence hovering on the edges of vision. They're both close, pressing in but not disturbing. I hate my body for responding, the fine hairs on the back of my neck standing on end, but I don't let it show.

We file out of the room in silence, respectful distances being kept. I pretend not to notice how they bump shoulders trying to follow me into the elevator, not expecting them to be on their best behavior all of the time. Something has to give.

The top floor opens into a food hall, the sterile gleam replaced by the comforting smell of coffee and freshly baked bread. A section has been cordoned off for our group with a long table piled with sandwiches and cakes.

I barely register Rhys dropping in beside me, my focus on disconnecting the hearing loop and letting the room blur into the background. Clay is quickly trapped in conversation with the redhead again, much to his irritation but at least he's sitting opposite me. Stacking a plate high with sandwiches and pastries, building a small fortress of carbs, an inked hand pushes a coffee cup in front of me.

"*Shhhh,*" Rhys says, pushing another sandwich into my mouth. "*Talk to me when you're not hangry.*" I scrunch my features up at him but keep eating, one rough tear of teeth on bread at a time. Drawing my attention across the table, I latch onto parts of Clayton's conversation, struggling to keep up with the clench of his jaw.

"*Get - fuck - from me.*"

"*But...we made a deal,*" the redhead replies, appearing to be on the verge of tears. "*You promised – we're friends - didn't speak.*"

"*- deal wasn't - leave me in - gay porno.*"

Wait, that can't be right. I must be way off my game. Shaking my head, I spot Rhys stifling a laugh into a cinnamon roll, licking the icing from his lip ring. My gaze lingers for a beat too long and it doesn't go unnoticed. Beneath the table, Clay's foot tangles with mine, breaking the spell in the most Clayton way possible. Gentle yet meaningful. What is it with these men mind-fucking me today.

Lunch finishes in a blur, two coffees in my system and a small food baby in my gut. Peterson clears away his trash and rounds us all up for the next part of the tour. I switch the hearing loop back on in time to hear Clayton talking to Vikki off to one side. I don't want to make it obvious, even though I should know better than to eavesdrop.

"-really quite brilliant," Clay says. "I would keep her name on file if I were you."

"Thanks for the heads up," Vikki replies before taking the lead ahead of the group. I blink a few times, unable to clear my face of the surprise when Clay approaches.

"Everything okay?" he raises a brow. I bite my bottom lip.

"Yeah, yes. Ahh, sorry about earlier. I didn't sleep well." It's a weak excuse but it's all I've got. I can't come out and say he's half of the duo making me so crazy. Clay smiles as he falls into step.

"I get it. I rarely get a full night these days. Next time, drop me a message. Chances are I'm already awake."

Opening my mouth to respond that I might just do that, Rhys cuts in front of us and I nearly run straight into his chest. *"Or, next time you have trouble sleeping, you can wander over to mine and I can tire you out."* A snort escapes me and I push him aside.

"Ahh, but that would go against your one night only rule." Moving on, we reconvene with the others on the third floor, entering a room that mirrors the lab back at school. Well, the lab before I blew it up. But I'm sure after the renovations are finished, it will be just as... clinical.

"Time for an experiment," Vikki announces to us from behind a bench pre-set with perfectly arranged equipment. "What do you think would happen if we combined sugar and sulphuric acid?"

A few guesses fly around and more than a few snickers sound when it's suggested that 'the deaf girl' can make anything explode. I'm not too sure where it comes from, but my trusty meerkats sit upright at the comment, glaring in the general direction. I don't care either way, raising my hand high in the air.

"The carbon would cause the mixture to blacken and expand."

Vikki smiles at me, seemingly pleased. "Exactly. Now, who would like to come up and try?"

The demonstration begins with Millie tipping sugar into the beaker already sitting inside the fume hood. The liquid darkens, shifts to brown, then black. The mixture bubbles into a grotesque sponge that claws its way above the rim. Next, she adds hydrated copper sulphate, tipping it in carefully and as the mass retracts, the liquid blanching to white.

Steam hisses when Vikki flicks water onto the glass, and whilst more jokes are cracked about ducking for cover, I pull out my phone. Something in the way Peterson is leaning forward, his eyes keen and watchful, tells me that this experiment might make an appearance in an upcoming pop quiz. Even after the class begins drifting toward the exit, I circle back, snapping photos of the leftover solutions. Five stars to Harper for finally committing herself to her studies.

Vikki's voice drowns out as she walks too far out of the loop's range, signaling I need to get a move on. Just as I'm turning, the door slams shut and lights inside go out, plunging me in complete darkness. What the hell? I rush forward, catching my hip on the edge of the table and cursing. Pain blossoms instantly but I ignore it in favor of swiping my phone to turn on the flashlight. Suddenly and silently, a body barrels into mine. My phone skitters away, my back slamming onto the hard floor beneath whoever is pinning me down. Three guesses who it could be.

"Fuck's sake Rhys, this isn't the time!" I grunt, throwing my fists upwards to connect with his torso a few times before he manages to trap my arms beneath his knees either side of me. He really thinks after all this time and everything we've been through that he can pull another hazing stunt on me? Without holding back, I struggle and jerk with all my might. He is easily dislodged a few times, scrambling to pin me back into place. I'm starting to win, quickly learning his weak spots, until my hair is tugged so hard, my head is forced to the side.

"Okay this really isn't funny anymore," I snarl, white hot anger filling me. If Rhys thinks I find this sort of thing sexy, I'm going to show him just how wrong he is. Something cold brushes my cheek, metallic I reckon, working its way towards my ear. Locating my implant, my skull denotes.

I scream, my body arching against the unbearable shriek ricocheting through me. He thrusts my head to the other side, pressing the device behind my ear and it happens again. Tears stream down my face as I thrash, finally managing to break free. My hands fly to my ears though it does nothing, the shrill static carving me apart from the inside out. My voice breaks into pleas that beg for the agony to stop.

"Why would you do that to me?" I sob into the darkness. The weight lifts from my body and I curl up into a ball, unable to think or react. Barely able to breathe. Over and over, the high-pitched noise that feels like electricity crackling through my head bounces back and fro. Writhing around on the floor, I scream for Clayton, then for anyone. The dark envelopes me, and for longer than I want to know, I lie there completely alone in a world where only suffering exists.

Light brightens beyond my eyelids, a shadowed figure coming into view. Even without being able to focus properly, I can tell whose strong arms collect me from the ground and pull me into his hard chest. Clay's earthy scent mingles with my senses, my nails clawing into his arms as I come back to reality.

The pain ebbs away too slowly, my limbs remaining heavy and sluggish whilst we remain huddled together. I feel the rumbles of his chest but I can't hear or read his words. More people surround us, their movements erratic and painful to look at. Although, through my squinted blinks, there's one person distinctively missing.

"Where is he?" I croak, peering up at Clayton's face. He frowns, looking around and then realizing who I'm asking for.

"He went outside-" I don't want around for the end of that sentence. Pushing upright, my legs threaten to give out but the crowd separates, allowing me to stumble into the elevator. I shrug off any attempts of support, being guided by more than just rage. There's sadness there, and a whole load of regret. I truly thought Rhys' threats were empty, that I was safe with him. I let my guard down, and he struck where it would hurt me most. At the small chance of hearing I have left.

I stagger out of the elevator on the bottom floor, making a beeline for the Porsche still parked at an angle out front. Rhys is leaning against it, a cigarette in his hand and a smirk on his mouth.

"Hey Babygirl, couldn't keep away from me," he grins as I approach and punch him straight in the face.

"You're a coward, Rhys Waversea. A fucking coward!" I hit him a few more times before he straightens and grabs my wrists. I can't stop my legs from buckling, the migraine in my head and ringing in my eardrums all too much. Rhys follows me down to the floor, softening the fall and holding me upright as I start to cry again. "I hate you. I hate myself for giving you a chance."

Trying to shove him away, I pitch forward and end up crying into his chest. I feel the vibrations of him talking, presumably to someone else because his fingers release me and seek out the patches of skin behind my ears. I try to swatch him away but he's strong. Stronger than the person who was holding me down.

This thought causes me to falter, and in the next second I'm being scooped up and placed into his passenger seat. I don't care to ask where we're going, my headache talking over all reasoning and as the Porsche speeds into motion, my world goes dark once more.

RHYS

CHAPTER TWENTY EIGHT

Not for the first time, I question why the fuck I am still sitting here. I may talk the talk about thriving in places steeped in despair, but hospitals make my skin crawl.

Even this so-called private clinic, chosen after I refused to waste my afternoon in a public one, reeks of death. Over-priced, pitiful death. Fancy artwork on sterile walls and plush carpets cannot mask the staleness of last wishes. Behind every door lies a rich body rotting slowly, dragging out the inevitable in designer pajamas. Wow, I'm gloomy today.

It has nothing to do with Harper crying in my arms, hissing words she knew would cut me the deepest. Or that when she passed out in my car, my heart rate rivaled the beat of a train hurtling down its tracks. I carried her into the reception and barked at a nearby nurse to get her a bed immediately. Just as Harper was stirring, I stepped out to give her some privacy.

The doctor has interrupted my brooding a few times, asking for more details I don't have. All I've got is the hollering Clayton gave me through my Porsche's Bluetooth speakers, something about a prank I supposedly took too far.

Trust me, if I wanted to prank Harper, it wouldn't be shutting her in the dark and jamming a harmful device against her head. It would be removing one of my cock piercings and convincing her it was lost inside her, so I'll have to fish it out with my tongue. Clayton did not care for this response. He ordered me to update him on where I took her, as if we're texty little bitch friends. I don't think so somehow.

Time bleeds slowly on the face of my Rolex. I chew my lip ring, craving a cigarette, but I remain here, sprawled across a mustard yellow sofa meant for three. Arms spread along the back, legs wide, I claim it as mine so no one dares to join me. Seriously, how freaking long does it take to check an implant? With the money this will cost me, they could have ripped hers out and built her brand-new ones from scratch by now.

My only amusement came when Malibu Barbie wobbled out of the elevator, immediately realizing this wasn't the cosmetic level, and tried to retreat. Her heel caught, and she folded on herself as the doors closed. I can confirm I heard the snap of bone. If I had seen it pierce her tanned flesh, my day would have been made.

I have tolerated enough 'aspiring models' swanning around my father's house to build a lasting hatred for the plastic and fake. That's where the two rules for ending up in my bed came from. No STDs and no silicone.

Nurses and receptionists click past on heels designed more for catwalks than clinics. They eye me like I am the anomaly, even though they are the ones dressing up an impending morgue with coffee machines. If one more of them asks me if I want an icepack for where Harper nailed my jaw, I'm going to rip the vending machine off the wall.

I stand and crack my knuckles, pacing. Not because I'm worried or anything. Because I'm bored. It's not like Harper Addams is the only person alive who has me tethered to the hallway outside her door like this. Except she is. Fuck.

I hate how she intrigues me. How she came into my life when I didn't need the distraction, teaching me what real desire is. For a kid who had everything he could have ever wanted, even though I never asked for any of it, I've come to understand that possessions are pointless if they do not come with a chase.

Finally, just before I consider jumping out of the nearest window to avoid these internal therapy sessions, Harper emerges. I'm stretched across a table that once displayed cupcakes for some charity farce, licking frosting from my thumb when she appears. Her pink hair is tousled, her expression as bored as I feel. Missing her hoodie, she rolls her shoulders in a t-shirt that states, *'Deaf-inatley Too Good For You'*. I snort, resolutely agreeing as I swing my legs beneath the table.

"Are we done here?" I ask the doctor accompanying her.

"Almost," Harper answers for him, lifting her hair to reveal a pair of new receivers. They're clunky and industrial looking. I'll be sure to order bespoke, slimline versions and mail these stone-age monstrosities back as soon as we get back home. I mean my house. My frat house, where I'll be returning to alone once Harper is safely back in her dorm.

Harper nudges my head aside, picking up a cupcake as she sits and somehow ends up with my head in her lap. I'm not sure how that happened.

"We just have to wait for the X-rays and a report to be written up," she mumbles, taking a delicate bite. I groan, dragging my palm down my face. That will be at least another hour they'll want to charge me for. "You didn't have to stay, you know."

Irritation slices through me. Didn't have to stay? I've read several leaflets on cervical cancer, re-evaluated my life choices and eaten my body weight in sugar but it's okay, I didn't *have* to stay. I roll my head against her thigh and glance up at her, half tempted to swipe the cake from her hand just for the reaction.

"If I didn't want to stay, I wouldn't be here." At Harper's quirked brow, I look away before she mistakes my words for sentiment. "I'm mad at you. I stayed to tell you that."

"You're mad at me?" Her hand freezes halfway to her mouth, lips parted and far too kissable for our current predicament. "That's rich." I sit upright, removing the cake from her hand before I become too jealous and tossing it into a trash can. The only thing allowed in Harper's mouth should be me. Oh right, I'm supposed to be angry.

"You doubted me," I clench my jaw and turn away. I don't know how far her historical receivers can hear, but maybe it's best this one is kept to myself anyway. "Something terrible happened, and you assumed I was to blame. I don't give a shit when others do that, but not you. You're supposed to know I only hurt you when it's for my pleasure."

A nurse who was walking past stumbles, and it serves her right for eavesdropping. Harper's hand slides over my shoulder, the heat of her body pressing against my back. I twist my head to the side, finding her right there, nose nudging my jaw.

"You suffocate me with your presence, rarely giving me an inch of space. Yet when something terrible happens, you were the only person missing. What was I supposed to think?" This is a valid point that I've also been considering. Someone tried to set me up, and I have a PI already on the case to find out who. By the time I leave here, I should have their identity sitting in my inbox and a new life to destroy. Until then, I won't be letting Harper out of my sight.

"You could have just, I don't know, trusted me." I roll my eyes, more at myself. My mouth is moving without my brain doing any of the work. Do I even want her to trust me? When someone trusts you, they come to rely on you. I'll reflect on that later. "I just needed a smoke, that's all. I thought your loyal foot soldier could look after you for five minutes without a war breaking out."

Harper's mouth goes on a journey, her lips against my neck. At the same time, her hands slip beneath my t-shirt, spreading across my lower back. If this is her apology for doubting me, maybe I wouldn't mind her doubting me more often. The tightness in my muscles loosens and a lengthy exhale leaves me.

"You know what the moral of this is, right?" Harper asks, nudging me again with her nose. She's like a cat seeking affection.

"That we need to hack Clayton's student record and have him dismissed?" I reply, not an ounce of sarcasm in my tone. I've already decided it's the only course of action for his colossal fuck up this afternoon, and having Harper on board means I don't have to sneak around about it. She laughs softly, dousing that plan. Looks like I'm sneaking around after all.

"That you need to stop smoking." This time, it's me that laughs. A thunderous sound that shakes the table.

"I have many vices, and I'm not giving up a single one. Not even for you, Babygirl."

Harper pouts but clearly expected as much. I turn back towards her, enjoying the press of her body and the weight of her attention far too much.

"Okay, well, maybe you should lay off Clay then. You two have a lot in common, you know."

"No, we don't," I roll my eyes, all the way leaning closer. Harper smells like all the lotions and ointments they've used on her, but she isn't any less appealing to my poisoned brain. Even the smell of the hospital isn't enough to deter me from wanting to be close to her.

"Yes, you really do. You both go to extreme lengths to cover up your sadness." Jerking back, I give Harper a crazed, wide-eyed expression.

"I'm not sad." This time, she rolls her eyes.

"Okay fine, you're downright miserable." My sour mood returns. What a way to destroy any hopes of lightening the atmosphere around here. The nurse's station was about to get a show.

Despite giving her the cold shoulder, Harper continues to stroke and attend to me like we're lovers. Like we're more than the bully and the deaf girl who have no business wasting their time on each other. I've almost started to relax into her touch again, until her hand travels upwards to where another one of my vices is located, and my throat suddenly constricts.

"What..." Harper tilts her head, her fingers running over the circular bumps. I jolt upright, trying to shove her hands out of my t-shirt but it's too late. She's already found them. "What are these? They weren't there the other week."

"Alright, alright. Exploration time is over." I jump down from the table, but Harper grabs my t-shirt in her fist and drags me in between her legs. When I dare to look down, I note the fury in her green eyes.

"What the hell are they?"

"Fine, you win. I get sad sometimes."

"Rhys," she breathes. Too quietly, too softly. I loathe it.

"Don't *Rhys* me. I don't want your pity." I step back but she doesn't give me an inch. Dragging me back into her body, Harper puts her face up close to mine, her words harsh.

"And you're not going to get it. Forget mad, I'm furious! Don't ever do that again, you hear me."

"Why do you even care?"

"Don't make me answer that question. You know you wouldn't." I hold Harper's stare, and then relent on a shrug. That's fair, but this conversation is done. Attempting to leave, Harper refuses to release her hold on my t-shirt. Her features are still pinched, her nostrils flaring and jaw tight.

All the signs are there to indicate she's about to lose her mind, except for the first time in life, the person who claims to be angry at me isn't lashing out. She isn't screaming or ordering me around. Harper surprises me like she always does, by winding her arms around my middle and keeping me pinned against her. She's disappointed in my actions, yet she hugs me harder. I stand in a state of confusion, stiff and uncomfortable.

Gently, my arms wrap around her as well. Harper presses her face against my chest and breathes me in as if she's resolute on staying. The tightness in my throat deepens, not from holding back words but from something I cannot name. It burns. It soothes. It terrifies me.

I do not get hugged. In fact, I can't remember the last time I was hugged, and no, Klara hanging off my neck does not count. The few times I have returned Klara's affections, it's been because there's a string attached, a threat held over my head, a performance to uphold. But Harper doesn't seem to be using me for her own selfish interests. She just holds me as though I earned her comfort. I didn't, but I take it anyway.

Something unwanted and dangerous pushes against the inner walls I have carefully constructed over the years. It is not lust. Lust is easy. Lust is mine to command. This is different, slow and warm, creeping in through cracks I did not know existed. I want to shove it back out. I want to keep it. Yet I just stand here, rigid as stone, my cheek finding the crown of her pink hair almost by accident.

As time stretches on, I hunt for a way to break the contact. For something to drive between us and give my mind a focus. Her disgust would be easiest if I were to say something vile, but Harper doesn't deserve the easy route. Dare I say, she deserves the truth. Just a snippet, just a tiny thread to prove to her that I'm not just a monster. Well, not one of my own making at least.

Reaching back, I peel her arms free and take her left hand in mine. I bring the back of it to my mouth, pressing a soft kiss there with the faintest tremble of my lips. On a deep inhale, I close my eyes as I raise that same hand to my neck, brushing her fingers against the raised scar hidden beneath an emancipated demon tattooed there.

"I've hated hospitals since the first time my father burnt me. He believed leaving a permanent mark would be a visible reminder to keep me in line. It didn't work. As soon as I became old enough, I had the scars tattooed over and realized I could just keep doing it. My father's attempt to discipline me became a twisted craving. I yearned for the pain. The burn of the cigarette, the burn of the tattoo gun. It's one of the only ways I feel alive anymore. It's how I remember who I am and why I can never be..."

I stop myself short. It's pointless to hope for something that will never happen. Opening my eyes, I see a pinch to Harper's eyebrows and glassy glaze to her green eyes. Her fingers smooth over the bump, too intensely for my liking. I've never let anyone this close to seeing my soul bared, but it's clear now that I've been longing for someone to share that with. Someone who actually cares to listen.

She parts her lips and I grit my teeth, ready for it. *'Ahh poor Rhys, you never stood a chance.'* But I should know better than to think Harper is predictable.

"Follow me." She tugs me down the hallway like she has every right to command me, her small hand clutching mine with a force that brooks no argument. We pass a trolley of medical supplies which holds a cooler box marked, 'Blood Products in Transit'. I pause, dragging on Harper's arm to flick open the lid and take a packet of blood. She raises a brow as I shove it into my pocket and gesture for her to keep walking. She doesn't need to know about the length my hazing tactics go to.

Down the corridor, past a row of silent doors, Harper pauses at a cupboard marked *Storage* and slips inside. There's no hesitation from me, shutting us into a dark room smelling of bleach and cotton sheets. She turns to me, her green eyes shining in the strip of light spilling beneath the door, and then she launches. Her mouth collides with mine, no hesitation, no doubt. She kisses like she's burning alive and I am the only oxygen she has left.

This is good. This is safe. I can do desire any day of the week, but talking emotions? Fuck no. I press Harper against the shelving, the metal rattling, her gasp swallowed by my tongue pushing past her lips. Her fingers claw at the back of my neck, dragging me closer, desperate and unapologetic.

I want to consume her. I want her to consume me right back. But then her pace falters, dragging me down a strange and unfamiliar path. She cups my face with both hands, softening the kiss, brushing her mouth across mine in a slow sweep that leaves me shuddering. Tenderness. That is what this is. I almost recoil from it, but she will not let me. Her thumbs stroke my cheeks and her lips press into mine like a vow.

I hold her waist, not to control, not to pin, but to keep her steady. The heat in my being surges to the surface, but it doesn't take over. It aches to blend into Harper's seamlessly, to be a part of whatever she's offering. Her thighs press against me, and I want to lose myself, yet I ease the pressure of my hold, tasting the sweetness of delayed gratification. She taught me this on our night together. She restrained me, made me wait, made me crave. It's as if the cuffs she used on me that night seeped into my skin, tugging me back to her every time I try to pull away.

Her back arches, pushing her chest into me on a gasp. I shouldn't still want her this much. I've never wanted anyone this much. I kiss her jaw, the corner of her mouth, her throat, every touch fevered but careful. Harper winds her arms around me, chest to chest, whispering against my lips between kisses.

"Thank you for giving me something real."

A sharp crack carves through my chest, a small, choked sound in the back of my throat. She's thanking *me*? The man who planned to have her expelled the moment she set foot on campus. The fiend who couldn't take no for an answer when he decided he must have a taste of her first. The bully who's given her nothing but grief.

"Don't thank me, Babygirl. You should hate me." I bury my face in the curve of her neck, inhaling her warmth, my teeth grazing the soft skin there. She tilts her head back and I hear the faintest sound escape her, a breathy moan that makes my blood thunder.

"Why?"

I snort. Why? Because everyone else does. Because it's what I want. Because it's easier. Yet none of that makes it out of my mouth. Whatever spell Harper has cast over me, I find that I don't want to give her basic answers. I don't want to give her the version of myself that everyone else gets to see.

"Because I'm broken." I keep my face hidden from her view, pressing my lips to her collarbone like a coward. No doubt she already knew. Harper sees the world through silent eyes without prejudice. Lord knows she saw straight through me, into the secrets I have buried, beyond the broken pieces I hide behind ink and smoke.

"I think that's why I appeal to you. I'm a little broken too."

I keep my response to myself, grinding against her and licking a trail from her neck to her jaw, until my mouth finds hers.

Harper appeals to me for many reasons, and only a fraction of that is the darkness inside her which is all too similar to mine. Every time she's backed into a corner, it appears with a vengeance, clawing and battling until she's back on top. I know, no matter what I throw at her, Harper will continue to surpass my expectations, and I can't fucking wait to see it.

CHAPTER TWENTY NINE

"Hey Harp, how are—", Addy's voice cuts off as she takes in my appearance.

My bags have bags, my hair a catastrophic mess that could rival a rock back from the eighties, and there's a coffee spill on my pajama top. I'd momentarily tricked myself into thinking I might have that cute bedhead thing going on, but judging by Addy's shocked expression, I was totally kidding myself. It might be the weekend and the sun may be shining, but sleep continues to evade me.

The restless dreams worrying about Clayton and Rhys killing each other over me were bad enough, but that was before the lab. Before I realized the person I'm fearing doesn't have a face. Now, sleep would be a mercy. Anything to switch my brain off, to stop the possibilities from running through my mind's eye.

My only saving grace has been Clay's own insomnia. Each night since the field trip, he's stayed up to message with me for hours on end. It's amazing how much one can say whilst remaining surface level, but we share reels and memes, finding a way to communicate without Rhys' looming shadow always pressing in. Clay tells me what I've missed in classes while I'm taking the 'rest' Dean O'Sullivan has ordered. He sends over his notes, and keeps me up to date on the disciplinary Peterson received for his negligence on an academy-funded outing. He's been my link to the world whilst I hide away and pretend it doesn't exist for a while longer.

Some of us aren't having the same inner turmoil. Perky-and-Pink across the room has just returned from a morning jog in tight lycra that shows off her mid-section. Ugh, I hate her sometimes. Groaning, I slip back beneath my covers and pick up a crumbled paperback that I'm halfway through. My mattress dips, giving a moment's warning before she wrestles the duvet off my face.

"Nope, we're not doing this again. Get out of bed." I wriggle and shout. The neighbors probably think there's a cat fight happening in here. For a split second, I manage to grab the cover back and roll in it like a sausage, until Addy and her surprising strength whips it back off and sends me flying onto the floor. Giving up the will to live, I just lie there like a suicidal starfish waiting for a seagull to finish me off.

"What's got you all miserable? Ooo look at me I'm Harper," she steps over me to do a terrible impression of swaying hips and expressive arms that I have never done. "I'm super smart and gorgeous, and have two of the hottest guys in school fighting over me but I am *soooo* not secretively dating both of them."

"I'm not dating Rhys," I grumble, frowning at myself. Although, a quickie in a hospital storeroom might be Rhys' idea of romance.

Refusing to move from my new spot, I reach up to switch off the slimline receivers which were waiting for me on the doorstep this morning. I was just trying out the weight of them when Addy got back, her bossy orders proving that I can hear with astonishing clarity. Rhys must have paid a fortune for express delivery on the latest processor upgrade. I've made a promise to myself to pay back every cent by the end of the semester.

On a shrug, Addy walks out of view and I return to my pity party for one, inspecting the ceiling from a new angle. How long has the lampshade been so dusty and where is the spider responsible for all of the cobwebs inside? Looking from corner to corner, on the hunt for a valid distraction, Addy suddenly dives onto me, grabbing my thumb and pressing it on my phone's home button.

"What the fuck are you doing?!" I yell, shoving her aside and sitting upright. Her chocolate brown eyes are glimmering as she leans across to switch my receivers back on and tosses my phone into my lap.

"Oh, me? I'm not doing anything. You, however, have just booked a last minute slot at the gymnasium."

"What on earth am I going to do at the gymnasium?"

"You'll see," Addy grins, dragging me upright. She's already dressed for a round of fitness, but thankfully, it's not spandex she shoves into my arms. I quirk a brow at my bikini and a fluffy sweatsuit, allowing her to usher me into the hallway in the direction of the bathroom.

"Make sure you shave!" she shouts through the throng of students milling around me, all of whom stop to snigger. The door is slammed closed, leaving me to either stand long enough for someone to post my humiliation online or rush in the bathroom before anyone else does.

Fine, Addy wins this round, but if she thinks she's tricking me into a weekend workout, she's seriously underestimated my upper body strength.

By the time I'm convinced Addy hasn't lured me into some sadistic spin class, I am already melting into the bench of the newly installed sauna. The dry heat presses down like a heavy blanket, loosening the knots buried deep in my shoulders, forcing the weight of sleepless nights to bleed out through every pore.

Addy sits opposite me, hair pinned high, her expression caught somewhere between smug satisfaction and blissful surrender. She closes her eyes with a sigh that looks theatrical. I let my head fall back too, because I can finally take a break from Clayton's insecurities and Rhys' twisted perceptions. Better yet, I can relax with the knowledge that no one is watching from the shadows, waiting for another opportunity to strike.

Before long, we abandon the smothering heat and move into the adjoining room which hosts a line of three hot tubs. The bubbling water greets us with a rush of steam that fogs up the windows and curls around the edges of the tiled floor. Sliding into the water, I feel my bones go soft, dissolving into the warmth until I am convinced I could live here forever.

Addy stretches her colorfully tattooed arms legs dramatically, bringing forth a memory of Rhys's tattoos shimmering within the water, his blue eyes focused on me as I straddled him in his own jacuzzi. More flashes from that evening assault me, drawing my thighs together tightly. Luckily, I can pass off my sudden blush as a reaction to the temperature when Addy turns to me.

'I told you I have the best ideas,' she signs lazily from across the other side.

'Yes you do.' I sign back and grin. *'How did you know this place was open?'*

'The track team was given a heads up before the official reveal next week. We won the AAU championships last week, we deserve a reward.'

'And I happily accept that reward on your behalf.' My arms float gently by my sides as I curve into the provided seat and groan in pure bliss. Not for the first time, I thank whatever ultimate power ruling over us for placing Addy in my life.

Of course, peace never lasts long around here. The glass door opens and Klara sweeps in with a towel slung over her shoulder, her designer bikini barely a scrap of material that does nothing to cover her. She steps into the hot tub without waiting for an invitation, despite there being two others which are empty. Arranging herself between Addy and I, her eyes flick to me first, traveling down and back up with all the subtlety of a knife blade.

Addy lifts one eyebrow and grins lazily, not bothering to adjust her seat. *'Well, look at that. The water just got colder.'* She signs with a smirk, fully aware that Klara can't read it.

Unaffected, Klara leans back, dipping her hair into the froth of the water. Tension clings to the steam, thick and inescapable. Her painted nails drumming along the edge of the tub as if she is waiting for me to leave. Fuck that.

I force my shoulders back and meet Klara's stare, unwilling to look away first. I'd hoped our drama was over with, my revenge exacted for screwing with my hair and our rivalry settled at the party. How naïve of me. There is still a war brewing in Klara's blue eyes, and judging by the smirk tugging at her lips, Klara thinks she's going to win it.

"Doesn't a part of you think this is a little bit ridiculous?" I finally give in and attempt to break the tension. Brownie points to me for trying to be the bigger person. "We don't have any real grievances, Klara. There's no need for...this," I wave a wet hand in between us. Klara doesn't seem convinced.

"Do you know he's shut me out completely?" I read her words, my brow raising. *"At least he would let me hang around as long as I stayed out of his way. Now, the only person he lets close is you."*

Addy catches my eye with a demented expression but I subtly shake my head. We're not going to even touch on how tragic that is. Klara is a fully grown woman, if she hasn't learned self-respect by now, it's beyond us to explain it to her. Instead, I keep on track, trying to defuse our conflict amicably.

"Isn't it archaic for women to fight over a man these days? It's not like his attention didn't stray before I came onto the scene." Klara sniffs, twisting her head away. Luckily, Addy is there to interpret for me.

"It's part of the deal he has with my parents. Whilst at school, Rhys can do whatever or whoever," cue bitchy up-and-down glare which

Addy unhelpfully mimics, *"he wants. But once he graduates, he's all mine."*

"Unfortunately, I don't think he'll ever be yours. Surely you want better for yourself?" I ask, unable to keep the pity from showing. Addy bites back a grin, clearly enjoying herself as the third wheel in this fight. Scoffing, Klara's brow tilts, her expression filled with conceited attitude.

"Better for myself?" she repeats back. Her eyes sweep over me with cruel precision, the frost settling between us contradicting the heat of the water. Her lips twitch into a faint smirk as she leans forward, her voice no doubt sharp enough to cut through glass. *"Bitch please, I'm doing better. You're the distraction. A pretty toy for him to play with until he remembers he already belongs to me. Don't fool yourself into thinking you're anything special. He's just getting a taste of trash before he comes back to quality."*

Addy's hands slow towards the end, her disbelief stalling her signing but it's fine. I caught the gist. My heart pounds, a mix of fury and adrenaline flooding every inch of me. Heat bubbles inside me, hotter than the water lapping against my shoulders. I tried. I offered peace, trying to put an end to this stupidity. Klara took it, twisted it, and shoved it back down my throat.

Rising from the tub, every muscle strung tight with purpose, I grab my bag from where it was waiting right where I left it. Droplets cascade down my simplistic black bikini as I roughly dry myself off and push my receivers into place.

"Fine, Klara. You want a fight, you've got one." I let my mouth curve into a smile, though there is no humor in it. Pulling Rhys' jersey from my bag, I shake out the fabric and slip it on. We're not going to talk about why I had it on me, or how many times I sneakily inhale the lingering scent every now and then.

Klara's reaction is brief, quickly smoothed over with practiced poise, but I catch it. She's stunned that I've accepted her challenge, proving that she's done this before. Intimidated women that Rhys has shown a margin of interest in. Addy is silently cheering in the background, signing to *'go fuck his brains out'* in the air. The last thing I see as I close the door is the fury in Klara's eyes, the promise to see this war through until only one of us is left standing.

I suppose it's lucky that I have no self-preservation then.

RHYS

CHAPTER THIRTY

The basketball leaves my hands and sinks through the net with a clean dunk. I catch it on the rebound, bouncing it lazily as I drift back across the court and repeat the motion again. And again.

Practice ended over an hour ago, but I stayed behind because moving is easier than thinking. Thinking leads me back to the same place, back to her, and I'm starting to admit that no amount of weed, video games, or bad decisions can scrub Harper from my mind. Those green eyes haunt, following me around campus without her even being nearby. She's been ordered to rest, and I've forced myself to stay away. To allow enough time for this fluttery feeling to shrivel up and die. If only I were so lucky.

Every time I picture her, I end up inventing new ways to get under her skin, just to see that fiery glare. Ways to antagonise, to push her to breaking point. And in every fantasy, we end up hate fucking across my mind in every angle imaginable.

Again, that's the easy option. Destroying my father's empire was supposed to be my life's singular obsession, but lately...it's her. I ache to take a cigarette to my ribs just so I can bleed some of this poison out, but the thought of her cutting me off is enough of a deterrent. That in itself speaks volumes, because damn if I've ever allowed anyone to have this much power over me.

I'm so tangled in confusion that I don't notice I've lost the ball until it's snatched away mid-bounce. My fists twitch on instinct, my gut reaction to lash out. Then, pink-tipped waves of hair and the kind of ass I'd recognize even in a blackout come into focus. Harper looks scandalous in my jersey and a pair of tiny shorts. I blink a few times to make sure this isn't a mirage I've conjured up, some cruel trick of my imagination.

Harper stops on the arc line to do a cute little bop, her hands remaining in a flick as she propels the ball straight into the net. My eyebrow raises.

"I thought you could use a worthy opponent," she grins and my stomach does some weird swoop I never want to feel again. Cracking my neck, I shake out my shoulders and paint a smirk on my face.

"You sure you want to play this game, Babygirl? You've seen how rough I get, on and off the court." I speak as if I'm giving her an out, as if I haven't already decided Harper isn't leaving until I've had my fill of whatever it is I need. I'm sure I'll figure out what that is along the way. Harper walks towards me, forgetting about the ball as it dribbles itself away.

"I'm pretty sure I've held my own up to now. And maybe you'll find you've met your match because," she leans in close to whisper into my ear, "I happen to like it rough." A laugh is lodged in my throat as her elbow cracks me in the jaw. My teeth bite down on the inside of my cheek, blood exploding into my mouth and a shudder ripples down my spine, feeding both my hunger for lust and pain. Oh, that saucy minx knows exactly what I need.

I catch her wrist before she can escape, whipping her back into me and pinning her there using my hand in her hair. Our mouths crash, her lips clashing with mine, and the sound that rips out of me isn't human. Her jacket hits the floor with a shove, my hand sliding under her shirt to the soft curve of her stomach just as her knee slams into my groin, an inch above my dick, packing a harder hit than I thought her possible of.

I stumble back and lose my footing, falling hard on my ass. It wasn't graceful, yet I can't stop grinning. I always smirk out of habit, because life's always one bad joke away from collapse, but this smile is real. The kind that hurts in a good way, like stretching muscles I forgot I had. Even doubled over, I'm more alive at this moment than I've been in years.

The whoosh of another basket snaps me back. Harper cheers for herself, prancing in a half-ass moonwalk near enough for me to grab her ankle and yank her down with me. Her squeal turns into laughter as she tumbles, but I'm already gunning for the ball. Winning still matters. Always. There'll be time for sex, for more of that wild, bruising fire she stirs in me, but right now? I don't fucking lose.

I tear across the court, ball tucked tight, launching up for another slam dunk. It rattles through the hoop, and I land with my fist in the air, victorious. Only... she's gone. For a split second, I wonder if I've finally lost it, if I summoned her out of loneliness and obsession. Then there's a shuffle by the bleachers.

"Come out, come out wherever you are, Babygirl," I call, cupping my hands. Maybe she hears, maybe she doesn't, but the giggle from my right gives her away. She pops up with that devilish spark in her eyes, throwing the loser sign across her forehead with her tongue sticking out. I bite my lip ring hard, the grin trying to break free. Around her, I don't have to posture or pretend. Around her, I'm just... me. Or at least a fraction of who I could have been.

Finally, I give chase, eating up the distance in long strides that span multiple steps. Her giggles echo around the arena, bouncing off the walls like a soundtrack to my madness. Harper runs the length of a bench before darting into the stairwell, keeping rows of plastic between us like a barricade. Cracking my neck for effect, I hop onto the nearest row, sprinting across the yellow seats, grateful for the grip of my high-tops that prevents any sliding.

She bolts up the stairs, nimble as hell but I'm right on her tail, leaping over benches until I close the gap. Harper squeaks with laughter, attempting to pivot back in the direction she came but I lunge, managing to snag her waist and carry her back to the court again. She makes a show trying to wrangle free without enough effort to do so, my naughty little minx who's aching to be chased and bound.

I don't falter, ramming her back against the basketball pole. The clang reverberates through my palms as I cage her in with my arms. My body grinds against hers, cock hard enough to pulse. Harper doesn't flinch, she pushes right back. The arch of her spine puts her chest firmer against mine, and I can't resist tracing her collar bone with a tattooed finger.

"I forgot to say that I don't play fair," I lick my lips, appreciating the sight before me. She's flushed, breathing heavy, and far too sexy in my jersey. I'd give anything to tie her to my bed and never let her see the light of day again, but I must confess, I'm rather enjoying the chase too.

"I hope you don't pin your teammates like this." Harper fires back, her green eyes alight with mischief. I bite down on my tongue, pulling back the smile that tries to break free. I need to get a hold of myself, to stop letting her trample all over the rules I spent years putting in place. Yet, my mouth doesn't get the memory and I lean over her, forcing her head to tilt back.

"Are you jealous, Babygirl?" I lick my lips and she tracks the movement. "I don't do this, but I'd be willing to make you a deal. I won't press up against any of the Waversea Warriors if you vow the same."

"Mmmm, nice try," she grins, leaning up for a kiss. I lean away, revealing in the sweet satisfaction of her mouth pursuing mine before I relent. I knew she wouldn't agree, but it was worth a shot. For reasons beyond my comprehension, Clayton has a hold on Harper. A situation I intend on rectifying, but not today. Right now, my focus is on dragging my teeth along Harper's jaw, a growl more beast than man vibrating from me. It's possessive and animalistic, and it's exactly what she does to me.

My lips return to hers, kissing her until we're both consumed by it. She shudders as if I've short-circuited her whole system, something I understand all too well. Harper isn't like anyone else. Her stubbornness, her grit, her refusal to bend, they have me hooked. Addicted. I can't stop thinking about ways to have her at my mercy, ways to push her to the edge of her limits. It's no longer enough just to ruin her, I want the right to piece her back together and lick her wounds better. I want it all. The depravity, the discomfort and the—Holy fuck, she's grabbing my dick.

Harper's hand has dipped into my waistband, the smooth surface of her palm reacquainting with my piercings. That simple touch alone sends me into a frenzy, like a virgin getting his first handjob. She moves with slow, deliberate strokes, dragging up every ounce of frustration I've been choking on all weekend. I crush her against me, my hands growing white against the metal pole at her back. Resting my head on hers, I drown in her vanilla-scented shampoo, my eyes screwed shut.

The urge to explode rises too soon, but I hold it back. I'd rather let my balls rupture than give Harper the victory of making me fall apart this fast. My head is reeling, every nerve ending firing as she toys with me, teasing the piercing at the tip until my pants become lost in her hair. She's winning. She knows it, and I hate how quickly I change my mind. Give her the satisfaction. Give her whatever she damn wants whilst stroking me like this.

"Well," a voice cuts through the haze, freezing me where I stand. Not just any voice, but the one I'd rather never hear again. "When you said you never missed basketball practice, this isn't exactly what I had in mind. Good to see all the money I'm spending on your education is being put to good use."

My cock sinks faster than the Titanic. I bare my teeth as I glance sideways, and by whatever cruel trick of fate, there he is. The same shrewd blue eyes and same air of superiority. A navy suit is stretched perfectly over his aging frame. His hair is more gray than black now, but still styled within an inch of its life. Shiny black loafers gleam on the court, polished and out of place, like he's allergic to the world the rest of us live in.

"Hello, Father," I grind out. Harper stiffens against me, but her face is otherwise a mask of indifference. Smoothly withdrawing her hand from my shorts, she thrusts it straight out towards the man staring at us.

"Pleasure to meet you, Mr Waversea. I'm Harper Addams." She holds her hand out, steady and sure, much to my delight. My father sneers at her cock-contagious hand, making absolutely no move to shake it.

Shrugging, Harper lowers her arm and links her fingers with mine instead. Hot damn. If the bastard who spawned me wasn't standing right there, I'd be tempted to propose. This girl, this incredibly beautiful and ballsy girl, is the one. End of conversation.

"I see my son is doing a fine job mentoring you," he finally says, voice laced with disgust. "I'm attending a meeting with the board, then we're having lunch with the Kavanagh's. Try to look presentable," my father looks me up and down, clearly unimpressed.

"I have plans," I grunt, tugging Harper in front of me and curling my arm around her shoulders.

"Send your plans out to get her nails done. Lunch is non-negotiable."

I bristle, about to call him out for speaking about Harper as if she's dispensable. To him, everything can be bought, and everyone has a price. It's exactly why lunch with the Kavanagh's is happening. I'm being sold to the highest bidder, my future mapped out by a man who has no idea I'm going to burn my own legacy to the ground before we get there.

Before a single word makes it past my lips, my father turns on his heel and strides away. Harper wiggles in my loosened grip, turning until her cheek rests against my chest. Here we go again with the hugging, but no one is around to see my street cred going up in flames. Regardless, my arms circle her, holding her against me whilst my pulse begins to ease.

"He didn't look like the monster I pictured," she murmurs, her voice threading into the quiet.

"They never do, Babygirl." My hand drifts to the scar at my neck, fingers brushing over it as if to remind myself it's real. That the nightmares were real, because sometimes, around her, I almost forget. Or more rather, I can buy into the fantasies Harper offers and pretend none of it happened.

Leaning forward to press a kiss to her head, I freeze halfway, horror ripping through me at the realization of what I was about to do. I wasn't going to bite her or mark her or mock her. I was about to show *affection*. My stomach twists. Fuck. With a sharp pull, I peel her away before my brain short-circuits completely.

"I'd better hit the showers. Come over tonight." I just about manage to force some authority into my tone, pushing the balance of power back into place. Harper smirks, seeing straight through me but nodding anyway. My eyes track her to the bleachers, noting the slight skip in her step as if she's the Queen of the court wearing her King's jersey. She swings her bag onto her shoulder and leaves, every step echoing like the crack of a whip down my spine.

I refuse to think about where she's going next, and with who. There's only so much torture my brain can handle at once, and it seems my father is hellbent on taking the mantle today.

CHAPTER THIRTY ONE

The hallway smells faintly of coffee and dashed hope, students dragging their feet away from the lure of the cafeteria. I'm amongst them, clinging to the strap of my backpack and trying to remember the reasons I left Aunt's Marg's dusty attic. Things were simpler there. Online coursework was easier, and my friendships were mostly virtual. I've never had to deal with walking into a room and wondering who is out to get me, and why.

Due to the ongoing investigation, Peterson's classes have been moved to an adjacent building to be led by Professor Hargreaves. Rumor has it his lab and onsite apartment are being ransacked, the police becoming frantic in their search for the device that interfered with my implants.

I can't believe Peterson has anything to do with it, even if he does think I'm merely a distraction to his class. It was too risky. There were too many witnesses who would have noticed his absence. No, whoever attacked me was able to disappear without being noticed. Someone who lives under the radar. Not for much longer, if I have anything to say about it.

Steadying myself, I push the door open because avoidance is no longer a luxury I can afford. The lecture hall is half-full, a scatter of hoodies and backpacks spread evenly across the faded blue seats. Rhys is lounging with the ease he wears like a second skin, one arm slung over the back of a chair no doubt intended for me. Clay is the opposite, rigid on the edge of his seat, all contained tension and careful eyes. My chest tightens at the sight of them near one another without fists between thrown and blood being spilled. Rhys appears more invested in his cuticles and Clay is jotting in his notebook.

Making my way through the aisles, I catalogue each student, on high alert for a hint of a sneer or feigned shock. This is my first class back, and someone amongst these masses didn't want me here. Or perhaps it's who isn't present I should be focusing on. By the time I make it to my seat, I sag with deflation, my head swimming. I don't know these people well enough. I was too content staying wrapped in my silent world, I didn't bother to notice those around me.

Clayton nudges closer, the movement so small I almost miss it, but his heat at my shoulder is impossible to ignore. He slides a disposable cup of coffee into my hands and retreats before anyone notices. I smile then. It's like our texted conversations each night. Private, secret, and solely ours. My fingers close around the cardboard, grateful for the warmth that seeps through me as I take a sip. Over the rim of the cup, I slyly watch Clay finish his notes. There is a new ease about him now I'm near, a softness in his eyes that betrays the monster everyone assumes he is. He says nothing as Hargreaves clears his throat and launches into a dry lecture about electrophysiology, but his presence is everything I need to get through it.

On my other side, Rhys' knuckles brush the back of my chair, a ghost of contact to remind me that he's there. As if I could forget. I turn my head to the side and drop my voice to a whisper.

"How was your lunch with the Kavanagh's?"

Rhys rolls his tongue over his lip ring, just about covering up the bitterness that ripples through him.

"You'd know if you came over last night, as requested."

"Oh, that was a request? I thought it was an order. I've never been very good dealing with authority."

"I heard practice makes perfect. Let's try again. Come over to mine tonight, or else."

I lean back against the seat and let a grin spread slowly across my face, enjoying the small, wicked pleasure of riling him up so early in the morning. I half-expected him to chase me down last night and drag me back to his, kicking and screaming.

"I thought I should give you space, you know, in case Klara wanted to—" Rhys' hand shoots from the chair to the back of my neck. A low growl emanates from his chest, startling a few nearby students. I simply chuckle beneath the firm hold at my nape.

"You want me to work harder, is that it? Send you flowers, little love notes under your door? Maybe I'll put a little apron on and bake you cupcakes?"

"Quiet back there!" Hargreaves shouts, his whiteboard now a blurred landscape of arrows and brackets. I sink lower in my seat, covering my mouth behind my hand.

"Now that you mention it," I mutter low, my cheeks aching with the need to laugh. "You could give it a shot. What's the worst that could happen?" Rhys shoots a death stare at the side of my face,

"Hard pass. If you want sappy shit, you know where to find it," Rhys leans forward and glares in Clayton's direction. Clay's throat bobs, his temper working its way to the surface. I give him a sly wink until Rhys uses his grip on my nape to jerk me back forward.

"Focus. I'm here for your sake, not mine." I bite down on my bottom lip, mustering the sarcastic response that dances on the end of my tongue. Rhys won't realize it, but that's probably the most romantic thing he's ever said. Settling into Hargreaves' bland drone, I make vague notes, scribbling random words that might be relevant in a future assignment, but let's face it. My attention is on those shifting in closer, a millimeter at a time. Rhys rearranges his junk, pushing his thighs wider. Clay fakes a yawn and smacks Rhys' arm off the back of my chair.

I've been trapped between them like this before, but thankfully the tension is lighter now. Instead of being at each other's throats, they're resolute on being my sentinel bodyguards, warding off external threats. No one dares to look around for more than a second, giving me time to memorize each person in the room. Soon enough, my jottings turn into a list of names and in failing that, a brief description. After that, I start crossing out names that have no reason to harm me. Class ends as I cross out the last name, coming to a dead end.

Moving to pack my stuff away, Rhys grabs my notepad and tears the scribbled page clean out. I call out in protest, reaching for it back but he scrunches it up in his fist and tosses it aside.

"Stop worrying. I've got someone already on the case."

"Who?" I frown, crossing my arms. I'll be the first to admit I'm stubborn to a fault, preferring to save myself than rely on others, but something else about Rhys' nonchalant shrug doesn't sit right with me.

"An online hacker. Highly overpriced, but he's the best there is. If there's anything to find on the surveillance cameras, he'll find it." Under my careful watch, Rhys packs the rest of my bag and shoulders it himself, jerking his head to the exit. I might as well be wearing that collar I stung him up on. I hang back with Clay, my thoughts suddenly colliding.

A small voice trickles into my psyche, reminding me that there were two names I didn't put on that list. Clayton and Rhys. Clay ruled himself out by being the one who rushed back to save me, and I know Rhys was supposedly outside smoking, but what if he wasn't? What if I'm giving my trust far too easily to a man who, by his own admission, doesn't deserve it? How convenient would it be to leave my digging in the hands of an anonymous hacker, especially if the man he's tracking is the man sending the paycheck - if the hacker is even real. No, that's ludicrous. I know Rhys, possibly better than anyone else, and I owe it to him not to think the worst all the time.

"Harper," Clay gently shakes my shoulder. I blink, returning to myself. Rhys has vanished, taking my belongings and my phone with him. I open my mouth, stuttering until Clay links his fingers with mine. "Do you...I mean, is it what you want...the sappy shit?" he winces, his eyes looking everywhere except at me. The room has emptied out, leaving just us in the huge lecture hall.

"What exactly are you asking me?" I tilt my head until he has no choice but to stare into my eyes. Squeezing his fingers, I smile tenderly, yet the breath that saws out of Clay isn't a light one.

"I can't stand back and watch any longer." His jaw tenses and I reach up to soften it. Clay turns his face into my palm, brushing his lips over my skin. "I'm not a good man. I've done things I'll never be able to fix. I live with regret and shame on a daily basis. But I know deep down, I'm still better than him."

I keep my mouth pressed closed, allowing Clayton the space he needs to speak freely. That, and I won't be caught bad mouthing one of the men holding my interest to the other. They're both damaged in their own right, and they cope differently. Clay shakes the tension from his shoulders and lowers my hand to his chest.

"I won't make you any false promises, but I can show you the kind of man you deserve. The only kind that should catch your attention and have your heart one day. So, if you want, I'll pick you up from outside your dorm tonight. Say seven o'clock?"

"Okay," I reply simply, finding myself in a daze. Clay just asked me out. For a second, the whole lecture hall shrinks to the space between my palm and Clay's chest, the steady thud of his heartbeat a perfect anchor for the storm brewing inside of me. This is what it's supposed to feel like. Dizzying, exciting, a hint of anxiety. Not a constant migraine from being pulled here and there whilst a bucket of lust is dumped over my head.

He smiles in that quiet, almost embarrassed way he does and nods, before releasing my hands and starts to walk away. My mouth opens a few times with follow up questions but I manage to reign myself in. Be cool Harper. Cool, calm and collected. Clay pauses in the doorway, the hallway light catching at the edge of his jaw.

"Oh, and don't worry about bringing your receivers. You won't need them."

Okay, now I have so many more questions! Luckily for him, Clayton leaves before any of them make it past my lips. I stumble forward on weak legs, feeling all too giddy for a girl who still needs to reclaim her shit from the campus bully. I hope Rhys isn't intent on getting a rise out of me today because I'm too busy walking on cloud nine. It turns out I do want the sappy shit after all.

CLAYTON

CHAPTER THIRTY TWO

Resting my arm against the back of her headrest, I reverse my battered old truck onto the road behind McAllister dorms. The thing rattles like it's one pothole away from the scrapyard, yet Harper smiles from the passenger seat as if I can compete with Wavershit's Porsche.

Crossing her legs, my gaze dips back to the knee-high black boots, the dark denim painted onto her thighs, the leather jacket pulled tight around her chest. Her hair is tied high with waves spilling over her shoulder like ribbons of magenta. A single curl frames her face on each side, and I just about manage to drive straight.

Harper is a vision of purity. I'd almost changed my mind about this date, halting her from entering the truck as if its cracked seats and rusty parts would sully her. As if going out with me isn't going to tarnish her enough. Then I remembered that she shares Rhys' company and figured she doesn't give a shit about public image whilst I opened the truck door and helped her hop inside.

As campus and the sleepy town shrink in the rearview, I let out a breath that has been strangling me all week. I don't bother with the radio, or any small talk that would be awkward for Harper to decipher in the passing streetlamps. I simply sit, nervously tapping my thumb on the steering wheel, the growl of the engine filling the cab. This is my first date. My first real chance to impress her.

All afternoon, I've been solely focused on planning where to take her, how to make her laugh, what it might feel like to hold her hand and never let go. Daydreaming kept me alive in the JDC, building a barrier between the heavy, cold locks and the reasons that put me there. But with Harper, those visions dig deeper. I picture myself as the kind of man who could give her everything, who could pleasure her in a way that Rhys won't be able to compete with. Those fantasies are safer locked inside my head.

The reality is different. The reality is Harper sitting right here, eyes focused on the road ahead, no doubt trying to decipher where we're heading. Remembering my promise to set the bar for all future dates, I slide my hand onto her thigh with a smile that feels foreign on my face. As usual, her body is so warm, radiating pure energy and an unbreakable spirit. If I had anything to give, I'd exchange it all to be worthy of someone like her.

The freeway signs loom, and I take the exit I memorized last night in the library. I can't afford a GPS, but every junction is signposted and in no time, I'm pulling into a parking lot by a brick-built hall. I kill the engine and hurry out, circling around before Harper can touch the handle. Taking her hand to help her down, I keep it in my grasp as the night swallows the path ahead. There's no moon tonight, only the lights surrounding a pair of large, double doors.

The lobby looks like a retirement home threw up on itself. Brown carpets, faded curtains, armchairs that quite possibly were stolen from a yard sale. A fish tank bubbles against the far wall, the two fish inside appearing that look more depressed than the woman seated at a makeshift desk. A paper banner hangs limply over the folding table, the words '*Silent Disco*' printed in bold letters. Harper halts, her hand pulling from mine.

"Are you mocking me?" Her green eyes narrow. "I can go to regular disco's, you know." My gut flips and I scramble for an explanation. Fuck, I knew I'd screw this up.

"*No, no,*" I shake my head vigorously. *"Just trust me, please. Let me show you, if you don't like it I'll drive you straight back."* Harper raises an eyebrow skeptically whilst reading my words, gesturing for me to lead the way. Damn, I really hope I'm right about this. It's not like I've got the charm, tattoos or smart mouth to fall back on.

Borrowed cash changes hands at the desk, money I'll pay back to Kenneth later. He was overjoyed I was simply speaking to him again, even if it was for my own gain. I ask for one pair of wireless headphones and explain that I'm the guy who emailed ahead about Harper's receivers. Ahead of this evening, I downloaded the transmitter app onto my phone, which I now connect to her implants. Harper watches on, giving me time to see my plan through and by the time I hold out my hand again, she's softened enough to take it back.

We enter an enclosed room that appears dark from the outside, but the contrast to the limp lobby area almost knocks me back. It's even better than I'd hoped. LED strips light up the wooden dance floor, a disco ball scattering fractured stars across the walls. Refreshments glimmer on a plastic table. A few couples sway, bodies pressed close in complete silence. I turn to Harper before the door clicks shut behind us, swallowing the last of the outside world.

"Now everyone is just like you." Her eyes follow my lips, catching the words, and something in them shifts. She steps closer, her forehead briefly touching my chest.

"Sorry, Clay. I—" I don't let her finish that sentence. Harper is used to a world that treats her differently, that mocks and excludes her because she's different. I relate to that, and it's something she never has to apologize for.

Handing Harper my phone, I encourage her to pick a music channel and then set my headphones to match. 'All My Life' by K-Ci and JoJo filters into my ears, the first notes tugging at something raw and unguarded inside me. In the dark, she cannot see the tiny smile that slips free, but I feel it pressing against my lips like it has been waiting years to escape.

I trail my fingers along the inside of her arm until I find her hand, guiding her into the hall and then to rest over my chest where my heartbeat hammers like a drum. My other arm slides carefully around her back, pulling her in until I can lean my forehead against hers. Her sway is soft, instinctive, and I let her movements guide mine, grateful to give her the lead.

For the first time in longer than I can remember, I feel something other than a hatred for the world that swallowed me whole and then told me I'm the blame for the outcome. It's more than her warmth seeping into me. It's her presence, the way she centers me without even trying, pulling me out of the storm that never leaves my head.

I spent so many nights in a cell imagining what it would feel like to hold someone like this, someone who made the walls vanish and gave me the illusion of freedom. Not once did my fantasies come close to this reality. This is too sharp, too sweet, too much for me to take in all at once, and my lungs stumble against the weight of it.

When her arms slip around my neck and her lips brush the corner of my cheek, my chest ignites with intensity I do not know how to contain. My throat tightens, and it takes all of my strength to keep my arms from trembling. She's too precious for a beast like me to be holding, yet I can't tear myself away now.

The playlist leaks from one song into the next, each as heartfelt and romantic as the last until Harper has fully melted into my body. The thin cotton of my black t-shirt is the only barrier between her cheek and my chest, her leather jacket long forgotten on a metal chair off to the side. My hands move instinctively across her back, greedy in their need to keep her as close as humanly possible. She smells of vanilla and something uniquely her, and I know it will ruin me forever. Her fingers brush against the edge of my beanie, trailing across the nape of my neck with feather-light strokes that nearly undo me.

I could stay like this forever, wrapped in the illusion that she belongs here in my arms. Too easily I imagine a life with her, a world where I could care for her so deeply that misery itself would never touch her again. A dangerous thought, because I almost let myself believe it.

But I know better. It is a pipe dream. She doesn't know who I am, what I have done, or the kind of filth that stains me. When she finds out, she will see I am no savior but the very thing she should fear. I have nothing to give her, nothing worth her light. Not money, not power, not even a clean conscience. Rhys may be poison, but at least he can wrap that poison in gold. What do I have offer but meaningless words?

We stay until the disco ends and the lights switch back on. Squinting against the harshness, the silence suddenly presses in. There's no more hiding who has his arms wrapped around her, who can't seem to look away. My body screams to keep her here, but I force myself to pull back, creating a space between us. It hurts like hell, worse than any bruise or scar I have carried, but this isn't about me.

This is about showing Harper there's better for her out there. Better than me, better than Wavershit. She deserves more. Straightening my shoulders, I jerk my head towards the lobby, indicating it's time to go. My chest feels even more hollow than when I arrived, void of the peace she carved within me, but I walk her out anyway.

Every step feels like she is dragging her feet, reluctant to leave the cocoon we built out on that dance floor. I keep my shoulders squared, my stride purposeful, but inside I'm fraying with every second. I feel her eyes on me, searching for answers, searching for what changed between one beat of a song and the next. I don't dare look back at her, because if I do, I'll crumble, and I'll drag her into a world she has no business being part of.

Reaching the truck, Harper's hand lingers in mine a second longer than I should allow it to, and when I ease away, she looks up at me with a furrow in her brow. I can't quite interpret her expression, but quickly decide it's not anger. Not quite confusion either. It's heavier, and lands in the pit of my stomach like a stone. She doesn't say anything, but the faint downturn of her mouth feels louder than a scream. For a girl who has mastered silence, she doesn't need words to make me feel like I just took something precious and crushed it in my palm.

Opening the truck door, Harper refuses to get in. She stands there, her head tilted slightly, as if she is trying to piece me together, like I'm a puzzle with missing edges. There's a challenge there too. The faintest spark that she won't let me retreat so easily. For a terrifying heartbeat, I almost confess everything just to erase the look in her eyes.

"*Did you...did you have a good evening?*" I ask weakly, just to divert her attention. It doesn't work.

"You know it's not fair when you shut me out like that." Running a hand over the back of my beanie, I try to sidestep her but the palm slamming into the center of my chest refuses to let me leave. "I mean it, Clay. You can't bring me here and let me feel all these things, and then close yourself off as it it means nothing."

"*Believe me, it means something,*" I mouth back slowly, allowing Harper to read my words by the light tumbling out from my truck. I hang my head, shaking it slightly at the mess I've made. I was trying to prove a point, but the only thing I've proved is that I'm not worthy of her.

"Since the moment I stepped on campus, you've made me swoon and then disappeared. Filled me with hope and then frustrated the shit out of me. This is new territory for us both, but we're finally here." Harper holds out her arms. "I'm not going to let you backtrack now."

"I'm not a good man," I repeat from the other day, hanging on those words like a mantra. It's an excuse really, something I say to hold myself back from trying before I've had a chance to fail. Harper is the one person I don't want to fail, so I swallow down the desire to run and keep myself planted before her.

"Clayton, look at me," Harper demands, cupping my jaw. I spare her a glance long enough to show her my fractured soul. Her eyes are glinting as they bore into mine, leaving me vulnerable and bared.

"Everyone has a past and everyone has their issues. But I know a decent man when I see one."

The sincerity in her steady gaze floors me, a lump rising in my throat as I sift through her words. My mind snags on one part, but luckily her lips capture mine just before I ask if that's what she sees in Wavershit.

CHAPTER THIRTY THREE

I'm happy to report sleep didn't evade me last night. I passed out straight after Clay dropped me back to my dorm, my head filled with notions of romance and breakthroughs. So much so, that I missed an apparent storm that rolled through overnight, dousing the campus in an excess of slushy mud.

The soles of my boots slip on the slick grass as I head toward the library, intent on hiding myself between silent stacks and over-ambitious notes I've been collecting for weeks. Especially as winter break is looming and I suspect a host of lengthy assignments are about to be set.

Reaching the library's stone steps, I don't see Rhys until his shadow stretches long across my path, blocking the weak sunlight. He moves with the intent of a viper, slipping an arm around my waist and guiding me back toward the street with a decisive tug.

"*No studying today,*" he mouths, his mouth tight and eyes hooded. "*You're coming with me.*" I stumble once, my protest half-formed, but his grip is unwilling to release me. I'll pretend that's the reason I follow without more than a huff, and not that I'm avoiding doing real work by any means necessary. The hold shifts from my middle to around my shoulders, keeping me closely tucked into his side. Rhys is leaning onto me slightly, the first hint that something isn't quite right.

Escaping the bleakness of outside, we enter the veterinary medical block and stroll into a coffee house on the lower level. I've heard there's no strict rule that students can only use their own facilities, but it's implied. Everyone present is wearing a white coat, green lanyard and ID badge, setting them up for becoming real veterinarians one day. They cradle their steaming mugs whilst hunched over textbooks, too engrossed in their work to notice two outsiders amongst them. Their commitment is putting me to shame.

The soothing deep roast smell washes over me immediately, the scent embodied by wood panes covering every wall and rustic art hanging sporadically throughout. Large windows sit pointlessly along the right side, a view of the hallway beyond drawing away from the small corner of refuge. Symmetric patterns in black and yellow spread across the carpet beneath my sneakers, the only link to the Academy that this place has.

Walking the length of the counter, Rhys orders a black coffee for himself and something sweeter for me. He picks out a few pastries, more than we could possibly eat, and I leave him to it. My gaze wanders to the quivering stick of a boy behind the glass with an unfortunate shade of orange covering his head. A smile pulls at my mouth as I wave to Clayton's roommate, but Rhys is quick to step into my way. I peer around him, noting Kenneth's eyes have gone wide and glassy.

Without my receivers on, I struggle to catch the apparent argument the two of them get into, until Kenneth slams down the tray before us. Whilst my coffee sloshes in a tall, glass mug, Rhys' is in a takeaway cup with the implication he should leave. *"It's Dockerson!"* Kenneth seems to shout before running out back to cry into his apron.

I wrench Rhys into a corner booth, clicking a mini microphone to his t-shirt collar.

"Do I want to know what that was about?" I purse my lips. Rhys' attention is on stirring his drink mindlessly, and when he looks up, he seems more vacant than usual.

"Hmm? Oh, with Dickerson? Just the usual banter. It's part of our daily routine." Rolling my eyes, I offer him the pastries first and he waves them off. Apparently, they're all for me.

"You shouldn't tease him. Not everyone is able to take your taunting as easily as others."

"Are you offering to take it on his behalf?" The ghost of a smirk twitches at the corner of his mouth, but the light doesn't meet his eyes.

"Sure, lay it on me. I can handle you." Rhys huffs a small laugh, keeping his jaw tight. I distract myself, nibbling on a butter croissant and settling into the chatter and clinking cups around us. I'm more than happy with comfortable silences if that's all this is about. Rhys is absent today, but it speaks volumes that he sought me out. He didn't want to be alone. Draining my coffee, Rhys lurches out of his seat and returns with another, keen to keep me here. I'm not complaining.

"This is my favorite place to come after early basketball practice," Rhys finally says, his head resting on the back of the booth's bench. "They're a weird bunch. Sometimes they bring in roadkill and gush over the amount of organs they can see, but the coffee is damn good. Plus," Rhys rolls his head to the side, the sharp ridges of his profile pulling taut, "no one cares who I am in here. It's one of the only places on campus I can just sit unbothered."

"Except today, you've brought me here to bother you," I quirk a brow. Rhys lifts his mug to his lips, hiding his words but the microphone picks up on them anyway.

"You're never bothering me."

I study him quietly, the restless tap of his fingers against the tabletop, the twitch of his shoulders that betray whatever is raging beneath the surface. He wants to be destructive, I know enough about him to sense that, but right now he just looks... tired.

"Are you going to tell me what's wrong, or am I supposed to guess?" I ask, nudging my knee against his under the table. Rhys takes another minute to organize his thoughts, and when he eventually speaks, it's on a deflated exhale.

"My father called." His lip curls over the edge of his takeaway cup before he drowns the rest. I nod slowly, starting to understand. Encounters with his father seem to be a constant strain, no matter if they're in person or simply a phone call.

"Another dinner to attend?"

"Worse," Rhys shakes his head lazily, already resigned. "He spoke with the Dean. Wanted to let me know he's *proud* of the rise in my attendance. He *commended* my efforts rebuilding Peterson's lab. Several professors have noted that I've settled down and taken a real interest in my education. Fucking joke," Rhys flares his nostrils, his breathing becoming labored.

I'm careful to mask my reaction, fully aware that I'm treading in unknown territory. Others work endlessly for the type of validation Rhys has been given, yet to him, it's the desecration of what he's working towards. From the little I know, his dad was a monster to him, and he's constantly seeking his revenge.

Reaching across the table, I take his hand in mine. "I'm glad you sought me out." Rhys brushes his thumb over my knuckles, tracking the motion with his eyes, before withdrawing.

"Don't be. I blame you," he glares with harsh blue eyes. "I'm just trying to decide what would piss my father off more. If I killed you and left your body for the board of investors to find on his next yacht party."

"I'm eager to hear plan B," I slowly pull my arm back, holding Rhys' level stare.

"Or if I kidnap you, drive to Vegas and get us hitched so his arrangement with Mr. Kavanagh goes up in flames." Ahh, of course. Both sound like completely logical conclusions for a freaking maniac.

"So I'm either dead or bound to your mood swings. What great prospects I have." I let out a strained laugh that bounces around in the small booth. How can I be having coffee with a man who buys me every pastry, and then tells me he's plotting to kill me? But alas, that is the whirlwind of Rhys' psyche. "Counterproposal. I help you plan a revenge scheme for the *outlandish* praise he gave you, and you let me live another day as an unmarried woman.”

“You want to...help me...get revenge?” Rhys tilts his head, considering my face with sharp precision. *Uh oh.* I instantly realize my mistake as the malicious glint returns to his eyes. Rhys’ entire mental state evolves around pain and punishment. He thrives on destruction, only happy when he’s leaving a trail of anarchy in his wake, and I’ve just stepped into the circle of fire.

“I will help you brainstorm ways to get revenge,” I say carefully, “if you tell me why this is so important to you. I know he’s a bastard, I get that, but you could leave him behind. Leave it all behind and start fresh. You have the means to do so.” The rush of fury that radiates from Rhys’ being is palpable. Danger flashes through his features, and I almost forget we’re sitting in public. Holding my breath, I watch him shudder and roll his neck as if he’s itching to be free of his own skin.

“I can’t live in a world where he’s roaming around, respected and smug. He doesn’t deserve to get away with everything he’s done to me, and to my mom.” An arrow strikes me directly through the chest, my sternum spasming with an ache I wasn’t prepared for. Rhys never talks about his mom. I don’t know anything about her, and now, I’m not sure I want to. I don’t know if my heart could handle it.

“Okay. I’ll help you, on one condition. No one else gets hurt.” Rhys exhales a disappointed sound, but I drag my backpack up onto the bench, fishing out the notebook and highlighters that were meant to be filled with study annotations by now.

“What are you thinking?” Rhys leans forward to watch me write. I have no idea what I’m thinking, but it’s okay. This is good. Rhys could have easily blown up this morning and done something awful in the name of his reputation. Instead, we’re sitting here, working out a solution. He’s like a chaotic kitten and I’m now holding the laser pointer.

“Something public. Extremely messy. Controversial, maybe,” I shrug. Rhys comes more to life with each suggestion. Writing Mr. Waversea in the center of the page, I underline it, circle it, and then draw a mini skull and crossbones underneath. Totally not stalling. "What's something your dad cares about?"

"Money," Rhys shoots back sharply. "Reputation. Power." I write down each one, scoffing lightly to myself.

"Wow, are you sure he's your real dad? Maybe you should seek a DNA test," I raise my brows, dripping with sarcasm. There's no trace of humor in Rhys' responding glare.

"I'm nothing like him," he growls down the microphone. Sore subject, got it. Sitting with his elbows on the table, chin in his hands, Rhys watches me draw arrows and mess around with different colored highlighters.

"He cares about the scholarships." My highlighter stalls mid-air.

"Absolutely not." Inside our corner booth, the air compresses, the weight of the pen in my hand becoming heavier. Rhys' lip curls, and he leans further forward, angling his head like a predator going in for the kill.

"Do you know why Clayton is so special?" he hisses. I prop my head on my hand, bat my lashes and sigh dreamily.

"Thickly, corded muscles. Brooding personality with a soft, gooey center. Huge—"

Kenneth suddenly appears at our table with two steaming cups on a tray, but he only sets one down for me and leaves, ignoring Rhys completely. I manage to hide my smirk behind the cup, thankful for the distraction from Rhys' narrowed stare.

"Clayton's scholarship is state funded due to his criminal record. It's not just the board of trustees and the investors who will get involved if he leaves, it'll be the secretary of education. They will want a full report detailing my father's failures and sitting right in the center of it, will be me." Rhys grins, far too smugly for a man who's planning to sink along with his own ship.

"If Clayton goes, you'll get kicked out as well."

"My being here is a means to an end. I never intended to stay." A trace of his usual cockiness floods back. Spreading his legs, Rhys adjusts his posture and centers his focus on his cuticles. I could roll my eyes at the display, but dealing with Rhys' self-destructive behavior will have to wait for another day.

"We're not using anyone else as a pawn to get back at your father. There must be other ways." Finally, Rhys relents and we stretch our brains to the depths of our imaginations, coming up with plans involving botched charity galas, press leaks, even straight up robbery from his private art collection. With every idea his shoulders drop, the tightness around his mouth loosening, the black edge of him softening into something I am becoming rapidly addicted to. I quickly find I'm not helping out of a necessity to save everyone else from his wrath, but because he needs someone to lean on. Because I want to be the person he seeks out this time and every time.

Easing the page from the notebook, I hand it over, content that I've done my bit. I've given Rhys plenty of ways to fulfill his need to harm, without causing pain to anyone else.

Kenneth has kept my coffee topped up, the latest cup burning hot as I sit back, cradling it in my palms. I sip gently, and it tastes like heaven, sweet enough to ease the edge in my chest. The shop buzzes around us, the echoes of the espresso machines hissing and a playlist of indie ballads humming through Rhys' microphone. It's dulled beneath the even sawing of his breath as he reads over what we've created and nods slowly.

"I'll edge him out, make him see what he's turned me into." Rhys mutters, mostly to himself. My heart aches to watch Rhys shoulder his burdens alone, cocooning himself in hatred rather than see how broken he really is. Quirking my lips, I don the mask he usually wears.

"You do like a bit of edging."

The corner of his mouth lifts and for the first time all morning, his face relaxes. Rhys shifts, rounding to my bench seat and pressing firm against me. His leg lines mine, his shoulder pressed close as long, inked fingers slip over my thigh. Taking my coffee, Rhys sips it himself, his throat working and limbs easing. It takes everything in me to pretend that the heat of him isn't overriding my senses. That the patterns he's tracing on my thigh aren't carving themselves into my very being.

"May I offer an alternative approach? Something completely off script?" I tilt my head. With him so close, my chin practically rests on his shoulder. Rhys hums thoughtfully, leaning closer still until my lips are beside his ear. "Have you ever thought, instead of destroying your father's legacy, you surpass it?"

Rhys stills, the cup in his hand forgotten. I'm glad I have his full attention, because I reckon I'm only going to get one shot at this.

"You could be so much more, Rhys. You're smart, deceivingly so. And committed. At some point, maybe you should stop holding yourself back, pressed beneath his heel with nothing but devious plans to cut him at the ankles. You could see what you can be without anyone pinning you down. Maybe the best way to bury your father would be to drown him in your shadow. Don't wound him, overthrow him."

Rhys' eyes lift to mine like he's searching for the trick, the punchline where I laugh in his face and tell him he's not capable of it. All he finds is quiet confidence and something I doubt anyone has ever given him. Encouragement. The entire cafe narrows to the distance, the warm steam and clatter receding until I hear nothing but the faint thump of my own heart. Every tiny intake of air he takes sends a ripple through my ribs. His fingers pause on my thigh, the pads of them pressing in a way that is both ownership and question, and I answer by curling my hand into his t-shirt, clinging with the plea to believe in himself.

Rhys leans in a fraction, and the warmth of him spills across my cheek, his jaw brushing against my skin as if he is deciding whether he can cross an invisible line he set himself. Tilting his head upwards, he presses the tenderest kiss to my temple.

"I'll consider it," Rhys mumbles into the microphone, his tone hoarse.

"Thank you," I beam a genuine smile. Releasing his t-shirt, before we end up becoming a scandal on the student portal ourselves, I remove the cup from his hands and nudge him out of the booth. "And now we're finished with your crisis, you need to help me with mine. The library is calling."

"Oh, I actually have a thing—" Rhys tries to duck out but I grab his hand, hiking my backpack onto my opposite shoulder and tug him towards the exit. He digs in his heels like a petulant child, knowing full well this mama isn't opposed to a bit of spanking. On full grown men that beg for it, that is.

"Too bad. It's my turn for a pre-life crisis."

CLAYTON

CHAPTER THIRTY FOUR

Leaning back with a frustrated huff, I slam the laptop shut and press the heels of my hands into my eyes. One more line of my thesis and I'll claw my own brain out. I've been slipping lately, but not because I don't care. It's because every time I try to focus, a pair of green eyes and the curve of a body that fits against mine too damn perfectly hijacks my concentration.

I've started looking forward to sleep, because at least in dreams I get to relive that night. Our date plays on a loop in my head, over and over. And in those dreams, I'm someone else entirely. A man with no scars, no shadows, no weight dragging behind me. A man who takes Harper on picnics, drives her through town in some classic car with the top down, shows her off to the world instead of hiding her in the dark. Waking up has become a cruelty.

The dorm is quiet today, Kenneth off dealing with some family crisis. Perfect conditions for catching up on work. Or it should be. Instead, I'm standing at the window watching a group of guys kick a ball around on the lawn. Their laughter carries through the glass, jeering and playful taunting leaking in. The setting sun slants across the field, dipping low, dragging the day down with it.

Not for the first time, I wonder what it would feel like to join them. To grab a beer afterward. To be someone who doesn't feel like every laugh is borrowed from a life that isn't his. Would Jeremy think I was insulting his memory if I tried? Or would he tell me to stop punishing myself and live a little? Lately, the question has shifted. It's not '*What would Jeremy do?*' anymore. It's '*What would Harper's dream man do?*' And that's an impossible mantle to live up to.

Sighing, I decide to take a boredom shower when a knock comes at the door. My shoulders stiffen instantly. Huxley better not be back for another round of his twisted mind games. I've been attending his friend's online therapy sessions as promised, and saving up what I can to pay him back sooner rather than later. Although, another bill came in from the care home the other day and I don't know how I'm going to keep scraping by like this.

Throwing the door open, any protest dies on my tongue as Harper stands in front of me. Her eyes widen before travelling down my body as I suddenly remember I'm only wearing a pair of black lounge pants. Swallowing thickly, she tucks her hair behind her receiver and returns her gaze to my face.

"Oh hey. You didn't come for our usual study session in the library, and I wanted to check if everything is okay? I brought coffee, unless you had other plans this evening?" Pushing one of the takeaway cups into my hands with a slanted smile, she waits for my answer. Or maybe an excuse, as I look up and down the hallway.

"How did you–"

"Oh wow, do you play?" Harper interrupts me, gesturing to Jeremy's guitar propped against my bed. She doesn't wait for an answer, just slips past me and hops onto the mattress, crossing her legs. My pulse trips over itself. Closing the door, I gently sit beside her, equally admiring the cedar wood instrument.

"It was my...I mean, it has sentimental value to me."

Harper nudges forward to get a closer look but is careful not to touch it. She smiles, murmuring about its beauty.

"Do you think you could play something for me?"

"Um...sure, I guess. What would you want to hear?" I reach up to scratch my hair and realize I don't have a beanie on. Vulnerability hits me like a punch to the face, but Harper remains oblivious. Jumping up, she opens my borrowed laptop and searches for sheet music online.

After slyly dragging on a T-shirt, I drink the coffee as she searches, scrolling through several sites before finding whatever she's looking for. She swivels the screen toward me when she finds what she wants, and I glance through the notes, letting my fingers brush over the strings for practice.

Before I can settle into it, Harper shifts again, moving behind me. Her cheek rests lightly against my back, the warmth of it seeping straight through the thin cotton of my shirt. My hands hesitate on the strings, because her touch and her trust feel like a gift I'm not built to keep.

"Ready?" I ask, my voice low, feeling the faint nod against my back. Her arms slip tighter around my middle, anchoring me as I let my fingers skim the nylon strings. I've always preferred playing without a pick, the bite of the cords grounding me in a way smooth plastic never could. At first, I falter, running the opening bar more than once, unwilling to butcher whatever song she's chosen. If it matters enough for Harper to request it, then I have to play it right.

A few measures in, recognition sparks. The melody is familiar, muscle memory kicking in and guiding my hands. The guitar hums against my chest, vibrations sinking bone-deep until the sound feels less like music and more like a tether keeping me steady. With each chord, the tension in me loosens. By the time I reach the chorus, I can close my eyes and surrender, Harper's hold at my waist keeping me from unraveling completely.

The music fills the room, cocooning us in something untouchable. Ghosts from Harper's past dance around us, and Jeremy is here too. He always is when I play. I see his face, feel his presence in every note, as if he's been trapped inside this wood all along and the only way to free him is to let the strings bleed out his memory. My chest tightens, but I keep going until Harper's hand darts forward, cutting the sound dead.

"That was..." Her breath stumbles, breaking before she can finish her sentence. Her arms have gone rigid around me, and a drop of wetness trails slow and cold down my back. My gut seizes. The guitar is abandoned on my pillow as I turn, dragging her into my lap.

"Why are you crying?" My hand lifts her chin when she tries to hide, forcing her to look up very much the way she did to me on our date. Her cheeks glisten with streaks, her eyes shine with fresh tears threatening to fall.

"That was the last song I properly heard," she whispers, her voice so fragile, I feel a fracture in my chest crack wide open. "It was playing in the car when the accident happened. The one that killed my parents." The air leaves my lungs in a rush. I stare at her dumbstruck, wanting to give comfort but not knowing how. If I did, I would have tried it on myself years ago.

"Why—why would you ask me to play that?" The words rasp out before I can stop them, equal parts shock and self-loathing. She only shrugs, gaze slipping away, but the guilt surges anyway. I hate that I'm the reason for the tears streaking her face, and worse, that I have no way to erase them.

"Running from our fears only feeds them," she replies steadier now. "If we own our pain, it won't have the power to hurt us anymore."

Her words cut straight through my defenses. I let her chin go, let her melt into me, and I sit there processing. She's doing something I've never been able to. Turning toward the pain instead of letting it rot in the dark. She chooses when to bleed, when to remember, so the past can't ambush her. And in this moment, I'm in complete awe.

"I wish I had your strength," I whisper before I can stop myself. The admission feels like handing her a weapon, but she's the only person I'd trust to wield it. The only person I'd allow to have any power over me. Sitting back, Harper levels me with a look that shatters every shred of my resolve.

"Then take some." Her lips crash against mine. Every conflict within me, the want, the fear, the guilt, the obsession, collides at once, a violent storm threatening to tear me apart. I can't cage it, I can't fight it, so I choose to welcome it in. To embrace it, like Harper does.

The salt of her tears mixes with the heat of her mouth, grief bleeding straight into me. I take it willingly. If I could shoulder every ounce of her sorrow, I would, burying it inside myself until it crushed me flat. A light like hers should never dim. My hands tremble as they skate across her back, pulling her tight against me, desperate to make her believe she's safe here, in my arms.

Her lips part, and when her tongue skates over mine, it steals the air from my lungs. Every stroke ignites and destroys me in equal measure, a war raging inside my ribcage. Her fingers dive into my hair, a shock of intimacy that tears me open. Guilt surges, and I break the kiss too soon, mumbling a useless apology. I want to let her drag me out of the pit I've dug, but I know I deserve to rot there.

"Who did you lose?" she whispers. I look away, a lump stuck in my throat but she cups my cheeks to bring my focus back to her. "Own your pain." Her command and sea green eyes calm the storm happening within, a desperation to prove myself pushing me through.

"My brother." I run the pad of my thumb over the guitar strings once more before carefully placing it on the floor. Leaning back, I drag Harper down with me so her head is on my chest. "He was four years older. More like a father than a brother. It was his dream to come here, to play guitar in the courtyard, to wear that damn jersey and lead the team. When I lost him...I didn't know what else to do, so I tried to live his dreams for him."

Harper makes no attempt to chastise me for making the wrong choice, she doesn't try to convince me I should start living for myself. Her fingers trace idle patterns across my chest, each line sparking fire beneath my skin. My heart pounds beneath her cheek as I stroke her arms, goose bumps rising in the wake of my touch. I ache to fill the lasting silence, to expel the weight I've carried for far too long. It's tearing me apart from the inside.

"It's my fault," I force out, my voice tight with grief. "He's gone because of me. I was a stupid kid, and he paid the price. I...got him killed." Harper shifts, pushing up onto her forearms, her face filling my vision. Her pink hair spills over us like a curtain, her expression unshaken by my confession.

"And how long are you going to punish yourself for that?" My mouth drops open, no sound coming out. My brain is stuttering, unsure how to divert this conversation back to familiar ground. I want her to shout at me, to scream and insult me. To cut me out of her life before I give her another reason to.

"You don't understand. He's dead because of me. It's all my fault," I repeat pathetically. I shift us onto our sides so I can half-bury my face in the pillow, turning away from her probing stare.

"Clay, I don't need the details. I know your character. I know you protect me when I don't have to ask for it. I know you're a good man." Her hands drag down my chest, settling over my heart. "I know I feel safe when I'm with you."

Her certainty shatters me. This time, when I kiss her, it's not careful. It's desperate. My lips tremble against hers, my hands clutch her closer like I might drown without her. My heart claws for hers, a lifeline in the dark. Her hands explore me too, nails dragging lightly down my chest, skimming my abs. She tastes like caffeine, intoxicating and addictive.

I fist the hem of her shirt whilst my other hand tangles in her hair, thumb brushing over the cool disc hidden beneath her skin. She breaks the kiss, eyes fluttering open, and for a breathless moment, we just stare. Her innocence cages my fire, taming it into a single flame I can manage.

"I hate that you've seen me weak," I rasp.

"I've never seen anyone so strong."

No more words are passed, nothing left to be said. I roll her onto her back, bracing on my forearms, caging her beneath me. She hooks her legs around my waist, locking me to her, pulling more of my weight down until there's nothing left between us. With the heightened emotions clashing in my chest, an erection should be impossible. But with Harper spread across my sheets, her pink hair fanned out like a halo, I've never been harder.

My thumb drags along her jaw, tilting her lips up so I can claim them again. Own them. This time, when her fingers clutch my hair, I don't retreat. A shudder runs the length of my spine, the thin material of my pants doing nothing to hide my hard length. But I don't want to hide it, I want her to feel it. Feel how she captivates me, how I am merely a man at her mercy.

Her hands roam my back, stroking every tense line of muscle, worship and torment in each slow caress. I'm unraveling, piece by piece, and I can't bring myself to stop. Travelling down to slip beneath my waistband, she brushes the tip of my dick just as the door bursts open.

Jerking upright, a vicious rage bleeds into my veins as the freckled-fuckface I didn't expect to see for at least two days rushes into the room. Throwing his bag onto his bed, he storms back and forth in an angry pace whilst muttering to himself.

"Fuck's sake Kenneth! I thought you'd be gone until Wednesday!" Kenneth freezes mid-step, his head swiveling toward me like he's just noticed the scene. Me, positioned over a girl with a beautiful soul to match her outer appearance. The moment has well and truly evaporated as Harper wriggles out from beneath me giggling, although my blue balls fail to see the funny side.

"Hey, I'm Harper. We're in the same bio class," she smiles kindly with her hand outstretched. Kenneth takes it in his sweaty grip, a strangely predatory grin sweeping across his face.

"Yes, you are. Kenneth Dockerson. It's a pleasure to be properly introduced at last." His hold on her hand lingers a beat too long, spiraling this encounter to a level of awkward I refuse to sit through. Especially when my dick is aching to be set free. Grabbing a hoodie and sneakers from under the bed, I pull Harper beneath my arm and usher her out the room. I'll deal with Kenneth the Cockblocker later.

Right now, there's a gorgeous girl by my side and a free taster session about to start in the food technology department.

"Come on, we're going to get some dinner."

CHAPTER THIRTY FIVE

Dinner in the catering area became a fully fledged party when Clayton walked me back to my dorm, discovering Addy in the throes of another messy break up. I swear she goes through partners faster than I go through cups of coffee.

At least this time, instead of crying in a heap, Addy is on the cheery side of lone drinking, a plastic bag filled with wine bottles at the end of her bed. Dragging Clay inside to help her drink them seemed like the responsible thing to do. And somewhere between giving Addy relationship advice I have no experience with and rubbing shoulders with Clay, a plan was hatched. A day trip, fueled by liquor and desperation to get off campus.

"Come on, Sleeping Beauty," I tug at the covers wrapped around Addy's body. "You told Clayton we'd meet him in the parking lot in twenty minutes."

"Head. Ow. Leave me," Addy mutters, dragging the cover back over her face. I shake my head at the ceiling. This was her plan, to take us to a small, private beach she saw online. The drive alone is going to take up most of the morning, so we stupidly agreed to leave at dawn.

After one last attempt to get Addy back from her sleeping death, I abandon her. Clayton is already waiting, his beanie tugged low and hands shoved in his jeans pockets. His usual, worn military jacket is doing nothing to protect him from the chilly air, but he straightens and smiles when he sees me.

"Where's Addy?" he asks, looking behind me at the closing door.

"Hungover," I roll my eyes. "Although, I'm starting to doubt she ever intended to come anyway. Looks like it's just us, if you still want to go, that is?" Clay blinks a few times, his shoulders drawing up to fight off the breeze.

"Oh, yes. Yeah, I'd love to." He clears his throat and runs a hand over his beanie. "I'll grab the keys to the truck."

"Don't worry about it, I'll drive," I smile, swirling my keys around my finger. I don't wait around for the protest, skipping over to my cherry red Audi. Oh, how I've missed driving my baby. I should get out more, but with the town so close to campus, I haven't found the excuse to.

Shedding my thick sweater for the drive, I drop into the driver's seat and watch Clay fold himself into the passenger seat, his knees brushing the glovebox. My Audi is many things, but generous with legroom isn't one of them.

"Uh, hang on," I lean over him to fiddle with the seat lever, attempting to push his seat back further. However, with Clay's muscular weight, I need to jerk the lever a few times before the seat shoots back, taking my arm with it.

"Ahh!" Clay half grunts, half hisses, his entire body going stiff.

"Oh my god, I'm so sorry!" I gasp, removing my elbow from where it artfully pounded into his crotch. Hovering my hand over his privates, I scramble for a way to help. "Is there anything, I mean, do you need..."

"It's fine, it's fine," Clay insists, although his face is a shade redder than my car. "Just drive, I'll be alright in a minute." I know I shouldn't laugh, but there's something inherently funny about a man squirting in his chair, trying to cushion his dick while there are tears springing to his eyes. I cover my mouth with my hand to hide my smile.

"I am *so* sorry. I was just trying to give you more room."

"I definitely have more room," he croaks, and I lose it. My laughter fills the entire car, reverberating through the soft-top roof. A rumbling from Clay's chest follows as he thankfully sees the funny side of his morning assault. I put my beloved car in drive and get us the hell out of dodge before I damage the poor guy any further.

There's nothing quite like the freedom of the open road. Once we've left campus and stopped off at a gas station for make-shift picnic snacks, the atmosphere between Clay and I becomes light. Nothing matters but the wind streaming through the cracked windows, the vague cry of gulls and the view of the coast growing closer. The sun has risen higher, painting the waves in silver light as I pull onto a gravel lay-by.

For a long moment, neither of us moves. We just sit, side by side, staring out at the horizon as if the world has finally granted us space to breathe. I hadn't noticed the weight that had been dragging me down until it just lifted. The stares, the gossip, the constant spotlight that comes from being associated with Rhys. Waversea is nothing like I expected, and maybe that's not a bad thing. I might not be cracking down with my education the way I'd hoped, but I've also been studying hard for years. In an attic room, completely isolated from the world. At least now, I'm actually living.

Clay exhales softly beside me, his breath fogging the glass before disappearing into nothing. I sneak a glance at him, his features eased and soft, his dark eyes locked on the waves. My chest tightens as I notice the vast difference in him. There's no barrier held high, no defensive posture ready to ward off an oncoming attack. He's simply at peace.

I leave him to his thoughts, making no rush to disturb the silence, despite the need to stretch my legs. I once shared with Clay that my parents used to take me to the beach regularly, which is partly the reason I jumped at Addy's suggestion to come here. Now that I'm staring at the water, I don't know if I'm ready to hear the crash of the waves again. Clayton seems to also be taking a trip down memory lane, because when he turns to look at me, his expression is stripped bare of the guarded mask he wears on campus.

"My brother's name was Jeremy." His eyes shift to the window, and he swallows thickly. "I just...I wanted someone to know that." Chewing on my lip, I try my luck and press a little further. Something tells me Clay has been waiting for this.

"Do you want to tell me about him?" At Clay's nod, I settle back and wait patiently, letting him organize his thoughts.

"He was shit scared of spiders."

I burst out laughing, only because I wasn't expecting that. Clayton chuckles too, reaching up to tug the beanie from his head. I don't comment on the state of his blond waves. I find his bedhead vibe endearing. "If I was in trouble, he would take on a gang without blinking an eye, but if a spider crawled across the bed we shared, he screamed like a little girl. It was the only time I got to take care of him." Clayton's smile melts my heart.

Reaching over, I take his hand and squeeze tight. He suddenly looks younger somehow, as though the years of loss and betrayal have fallen away for a mere heartbeat. He squeezes my hand right back, a little hard but I don't let it show. Instead, I brush the back of his hand with my thumb and smile encouragingly.

"I reckon he would have loved you. In a big brotherly sense."

"Of course," I chuckle. It's obvious that Clayton puts his brother on a pedestal, valuing him far above himself. Perhaps that's what draws me to him. I know all too well how easy it is to believe we are unworthy of love because those who used to give it to us are no longer around. By some stroke of luck, Clay and I have found each other instead.

"It's okay to step out of his shadow, you know. You've honored him well, but I'd really like to see what Clayton Michaels has to offer." I shift closer on instinct, my shoulder brushing his. Clay's hand twitches, a mental block lowering behind his eyes. I can't help but smile in response. "WWCD. What would Clayton do?"

Clay goes still beside me, his gaze sharpening as though my words have struck something deeper than either of us expected. For a moment he just watches me, those black eyes glinting with something dangerous and alive, like a storm breaking free from the horizon. Then, without warning, he shoves open the passenger door and rounds the front of the car. Tugging at my handle, I blink up in shock, the wind lapping around my face and hair.

He doesn't give either of us the chance to overthink. His fingers wrap firmly around mine, hauling me out of the seat with a determination that steals my breath, his palm rough against my skin as he pulls me toward the cliff's edge. Gravel crunches beneath our shoes, the salty sting of the ocean air colliding with the sound of waves crashing in my receivers.

We stop so close to the edge that my stomach flips, the expanse of sky and sea stretching out below us, terrifyingly beautiful from this vantage point. My heart is in my throat, my legs trembling as I brave a look over the ledge. The beach is far enough below that a rush of dizziness floods through me, and if it wasn't for Clay's hold on my arms, I might have collapsed. When he turns to me, his chest rising and falling in quick bursts, I gasp at the clarity in his face. The steadfast assurance he usually hides.

"If I were living for myself, I would risk everything to feel alive. I would take control of my fate alongside the girl I'm falling for," he breathes. Now I understand the thrill he's chasing. The world sharpens when you are living on the edge, fear and longing blurring until they are one of the same.

Before I can respond, Clay's mouth is on mine. The kiss crashes into me with the same force as the ocean below, leaving no room for hesitation. His lips are insistent, desperate, tasting of salt and heat and the hunger of someone who has been starving for too long. My hands fist in the front of his jacket as though I need the anchor, as though letting go would mean tumbling straight into the sea.

For a split second I think I might fall anyway, because nothing has ever felt this overwhelming. My head is spinning, my lungs burning, but I don't care. Each brush of his tongue, each press of his mouth, each gasp we share is a reminder that we're alive. We're the survivors who have been wandering blindly for too long. Maybe together, we can claw something beautiful from the wreckage we've been left with.

Clayton deepens the kiss, angling me closer until there is no space left between us, until my entire body is molded to his. His hand cups the back of my neck, and I let myself melt into his hold, surrendering to the wild rush that screams louder than the waves. I want to memorize this feeling, to finally be embraced by the man who has danced around his feelings for so long. To be standing on the edge of the world, lips bruised and heart thrashing until I might just burst.

Reluctantly, Clay pulls back, our lips raw and tingling, both of us breathing in an erratic rhythm. I come up blank, unable to form a single word, when Clay tilts his head to the right, pointing with a little jerk of his chin. Following his gaze, I notice a narrow trail cut into the cliffside, jagged rocks winding down toward the beach below. It's steep, dangerously so, but the thought of retreating now doesn't even cross my mind.

"Come on then," I challenge, and Clay grins like I've just given him permission to live. That's a sight I'll never tire of. Stopping only to grab my backpack and our mismatched gas station snacks, neither of us can stop reaching for the other, his hand finding my waist as I wobble over loose gravel, my fingers curling around his wrist for balance. Our touches are clumsy but constant, as though the connection so recently forged can't be denied.

The descent is awkward, an even amount of stumbling and laughter. Clay steadies me with every slide of my boots on damp stone, the heat of his palm burning through my sweater. Our shoes finally sink into the cool sand, but there's no time to appreciate how far up the cliffside really is. The bag is dropped in a heap, our shoes kicked off, my hearing receivers unclipped and tossed aside with the rest of our clothes until we're stripped down to our underwear. It's sea breeze is shocking against my bare midsection, and no doubt the water will be glacial, but we don't hang around long enough to care.

"Last one in drives back," I call out, already racing over the sand on bare feet. I wouldn't be able to hear Clay's response anyway, and I'm not missing out on the chance to see him mashed up against my steering wheel. I'm already cackling when an arm winds around my waist and lifts me far too easily. Clay holds me high, cradling me as he runs straight into the tide. I scream, wrapping my arms around his neck as the sea crashes over his knees and thighs, his strides undeterred. Specks of icy water prick my body and I shiver.

"Okay, okay! You win," I squeal and wriggle. "I've changed my mind! Take me back to safety." Usually, this would have been Clay's trigger word. He keeps me safe. He's my valiant protector. However, this version of Clay simply cocks his brow and widens his grin. I know what he's thinking without needing to hear it. *Not a fucking chance.*

I'm plunged south in the next second, my entire body dunked into the waves. To his credit, Clay comes with me, his arms remaining wrapped around me, his chest a solid presence beneath my face. All I can do is scream with delight as the salt burns my tongue and the current drags at my body. The ocean roars silently in my ears, the horizon spinning, and Clay's laughter rumbles through his chest. I laugh with him, as though we're both escaped a mental asylum after years of being chained.

After becoming slightly accustomed to the water, I reach up and attempt to shove Clay's head beneath the surface. It doesn't go well as he stands at this full height and flings me several feet. I gasp, brushing away the hair plastered to my face and splash him right right back.

"You've done it now!" I threaten, making a beeline for his boxers. Clay bats me away, diving and swimming further into the sea as if I won't chase him. The sun watches us play like children, passing over the sky until hunger drives us back to shore.

Stretching across a towel, Clay hands me the fizzy sweets I picked out, but I knock them aside. There's only one thing I'm hungry for right now. Leaping over him, I capture Clay's lips again, propelled by sheer instinct.

Despite the worry that I won't regain sensation in my limbs, I don't want this to end. I don't want to think about what will happen when we return to campus, what Rhys might say or how fragile this thing between Clay and I really is.

Right now, I just want to feel the freedom of my heart hammering without fear. The freedom I found whilst Clay cradled me beneath the waves, gripping tight as the surf crashed around us. The freedom of knowing that for one single moment, we don't have to hold back. We can just be.

CHAPTER THIRTY SIX

By the time we pull into campus the sun has sunk low, painting the dorm building in streaks of orange and gold, salt still clinging to my skin. My hair is tangled beyond belief, and Clayton beside me looks completely exhausted. The sea air will do that to you. Thankfully, there's barely anyone around to note our return. Not that I'm embarrassed to be seen with Clay, but that I want something for myself. Something that isn't publicized all over social media with an unsavory hashtag.

But I should know better than to expect a little privacy. Turning into the parking lot, I pull up beside a black Porsche parked crooked across two spaces, already rolling my eyes. Rhys is leaning against the brick wall, his jaw tight in the light of his phone as he scrolls endlessly. Clayton bristles but I place a hand on his thigh and shake my head. I'm not ending this perfect day on an argument, finding myself swiftly back in the middle of their cockfight. Apparently, Rhys didn't get the memo. He's on me the moment I slide out from the driver's seat.

"Where the fuck have you been?" Rhys spits, his voice slicing through the buzz of contentment still humming in my chest. I take my time to shoulder my backpack, close my door and lock the car once Clay has also vacated.

"We went out," I shrug, attempting to move past him. It's not that I don't enjoy Rhys' delusion of keeping me strung up as his personal puppet, at his beck and call for whenever his boredom strikes, but he needs to learn this lesson the hard way. A lesson that, apparently, only I can teach. If he wants my attention, there are better ways to get it.

Growling, Rhys' hand curls around my arm and Clay moves in, placing me exactly where I didn't want to be. Right in the middle of them.

"Clay, don't—" I start, bracing to physically pry them apart when he catches my chin between his fingers and tilts my head upwards. The breath saws out of my parted lips as he swoops in, kissing me slow and deep as if intent on burning himself into my memory. I melt, letting myself drown in the taste of him, despite Rhys' hand clamping down on my arm, determined on leaving a mark.

Pulling back, Clay smirks as I sway slightly, his thumb brushing over my cheek. "I'll see you later," he promises and slinks away. I watch him go, my mind short-circuiting. What the hell just happened?

The silence that follows is suffocating, the air thick with Rhys's fury, and when I finally look at him his lips are curled, his chest heaving like he might tear the world apart just to make a point.

"Get in the car," he growls, jerking his head toward the Porsche. I start to refuse, but Rhys drags me there anyway, popping his passenger door. Shoving me into the seat, the door is slammed and he's behind the wheel in the next moment.

"Rhys, it's been a long day. I just want to shower and collapse."

"You can do both of those things at my house." The tires skid, speeding us back out the way I just came. We pass Clayton walking along the sidewalk but he can't see me through the blackened windows. There's not much he could do anyway. The beast has been unlocked in Rhys and there's only one way to lure it back into its cage. Complete submission.

Arriving in record time, Rhys manhandles me into his frat house, up the stairs and tosses me onto his bed. He paces back and forth, making a valiant effort to ease his rage.

"So you're dating him now?" he hisses, his fists clenching and opening. I force my voice to stay level, not betraying the sarcasm that wants to jump to my defense.

"We went for a day out." Rhys stops to glare at me, his eye twitching.

"Was there laughter and touching and kissing and *food*?" I roll my tongue between my teeth, considering these points.

"Okay fine, I suppose I'm dating him now." I admit. Rhys' blue eyes darken, a predatory exhale leaving his nostrils. I chew on my lip, wrapping my arms around myself. After such a peaceful, liberating day, losing Rhys is the last thing I wanted to do. Selfish, I know, but just for one more day, I wanted to live within the blurred lines of being wanted by two gorgeous, overpowering men. Sighing, I ask the question I don't want the answer to. "What does that mean for us?"

As per usual, Rhys does what I least expect. His grin snaps back into place, the only warning before he lunges. His fingers tighten around my throat, his thumb pressing against my pulse. I barely have time to gasp, the length of his body crushing mine back into his mattress.

"Well, you clearly aren't fucking him, or you wouldn't respond to me so beautifully. Let me remind you who you really belong to." Tilting my jaw upwards, exposing my throat to him like an offering, the heat of his mouth descends, brutally marking for all to see.

"Rhys," I groan. His smile curves against my skin.

"Say my name, Babygirl. Say it loud and proud." His crotch grinds against my center, already hardening and rubbing my jeans in the right kind of way. It's ridiculous how quickly Rhys affects me, his lean muscles and confident swagger straight out of a porno I'd play on repeat. Each roll of his hips draws a strangled sound from my throat. I reach up to remove my receivers, but Rhys clamps down on my wrists and pins them either side of my head.

"Don't," he warns, flashing me a narrowed glare. "I want to see how wet I can make you with just my filthy mouth." I close my eyes, a bolt of pleasure zipping straight to my clit. Mission already accomplished. As if he enjoys watching me squirm beneath the weight of his stare, Rhys memorizes my face, the way it pinches when he grinds against me again. Giving into him goes against my nature, the part of me that despises bullies humming with curiosity now that I'm pinned beneath one.

When he finally leans in, his kiss is not gentle. It's harsh, slipping the imaginary leash around my neck and pulling hard. The only solace I have is that I chained him first. Rhys' mouth crashes over mine with a hunger that pushes air from my lungs, driven by the need to claim and ruin. His hands round my ass and pull me flush against him, inked fingers splayed across my jean pockets. I twist uncomfortably, agitated by the denim.

"Take them off," I groan between Rhys biting down on my lower lip hard enough to hurt and then licking it better.

"If that's what you want," Rhys reaches for my waistband. "Then no." Hiking them up higher on my hips, I almost cry with frustrated relief. The rugged seam gives me a hint of the release I'm chasing but my hips are bucking in Rhys' direction.

His laugh is wicked, the smug bastard that he is coming out in full force. I try to twist away, ashamed by my reactions but Rhys grabs my chin and forces me to stare straight ahead.

"Let me look at you," he rasps, dragging his thumb over my bottom lip. "All restless and needy. I could watch you squirm all night."

The words sear through me, hotter than the friction of his hips. I want to deny it, to throw something sharp back at him, but my brain is nothing but fog and static as he drags his nose along my cheek, inhaling me like I'm his oxygen. His hand slips between us, skating over my breasts to cup me through my jeans.

"You like it when I press here, don't you?" The heel of his palm applies pressure to my clit and I mewl. Actually mewl for this crazed, possessive man. "You like it when I keep you right on the edge, quivering for more. And best of all, you hate that I'm the one who does this to you."

It's like he's in my head, voicing my very thoughts.

"I—Rhys—" My protest chokes into a gasp when his thigh slides between mine, forcing them wider. His hand has full access now, rubbing in firm, slow circles. He's driving me crazy and I'm not even undressed yet.

"Here's how this is going to go, Babygirl. You're going to get on your knees and take my cock in that pretty mouth of yours. If you do a good job, I'll rip your jeans off and take you hard and fast until you're crying with pleasure." His blue eyes are consuming my vision, sparkling with lust as he speaks. I'm hanging on every word. "Are you going to do a good job for me?"

Swallowing, I nod. Rhys' smile is demon worthy. He flips us, angling me off the mattress and onto the floor. Before I can reach for his sweatpants, he tugs my sweater and t-shirt over my head. I'm adjusting the tatted mess that is my hair when he releases the clip of my bra, baring my top half to him. My nipples pucker at Rhys' undivided attention more than the cool air.

"Make it rough. Suck, bite, scratch. Make it hurt," he orders, pulling his cock free. It bobs against his stomach, the Jacob's ladder piercings catching the light. I lick my lips on instinct. I don't hesitate, urged on by this need to be satisfied one way or another, taking a solid grip of his shaft and guiding it into my mouth before Rhys has fully shed his sweatpants.

Despite the metal gliding over my tongue, he's so smooth. We groan in unison, my throat adjusting his size and the pierced stud at the tip of his plump head, then I deliver on his request. I lay my tongue flat, taking him as far as I can, and bite down between his piercings.

"*Fuck yes,*" Rhys groans, filling the room with his approval. At first, I'm cautious, choosing my timing and placements carefully. Encouraged by his hands either side of my face, I suck until my cheeks hollow out and I'm fairly certain Rhys' soul leaves his body. He hardens impossibly further, his hands becoming lost in my hair, pushing me to take him deeper than I thought possible. Tears spring from my eyes, my throat constricting. He releases me long enough to take back and thrusts back in, blinded by his desire.

"You're mine," he grunts in deluded ramblings. "Not Clayton's. No one else's. Mine. Fuck, you drive me insane, Harper." I don't often hear him mutter my name and I smirk around his shaft, twisting my tongue around his head, toying with the stud. All the while, my nails scratch angry patterns over Rhys' thighs and my hips roll to gain friction from my jeans. I'm a frenzied mess, frantic and needy.

"That's enough," Rhys tugs my head free. I sit back on my heels but he doesn't give me a moment to catch my breath. Joining me on the floor, Rhys throws me onto my hands and knees, tugging at my waistband with eager desperation. They make it to my thighs before he gives up, thrusting two fingers straight inside me. I scream out in shock, jolting when they pump twice and pull out just as fast.

"So fucking wet. So fucking beautiful," he moans, lining up his cock with my center. A spark of panic bursts through me until I feel the telltale sensation of latex. I don't have time to be impressed by his speed in suiting up, as Rhys simultaneously pushes his dick into my pussy and his two fingers into my mouth. "Can you taste how much your body wants me? How it's begging me to carve my mark into your cunt?"

The taste of my desire explodes within my mouth. He uses those fingers to hold me in place, not giving any room between us as his powerful jerks reach higher and deeper inside of me. The room blurs around the edges, the entire world ceasing to exist as I spiral closer to the climax that tears me apart.

Rhys is everything I both fear and yearn for, brutal in the way he moves. Yet somehow, every movement is methodically precise, like he knows exactly how to make me forget myself. His hands map my ribs and his mouth claims my skin, not leaving an inch of space untouched.

I scream louder than I care to admit, cum more times than I can count, until we collapse in a sweaty heap on the floor, breathless and exhausted. I'm fully prepared to fall asleep right then and there, but for the second time this evening, Rhys surprises me.

His arms curl around my body, lifting and easing me beneath his covers. He slides in behind, the evidence of what we've done making a mess on his sheets, but he doesn't care. Instead, the ghost of a kiss touches my hair just as I doze off, unsure if I actually got the answer to my question – what does this mean for us? All I do know is that my interest in Clayton threatened whatever this is, a passion we can't explain or resist. Rhys Waversea doesn't do threatened, and he definitely doesn't do losing.

RHYS

CHAPTER THIRTY SEVEN

Harper's tongue pokes out in concentration as she lowers each careful drop of potassium ferrocyanide into the diluted sulphate. She leans in close, eyes narrowed, waiting for the shift. The liquid deepens into a royal blue and she beams at me like I had a single thing to do with it.

I've point-blank refused to contribute all lesson. The fact that I arrived here *with her* is insult to my reputation enough. Setting me in a self-destructive mood, I've spent that last forty minutes trying to shift the power balance back to normal.

Switch her chemicals when she isn't looking, scattering her notes across the floor. Although that just gave me a perfect view of her ass in those tight leggings. On her phone between us, I've turned off her microphone app twice. If only I can get her to yell or slap me, if I get any rise at all, I'm sure I'll stop. I just need that palette cleanser to settle the jittering inside of me, which has absolutely nothing to do with the decision I made while she slept in my bed *again* last night.

I woke before the sun, sheets tangled around our legs, her scent still clinging to my skin like a brand I can't scrub off. Not that I didn't try in the shower for forty five minutes. I let her in too far, let her strip away the armor I've spent years perfecting. Now, I'm raw and exposed in a way I don't fucking recognize. I don't know how to live in a world where she holds that kind of power over me.

But as per usual, Harper isn't one to be goaded easily. She just steadies her breath and carries on, like a soldier trudging through the battlefield. And in the end, she rewards me with a smile that empties my lungs and fills them all at once.

I can't say I'm surprised. Her resilience is part of her allure. It's carved into her bones and tattooed across her soul. She doesn't shatter when pushed, she refines. I need to keep pressing, keep tearing at the edges of her calm until she has no choice but to react. When she does, when her power burns bright through the cracks I've made, I swear it is the most exquisite thing I've ever seen.

Peterson cuts the lesson short, checking his watch like he has some-where better to be, and slips out the door. Students shuffle into line for the basin. Harper gathers her test tubes, carrying them across the room where Clayton is already stationed, sleeves rolled up like some golden boy hero. He takes her rack without hesitation, *no pun intended*, rinsing her glassware while she stands close, smiling at something he says. Her hand drifts to his arm, a soft laugh escaping her lips.

My jaw locks until my teeth threaten to crack. Bile licks the back of my throat. How the fuck does he hold her attention when he doesn't understand a single piece of her? He doesn't push her. He doesn't force her to prove herself. He doesn't give her the gift of pain that makes her shine.

I watch her laugh while I sit here with my chest tearing itself apart and wonder how long it will take before she finally recognizes what it is she really needs. Not his shielding. Not his comfort. She just needs... me.

Class empties one by one, voices rising with relief at the promise of lunch. Harper clears every trace of her presence but leaves my mess scattered across the bench, her satisfied grin marking it as deliberate. When she shoulders her backpack, Clayton swoops in to accompany her, only to find me stepping into his way.

"You go ahead, Babygirl," I tell her, leaning casually against the table. "Dr. Jekyll and I have business to discuss." Clayton visibly bristles, his shoulders squaring and an impatient breath humming through his nose. Harper hesitates, her eyes flicking between us both standing either side of her.

"Are you going to behave yourself?" she asks me. I roll my eyes.

"Never." A flash of red appears, his freckled face stretched wide with a serial killer's smile. Dickerson fumbles with his bag strap whilst addressing Harper.

"I'm heading to the cafeteria if you want to come with. We can save Clayton a seat." He offers her a clammy hand and I slap it away. Harper is quick to glare at me and finally, at fucking last, a tremor rolls down my spine. If hurting Dickerson is what gets a rise out of Harper, I could rid him of all his teeth.

Sweeping him out of my reach, Harper tells Clayton to come find her at lunch and leaves me alone with my longtime rival. Waiting for the door to click shut, I crack my neck, gearing myself up for what might be the stupidest thing I've ever done.

"We have a problem." I state evenly, hopping back onto my stool.

"My thoughts exactly," Clayton growls and drops his bag to the floor to take a fighter's stance. "You keep wasting my fucking time."

"Relax. We're not going to fight today." I chew my lip ring, savoring the bite of metal on flesh as I rein in the urge to lunge across the aisle. It's truly not my intention to fight, but I could be convinced quite easily. Especially after Harper refused to take the bait all lesson, leaving me pent-up. I swear I need her hostility as much as I need her sweet pussy, but I digress.

"We're going to resolve this the civilized way. Take a seat," I demand. Clayton scoffs but he lowers onto a stool across the aisle, crossing his arms and raising a bored brow. "I'm going to offer you a one-time deal which expires the moment you step out of this room. We both have something the other wants, so a simple trade should suffice."

"What the hell could I have that you would want? You've already have everything." Clay's eyes narrow, his distaste for me palpable.

"Apparently not," I drawl, resting my forearms on the desk. "Having everything makes it impossible to really want anything. Nothing holds my interest. Except lately, I've found a rare possession that I've decided I want to keep."

Clayton's shoulders bunch as he realizes exactly what, or rather who, I'm referring to.

"She's not a possession. You can't own her." My lips curl into a slow smile. Oh, but I can.

Clayton lives in a fake version of the world, where people's choices aren't dictated by others. I've had every decision made for me my entire life. My future is already set on who I'm supposed to marry, what job I'll have, where I'll live. I'm a dog on a chain, living out his last few years of freedom until his master jerks on the leash. That's if I haven't managed to destroy my father and everything he stands for by then.

And then Harper appears. Sweet, unfathomable Harper. The temptress who has shifted my perception, who has given me an out from the world I despise. She's smart, beautiful, stubborn in a way that makes me yearn for a moment of her attention. Imagine if I had all of it. Imagine if, after I've burnt my father's mansion to the ground with him inside it, she was standing by my side, bathed in ash and desire.

My mind runs away with me, much like it has been lately, and Clayton clears his throat. Oh yeah, loose ends to tie up.

"Your mom has extortionate debts, is that right? And the care home fees. They must be a killer." A tick beats in his jaw, causing my smirk to widen. Rule 101 in destroying your enemy, *know everything*. "And even if you do graduate, that juvie record will haunt you everywhere you go. It looks like I'm not the only one with a noose around his neck."

"What exactly is it you're offering?" Clayton frowns, his posture guarded. I lift my shoulders in a shrug, pretending that I haven't already set this plan in motion by calling the bank and a solicitor this morning.

"Your mom's debts cleared and her care fees paid up for the next five years. I'll have your record redacted, and your scholarship moved to an online, *off-campus*, program. All you have to do it pack your shit and fuck off before nightfall."

I watch the weight of my words pass through his face. The way his eyes flicker, thoughts running a million miles a minute. This is more than he could have ever hoped for. An easy solution to all of his problems. Releasing his arms to let them hang by his side, Clayton inhales deeply.

"No."

For a moment, I stare at him, waiting for the word to rearrange itself into a hell yeah. I expected hesitation. A flicker of doubt at the very least. Maybe even greed, demanding more. Yet he simply holds my gaze, far too steadily for a man who just threw away the chance at a fresh start.

"Apparently, you don't understand," I say mockingly. "I'm handing you a fucking life raft while you're already drowning." Clayton leans forward, his black eyes burning into mine.

"No, Rhys, it's you who doesn't understand. Some of us don't sit around waiting to be handed everything, and not everyone can be bought. I haven't come this far just to throw it all away."

"Throw what away?!" I throw my head back and cackle. "You have nothing. You are nothing."

"It might look that way to you," Clayton stands and gives me a look that's too close to pity for my liking. Why the fuck would he be pitying me? "But I'd rather lose it all than sell out to you."

Something inside me twists violently. For the first time in years, I feel off balance. People bend to me. They always bend, just before they break. Yet Clayton stands there like a brick wall, steady, immovable, making my carefully laid plan look pathetic.

"You're even stupider than I thought," I force out, though the edge of my voice betrays the rambling grasp for control I can't quite reach. "You would sacrifice your future, everything you've ever fought for, just to play house with Harper? You're not even in the same league as me."

"Maybe not," Clayton admits, though there's no shame in his features. "But I have integrity, something Harper *adores*. So, if we're done here, I have a lunch to get to."

I sit frozen, rage boiling in my chest, fighting against the bitter taste of shock. Who even is this man? He's not the bull-headed jock I first met, not the immovable asshole who always rose to my challenges. No, Clayton has changed, and I have a feeling I know why. Harper got to him, exactly the same way she's dug her claws into me.

Shouldering his bag, Clayton tries to walk away from me. He must have missed the memo. No one makes me look like a fool. Shooting around the table, I shove him hard in the chest, forcing him a step back. I've tried to be civil, generous even, but Clayton seems to have forgotten who he's dealing with. I'll happily remind him.

Slamming my shoulder into his ribs, I drive him onto Peterson's desk with enough force to rattle the glassware. I snatch the metal pointer, pressing it against his throat until his face reddens and his breath catches. Clayton grits his teeth, jams his leg between us, and boots me across the room. My back skids along the polished floor, a white-hot sting cutting through me in a way that almost feels good. He's on me instantly, hauling me up by the scruff of my Gucci collar.

"As if I'd ever trust you with her," he growls, slamming me down hard. I chuckle, sprawled on the floor, watching him stride away muttering about Harper being too special.

"I didn't realize you were so selfish." The words stop him dead, a tremor of fury passing through his shoulders before he spins back toward me. Grinning, I stand and make a show of brushing dust from my sleeves. "I'm giving you an out. A clean fix to all your problems, and as an added bonus, you'd never see me again. All you'd have to do is leave behind a girl you barely know."

"And read about her *'accidental death'* in the papers when you finally go too far?" His eyes burn a hole through me. It appears I'm not the only one who is possessive. "Not happening. One day I'll pay off my mom's debts myself, through hard work and perseverance. Right now, I have a real shot at turning my life around and finding happiness with someone. I won't let you ruin that for any amount of money."

Clapping slowly, I give his little speech the deluded applause it deserves. Leaning against a table, I drag my eyes over him deliberately.

"I'll be honest, in another lifetime, I reckon we could have been somewhat civil. If only you weren't always standing right in my fucking way." I make a dramatic show of checking my cuticles. "You will be leaving Waversea. Whether as a rich man today or through force tomorrow, I won't stop making your life a living hell until you've gone."

A noise cracks through the room, one I've never heard before. It takes me a second to place it, Clayton's rambling laughter wrapping around me like a vice. I didn't know he was capable of more than a small smile. For a split second, it's like looking in a mirror, his head held high with an air of superiority he's done nothing to deserve.

"I've never understood the saying that money can't buy happiness until I saw you. You must be the loneliest, most miserable person I've ever had the displeasure to meet. I may have no money, but I'll always be richer than you. And the funniest part is," he leans into my face so we are nose to nose, "Harper tolerates you, but she actually likes me. She comes to my room without being forced and waits for me in the library every evening. How many times has she willingly spent time with you?"

For whatever senseless reason, I let myself feel the weight of that truth pressing against my ribs, squeezing until my chest carves in. Clayton turns to leave, his hand bracing on the handle, and my chest lurches. I've failed. I've finally found something money can't buy, and it hurts in a way I don't like. It burns harsher than any cigarette stub against my skin.

"You're making a huge mistake," I state, one last pitiful attempt to change his mind.

"So have you. You've shown your hand. Revealed what your dead heart desires, and you've given me the power to tell you no. What a successful morning this has turned out to be."

The slamming of the door ricochets through my body, igniting a dull ache I thought I'd outgrown, but it always finds its way back. The kind of ache that is so unbearable, I do what comes naturally. I submerge it in rage. Clayton can think he's better than me, that he's noble and deserving of Harper. Who's to say I don't deserve her? That I haven't suffered enough to earn a little light in my life.

Returning my attention to the desk, I rip the microscope from its station and throw it directly into the whiteboard at the front. The table goes next, flipped across the room I recently spent a week renovating. It all seems pointless now. The pining, the infatuation. I can't share her. I'll end up killing one of us and she'll never speak to me again once I've picked out Clayton's coffin.

He's no one. He has nothing to offer. Yet he's clawed back from the brink and found himself worthy of *her* attention. And why do I even care? Am I jealous of the way she looks at him or the way she—Holy fuck, I'm jealous. An emotion I was incapable of before I set my sights on Harper fucking Addams.

I suppose I've never allowed myself to be vulnerable enough for such feelings to exist but she's cut me open and left me to deal with the wound. I'm bleeding for her and she doesn't even know it.

Lifting a steel ruler, I walk over to the washed test tubes next. Let her see the carnage she's caused, the resulting mess of luring me into an exposed state I can't handle. By the time every breakable item is broken, including Peterson's desktop, I've begun to relax. The red curtaining my vision fades and my breathing levels out.

This is what emotions do to me. What she does to me. But even still, I know I won't be able to stop pursuing her. I must feed on her rage to ease my own, revel in her brutal honesty to clear a pathway for my mind to briefly function. And I want her to want it too. To want me too. Not for the money or the parties or the fame. Just for me, in all my fucked-up glory.

CLAYTON

CHAPTER THIRTY EIGHT

"What are you doing?"

Kenneth's voice makes me jolt so hard I nearly slam my laptop instead of just closing it. The tinny sound of *How to Learn Basic Sign Language* still plays from beneath the lid. I'd been so focused I hadn't even heard him enter our dorm.

"Oooh, are you trying to impress a certain lady?" Kenneth's eyes light up like he's just unearthed my deepest secret. "Does she know? Please tell me it's a surprise, like you're gonna sweep her off her feet, carry her into the sunset, the whole deal." He twirls in the middle of the room, arms spread wide like he's waltzing with a ghost. I'm starting to wonder if he needs professional help.

"Fuck off, Kenneth." I snap, sharper than necessary. My temple throbs, so I press a hand there and let out a breath. Kenneth has been... well, the closest thing I've got to a friend here. Even if his actions are questionable and I will never forgive him for Iron Man 2.0, it doesn't mean I have to be a complete dick every time he opens his mouth.

"I just thought it'd be a useful skill to learn, alright?" I shrug, playing it off. He smirks like he knows better, but I swiftly change the conversation. "Why are you even back? Didn't you have a double shift at the café today?" I grumble as I shove the laptop deeper under my pillow. After yesterday's blow up with Wavershit and an awkward lunch where Kenneth talked to the side of Harper's face, even though it was obvious she'd switched her receivers off, I was counting on some time alone.

"Oh, that!" Kenneth stops spinning and launches straight into a monologue at machine-gun pace. "So, Danny called in sick, right, but it turns out he was just hungover, and the boss dragged him in. It was so funny. He was in his dressing gown and I was like how's he going to work in that, and the boss was like give him your shirt so I said okay but it's lined with baby powder to stop the polyester from irritating my skin, but boss said give it over so I stripped off in the middle of—"

"Okay, *okay*. I get it!" I cut him off before the image gets any worse. Now I can't help but notice his powdery skin is bare beneath his half-zipped hoodie. "Christ. Go wash that shit off before someone thinks you've been rolling in chalk." Thankfully, my phone buzzes on the mattress. There's a message from Coach.

Get to the basketball court. Now.

Without hesitating, I scramble for gym clothes. Any excuse to get me out of here. Of course, half my wardrobe has been swallowed by the dorm washers again. I swear those machines eat fabric for fun. Socks vanish, T-shirts too. At this rate I'll end up a nudist out of sheer necessity.

After a hunt that takes longer than it should, I drag on a pair of black sweatpants from under the bed, two mismatched socks with identical holes, and a hoodie that smells faintly of stale laundry detergent.

When I glance up, I find that Kenneth has ignored my instruction to shower completely. He's sitting cross-legged on the floor, organizing his bottle caps collection. "Don't follow me," I tell him as I grab my phone and head for the door. My eyes snag on the dried mud caked into his work shoes and trousers, all crusted up his laces, and I cringe. I don't even want to know.

For once I leave the beanie behind, letting the winter wind run its fingers through my hair. The season's shifting, rolling into a bitter cold I'm not prepared for. The air feels fresher, like it's trying to scrub off the last of the frost. The grass edging the pathways is starting to turn green again, a green that reminds me of Harper's eyes. Maybe it's not just the weather making the weight on my shoulders feel a little lighter.

That vaguely blissful feeling evaporates when I round the corner to the gymnasium. Coach is pacing by the back door, rubbing his bald patch like it's a lucky charm. I'm about to pass without caring what's got him all riled up until I see Huxley and Garrett are also waiting for me just inside the doorway.

"What's wrong?" I breathe deeply, knowing from experience not to let emotions rise until I know what I'm dealing with. Too many times in the JDC, I leapt into a fight too fast, letting my anger rob me of the advantage. Some instincts can't be taught, but scars carve lessons you'll never forget, and I learned mine the hard way.

When no one answers, I push through the cluster of bodies and stride into the locker room. At first nothing looks out of place. The showers stand empty, patiently awaiting their next visitor, no flickering bulbs overhead, no eerie shadows creeping in the corners like every horror film has conditioned me to expect. The tiled floor even looks freshly mopped, the sharp scent of disinfectant clinging to the air. Then I round the bench and see the lockers.

Liquid has been splashed across the grey metal, thick and glistening, and the way the overhead light hits it confirms what my gut already suspects. It's blood. Real, fresh blood. A soft pattering drips to the floor, the sound slicing through the silence like a clock counting down to detonation. My combination lock dangles open, smeared red, swinging like someone wanted me to know exactly where they'd been. Shoving it aside, I wrench the door open.

Something bulky has been crammed inside, shoved in a heap so I can't make it out until I grab hold and drag it free. Eyes burn into my back as I unfurl the cotton, and when the heavy fabric falls open, I almost drop it.

A black Waversea Weavers jacket with yellow sleeves, the crest stitched neatly on the chest. It should be a symbol of pride, but masses of shredded paper pour out of the lining, scattering over the bloody tiles at my feet. My knuckles tighten around the thick trim, the weight dragging at my arms like an anchor, but when I flip it over, the floor disappears from beneath me.

The number seven stretches bold and proud across the back, but around it, stitched into the material in neat yellow thread, is a name. Jeremy Michaels. My brother. And slashed across that name in white paint is the word **MURDERER**.

I can't move. Can't breathe. The world tunnels until all I see is that word carved into the fabric of his memory. My mind stutters, unable to comprehend what I'm looking at. Huxley crouches to snatch up strips of paper. He turns one toward me, a grave look on his face. *You don't belong here,* is typed over and over onto every strip.

The last thread of resolve snaps. Wavershit has gone too far. This time I'll kill him. A rush of blood floods my ears, my chest tightening to the point of suffocating. I've stayed indifferent for long enough, refused to give him the rise he so obviously craves, but not anymore. Now I'll break every bone in his body until he begs for mercy that will never come. He'll finally learn I'm the bear you don't poke unless you want your throat ripped out.

But the thought ices over with doubt almost instantly. How the hell could Rhys know I blame myself for Jeremy's death? That I'm responsible. All of the police reports stated that I wasn't even there when the knife that took Jeremy's life was plunged into his neck, and my actions afterward were out of grief.

My chest caves in as another possibility slams through me. She wouldn't. Harper wouldn't have told him, sharing my deepest secrets with the man who wants to destroy me. She promised. But what if…

My throat constricts, nausea choking me. What if she ran straight into his arms with my confession, with my shame, dangling it like a trophy? What if they've both been playing me from the start, laughing behind my back, testing how far I'd go for a pair of fluttering lashes and curves I never stood a chance against? What a fucking idiot I am.

I slam my fist into the locker next to mine. Metal crunches under my knuckles, skin splits, but I don't even feel the pain. All I see is red. The wall I'd stupidly started to let crumble, brick by brick, comes crashing back down with brutal finality. My armor is all I've ever had to rely on, and I should've known better than to let it slip for anyone.

Hands grab my shoulders, voices blur around me, but I shrug them off with a violent jerk, shouting at everyone to get the fuck out. No one moves. Their hesitation fuels the fire roaring through me, turning it to wildfire.

The jacket is still clenched in my fist, heavy as lead, and all I want is to swing it into someone's face. My fists fly instead, air splitting around me as I throw punches at ghosts, at anyone stupid enough to step closer. My vision's gone scarlet, my thoughts gone black. Only one thing remains, the raw need to hurt, to burn down every obstacle until I get to the bastard who dared drag my brother's name into this.

Dropping low with a roar, I grip the wooden bench and hurl it across the room with every ounce of rage burning inside me. It slams into Coach's metal grate-caged office with a deafening crash, the sound ricocheting through the locker room but doing nothing to ease the inferno tearing through me. A guttural noise spills from between my clenched teeth, half growl, half sob, raw enough to scrape my throat. My fist connects with a jaw before I can even register whose it is, and the shockwave of bone against bone floods me with a twisted kind of satisfaction. A blood bath is coming, and I'll be the one to paint the walls.

Two bodies ram into me, smashing me back into the lockers several doors down from mine. Metal bites into my shoulder blades, the clang reverberating up my spine. I thrash wildly, almost managing to shake one off until another pair of hands clamps down on my wrists, dragging my arms wide. Strained voices shout over me, but all I can hear is my own pulse pounding in my skull. I buck against their hold until it finally hits me. This fight is wasted. I need to save the hatred for the bastard who deserves every last shred of it.

The second I stop struggling, I expect them to let me go, but they don't. Instead, the two in front of me press closer, lowering their heads onto my shoulders, wrapping their arms around my middle like a pair of idiots.

"What the fuck are you doing?" I snarl, trying to shove them off, but their hold only tightens, tangled arms locking me in place like some fucked-up version of family therapy.

"This is the Shadowed Soul way. We hug it out, then fuck shit up," Huxley grunts.

"That's the gayest shit I've ever heard," I snap back, pressing my head back against the lockers like I can somehow put distance between myself and whatever the hell this is.

"Barely. I'm not even hard yet." Garrett lifts his head, earning a sharp slap to the back of his head from his friend, though the bastard chuckles low like he finds himself hilarious. Eventually I realise this isn't ending until I let it, so I stand there, seething, waiting it out with whatever shred of dignity I can salvage. Coach peeks around the back door, eyes wide, only to duck back again when I bare my teeth in his direction like a cornered dog.

Finally, the pair release me, stepping back with smug grins plastered across their faces like they've solved the world's problems. I roll my neck, flex my fists, and spot the jacket on the floor. Jeremy's name is there as it always should have been, but now it's tainted. Marked with the very thing I've been running from. I can't bring myself to let it go, so I scoop it up, clutching it like I've won back a piece of him, even if it's been desecrated.

"Now you're calmer, let's think rationally about this," Garrett says as he and Huxley drag the bench back into place and drop onto it, staring at me like they're some jury panel. "Who would—"

"Wavershit, obviously," I cut in, my voice dripping with venom. The long exhale through my nose is more animal than human.

"Are you sure it's him?" Huxley asks, and I scoff.

"Of course I'm sure. He's had it out for me since day one, and he threatened me just yesterday. He...he tried to make a deal with me and I said no." My eyes burn with unshed tears of frustration. I fucking said no, thinking I had a brighter future here than elsewhere. Yet Harper stabbed me in the back and left me to bleed out.

They exchange glances like they've been watching a different game than the one I've been living, like from their perch at the back of the bleachers they've mistaken my survival for a performance.

"Okay then," Garrett shrugs, his tone maddeningly casual. "Rule one of revenge, know your target. What does he want, how does he move, where are his weaknesses? You calculate it, then you hit him where it hurts most. So, what can we use against him?"

"We? This is my beef. Stay out of it." I take two strides, but Huxley appears in front of me. He refuses to let me sidestep around him, carefully easing a hand onto my shoulder.

"I met Jeremy," he says, the words I never expected to hear. I shake my head, tired of the trickery, sick of people trying to fuck with my mind.

"There's no way—"

"We did our trial days together. We would have been in the same year." The floor seems to tilt under me, my balance knocked sideways. I search Huxley's eyes for the lie, for the smug flicker of satisfaction that would tell me he's full of shit, but I don't find it. His face is open and carrying something close to reverence.

"He talked about you all the time, Clay. Said his little brother was coming up right behind him and how proud he was. You were all he mentioned, every fucking break, every conversation. He kept saying he couldn't wait for you to walk the same halls, for everyone to see the kid he knew would make it big. Said we'd have to look out for you when you got here."

My chest caves with the force of it, like his words are a hammer striking bone. I grip the jacket tighter in my hands, Jeremy's name burning through my palm. Huxley doesn't stop, doesn't give me a chance to run.

"He was so excited. He said you'd been through too much already, that this place had to be different for you. He made us promise to have your back, no matter what. We promised to keep you safe." His jaw works as his gaze searches my face, his hand still anchored to my shoulder like he's afraid if he lets go I'll disappear. "I have a feeling he knew he wouldn't make it out of the slums. There were always demons chasing him, shadows in his black eyes. So you might not want it, but I'm not letting you crash and burn while I'm around. Now tell us what you need."

I want to shove him off, to tell him he doesn't know a damn thing about me, that I don't need anyone to babysit me. But the words don't come. They stick in my throat like barbed wire, because even in my fury, I can see Jeremy in the way Huxley holds himself, in the way his voice steadies like he's forcing it not to break.

Jeremy always did that too. Shouldered the weight so I didn't have to, made jokes when I wanted to rage, supported me even when he was breaking. And now, with my fists still trembling and blood still roaring through my head, I realise Huxley means it. He's not mocking me. He's not trying to take my fight away. He's trying to give me what Jeremy would have wanted.

"It's Harper. She's his weakness," I breathe, regret lacing my tone. Not because I'm about to break everything we had, but because she threw it away before it stood a chance to flourish. Stolen moments in the library, the silent disco, on the cliffside, in my bed. All wasted. She ripped me open and stole my secrets to sell to the devil, and now, no one is getting out of this unscathed.

HARPER

CHAPTER THIRTY NINE

"Erm, what's going on in here?" My voice sounds smaller than intended, thin against the darkened lecture hall. The only light comes from a harsh beam fixed on the front desk, leaving the tiered seats swallowed in shadow. The silence makes my footsteps louder as I approach, each one echoing like a warning I'm ignoring. The strangeness doesn't stop there.

Clay is in Hargreaves' chair, hunched over a laptop that isn't his. He doesn't acknowledge me, just keeps typing with sharp keystrokes, his face drenched in light and resentment.

"Rhys text me to meet him here."

"And like an obedient assistant, you came running." Clay responds without even lifting his eyes but it's the slice of his words that give me pause. A coldness washes over him and my eyebrows pinch together.

I'd actually marched here intending to tell Rhys to stop treating me like one of his cronies. Although, I must admit the tiniest part of me had been curious, wondering what stunt Rhys was pulling this time. But whatever words I had planned die instantly on my tongue as I step closer, rounding the desk to see *student profile deactivated* splashed across grayed out screen as Clay pushes to his feet.

"I don't understand," I shake my head slightly. Clay stares at me, vacant of the warmth he was starting to drip feed me. There's no fleeting smile or gentle brush of companionship, but a storm swirling his black eyes.

"How could you?" Despite having my receivers on, I have to watch his lips since his voice is so low. Dangerously low. Suddenly, he swipes a stack of textbooks to the floor by my side with a roar. "I trusted you!" I flinch and cover the sides of my head with my hands.

"I don't know what—"

"Don't play ignorant, Harper." My name isn't just a name anymore. It's a verdict, a curse spat into the air with enough sharpness to make my ears ring. I'm being blamed for something I can't comprehend. My chest feels tight, my pulse a hammer in my throat.

"Clay, talk to me. What happened?" I reach out, desperate, my fingertips barely brushing the fabric of his sleeve before he recoils as if my touch is toxic.

"You happened. You used me. You broke me." His words drip like acid, each one eating into me until I can hardly breathe. "I hope you got whatever it is you wanted." Leaning over the laptop, he clicks a tab open and shoves the screen back towards me.

The image burns itself into my eyes instantly. Locker doors slick with red, the purest of red glistening against the metal. Streams trail downward to the floor, pooling under a black jacket laid out like a corpse on the bench. Jeremy's name stitched across the back, defiled by the word smeared in white across it. **MURDERER.**

My throat closes and my heart twists so violently it feels like it might rip in two. Who would do this? How could anyone desecrate the dead like that?

"You can't believe I had anything to do with this?!" My voice breaks, my eyes already stinging, tears prickling at the edges as I whip toward him. I need him to see it, to see the horror on my face, the ache in my chest, the proof that I couldn't, and wouldn't, ever be part of something so monstrous. "I know the pain of loss better than anyone, Clay. I would never—"

"I don't believe you." Any speech he can manage is guttural, shredded with betrayal. "Only a handful of people know about my past, and you are the only one I've told willingly. Did you even wait before running to Rhys? Did you two laugh in bed whilst I was trying to protect you? *Fuck.* How could I have been so stupid?"

The injustice snaps inside me, my grief twisting into fury. How dare he. How dare he think I would trade his secrets, the ones he'd bared like raw wounds, the ones I held with trembling hands, knowing how much it cost him to share them.

"Now hang on a second," I start to shake with barely restrained rage. "I opened up to you too. Do you think that was easy for me? What would I have to gain by betraying you?"

Clay's chest heaves, his eyes wild as he paces, raking a hand through his blond waves. He's on a path of self-destruction that I can't seem to slow, never mind stop. He's not listening to me anymore.

"I've been asking myself the same question all damn day," he growls. "At first I thought maybe Rhys hurt you, blackmailed you, but you're not scared of him. You stand up to him every chance you get and I defended you like a fucking idiot. So, it must be something else. His body. His money. Either way, you threw me under the bus. And I will never forgive you for this."

The words gut me, a clean slice straight through my chest as if he's aimed. My mouth falls open, though no sound comes out. He doesn't see the heartbreak tearing through me. He's too far gone, drowning in his own fury and dragging me under with him.

I turn back to the laptop, that cursed image still splattered across the screen. My hands tremble at my sides as fresh tears blur my vision. Anger spikes through the heartache, hot and uncontrollable. To mock the dead like that is to rip open the grave and force the soul to relive its pain, and for Clay to think I could ever, ever be capable of that...it's unbearable.

Rhys set me up. That's all I can think to make sense of the chaos happening around me. He had the means, the time, the desire to cause destruction wherever he goes. Somehow, and for some reason, he's hell-bent on forcing a wedge between Clayton and me. If only he wasn't too blind with grief to see it right now.

"Rhys is a leech," I hiss, every word sharp as broken glass. My fists tighten, nails biting into my palms. I've had enough of being accused, of being hunted, of being treated like a pawn in his sick game. "He drains the life from everyone around him because he has none of his own. I would never betray you to someone who survives on the weight of a name he didn't earn. Stripped of it, Rhys Waversea is nothing but a tattooed shell without a soul, and he knows it."

Slow clapping echoes around the curved walls, ricocheting from so many directions I can't tell where it's coming from, like the space itself is mocking me. Clay remains frozen beside the professor's chair, his eyes dark and unreadable. I raise my hand to block the harsh light cutting across the room and see a shadow striding toward the front. The spaces between the ink on Rhys's skin catch the beam, angels and demons staring at me as he steps in beside Clay, a predator walking into his prey's trap.

"I had my doubts, but you were right, Clayton. Utterly heartless. Deal's a deal," Rhys says, sliding an off-white slip of paper into Clay's pocket. Clay doesn't respond, eyes still fixed on me, and my stomach twists as the reality of what's happening sinks in. I've been deceived by both of them.

"Guess you win, Wavershit. Enjoy your consolation prize," Clay mutters, and I feel something crack inside me, sharp and cold like a bolt straight through my chest. He turns and leaves, the darkness coiling around him like an old friend, leaving me standing in the hollow ache of my own disbelief. Tears spill over, uninvited and unstoppable, as the loss I wasn't prepared to feel claws through me.

I storm forward but Rhys steps into my path. Rage boils over and I throw my fists into his chest, each strike a physical translation of the wrath ripping through my chest. He meets my force easily, pushing me back every time, my shrieks of frustration resounding against the walls, each shove louder than the last.

On the fourth, Rhys's hands curl around my waist and pin me against the nearest wall, his grip bruising, his fingers biting through the cotton of my t-shirt. His teeth brush my jaw with the slightest hint of threat, a tension so palpable it makes my blood run hot and my chest tighten.

"You know violence gets me off," he whispers, teasing me whilst twisting the knife further. "No matter how much I want to destroy you right now, if you hit me again, I will hate-fuck you against this wall and leave you writhing in a heap of pleasure on the floor. Then walk away for good."

My stomach lurches, torn between revulsion and the smallest flicker of desire I refuse to acknowledge. Anger wars with fear, with the deep, shattering sense of helplessness I hadn't felt in years. This isn't about him, it's not even about me. This is about Clay.

"You promised! You promised your revenge schemes wouldn't hurt anyone. That you'd leave him alone." I choke out, a sob catching in my throat. Rhys rumbles with laughter.

"Let's not try to shift the blame here, Babygirl." Rhys spins me around, using a hand on the back of my neck to force my face into the laptop screen. I can't bear to look, my eyes scrunching tight. "I have to say, nicely done. A little harsh, even by my standards, but I didn't know you had it in you."

"Me?!" I twist free, shoving Rhys a step away from me. I can't think when his hands are on my body, his push and pull, hot and cold routine scrambling my thoughts. Rhys yawns and stretches indicating that he's bored.

"Who else would have been able to get close enough to steal the bag of blood from my freezer?"

"You're the one that took it!" I scoff so hard, it scratches my throat. He's beyond ridiculous.

From the moment I stepped on campus, I've had no agency, no

control over anything. Not Rhys, not Clay, not the chaos that has swallowed me whole. And now, in his twisted logic, I'm the puppet master? My fingers curl into fists, knuckles turning white, as my chest tightens with the need to reclaim what little I can.

"You're the one who's been waiting for a way to devastate him. What did you do, wiretap my phone?" Rhys' tongue toys with his lip ring, considering me closely.

"Do I really look like I spend my evenings sitting around eavesdropping on conversations?" he drawls, and I hate how calm he is. How he won't give me a straight answer, as if I don't deserve one.

"No. You look like you chase deaf girls through the woods and beat them with a paddle. You look like you stalk me in the library and leave cute little notes that you're always watching. You look like the kind of guy to pay someone to lock me in the dark and attack my hearing implants. You look like—"

"Stop," Rhys frowns, holding up a hand. "I haven't done any of those things."

"Yes, yes you did," I nod, as if I can convince us both by nodding. "You attacked me in the woods, you...you hit me," I choke out, the tears burning hotter. I thought I'd got past this, passing it off as some freshman fuckery, but Rhys' eyes widen in confusion.

"Harper, I've never hit you. I watched you run off into the woods that night and then I left. I had to get the hog back before farmer Lee realized I'd borrowed it again."

"But if it wasn't you, then who?"

Our phones beep simultaneously. Rhys snatches his up first, jaw clenched, and I glance down. My own face is illuminated on his screen, my eyes staring beyond the camera as my mouth moves. "Rhys Waversea is nothing and he knows it," repeats across the screen, cut, chopped and edited to play over and over. My stomach drops. I follow the gaze to the open laptop on the desk and the small red light blinking beside the built-in webcam. Someone's watching, and they've made me into a gif.

Fury explodes from him, the phone slamming into the wall beside my head until the cracked screen splinters in his grip. His other hand moves to my neck, fingers tight enough to leave bruises, inked knuckles twitching with the restraint he barely maintains. Keeping my head held high and my expression neutral, I refuse to give him the satisfaction of my fear.

"If it's not obvious, we're done here," I say evenly, and he knows I mean it. I won't play this game anymore. Every second with him upends my world and mocks my resolve. His moods, his words, and his arrogance have already stolen my chance at a fresh start. I won't give him another second.

A tick beats through Rhys's jaw, his Adam's apple bobbing as he swallows. His thumb drags across my bottom lip and the look in his eyes makes my pulse stutter. Lust and danger coil together in a way that's almost unbearable. Flicking his gaze to his Rolex, Rhys gives a single nod.

"Yes, we are. An extra clause to Clayton's deal, stall you for ten minutes and I'll never have to see his face again. I've done my part." Rhys releases me as quickly as he grabbed me, sauntering away as if I didn't see the flicker of hurt in his blue eyes. His laughter ricochets through the auditorium, my heart slamming against my ribs. The pressure in my chest makes it hard to breathe, and suddenly I'm running. Bursting into the hallway, I refuse to overthink what I'm going to say or do. I just know that I need to stop him.

Stumbling through the corridors, I shove past a cluster of students clogging the doorway and sprint across the courtyard. Phones flash in my direction and heads swivel. The whispers quickly follow, no doubt the same gif reaching the entire campus by now. I've insulted their King, marking myself as enemy number one. I ignore them all for now.

All that matters is Clay believing I'd betray him. If I can make him see I'd never hurt him, even just for a second, maybe it won't be too late. After everything we've shared, the mountains we've conquered, I won't let him throw it all away on a lie.

McAllister Halls rises ahead, shadows pooling beneath its windows. I push inside, lungs burning, heart pleading. Scrambling up the five flights of stairs, mostly thanks to the use of the railing, I see a figure step out of the room halfway down the corridor. A pent-up breath escapes me, relief washing over me as I gain on the hooded figure. But as I near, I can tell merely from the body shape and size it's not him. He's too short, too skinny.

Kenneth turns to me with wide glistening eyes, his red hair poking out from beneath a hoodie that smells distinctly like Clay. Pointing to the made bed inside the open doorway, my heart breaks for the man I won't see again. The one who has been saving me since before I knew I needed it.

Arms slide around me from behind, our joined misery feeding the void spreading through my chest. For a moment, I can close my eyes on an inhale and pretend he's still here. Pretend I still have a chance to find out what he means to me. But Kenneth's voice beside my ear shatters the charade, bringing me back to the present.

"He isn't coming back, is he?"

I shake my head as tears begin to fall once again. I'd told Clay to own his pain. But now that I'm standing here looking at his empty open drawers, I feel like the biggest of hypocrites because there's no owning this. No fixing this. Like his past, his future is now bleak and the reality is starting to dawn that now mine is too.

Afterword

Thank you so much for reading Book One in the War at Waversea series! I have loved bringing Harper and the boys to life, and there is so much more to come! If Rhys thought he knew the meaning of groveling, he's about to be proven very wrong. Not to mention Clay, who is going to be forced to face the man in the mirror sooner than expected.

Book Two - Burned by Sin, rapid releases on November 21st! Just long enough for you to come down from the emotional rollercoaster that cliffhanger sent us all on.
Ensure you don't miss out by searching for:

www.books2read.com/burnedbysin

Thank you again for your support! A special acknowledgement to Amy Perkins for proofreading, Bianca and Amanda for being my betas, and Kris and Ella for continuing to be my emotional support blankets.

If you loved this story, **please leave a review** on Amazon and Goodreads. Your support is fundamental to indie authors like me. Then, make sure you're on my socials. I have so much character artwork and teasers stored away for this series, you do not want to miss out!

About the Author

If you're a new reader to Maddison – welcome to the Mole's Burrow!!

Maddison Cole is a Why Choose Dark Romance Author hailing from the south east of the UK. She is a creative through and through, whether my medium be pencil, paint, wool or words.

In her books, you'll find a heavy dose of dark humour, men with filthy mouths, shocking twists, an abundance of spice and always a feisty female lead. When not writing, you can find Maddison hiding from her two children, two cats and husband with a dirty book and a naughty dessert.

For regular updates and a FREE spicy snapshot download, join
my <u>Newsletter</u> , check out my website on
<u>www.authormaddisoncole.com</u>
and/or jump into my facebook readers group
<u>Cole's Reading Moles.</u>

Other Works

If you'd like to keep reading from Maddison's backlist, please check out...

Shadowed Souls Series – (set in Waversea)

RH Dark Academy Stepbrother Romance

Forged by Shadows

Bound by Obsession

Haunted by Secrets

The War at Waversea

Basketball College MFM Menage

Deafened by Silence

Burned by Sin

Scarred by Desire

Billionaire Brothers RH (set in Waversea) – Standalone

Beautiful Delusions

I Love Candy

Dark Humor RH - Completed Series

Findin' Candy (novella)

Crushin' Candy

Smashin' Candy

Friggin' Candy

<u>**All My Pretty Psychos**</u>

<u>Paranormal RH with mutants, ghosts and demons - Completed Series</u>

Queen of Crazy

Kings of Madness

Hoax: The Untold Story (novella)

Reign of Chaos

<u>**Bound by Fate**</u>

<u>Fated Mates RH Shifter – Standalone</u>

Moon Bound

<u>**A Deadly Sin**</u>

<u>MMA Fighter BSDM RH - Standalone</u>

A Night of Pleasure and Wrath

<u>**A Wonderlust Adventure**</u>

<u>A Twisted Menage Retellling Duet</u>

Descend into Madness

Embrace the Mayhem

<u>**Billionaire Badboys**</u>

<u>Con Artist/Billioanire RH Romance – Uncompleted</u>

Wreckin' Amethyst